To Lisa
Welcor[me]
Love and Music
♡ ♪

In And Out Of Love

Elizabeth St. John

Elizabeth St. John ♡

 **FriesenPress**

Suite 300 - 990 Fort St
Victoria, BC, V8V 3K2
Canada

www.friesenpress.com

Copyright © 2021 by Elizabeth St. John
First Edition — 2021

All rights reserved.

This book is a work of fiction, a product of the author's creative imagination. Some characters are based on real people and others are entirely fictitious. Names of all real people have been changed. Some locations/names of locations described are fictitious and others are real, but used fictitiously. All events described are fictitious. Any further resemblances are entirely coincidental.

No part of this publication may be reproduced in any form, or by any means, electronic or mechanical, including photocopying, recording, or any information browsing, storage, or retrieval system, without permission in writing from FriesenPress.

ISBN
978-1-5255-9392-5 (Hardcover)
978-1-5255-9391-8 (Paperback)
978-1-5255-9393-2 (eBook)

1. FICTION, ROMANCE

Distributed to the trade by The Ingram Book Company

This book is dedicated to:

Katrina – for getting me back into reading again after the most devastating time of my life

Christine – for introducing me to the authors who inspired me to continue this journey that I started so many years ago

Lindsay and Chelsea – for being in my corner and cheering me on while I wrote this labor of love

Ashley – for keeping me standing when all I wanted to do was fall down and never get back up

The Boys In The Band... You will never know how important you have been in making The Boys In MY Band come alive on these pages... ;)

Mom and Dad...
I love you...
I miss you...
Until we meet again
<3 <3

PROLOGUE

September 19, 2014

Krys

Krys was the Nurse Manager of the Labor & Delivery Unit at the local community hospital. She loved her job, but she was happy to be heading home after a particularly busy week delivering babies. She was more tired than usual and was looking forward to spending a relaxing weekend at home with her husband, Darryl, and their three kids – Julie, Lucas and Kayla.

"A few more miles to bliss..." Krys sighed as she exited the parking lot and turned her deep blue Mazda SUV towards home, a wave of exhaustion passing through her.

Happily married to Darryl for the past twenty years, they had an idyllic marriage. They were a match made in heaven except for the *bumpy patch* where they had split up for a year, just a few weeks before Krys' nineteenth birthday.

Who were they kidding?!

Bumpy patch?

It had been heartbreaking and utterly devastating to both of them, a matter of jealousy and deception from an unscrupulous outside third party that permitted no chance of forgiveness or redemption on either side.

Or so they believed...

After renewing their friendship and sorting things out, Krys and Darryl decided that they really couldn't live without each other after all. They just had too much history together to throw in the towel, so they chose to try again.

This time, their relationship was stronger than ever and they were closer than before. Within a short time, they were engaged and married.

They were meant to be – Krys and Darryl were the loves of each other's lives.

CHAPTER 1

April 1989 to October 1992
Krys & Natalie & Darryl

Krysten Harris and Natalie Sheridan had been best friends since they were children. Natalie's brother Darryl was two years older than the girls. The three of them had grown up together as their parents were friends who lived just down the street from each other.

Krys was 5'8" with a voluptuous, curvy figure. She had long, light blonde hair with bangs, sapphire blue eyes, a small dimple in her left cheek and a warm, compassionate personality.

Natalie stood at 5'6" and had shoulder-length, auburn hair with deep brown eyes and a generous, shapely figure. She was fun-loving and adventurous, but had a fiery temper and woe betide anyone who hurt someone close to her.

At 6'2", Darryl had longish, dark blond hair, ocean green eyes, dimples in both cheeks and an athletic physique from weightlifting, hockey and football. He was a genuinely nice guy with a soft heart and a wickedly funny sense of humor.

When Natalie started teasing Krys and Darryl that they were going to end up married someday, Darryl began looking at Krys differently. Cool and confident, he joined his sister's crusade and began dropping suggestive hints to Krys about dating him. Not only did he find her sweet, funny and totally alluring, she was also becoming quite a beauty, and Darryl noticed in a big way.

Krys noticed Darryl in a big way, too. He was so handsome, so charming and so charismatic that she secretly started dreaming that they *would* end up married someday. However, Krys didn't think Darryl was serious about dating her because, first and foremost, she was his little sister's best friend.

So, in the spring of 1989, she found herself interested in a cute boy in her grade who was sweet and kind, with a great sense of humor, much like Darryl.

His name was Connor Buchanan. He was 5'10" with ash blond hair and hazel eyes. He and Krys sat beside each other in several classes and soon began hanging out together outside of school. After a few weeks, they decided to start dating each other exclusively.

Darryl was devastated when he found out Krys had a boyfriend, but decided to wait it out until his chance to swoop in and win her heart for his own presented itself.

Because it would eventually...

And Darryl was a patient guy...

Krys and Connor gave their virginity to each other, but Krys' heart just wasn't in it. She wanted to be with Darryl and told Connor that she couldn't see him anymore because she had feelings for someone else.

He understood, seeing as he had his eye on another girl he was better suited with, so they ended their relationship and went back to being just friends.

Darryl's devastation turned to elation at the beginning of the summer when Natalie let it slip that Krys and Connor had split up. He had dated a few girls in school over the previous couple of years, made out with a few of them, and even had sex with one of them when he was fifteen, but his heart just wasn't in it. The only girl he wanted was Krys.

His two best buddies, Keith Jordan and Jeremy Phillips, knew of Darryl's feelings for Krys and razzed him relentlessly about it. They may have been high school boys, but they had a rock steady friendship based on mutual trust and respect. Plus, it was *guy code* not to be a jackhole to your buddy when he was trying to win the girl he loved.

With his wing men at his back, Darryl started his pursuit of Krys by capturing her attention any way he could. He would hang his arm around her shoulders and playfully hug her close to him, toy with her hair, compliment her, and ask her opinion on anything and everything.

Krys felt the shift in their dynamic as she realized Darryl wasn't teasing her anymore. She could see a sparkle in his eyes for her and that excited her. He asked her out after a week of relentless pursuit and she said yes.

Natalie was overjoyed at Krys and Darryl *finally* getting together!

For their first date, Darryl took Krys to Assiniboine Park to an outdoor concert of a local rock'n'roll band they both liked. He stood behind her with his arms wrapped around her, holding her close and whispering sweet things in her ear.

Krys leaned back into Darryl and snuggled into his warmth and strength, loving the feel of his arms around her, keeping her safe and feeling loved...

Loved?
Already?
Maybe...
They felt right, like they were meant to be.

After the concert, they drove home in Darryl's beat-up-on-the-outside-but-souped-up-under-the-hood gold 1970 Buick LeSabre, holding hands. He parked in front of Krys' house and turned to face her, placing his hand behind her head and pulling her to him while leaning towards her. His mouth formed a sexy, triumphant smile just before he lightly touched his lips to hers.

Their first kiss...

Krys wound her arms around Darryl's shoulders and pulled herself close to him. She revelled in his scent and his taste, overwhelmed with sensation as he slid his tongue between her teeth to tangle with hers. He gathered her close to him, making their first kiss absolutely unforgettable.

Krys and Darryl were pretty sure there were fireworks going on above them.

When they finished making out in his car, Darryl held her hand as he walked Krys to her door. They kissed again, slowly and sweetly, then reluctantly let each other go as Krys slipped inside with Darryl's promise of calling her the next day.

Which he did.

They spent all their free time together all summer long and when school started in September, they walked in with their arms around each other, leaving a trail of broken hearts in their wake.

Krys and Darryl shared similar taste in music, clothing, books, movies, TV shows, food, everything. They were compatible in every way and there was nothing they didn't talk about.

They were so in sync with each other, it seemed only natural that they carry their relationship to the next level. However, when they discussed having sex and Krys revealed to Darryl that she was no longer a virgin, he became jealous that she had not waited for him.

Krys fired back that he was behaving like a Neanderthal and refused to talk to him.

After three days of silence, Darryl showed up at her door, apologized for being a jackass and asked that they sit and talk. When they finished talking things over and sorted out their expectations, they kissed and made up.

Then they had sex for the first time.

It was nothing like Krys expected and certainly nothing like it had been with Connor. Because she had not been a virgin, it made the experience all that much better and even Darryl agreed.

Now they were truly connected in every way possible.

Bliss...

Pure bliss...

They remained happily together until THE EVENT happened that divided them, causing Krys to behave so out of character that it set up a chain of events devastating both of their lives. How she coped was the only way Krys could deal with the depth of betrayal she felt at the hands of the man she had loved so deeply and trusted so completely.

CHAPTER 2

October 1992

Darryl

Darryl and Krys had been together for just over three years. Both of them were in school – she in nursing school and he studying architecture.

Things couldn't have been better between them. Darryl was loving and thoughtfully attentive towards her, and Krys was adoring and completely devoted to him. Things were going so well that he was even thinking of popping the question as there was no doubt that this was the direction in which they were headed.

But there was one tiny thorn among the bouquet of roses in their idyllic existence that was set to cause the maximum amount of damage to their relationship.

Her name was Cynthia Rockford.

Cynthia worked as a secretary and was a total skank. She spent all her free time hanging out at ILLUSIONS, the local watering hole that showcased a popular local band called Diamond Angel. She thought she was a great catch, but couldn't figure out why she hadn't been caught yet. Cynthia had no clue how unappealing she was and had been trying for the past several months to get into the pants of any and all members of Diamond Angel.

She started with Bryan Davidson, the keyboardist, but that was a total bust because he had a steady girlfriend and was totally devoted to her.

Next she tried Diego Delgado, the drummer, since he banged anything in a skirt, but for some reason he was absolutely NOT interested in banging her.

Then she attempted to seduce Tony DiAngelo, the lead singer and rhythm guitarist, but that earned her a hearty laugh and a firm *getthefuckouttahere*.

With only two choices left, she opted for Alex Johnson, the bass player, who also had a randy reputation. Lo and behold, Alex was feeling off his game one night and obliged her. Come the morning, he had a pounding headache, cotton wool for a mouth and a suitcase full of regrets, wondering if she left him with any diseases and where he could have a bath in bleach.

Cynthia was satisfied for the time being after her not-too-shabby romp with Alex, so she left Rick Sutherland, the lead guitarist and backing vocalist, for another time.

One night a few months later, she was on the prowl at ILLUSIONS and laid eyes on Darryl Sheridan. One look at him was all it took – she *had* to have him. He was a Greek God come to life with his sexy green eyes, messy blond hair and muscled physique. She was in lust and *had* to have a piece of that dream all for herself, so that's what she set about doing.

She asked around and found out all she could about him. She tried get close to him, say something, try anything to get him to notice her, but he never gave her more than a passing glance because he was either wrapped around his girlfriend or hanging out with his friends. With each new piece of information she gathered, her lust grew to fever pitch until she decided that the next time she saw him, she was going to go for it, girlfriend or not.

It just so happened that she decided this when she saw him again at ILLUSIONS that night. He was drinking beer, shooting pool and having a good time with his buddies, Keith and Jeremy, on a guys' night out.

He's just so handsome...

If it's the last thing I do, he's going to be mine...

"D, she's here and she's watching you again," Keith stage-whispered to Darryl, nodding his head to where Cynthia was standing, sucking suggestively on a straw as she stared at Darryl. Keith was 6'1" with spiky, dirty blond hair, dark brown eyes and a lean body. He had a job with the City of Winnipeg, working for Manitoba Hydro.

"Yeah, D, you better watch your dick. She looks like she could do some serious damage to you," Jeremy guffawed, jumping out of the way to avoid Darryl's mean right hook. Jeremy worked in construction, giving him a more filled out physique. He was 6', had longish, light brown hair and light blue eyes.

Keith and Jeremy were single, but even if they were desperate to get laid, they knew to stay as far away from Cynthia as possible. She was a loathsome maneater and unfortunately for Darryl, she had the hots for him, the poor guy...

"Fuck off, you assholes," Darryl grinned at his two best buddies. "I've never given her any reason to believe I'm available to her or anybody. And it creeps me out the way she's always trying to get my attention. Can't she tell I'm not interested? Besides, I'm gearing up to ask Krys to marry me."

Keith and Jeremy's heads whipped around at the same time with identical looks of shock on their faces.

"Are you serious?" Jeremy asked, taking a swig of beer.

"Yeah, I am. She's *The One*," Darryl said, his lips tipped up into a grin.

"Seriously? Not that we don't think Krys is great, D. She is! But you're both kind of young to think about settling down, aren't you?" Keith wondered.

"We are, but there is no one else for me. She's been *The One* since the first time I laid eyes on her," Darryl replied.

"Yeah, it's been pretty obvious since high school. When are you planning to do it?" Jeremy asked.

"Soon. It has to be the right time for both of us and I'm still working out the details," Darryl responded, smiling happily at the thought of Krys being his bride.

"Let's hope your admirer doesn't fuck that up for you!" Keith joked, taking a pull from his beer.

"I can tell you boys right now, that will *never* happen. Anyway, we're here to celebrate Keith's promotion at work, so let's forget about her and have a good time, huh? Round two is on me!" Darryl said, rerouting the conversation.

He walked to the bar and chatted to Chuck the Bartender while he uncapped bottles of beer and poured shots of whiskey. Then Darryl felt a cold shiver up his back as Cynthia sidled up beside him, still sucking suggestively on her straw. He ignored her and walked away back to his friends, his hands full of beer and shots.

This didn't seem to faze Cynthia in the least. In fact, she felt fate and destiny shining upon her, delivering this hunky package of man to her feet. She was not above playing dirty to get into a guy's pants and she did enjoy a challenge now and again. And she could just imagine the challenge she would face with a man like Darryl...

She teetered on too-high heels over to the pool table where Keith was bent over the edge, ready to break. She stumbled up to Darryl and asked, "Nice stick, Darryl, can I chalk it for ya?"

Darryl closed his eyes, tipped his head up to the ceiling and exhaled as Jeremy choked on his beer, stifling a laugh. "No thanks, Cynthia. I got it," he replied, inching away from her.

"You sure about that, Handsome?" she asked as she stuck her finger into her mouth, then pulled it out slowly with her gum wrapped around it and twirled it in lazy circles.

Keith laughed so hard he missed his shot and nearly tore a hole in the green felt of the pool table.

"Yeah. I'm absolutely sure," Darryl repeated disgustedly.

She tried to entice Darryl by swivelling her hips at him suggestively, but he ignored her. Then she moved her hand up her side and grabbed her breast, showing him what she considered a *little slice of heaven*. To Darryl, it looked like a *huge slice of hell* and he continued to ignore her.

"You don't know what you're missing, not getting it on with me," she insisted.

He shifted away from her for his turn as he said clearly, "Cynthia, I have a girlfriend and I'm not interested in anyone but her. Now, would you please excuse me? It's my turn to shoot."

Cynthia was turned on by his refusal, energizing her to continue her pursuit of him. However, she realized she would have to change her tactics if she was going to be successful in this endeavor.

She knew that Darryl would inevitably have to go to the restroom at some point, so she was ready a while later after he and his buddies had imbibed in several more rounds of beer and whiskey shots. She could see him shaking his head as he laughed at something someone said, trying to clear the fog that the booze was starting to cause. He was stumbling slightly as he made his way down the narrow hallway where the bathrooms were located.

Time to strike!

She followed him at a safe distance, watching for his friends in case one of them tried to intervene, but both of them were busy at the pool table chatting up some young'n'lovlies.

When Darryl entered the men's room, Cynthia followed, placed the OUT OF ORDER sign on the outside, then locked the door from the inside. She turned towards Darryl and licked her lips as she watched his muscles move under the tight, faded jeans that curved around the best ass she'd ever seen.

He finished at the urinal and zipped up his jeans, leaving the top button undone, then turned and stumbled a little, catching himself on the edge of the sink.

Cynthia intercepted and pushed him so his ass was backed against the sink, then grabbed hold of his shoulders as she stuck her tongue in his mouth.

Darryl's head was jumbled from all the booze he had packed away. "Kryssie? That you, Blondie? Can you... take me home now? I... drank too much..." he slurred, blinking to clear his fuzzy vision.

Cynthia's eyes widened and an evil plan instantly hatched in her head.

"Sure Darryl, but can we fuck first? You know how I love to screw in the bathroom," Cynthia said in a higher pitched voice, making up dialogue that she thought Krys might say to turn him on.

"I'll try, but I've had a lot to drink..." Darryl grinned. He wrapped his arms around her, but she didn't feel like Krys. This person was much shorter, only 5'3", had short, mousy brown hair and rough skin that smelled of some sort of cheap perfume.

This was NOT his Kryssie, not by a long shot, but through the drunken haze of Darryl's brain, it WAS her. He had been looking forward to having wild jungle sex with her after his night out with the boys, but maybe she couldn't wait and came to the bar to surprise him.

Cynthia kissed him sloppily again, pulled down the zipper on his jeans and grabbed his dick.

He grinned and let his head fall back in anticipation, thinking it was Krys.

She hiked up her skirt, pushed Darryl against the wall and slipped his semi-hard dick inside her, trying to get herself off quickly.

Darryl groaned, closed his eyes and tried to get into it, but something felt very wrong. He opened his eyes and focused more clearly, then realized WHY this felt so different. This was NOT Krys he was screwing. "Cynthia?!" he croaked as he sobered up, pulled her off and pushed her far away from him.

"You betcha, Big Boy. I'll bet you never had it so good, huh?" she laughed, a wicked look of satisfaction on her face for the horrible deed which she had just committed.

"Cynthia! *What the fuck!* Why would you do this?" he yelled.

"Because, Darryl. You're mine," she replied as she adjusted her clothes.

"Are you fucking *insane*? I sure as hell am NOT!" he yelled louder.

"I think you are now, because when Blondie gets wind of what just happened between us, that'll be the end of you and her and the beginning of you and me, dontcha think?" she said gleefully.

Darryl gripped the sink, looking at himself in the mirror with a look of utter devastation on his face, wondering how he was going explain this to Krys.

Cynthia opened the door and pranced out, feeling like the cat who got the cream. Darryl's buddy Keith saw her coming out of the men's room and scowled at her.

"Hey Keith, nice night for a good fuck, huh?" she said and winked lewdly at him.

Keith shuddered in disgust as Darryl came stumbling out of the bathroom with a truly wrecked look on his face.

"Fuck, Keith... I think I just ruined my entire future!" Darryl whispered.

"I just saw Cynthia... What the hell, D?! Did you fuck her?" Keith asked, his jaw slack with disbelief.

"I thought she was Krys! I've had so much to drink... I thought Krys came here to surprise me," Darryl confessed, his eyes wild with worry.

Keith's eyes bugged out. "Darryl, fuuuck, man... What the *fuck* is the matter with you? HOW could you confuse Krys with HER, of all people, even after all the booze you put away?!"

"I'm telling you, man, I thought she was Krys! She does this sometimes, comes to surprise me for a bathroom quickie when I'm out with you and Jeremy!" Darryl revealed as he sagged against the wall and lifted his hands to his face, shaking it back and forth. "And to make it even worse, I didn't use a condom! What if she gave me something? I'm so FUCKED!!" Darryl said as he started to panic and hyperventilate at the devastating wake of destruction that Cynthia had created.

Keith was silent, agreeing with Darryl.

At that moment, Jeremy rounded the corner into the hallway. Keith noticed a look of appalled fury on Jeremy's face that he reserved for only his most disgusted thoughts.

"Dude, *what the fuck*? Cynthia the Skank Queen just sailed by me with a shit-eating grin on her face! She told me to tell you *'thanks'*. What the hell does that mean?" Jeremy bellowed, gesturing wildly with his hands, then saw the look on both Darryl and Keith's faces. "Holy shit!! She really did it! She finally fucked you, didn't she?" Jeremy deduced, sighing loudly and running a hand through his hair.

"What do you mean *'she really did it'*?" Keith questioned.

"I just overheard Mickey telling Chuck that he eavesdropped on her telling another skanky friend of hers a while back that she had her sights set on YOU, dude," Jeremy answered, aiming his eyes at Darryl. "That she would stop at nothing to fuck you and stoop to any level to make it happen. "I was coming to find you and warn you!"

"Why didn't *Mickey* warn me about her?" Darryl shouted.

"Because Mickey is a sleazeball asshole," Jeremy answered.

"Fuck! Krys is going to... I'm going to lose the best thing that's ever happened to me! I have to tell her what happened..." Darryl stammered, his hands fisting his hair.

Keith and Jeremy didn't know what to say to his predicament, so they decided to go seek out Mickey and have a word with him about this utter, complete and totally life-altering, colossal fuck-up of gigantic, mammoth proportions.

CHAPTER 3

October 1992

Darryl

"Mickey! You asshole! If you knew that skanky, devious slut wanted to get her claws into me so badly, why didn't you fucking WARN me!" Darryl screamed, cornering him in the office. Mickey was the owner of ILLUSIONS, a portly 5'6" with bugged-out hazel eyes and a balding head.

Mickey had the decency to look abashed as he whined, his hands doing double time waving in front of him. "I didn't think she would actually follow through with it! Who knew that when she set her eyes on Mr Gorgeous over here that she was going to pull a stunt like this!" he finished, jerking his thumb at Darryl.

"Well then, Mickey, since you knew all about this plan of hers, YOU get to be the one to explain this entire fucked up mess to Krysten. And I'm pretty sure that when you're done telling her, you're going to need medical attention!" Darryl yelled, curling his hands into fists so he didn't wrap them around Mickey's throat and squeeze the life out of him. He was barely able to control his fury, for his relationship with

Krys was absolutely over. This was something she was *never* going to forgive and absolutely NEVER going to forget. And Darryl could completely forget about asking her to marry him now...

"But..." Mickey started to say.

Darryl cut him off. "*But* nothing, Mickey. Forget it. I'll do it myself and face the consequences," he decided, a feeling of cold dread washing over him.

As Darryl, Keith and Jeremy left ILLUSIONS, Darryl was dreading what was going to be a volcanic explosion once Krys found out what happened here tonight.

CHAPTER 4

October 1992

Krys & Darryl

Because it was so late by the time the guys dropped Darryl off at home, he decided to sit on the atomic bomb he was going to drop on Krys until the morning. He got Jeremy to call Krys and tell her that Darryl was too hammered to come over for wild jungle sex, so they put his drunk ass to bed.

Krys just laughed and thought nothing more of it. She would see Darryl in the morning and find out what hilarity ensued, so she went to sleep and dreamed of them having wild jungle sex the next night instead.

CHAPTER 5

October 1992

Krys & Darryl

By the time Darryl woke up in the morning and thought about what he was going to say to Krys, his mouth was dry and his heart was pounding out of his chest with worry. He walked the few doors down to her place, wanting to vomit with every step he took to get to her, the panic and anxiety rising inside him like a tsunami.

When Krys opened the door, she reached for Darryl to kiss him, but he deftly moved out of her grasp. "Hey? What's up? You never pass up an opportunity to kiss me," she asked, feeling a little slighted.

"Come and sit, Krys. I need to tell you something..." Darryl began, feeling an icy cold wash over him. He directed her towards the family room and sat her in her favorite chair, then sat across from her on the ottoman, holding her hands in his. He looked up at her beautiful face, wanting to see her in the morning light one last time because he was certain that after telling her what he had to say, she would never look at him with a look of love ever again, likely only contempt and disgust.

Darryl took a deep breath and proceeded to explain to Krys everything that happened the previous night, wishing with the tiniest shred of hope that she would understand and turn her anger in the direction that warranted it – Cynthia and, to an extent, Mickey. With every word he spoke, he could feel her hands becoming lax in his. She just stared at him with her beautiful blue eyes, the ones he had hoped that their future children would inherit from her, and she shut right down.

When he was done talking, Darryl held Krys' frigid hands in his. He didn't know what else he could say as she remained silent. He decided against trying to apologize, knowing full well that would only make things worse. "Kryssie, talk to me..." he pleaded, leaning forward, trying to catch her vanilla and citrus scent that he loved so much.

Krys' face became glacially cold and hard as granite. She slowly pulled her trembling hands out of his warm grasp, closed her tortured, broken blue eyes, turned her head away from him and pointed to the door. "Get out... of my life... you cheating... sonofabitch..." she whispered.

Darryl was momentarily stunned. This was not what he was expecting her reaction to be. He was expecting tears, but there were none. He was expecting yelling and screaming, beating his chest with her fists, anything, but there was absolutely no other movement from her whatsoever. He stood up, looked at her curled into the big, comfy armchair they always cuddled in and dragged his feet to the door. Before he walked out, he whispered, "I'm so, so sorry, Kryssie."

Darryl didn't look back as he left. Tears slid down his cheeks, scorching a hot path down to his chin before they dropped to the ground beneath his feet as he walked briskly down the back lane. He had no idea how he made it home, his mind a flurry of thoughts in a million different directions.

He ran into Natalie on his way through the kitchen to the basement. She opened her mouth to ask him a question, but he ignored her as if she was invisible.

Once Darryl got to the safety of his bedroom, he closed the door softly in total defeat and slid down the wall, sitting on the floor. He pulled his legs up, rested his forearms over his knees and dangled his hands down in between them. His breath was tight in his chest as he hung his head and wept.

CHAPTER 6

October 1992
Natalie

When Darryl barrelled past her totally ignoring her, Natalie knew something *very* bad must have happened between him and Krys to make him behave that way.

But what?

Natalie followed her brother downstairs and pressed her ear against his door. She was shocked to hear him sobbing. Her heart broke for him, yet she had absolutely no idea what happened to cause this severe of a reaction.

She crept quietly away to her room and called Krys to find out what the hell was going on with her brother.

CHAPTER 7

October 1992
Krys & Natalie

They. Were. Done.

No forgiveness, no tears, no yelling, no screaming, no begging, nothing. Just a clean, swift cleaving of their relationship of over three years together because of one stupid, drunken, insane mistake.

Krys felt like she just had the wind knocked out of her and she'd never be able to breathe again.

The phone rang beside her and she turned mechanically towards it to see who was calling. The caller ID screen said *Sheridan's* and Krys recoiled in horror, thinking it might be Darryl trying to contact her, her mind a whirlwind of jumbled thoughts and emotions.

She tentatively answered, trying to wipe her mind, heart and soul of everything to do with him. "Hello?" Her voice was rough like sandpaper.

"Krys, it's me," Natalie said softly.

"Nat, I need you..." Krys croaked as she dropped the phone back in its cradle. She started shaking so violently that her teeth were clacking together. Then the tears began, cascading down her cheeks like a waterfall.

Natalie arrived at Krys' house minutes later and found Krys curled up into a ball in her chair, no wiser at what happened between her brother and her best friend. "Kryssie, I'm here," she said quietly, wanting to give her a measure of comfort. It was unbearable to see her best friend utterly shattered like this.

Krys looked up at her and whispered, "Natalie..."

"Kryssie, Darryl just came home, ignored me, went straight to his room and is now weeping, with his back barricaded against the door. I've never seen him like this. EVER. *What happened* between you two?" Natalie said, her voice soft and full of concern.

"He... He..." Krys rasped, her bloodshot eyes swollen, huge tears coursing down her cheeks.

"Kryssie, just tell me what happened. Please?" Natalie asked gently as she placed her arms around Krys and held her as she trembled.

Krys stopped crying for a moment and just sat there, cradled in Natalie's embrace. She turned her face into Nat's shoulder and spit out a strangled, "He cheated on me..."

Natalie stiffened. She loosened her grip on Krys, pulled back and looked in her eyes, trying to wrap her brain around what had just come out of her best friend's mouth. "I... What? I don't... I cannot believe what I'm hearing... What... The... FUCK???" she yelled in stunned disbelief.

Krys straightened up in her chair, pulled a tissue out of the box, blew her nose and mopped her eyes. She focused on her burgeoning fury, Nat's incensed words giving her the strength to pull herself together. Clearing her throat before she spoke, her voice started out quiet and steadily gained strength. "Last night at ILLUSIONS, Cynthia cornered Darryl in the bathroom and she fucked him – *WITHOUT A CONDOM* – and because he was so drunk, *he thought she was me*. Apparently she's been after him for a while and Mickey, that fucking weasel, knew all about it and said nothing!" Krys said, hoping that she would never have to repeat those words ever again.

Natalie managed to look astonished, heartbroken and infuriated all at the same time. "That... fucking... skanky... BIIIIIIITCH!!!" she cried out, fisting her hands at her sides and shaking with indignation.

Krys sat in her chair, staring straight ahead, frowning.

"I'm going to... rip her... fucking... hair out!!!" Nat continued.

Krys' lips tipped up slightly at the corners.

Natalie was far from finished her furious tirade of pure, vicious anger. "I'm going to... scratch her... fucking... eyes out..."

Krys sniffed and hid a giggle.

"I'm going to... rip her arms off... and beat her with them..." Nat said, then paused to catch her breath.

Krys had to suppress more giggles.

Natalie wasn't done yet. "Then... stuff them... down her throat!!"

Krys' lips were forming a smile now.

"Then, I'm going to... rip off her legs... and stuff them... up her ass... and... and..." Nat paused, trying to think of more awful things to do with the severed limbs.

Krys was shaking with silent laughter now.

"...light her on fire!!" Nat concluded, breathing heavily and panting from the mental exertion.

Krys let out a snort of laughter.

Nat whipped her head around to stare at her heartbroken friend. "Is that a smile I see and a giggle I hear?" she asked, astonished, not quite sure how to react.

Krys straightened up and nodded her head slightly, then brought her hand to her mouth to hide her grin.

Nat's face cracked into a huge smile and she busted out laughing at her creative rant. Then they hugged, laughing and crying together, releasing some of the tension.

Natalie pulled back from the embrace and dared to ask Krys the one burning question in her mind. "Krys, can't you forgive him? From what you tell me, it was all a horrible mistake!" she pleaded.

Krys wandered aimlessly around the family room. "No... I can't. He was so drunk he fucked someone else, thinking *she* was *me*, Natalie! How drunk does a guy have to be to *do* something like that?? And he fucked Cynthia! *CYNTHIA!* Of all people!! WITHOUT A CONDOM! I just... I can't, Nat... Even though he's your brother... and I've loved him... my entire life..." Krys' voice broke as she started to cry again.

Natalie decided to drop it and stayed with Krys for a while longer, sitting companionably side by side on the couch, watching a rerun of Three's Company that always made them both laugh.

This time, Krys wasn't laughing.

After a while, Krys turned to Natalie and said, "Nat, let's go to ILLUSIONS tonight. I really love Diamond Angel and you know I have the *tiniest crush* on Rick, the guitarist... I NEED to go out and distract myself with music. Besides, you kinda like Tony, the singer, dontcha? Pleeeeease, Nat?"

Natalie had to agree, Krys did need a night out to soothe her broken heart. And she was right, Rick was hot and Tony was *smokin'* hot. She smiled her up-to-no-good smile and said, "You betcha, Blondie."

That's how they ended up at ILLUSIONS that Saturday night where Krys met the second love of her life, Rick Sutherland, the lead guitarist and backing vocalist for the local house band that she and Darryl had seen in Assiniboine Park on their first date together three years earlier – Diamond Angel.

CHAPTER 8

October 1992
Krys & Natalie

Krys and Natalie were dressed to the rock'n'roll nines as they entered ILLUSIONS that night.

Krys decided that since she was a newly single gal, she was going to vamp it up. She wore a dark blue mini dress with a deep V neckline that dipped low in the back, the bottom hem just below the curve of her ass, and finished off with a pair of sexy black stilettos. She left her hair long and wild with her bangs side swept, did smoky eye makeup and glossed her lips to pink, kissable perfection.

Natalie was Krys' rock'n'roll wing woman, as always. She was wearing a short, tight dress of deep red with a low scoop neckline and a short hemline, showing off her snakeskin stilettos. Her auburn hair was partially upswept and her eye makeup was dark and smoky, her lips dark red.

They got drinks from Chuck the Bartender. He was 5'11", bald with deep gray eyes and a sexy, killer smile that matched his sexy, killer body.

Chuck looked at Krys and opened his mouth to say something, but she held up her hand and stopped him. "Chucky, stop right there. Not to be rude, but I can tell by the look on your face that I really don't want to hear whatever you're going to say to me. Just do what you do best and keep the drinks coming, wouldja?" She turned her back on him and glanced at Natalie, then focused on the stage.

Natalie said quietly to Chuck, "I'm so sorry! She's had a rough day."

Chuck replied, "I can imagine. I'm sorry, too."

Nat joined Krys as she turned her back to the bar and watched the band onstage.

Diamond Angel was absolutely fabulous!

They played a mix of cover tunes, old and new, covering several decades and styles, while intermingling their own original material in between. It was quite the eclectic musical combination. They were very popular and the whispered word was that there had been scouts in ILLUSIONS over the past few months, watching and waiting until the time was right to swoop in and change the world of rock'n'roll by signing them to a record deal.

Rick Sutherland, the lead guitarist, stood at 6', had longish, dark brown hair, dark brown eyes and was lean of build, with the best dimples Krys had ever seen. But the cleft in his chin was what she loved most. Her heart melted with how sexy and mischievous he looked.

And his voice...

That voice was pure panty remover...

She couldn't wait to hear him whisper something sexy in her ear with that voice...

CHAPTER 9

October 1992

Rick

Diamond Angel were in the middle of their second set with Rick singing and strumming out the hard rocking chords on his guitar. His eyes were locked on Krys as he sung the sexually charged lyrics that he had written about her.

He had noticed her several months ago in ILLUSIONS and was captivated by her beauty. Every time he saw her, he became nervous and couldn't muster up the guts to talk to her, which was completely out of character for him. He was usually charismatic and confident, especially around the ladies, but this Blonde Goddess had him tongue tied and shy as a schoolboy.

One night, when he had finally broken through his shyness and made a move to go talk to her, he saw a tall blond guy walk up behind her and slip one hand around her waist while the other swept her hair over her shoulder. He bent to kiss her neck, then brought his lips to her ear and whispered something to her. She smiled and laughed softly, a sexy sound that Rick heard from where he was standing. He felt the slow burn of longing for a woman like her to have as his own. He watched as she turned around into her man's embrace, kissed him sweetly and hugged him tightly, clearly in love with the lucky bastard.

Tony sidled up to Rick that night, observing him watching the loving couple's public display of affection and slapped him on the back, nearly making Rick drop his beer. "Don't worry, my friend, you'll find yourself someone like her one day, we all will. Except maybe Diego. He samples women like he's at a buffet," Tony joked. "And maybe Alex. He's a hound with questionable taste in women," he grinned, taking a pull from his beer.

Rick just stood there, silent and brooding over his loss and at how happy and content that gorgeous blonde looked in her man's arms.

But that had been a while ago.

Tonight, the atmosphere around her was entirely different. Rick didn't think she'd ever noticed him before because she looked so completely in love with her boyfriend and had eyes for no one but him. But the look on her face as she stared at him now was raw and hedonistic. The sexual signals she was firing out at him as she sucked suggestively on the straw between her glossy pink lips hit him square in the balls. He didn't believe she would act on them, like she was clearly doing so right now, unless things had somehow gone sideways between her and her boyfriend.

Could this be my chance with her?

Rick could feel right down to his bones that tonight was going to be a game changer for them both.

CHAPTER 10

October 1992

Krys & Natalie & Diamond Angel

"For the last song of the set, let's get our fantastic guitarist back up to the mic to sing. What do you say, ladies? Do you want to hear Rick sing to you?" Tony asked as he grinned sexily, cupping his hand around his ear to listen for the shrieks from the adoring females in the crowd. Tony was a lean and wiry 5'10", had long, blondish brown hair and piercing blue eyes.

Rick started playing the driving chords to the song, then started growling out the lyrics. All the girls went wild for him, but he didn't seem to notice. He scanned the audience until he found her, the Blonde Goddess, and locked eyes with her again. She made him weak in the knees and he had a hard time concentrating on playing the right notes and singing the right lyrics. He hoped he wouldn't screw it up because the guys would make sure he'd never live it down.

As Krys locked eyes with Rick, she could feel the electricity crackling between them. "Oh wow..." she breathed, feeling a fluttering in her belly.

Natalie glanced back and forth between them, not liking what she was seeing. She was still holding on to a shred of hope that Krys would change her mind, forgive Darryl and get back together with him. But after hearing those two little words escape her lips, that tiny flame of hope disappeared into a puff of smoke. Nat knew that Krys was a focused kind of girl and when she set her mind to something, there was no changing it.

Diamond Angel finished their set to a deafening round of applause and shrill whistles from both the guys and the girls in the audience. They jumped off the stage and all five of them headed towards the bar for beer, right where Krys and Natalie were standing.

Diego reached them first. He was only 5'7", but made up for his lack of height with his sultry personality, thick black hair and sexy black eyes. He smiled at them, thinking he might get lucky and have *both* of these delectable *chicas* in his bed in a couple of hours, but alas, it was not to be...

Bryan, the gentleman of the group, was hot on Diego's heels. He grabbed Diego's shirt collar and yanked him out of the way, recognizing Krys and Natalie from all the time they spent at ILLUSIONS. Bryan stood at 6'3", had long, curly, reddish blond hair, green eyes and was lean of build. He thrust out his hand and introduced himself politely to them, smiling and shaking both their hands. "Hello ladies, I'm Bryan and this is Diego, the Spanish fly of our illustrious musical group. Stay away from him, he's nothing but trouble," he smiled and faked feeling hurt as he rubbed the area where Diego punched him in the shoulder in retaliation.

Alex meandered his way to the bar, grabbing a few asses along the way. He was 5'8", had long, brownish black hair and hazel eyes. He was smaller in build like Diego, but made up for his height with his jovial personality. "Ladies, I'm Alex, at your service, day or night..." he started saying, but Tony moved in and shoved him aside to get close to Natalie.

"Hi. I'm Tony. And your lovely name is?" he asked Natalie, looking her directly in the eye.

Nat was momentarily tongue-tied, but she recovered quickly and replied, "Natalie."

Tony took Natalie's hand, turned it palm-down and kissed the back of her hand while looking up at her through his eyelashes, grinning seductively. "Natalie is such a pretty name, it suits you perfectly."

"Thank you," Nat replied, feeling heat pooling in her belly.

Tony straightened up, grasped Natalie by the hand and herded her off into a dark corner to talk.

While Tony was busy with Natalie, Rick walked over, stood beside Krys and took a sip from his beer. "Hi. I'm Rick," he said, flashing his dimples as he smiled at her.

"I'm Krys," she replied, turning to stand face to face with this handsome guitar player who had a silky smooth, sexy voice that could make her do anything he wanted...

"I sang that last song for you. And the other one I sang earlier? I wrote it about you," Rick admitted, snapping his mouth shut in humiliation.

HOLY SHIT!

What did I just say?

"Really? You wrote that for me?" Krys asked breathlessly, her eyes shining.

"Yeah. I see you in here a lot and you're just so pretty, you inspired me to write those songs," he revealed, then slapped his hand over his mouth to stop from spilling any more of his private thoughts.

"*Those* songs?" she asked, smiling sweetly and sipping her drink.

"Yeah, that last one I wrote about you, too," Rick replied, feeling his gut clench with anxiety.

"I'm flattered and kind of... turned on," Krys said, surprising herself and totally stunning Rick.

"You've become my muse, so it's pretty easy for me to write songs like that," he smirked, then let out a deep laugh that made her heart skip a few beats.

If I'm going to do it, I might as well do it all the way...

"Then perhaps I can provide you with a little more inspiration after you're done playing tonight?" Krys said boldly.

Rick nearly choked on the swig he took from his bottle of beer. "There's absolutely nothing I'd like more," he replied, smiling down at her.

They stood at the bar for a little longer and talked as Rick was genuinely interested in getting to know Krys. He could tell by how she held herself and spoke to him that she'd been incredibly hurt by her boyfriend and was looking for a one night stand to ease her heartbreak. He was more than willing to be the one to oblige her!

Rick found Krys easy to talk with. They found they had lots of things in common and their conversation became more interesting. She seemed more relaxed, so he made sure not to mention anything about her relationship status.

Then Tony, *damn the guy*, grabbed Rick and dragged him back to the stage for their last set of the night. "C'mon, Loverboy, we've got more songs to sing before we can blow this joint." Before they turned to go, Tony turned back to Krys and Nat and said, "Wait for us after our set's done? We can go back to our house and continue to party."

Tony looked at Natalie at the same time Rick looked at Krys.

"Absolutely!" Nat replied for both her and Krys, smiling from ear to ear.

Krys nodded and smiled shyly at Rick, her blue eyes sparkling with anticipation.

Natalie pounced on Krys when the boys departed for the stage. "Kryssie! We hit the hot guy jackpot! Tony is so hot and he's really into me! And *what's up* with you and Rick? He looks like he's totally in love with you!" she gushed.

"Rick is very interesting and I want to get to know him better," Krys said slowly, her eyes never leaving their destination – Rick.

"Ha! I'll bet! I can't wait to see where this night takes us!" Natalie squealed.

"Me either," Krys murmured.

Krys looked at how excited Nat was and had to agree – they were both in for an interesting night with these rock'n'rollers. It was time for Krys to misbehave for once and start to mend her broken heart.

CHAPTER 11

October 1992

Krys & Rick

After Diamond Angel finished their last set, they covered their gear and left Mickey and Chuck to lock everything up at closing time. Mickey came over to Krys as the lights went on and fumbled with his words when he tried to talk to her, but she shot him down.

Spectacularly.

"Mickey, you are an asshole of mammoth proportions with no scruples, no morals and no soul. It's inconceivable to me how you could sit on such information and not step in to ensure that what came to pass did not, in fact, need to happen. Ever. I'm a believer in karma and fate and I'm fairly certain that one of these days, they will team up and take a huge chunk out of your saggy ass. And you will deserve every bite it takes thereafter," she said bitterly, then grabbed Rick's hand and swept out of the bar with her head held high.

When they got outside, Rick asked, "Krys, are you gonna be alright?"

Krys huffed out a big breath and answered, "Yes, Rick. I will be. I'd rather spend the rest of the night with you instead of wasting any more time fuming about a situation that I can't change. Let's go to your place and continue the party like Tony suggested, okay?"

They walked hand in hand to Rick's car, a vintage navy blue 1968 Camaro. He opened the door for Krys and helped her in, then they drove the short way to the house the band lived in together, Rick holding Krys' hand the whole time.

The sexual tension between them was certainly palpable.

This is going to be more than just a one night stand...
For both of us...

When they arrived, Rick gave Krys his hand to help her out.

"Thank you, Rick. You're such a gentleman," Krys sighed happily as she stretched up on her tiptoes to kiss his cheek, enjoying the chivalrous gesture.

Rick almost blushed.

What IS it with me tonight?
WHY is Krys affecting me this way?

He smiled at her and kissed her cheek. "You're very welcome."

Once inside, Krys was surprised to find the old house was clean, tidy and in good repair for having five guys living there. "How did you guys end up living here?" she asked.

"It's one of a few properties my parents own and rent out. I learned general house maintenance from my Dad and I helped him fix this place up, so they let us rent it from them," Rick replied, grinning when he saw Krys' mouth drop open as she looked around.

"You've done a great job with it!" she marvelled.

"Thanks. Do you want the grand tour before everyone else gets back here? It'll be a madhouse," he said with true affection for his band mates.

"Yes, I'd like that," Krys said, feeling bold.

Rick gave her a quick tour of the house, leaving his attic bedroom for last. It was a large area with multiple windows that spanned the entire third floor of the house. The bathroom was clean and tidy, with a pedestal sink and claw-foot tub. The rest of the space was orderly with clothes neatly put away and a desk in the corner that held several textbooks along with other odds and ends. There was sheet music on a music stand, a couple of electric guitars on stands with a small amplifier on the floor and an acoustic guitar angled across the bed. He picked it up and placed gently on it's own stand, then turned on the stereo. Richie Sambora's "River Of Love" began playing softly, setting the mood.

"What's so funny?" he asked as Krys giggled.

"You're so neat! I was expecting you to be a slob!" Krys broke into a hearty belly laugh and Rick joined her.

He moved close, wrapping his arms around her as she collapsed against him, giggling. Then he cupped her chin and brought her face up to meet his. Her eyes caught the fire in his and she stopped laughing immediately.

Krys clutched Rick by his shoulders and reached up to kiss his lips, her eyes blazing with lust, fuelled by her heartbreak.

But that wasn't all...

She was honestly attracted to him. She *had* noticed him a while ago, but because she had a boyfriend, she never acted on her innocent little crush.

Now was another story...

Rick leaned down, meeting her half way as Krys reached up to him, touching his mouth to hers in a sweet, gentle kiss. He pulled back, dazed with excitement at finally getting his chance to kiss her. They both leaned in again, tongues out to touch and taste, soft and sweet. Then they moved closer together, the space between their bodies obliterated as their arms wound around each other in a sensual grasp.

Krys tilted her head back as Rick trailed his lips down her neck to her throat. "Mmm, Rick..." she murmured, her voice husky with desire. Her hands roamed over Rick's back, moving up to run her nails through his soft, silky hair.

Rick kept sliding down her body, nipping at her dress with his teeth to expose more of her soft skin. "I can't wait to get my hands and tongue on the rest of you," he growled.

Krys pushed Rick's hands away for a moment, her passion flaming even further at his sexy words. She grabbed hold of the hem of her dress, pulled it up over her head and threw it behind her onto the floor. Underneath, she wore a sexy bra-and-panty set in midnight blue satin, edged with black lace.

Rick's breath caught in his throat as he devoured Krys' shapely figure, driving him to tug off his black vintage Rolling Stones t-shirt. He yanked out his belt, then unbuttoned and pushed down his black jeans as he kicked off his shoes.

Krys inhaled sharply when she saw that Rick had gone commando. She admired his generous male endowment and tentatively reached forward to clasp it between her hands.

Rick groaned and tilted his head back to let the amazing feeling wash over him, but snapped back to attention when Krys was about to drop to her knees. "Things will be over before we start if you do that," he warned, removing her hands.

He lifted her up to stand with him, his lips tipped up in a sexy grin as Krys smiled and chuckled softly.

He took her hand and led her towards the bed. He stood there with his arms around her, feeling overwhelmed with such intense desire for her. He smiled and kissed her again as he slid his hands slowly down her shoulders, taking her bra straps with them. Then he moved his hands to her back, expertly undid the clasp, pulled the straps off her arms and let it fall to the floor.

Krys stood rooted to the spot with longing for him, letting Rick ravish her. She felt alive and excited at what other things they were going to do with each other.

Rick knelt down on one knee in front of Krys, hooked his thumbs into her panties and tugged them gently down her legs. He licked a wet trail down her belly to just above her cleft, where he lingered a moment, leaving a scorching kiss.

Krys had to place her hands on Rick's shoulders to keep her balance while she stepped out of her panties, one foot at a time. He ran his hands up and down her calves as he tenderly took off her stilettos, kissing the insides of her knees before letting each foot back to the floor.

Rick stood up, raised his arm out to the side with Krys' panties dangling from one finger and dropped them to the floor, grinning sexily. He swept her up in his arms and bent his knee to the bed, placing her in the middle. Then he lowered himself on top of her, keeping eye contact the entire time.

"You are the most beautiful woman I've ever laid my eyes on," Rick growled lustily as he leaned down and kissed her again, positioning himself off to her side so his hands could roam. He kept one hand up around her face and coiled her hair around it, the silky softness revving up his sex drive a few more notches for her. His other hand slid down Krys' body, stopping to knead her breast and roll her nipple between his thumb and forefinger, coaxing a whimper of pleasure out of her before moving to the other one for a repeat performance.

Rick's fingers were as talented with Krys' body as they were with his guitar...

When he was done worshipping her breasts, he traced little patterns on her belly down towards paradise. He cupped her between her legs with his palm and swirled his thumb on the sensitive area just inside her folds.

Krys' back arched as electricity shot through her body at Rick's touch. Her arms wrapped around him while he kissed her breathless, his finger sliding inside her.

Rick smirked with smug male pride as he watched Krys come apart at the seams. He kissed her once more, then began moving down her body, kissing and licking at her sweet smelling, oh-so-soft skin, his finger moving slowly in and out, his thumb on her sweet spot.

Krys raised her arms up above her head, drew her knees up and stretched luxuriously in anticipation at what was next on the sexual menu.

Rick reached his destination, withdrew his hand from her and threw Krys' legs over his shoulders as he settled in to devour her wet heat. He licked her and nipped at her until she was writhing in pure ecstasy. When he was sure she was close to coming, he thrust his tongue inside her.

Krys felt her body explode and was pretty sure she saw stars. Her orgasm was so strong, her hips bucked rhythmically in tune with Rick's tongue thrusts. Her hands threaded through his hair and she held him to her for maximum pleasure. As the shock waves of release subsided, Krys' arms fell to her sides, her eyes closed and a smile of absolute satisfaction decorated her lips.

Rick crawled up her liquefied body, licking and kissing his way up to her mouth. His own body was taut and hard as a rock, ready for the second half of the program. He leaned over to the side and dug in his night stand until he pulled out a condom, ripped it open with his teeth and rolled it down his hard length, one-handed. Then he positioned himself between Krys' thighs and wrapped her legs around his hips, prepared to enter heaven.

"Are you ready for me?" Rick asked in a low, husky voice.

Krys opened her eyes and saw a satisfied smirk on his face. "Sure am," she replied, her voice raspy with anticipation. She grabbed Rick and pulled him close, kissing him hungrily. Krys could taste herself on his tongue as she grabbed his hips and smoothly plunged him into her. She lifted her knees a little higher and Rick started moving slowly and sensuously, then began to increase his speed, pulling out and pushing back in a little faster with each thrust.

"Pure... heaven..." Rick growled.

"Don't... ever... stop..." Krys whispered, hugging him closer and kissing his jaw.

Rick braced himself on his elbows and thrust harder.

Krys came for the second time, squeezing her core around his cock, preparing him for his turn.

Rick was closing in on his own release, but he wanted to prolong the pleasure, so he pushed back into Krys and rolled them until he was on his back and she was sitting astride him.

He grabbed onto her hips and began thrusting up with his knees slightly bent while she ground her pelvis down onto him.

Sweat slicked both their bodies, allowing Krys to slide her hands up and down his lightly haired chest. She could feel his skin and muscles clenching and releasing in response to her touch.

Rick could feel the burn building back up in his dick as he watched Krys moving sensually on top of him. "Are you ready to get off yet, Krys?" he quipped.

"Are YOU ready to get off yet, Rick?" Krys fired back breathlessly, a hedonistic smile on her lips.

Rick smiled lustily and hung onto her while he thrust up again and again until the burn was *right there*. His cock erupted with a powerful orgasm, causing Krys to come for the third time, *with him*.

That had *NEVER* happened to him before!

Clearly this was the Universe telling him that he and this woman were meant to be together. He really hoped that this wasn't just a one night stand between them. They had a connection that was more than just sexual.

Krys collapsed on top of him with her cheek to his, breathing heavily.

Rick wound his arms around her and cuddled her close, never wanting to let her go, giving her baby kisses all over her face and neck.

She raised herself up, rested her forearms on his chest and smiled at him. "That was... I can't even think of how to describe what that just was," Krys said in a breathy voice.

"I know what it was," Rick said, grinning at her.

They said in unison as they looked at each other, "The best sex I've ever had!"

They stared at each other in stunned silence.

Krys leaned down and kissed Rick so tenderly, his heart nearly burst out of his chest.

Rick lifted Krys off him and tucked her in bed so he could dispose of the condom in the bathroom. When he came back, she was snuggled under the covers, facing away from him with her eyes closed and a frown on her lips. Rick noticed and asked, "Krys, What's wrong?"

She turned her head towards him and opened her eyes, wet with tears. "I... This... Oh, shit..."

Rick got under the covers and pulled her close to him. "What's got you so upset?"

Krys blew out a big breath and launched into her deepest, darkest feelings, exposing herself entirely to him. "Last night my boyfriend of three years cheated on me with a despicable bitch, but it's such a fucked up situation. She took advantage of him being really drunk and *he thought she was me*. I want to hurt him for breaking my heart, even though I know he's not totally at fault, but at the same time I've kind of had a *teeny weeny* crush on you for a while and this doesn't seem like a one night stand to me. I feel like we connected on a level I've never felt before, even with him," she explained.

"I felt it, too, Krys," Rick admitted, almost a whisper.

"You did?" she said, astonished.

"I sure did," he replied, cuddling her closer, then changed his tone. "Krys, I'm sorry that happened to both of you. I totally get where your head is at. And I think I know who the despicable bitch is that you're talking about," Rick added.

"You do?" Krys asked.

"It was Cynthia, wasn't it?" Rick said quietly.

Krys turned in his arms to face him, her eyes wide. "How did you guess? PLEASE tell me you've never fucked her!"

Rick laughed, "No way! But not for lack of trying on her part, with all five of us. She's only managed to snag Alex, but he's got shit taste in women, so that wasn't a surprise."

Krys sagged with relief at his answer, then spat out, "I could just kill her for ruining my life."

Rick winced at her anger and tightened his embrace around her. "I'm sorry you're hurting, Krys."

She noticed the shift in his touch, then continued her confession, softening her tone. "But if last night wouldn't have happened, I wouldn't be here with you right now, so I don't know what to make of this whole situation. I've never done anything like this before. I've been with... *was with*... Darryl since I was fifteen years old."

Rick didn't know what to say, so he just hugged Krys close to him, kissed her temple and asked her, "Stay the night with me?"

Krys turned to her other side and snuggled back into Rick's chest. She sighed tiredly, "I'd like nothing better," then closed her eyes.

Rick relaxed as they settled into each other's arms. He looked over at his clock – it read 3:28AM.

Soon they were sound asleep.

CHAPTER 12

October 1992
Krys & Rick

Krys awoke to Rick kissing her neck while his hands roamed over her breasts and belly. She could feel his hard cock pressing into her lower back and she smiled lazily, but said nothing. He moved away from her for a moment and she heard the tear of another condom wrapper.

Rick moved back in behind her and trailed his hand over her hip, gently burrowing between her legs, finding her wet and ready for him. He slipped his cock into her as she tipped her hips back. She was smooth and slick, warm and wet as he glided in and out of her in slow strokes, taking his time, making love to her instead of pounding the fuck out of her like he had earlier. He also kept up with circling her bundle of nerves to maximize her pleasure. He caressed her body lovingly, stroked her hair and kissed her cheek, her ear, her neck.

Krys reached back and held Rick's hip while he gently drove into and retreated from her wetness, making her breath hitch in her throat. After a few minutes of this intensity, he sped up only a little, but made sure she had her release before he groaned his, their breathing increasing in tandem. After they again came simultaneously, he cuddled her to him, kissing her all over her face and neck until they were both breathing normally again.

After a short time, he withdrew from her and went to the bathroom to dispose of the second condom of the night. When Rick came back to bed this time, Krys was fast asleep, a sweet smile on her lips.

I did that...

I put that smile there...

I'm going to make sure she smiles like this all the time, now that she's mine...

CHAPTER 13

October 1992

Krys & Rick

When Krys awoke, the sun was just rising. She turned in Rick's arms and kissed him until he opened his eyes. He looked even better in the early morning light, sleepy and utterly satisfied.

"Good morning, Gorgeous," Rick said to her, a lazy smile on his lips.

"Good morning yourself, Handsome," Krys said back to him, a shy smile on hers.

"When do you want me to take you home?" he asked tentatively, giving her a soft squeeze, hoping she'd want to stay with him a little longer.

She looked thoughtful for a moment before replying. "Later. I'm too warm and comfy to leave you and this bed just yet," she said as she snuggled closer to him.

They both closed their eyes and went back to sleep with their limbs tangled together, wrapped in each others' warmth.

CHAPTER 14

October 1992
Natalie & Tony

Tony took Natalie's hand as they left ILLUSIONS and walked towards his car, a black 1967 Shelby Mustang. He turned her to face him and wrapped one hand around her waist while cupping the back of her head with the other, bringing her mouth to his in a savagely sexual kiss.

Nat responded by shoving her hands through Tony's wild mane of hair, keeping his mouth fused with hers so they could continue their tongue duel.

The other guys waltzed out of the bar, laughing and gesturing about something, but stopped dead when they saw Tony and Natalie. Diego whistled and Alex clapped while Bryan just shook his head in amusement.

When Tony finished kissing Natalie, he grinned at her, then turned his head to smirk at the guys. "Go find your own women, you vultures." He turned his head back to Nat and kissed her one more time before helping her into his car.

They drove back to the band's house, holding hands. Natalie gave Tony the shortened version of the previous night and day's events, explaining Krys' scathing behavior towards Mickey the Weasel Asshole.

When they walked in the front door, they were expecting to find Krys and Rick in the living room or the kitchen, but all was quiet, even though a few lights were on.

"Hmm, the door to Rick's attic bedroom is closed... I don't have to wonder what's going on up there," Tony murmured to Natalie, unsure of what her reaction might be to what *her* best friend was likely doing with *his* best friend.

Natalie remained silent for a moment, then chose her words carefully. "I'm in a shitty position, Tony. Darryl is my brother, but Krys is my best friend and we're as close as sisters. I love them both and my heart is hurting for them equally," she sighed, leaning into Tony's side. "Part of me wants to see Darryl and Krys get back together, but another part of me saw how incredibly attentive Rick was with her tonight and she needs that. Now more than ever."

Tony spoke up. "Rick is a good guy, Natalie. He's had a crippling crush on her for a while now and he will treat her well. You don't have to worry about that."

Nat's eyes bugged out. "Really? Wow! Krys has had a tiny crush on him for a while, too! She would NEVER have acted on it before because she was with my brother, but now..." she said, her voice saddened.

Tony continued, "He's probably on cloud nine that he finally got a chance to talk to her and will be walking on air tomorrow because he's with her tonight. Which begs the question, what do YOU wanna do right now?" he smirked.

Natalie smirked back at him, winked suggestively and reached up to kiss him just as Bryan, Alex and Diego sauntered in. With their arms wrapped around each other, Natalie and Tony turned their heads to look at the guys.

"I'm going to show Natalie the new sheets on my bed. You guys steer clear, capisce?" Tony ordered, still smirking.

Bryan piped up. "I'm heading to April's. See you tomorrow afternoon. Pleasure to meet you, Natalie," he said, then went into his room at the back of the house, collected a bag and waved as he walked out the back door to his car and took off. April was Bryan's long-term girlfriend and he always took refuge with her on weekends because he didn't want to listen to any of his band mates getting it on with their female choices of the evening.

Alex and Diego looked at Tony and Natalie, shrugged their shoulders in silent defeat and shuffled in different directions. Alex went digging through the fridge while Diego got them beer.

Once they got their libations, the twosome went into the living room and settled in to watch an action movie on TV with the volume turned way up to drown out certain sounds that they were likely to be hearing soon. Both of their bedrooms were on the second floor and neither of them wanted to be sandwiched between Rick and Krys getting busy on the third floor attic and Tony and Nat going at it in the basement, so staying in the living room watching a movie turned up full blast was their only option.

Natalie and Tony stood off to the side watching Alex and Diego settle in, identical amused looks on their faces.

Tony whispered in Nat's ear, "They don't usually come home alone. They're just jealous and sulking."

Natalie giggled. "Then let's leave them to their jealousy and sulking, shall we? You and I have more important things to do than stand here and watch these two eat and drink themselves into oblivion."

"You're reading my mind, you vixen," Tony growled back in her ear as he took her hand and led them down the stairs to his bedroom.

Natalie looked around and was mildly surprised to find it wasn't as messy as she thought it would be. There were clothes strewn neatly across the back of a chair along with some books and a few magazines piled up on a desk in the corner. The closet door was open and orderly with some clothes piled in the laundry basket on the floor. In the middle of the room was the bed, which Natalie couldn't wait to test out...

Natalie had only had sex with five guys, her first was when she was sixteen. Two of the boys she had dated in high school, the other three she dated after she started University to become a teacher. None of them had been particularly bad, but none of them had knocked her socks off, either. She had a feeling that more than just her socks were about to be knocked off with Tony...

She made her intentions known by grabbing him and pushing him back onto the bed, then crawling on top of him, straddling him and kissing him hungrily. There was nothing ladylike or feminine about her behavior. She wanted to ravage him and be ravaged by him, and she was pretty sure he got the picture.

Tony liked that Natalie was taking charge and being aggressive. He plunged his hands into her hair and kissed her roughly, then rolled her to her back and ran his hands down her sides. He grabbed hold of the bottom of her dress and pulled it up while Nat lifted her hips, arched her back and pressed her breasts into Tony's chest, then he pulled it over her head and threw it across the room. He tugged his vintage Van Halen t-shirt off, revealing his sexy hairy chest, and threw it across the room where it landed on top of Nat's dress.

Natalie rolled them so she straddled his upper thighs, then undid her black lace bra and flung it onto the floor. She undid the button on Tony's jeans, lowered the zipper and reached in to grab his cock. He groaned and closed his eyes, smiling in anticipation.

Natalie certainly didn't disappoint! She tugged his jeans down enough to spring his hard cock free, then leaned down and wrapped her lips around him, sliding her tongue up and down his length. She used one hand to hold him steady while the other cupped his balls, massaging lightly.

Tony's hands clutched Nat's head, guiding her up and down at a faster pace until he was close to blowing his load. Before the party they were having ended too soon, he grabbed her under her arms, pulled her up to his chest and rolled them so he was on top, then pushed up to his knees and leaned back into his heels. He yanked her black lace panties off and flung them across the room where they landed on the lampshade, casting a sexy black lace pattern on the ceiling.

"Nice shot," Nat husked. "What other tricks do you have up your sleeve?"

"Just you wait," Tony teased as he crawled off the bed to pull off his jeans, socks and boots, leaving them lumped on the floor at the side of the bed.

Natalie lay back on the pillow watching him strip while biting her lip in anticipation.

Tony stood at the foot of the bed and admired Nat's beauty, feeling lucky that he was the one she wanted and not his sex-crazy band mates. And what a wildcat she was turning out to be! He climbed onto the bed and slowly crawled, licking and biting his way up Nat's body, pausing to give her wetness a few hungry licks, then continued until he reached her mouth.

Her eyes closed, savouring the plethora of feelings she was experiencing. She shifted so she was flat on her back, ready for what Tony had planned next.

He grabbed a condom from his bedside table and rolled it on. He placed his hands beside Natalie's head and positioned his pelvis above her own, his hard length poised at her opening. She opened her eyes and they smiled seductively at each other for a moment, then Tony dropped down onto his elbows, plunged into her and started thrusting.

Natalie wrapped her arms around Tony's back and her legs around his waist, tilting her hips so she could take him as deep as possible.

He vigorously pumped in and out of her, thrusting his tongue in and out of her mouth in tandem with his hips. Then he pulled out, moved back onto his knees and flipped her over onto her belly, pulled her hips up, plunged back in and began pumping into her again. She brought herself up to all fours and turned her head to watch his face contorting in pure pleasure.

Tony's hand left her hip and travelled around to her bundle of nerves, circling and lightly pinching, bringing Natalie to a shattering orgasm. When he felt her muscles clenching around his cock inside her, that was his cue to let go and blow his load.

He slammed in one last time, balls deep, feeling it from the top of his head to the tip of his toes as his orgasm drained him. He pulled Nat's torso up so her back was flush with his chest and she leaned her head back against his shoulder. Their faces were turned to each other, kissing lightly and panting against each other's mouths. He continued to pump lazily in and out of her, savoring the aftershocks of their mammoth orgasms.

When they came down from their orgasm high, Tony pulled out and lay Natalie down in the bed on her side with the covers tucked under her arm, then discarded the condom in the bathroom across the hall. He came back to bed to find her almost asleep, her feet dangling off the side of the bed.

She still had her stilettos on…

"Holy fuck, that is the sexiest thing I've ever seen," he breathed, looking at her messy hair and sated smile.

"What is?" she asked, a lazy, contented smile playing across her lips.

"You, laying in my bed with your stilettos still on, looking well fucked," he answered.

She grinned as she reached down and took them off. "I agree."

Tony crawled in behind her, pulled her into his arms and asked, "You staying the night with me?"

"Do you want me to?" Nat wondered.

"I wouldn't ask if I didn't," he replied.

"Then yes, I am," Nat said as she smiled happily.

Tony settled in bed with his arms wrapped around Natalie, their hands linked together. They sighed and closed their eyes, utterly satisfied smiles on their lips.

Shortly after, they fell asleep and slept through until morning.

CHAPTER 15

October 1992

Darryl

ILLUSIONS was loud and busy, like most Saturday nights.

When Darryl walked through the doors, he wasn't expecting to see Krys and Natalie there making goo-goo eyes at the band playing on stage. He kept to the shadows and meandered his way to the back bar to get a beer and ran into some friends. He stayed back there talking to them with his back to the wall so he could watch both girls.

He did not like what he was seeing.

My Kryssie flirting with another guy?

That's right, she isn't "my Kryssie" anymore, is she...

Cynthia fucked that up but good last night, didn't she...

He kept watch to see how the rest of evening was going to play out.

Darryl simmered with fury as Krys and the guitar player cozied up together. His own sister looked like she approved the match, *the traitor*, as busy as she was with her hands full of lead singer.

He watched as the two couples hooked up at the end of the night and walked out, hand in hand. Darryl felt like his heart was being ripped out of his chest.

Just then, some random, half-drunk girl sidled up to him and said something to him that he didn't quite register. He turned his head towards her and gave her a quick once over, a grim look on his face.

She'll do...

Darryl turned on the charm and after a few minutes of lame flirting, they went out the back door to her car, climbed into the back seat of the cramped sedan and had sex. He made sure he had a condom on before he continued down this path to complete moral bankruptcy and emotional ruin. He kept his eyes closed the entire time, wishing it was Krys on top of him and not this easy piece. His heart turned cold and as soon as he came, he pushed her off him and hauled ass out of there as fast as he could. He ditched the used condom and didn't look back, so he didn't hear her loudly complaining about not having gotten off and what a lousy lay he was.

Darryl didn't care. He didn't give a fast fuck about *anything* anymore. His heart was irreparably broken, splintered into a million jagged pieces. He and Krys were officially over and he just didn't know any other way to cope but to do what most red-blooded males do – harden his heart and screw anything that moves. He never would have imagined his life could get so out of control because of one person's heinous actions.

The next time he saw Cynthia, he was going to make her pay for ruining his life.

CHAPTER 16

October 1992

Krys & Natalie & Diamond Angel

Krys and Natalie met up in the kitchen of Diamond Angel's house in the morning, wearing only the t-shirts their guys wore the night before, big smiles plastered on their faces.

"Morning, Blondie! How'd you sleep?" Nat asked, her eyes glittering with mischief.

Krys managed a blush. "Pretty well, but not long enough," she admitted shyly.

"I'll bet," Nat replied, giggling.

It was then that they heard a strange noise coming from the living room, so they went to investigate. What they saw nearly brought them to their knees in fits of laughter.

Diego and Alex were cuddled together on the couch, chest to chest, limbs intertwined, faces smiling serenely and slightly turned upwards towards the ceiling, cheeks touching.

Krys heard footsteps on the stairs behind them. She turned to see Rick coming down from his attic space and Tony coming up from his basement space, where they met on the landing. They stared past the girls at the sight on the couch, their mouths gaping open.

Tony snapped out of his stunned stare first, turned and went back down the stairs, mumbling, "I have GOT to get a picture of this..." which made Rick snort with laughter, causing Krys and Natalie to fall against each other again, giggling loudly.

At the sound of the laughter, Diego cracked open an eyelid and looked at where the noise was coming from. Then he turned his head and saw who was cuddled in his arms. His eyes bugged out and he struggled to disentangle himself from Alex's vice-like grip.

Alex was still sound asleep with a sweet smile on his face, holding what he must have thought was a conquest close to him, hoping for a morning quickie before he booted her ass out the door.

Diego began cursing in rapid-fire Spanish, thrashing his arms and legs trying to wake Alex up, which caused them to roll off the couch and land on the floor in a tangled heap, finally rousing him awake.

"What the fuck, Al? Let go of me before I beat your ass into the damn carpet! *Ay Carumba!*" Diego cursed as he got up from the floor, leaving Alex there.

"What, dude? I'm a heavy sleeper and I thought you were a girl," Alex started to say, slowly getting up and rubbing his hip.

"You *idiota*, do I FEEL like a girl?" Diego asked, his hands on his hips with his head cocked to the side.

"Not really, but I'm not one to discriminate. I like to share all the love I have in me," Alex joked. "But you *look* like one with the way you're standing."

"Get away from me, you freaky *gringo,*" Diego said as he stalked up the stairs to the bathroom, mumbling something about weird-ass bass players and drinking too much cheap, watered-down booze, then slammed his way into his bedroom.

Alex just shrugged his shoulders and wandered into the kitchen to root around for something to eat.

Tony finally came back up the stairs, but had missed the entire scene, so Natalie relayed the entire scenario, doubling over in hysterics.

Rick moved behind Krys and wrapped his arms around her, kissing her cheek. "What's up for today?" he said to everyone.

Tony looked at Nat, Nat looked at Krys and Krys looked back to Rick.

Tony spoke first. "I got nothing planned, just wanted to take it easy today. Rick?"

"Maybe we should take our girls home to get a change of clothes? It's not fair to flaunt them in front of the boys wearing only our t-shirts and nothing else," Rick replied, then turned to the girls. "Do you both want to come back later? We always barbecue on Sundays."

Krys and Nat glanced at each other again and answered together, "Sure!"

They smelled the coffee that Alex had just finished brewing and they all went to the kitchen to get a cup, except for Krys. She didn't drink coffee, so she had orange juice instead.

Afterwards, Krys and Nat changed back into their clothes from the night before and threw on the guys' t-shirts over top, seeing as their clothes were slinky, going-out-clubbing clothes. Then Rick and Tony took them home with the promise that they would return later in the afternoon to pick them up for a barbecue at Diamond Angel's house.

Which they did.

This time, Krys and Nat were dressed appropriately in jeans and t-shirts, each with a zippered hoodie and sporty shoes, all in the name of comfort, and just a little bit of style.

Once they got back to the band's house and meandered their way out to the back yard, the girls got to meet April, Bryan's long-term girlfriend. She was a curvy 5'10" with long, curly, reddish blonde hair and bright green eyes. She looked like a female version of Bryan.

Alex's dad was a butcher, so he supplied his son with choice cuts of meat, which was why they barbecued as often as they did.

Bryan's mother hated that her son didn't live with her anymore, so she brought a cooler of food over for him and his housemates every week to ensure that he was eating properly.

Diego was a whiz in the kitchen, so he prepared everything for the grill.

Tony played bartender, pouring everyone drinks.

Rick was on clean-up duty.

When all the food was brought outside to the picnic table on the deck, Krys and Natalie couldn't believe their eyes at the spread before them. There was potato salad, coleslaw, mashed sweet potatoes, three-bean salad, fresh rolls with warmed sweet butter, steak, back ribs, BBQ chicken, grilled veggie skewers and for dessert, cherry cheesecake and chocolate cake with vanilla buttercream frosting.

Krys, Rick, Natalie, Tony, Alex, Diego, Bryan and April all fell on the food, enjoying the delicious tastes and textures of such lovingly prepared food. However, the heavenly atmosphere was about to take a sharp left turn at Albuquerque...

Alex began teasing Diego about the way they had woken up together on the couch that morning.

Diego had heard enough and, being a hot-headed Spaniard, he scooped up a handful of potato salad and overhanded it right at Alex's head. It splatted onto the right side of his face and slid down his cheek, some plopping onto the table and the rest into his lap.

Alex was momentarily stunned, then retaliated by grabbing a big serving spoon, loading it with mashed sweet potatoes and firing it back at Diego.

Diego saw out of the corner of his eye, waiting for retaliation, so he was ready and ducked.

The launch of mashed sweet potatoes found a new target of Bryan's face, but some landed on April's chest and slid down her top, shocking her into stunned silence.

Krys and Natalie gathered up their plates and hot-footed it inside to watch the chaos and mayhem play out from the safety of the kitchen window.

Tony was doubled over in his lawn chair laughing so hard, he missed the wicked looks coming his way. Alex and Bryan grabbed handfuls of three-bean salad and coleslaw, then advanced on Tony while his head was down and his eyes were closed. They came in from each side, tag-teaming him as Bryan stuffed the cold, oil-slicked bean salad down the back of his shirt and Alex mashed the coleslaw through his hair.

Rick laughed out loud and everyone realized he hadn't gotten involved yet. April grabbed a huge chunk of chocolate cake and hurled it through the air, right at him. It landed in the middle of his chest and splattered over his face and into his hair, knocking him back off the picnic table seat.

Diego nearly fell backwards out of his lawn chair at the huge chocolately mess all over Rick and he was about to pay the price. Rick picked up the remaining cheesecake and pitched it at Diego, but he ducked again and it hit Alex in the back of the head, cheesecake flying in all directions.

By this time, everyone had been hit with some form of flying foodstuffs, so they all moved in towards the table and decided to have a massive group food fight.

Then it was *game on* and any anger was quickly dispatched into hilarity. Everyone picked up whatever was closest to them and just threw it haphazardly in any direction, not caring if they hit someone or not.

Krys and Natalie caught the entire thing from inside the house, hooting and hollering at the hilarious melee going on outside on the deck.

"Hey, where are the girls?" Tony asked, drenched and dripping with a cornucopia of everything that was once on the table.

No one noticed until then that the girls were nowhere to be found.

"They went inside once I got hit," April replied. "Too bad they missed such great fun!"

Everyone turned to the kitchen window and saw the girls, clean and dry, staring at them and waving coyly, guilty looks on their faces at having been caught.

Rick looked directly at Krys and lifted his arm with his palm up, repeatedly curling his forefinger towards him with a sexy grin on his lips, drawing her out of the house. She was absolutely helpless and couldn't stop her feet if she tried.

When she reached him, Rick asked her, "Why did you leave the fun, Princess?"

All Krys could reply, in between giggling at the unbelievable mess of food strewn all around the deck and an undeniable desire to lick Rick clean from head to toe, was, "I didn't want to get my clothes dirty since I don't have any clean ones here."

"I'll make sure you have something to wear after we're done with you," he grinned wickedly as he playfully pulled her to him with her back to his chest and his arms firmly clamped around her. He nodded at Tony and Bryan, who teamed up and advanced on her, grinding a whole lot of mixed up food into her hair and down her shirt, all of them laughing and enjoying their rollicking good time.

All this time Natalie was cowering in the doorway, not sure if she wanted to join in the fun or run into the house and hide until the coast was clear of all the flying food!

Tony noticed her hesitation and walked over to her. "If you come out and play, I'll make it worth your while to get dirty," he leered lewdly, waggling his eyebrows up and down at her.

"Oh, all right, just not up my nose, okay? I can't stand that, but anything else goes..." she trailed off, knowing what Tony had in store for her was going to be well worth it.

Diego and Alex took their turns dressing Nat in what was left of the feast in her hair, on her face, down the front and back of her top and even down the back of her pants. She wasn't sure if she'd ever feel clean again, even after a thousand showers!

Once all the food had been scraped clean out of all the serving bowls and was plastered onto each and every person there, they stopped and just stared at each other in gut-busting hilarity. Then it came time to clean up, but Rick was let off the hook in having to do it himself, due to the sheer volume of work needed and time required for such a huge job, so everyone pitched in.

Bryan spied the garden hose attached to the tap at the back of the house, picked it up and turned on the faucet. "Okay everyone, line up!" he called out, waving the nozzle around.

Everyone fell in line, then Bryan pressed the trigger. He sprayed one after the other, getting them to lift their arms and twirl around in a circle, drenching them all from head to toe until they were squeaky clean.

When he was done, Rick took the nozzle from Bryan and hosed him down. The rest took the dishes and squished their way into the kitchen while Bryan stayed outside to hose off the deck.

April got a couple of towels from the closet and took them outside for her and Bryan to dry off with.

Tony disappeared with Natalie down to his basement domain.

Diego and Alex wandered their way to their bedrooms, shutting their doors at the same time.

Rick and Krys just looked at each other, shrugged their shoulders in fits of giggles and got busy cleaning up the kitchen.

Bryan and April came back inside with their arms around each other and headed towards his bedroom at the back of the house.

Once the dirty job of cleaning the dishes and the wet mess on the floor was done, Rick took Krys in his arms and kissed her. His tongue invaded her mouth and she turned to liquid in his embrace, bringing a smile of triumph to Rick's face.

"Why are you smiling at me like that?" she asked, feeling heat pooling in her belly.

"Because once I take your wet clothes off, I get to see you naked again and that will absolutely make my day," he replied seductively.

"Well then, let's not make you wait for me to make your day," Krys said as she grabbed Rick's hand and pulled him to the stairs that led up to his attic bedroom. Once there, she launched herself at him, wrapping her arms around his shoulders and her legs around his hips, kissing him with wild lust.

Rick held her easily in his arms and walked towards the bathroom. Before he reached the door, he let her legs down to stand in front of him. He stared into her eyes as he began undressing her, peeling away the wet layers of her clothes and tossing them aside into a pile.

She stayed still and enjoyed Rick's soft touch, feeling her desire for him rocketing up her body.

Once he completely divested Krys of her wet clothes, Rick took her hands in his and guided them to his own wet clothing, silently requesting her help in taking them off him.

She managed to strip off his clothes quickly, not wanting to waste any precious time that they could both be naked together. The air around them was so erotically charged, the anticipation of having sex with Rick again made Krys blush with excitement.

Rick placed his hands on Krys' shoulders and pressed her back against the wall as he kissed her, nudging her legs apart. He ran his hand down her torso and cupped her breast, rolling her nipple between his strong fingers, then bent down and suckled at the other.

Krys looked down and watched as Rick ravished her. He looked up at her with such wild passion that her breath caught in her throat. His eyes burned through her, making the heat in her belly expand until she was feeling flush from neck to knees. She had never felt quite so wanton, even with Darryl, and they'd had a pretty imaginative sex life...

But what was blooming between Krys and Rick was something else altogether.

Rick kissed Krys again and his cock slid into her as he pressed her up against the wall. He thrust into her slowly while Krys clutched at his shoulders. It didn't take long before the familiar burn was *right there* and they came together. Then he slid out of her and kissed her until they were breathless.

"Let's get clean," he husked as he lifted her legs around his hips again and walked into the bathroom, Krys' arms around his neck. He held her around her waist as he reached in and turned on the faucet in the claw-foot tub.

When the water was warm enough, Rick pulled back the shower curtain and climbed in with the spray at his back, holding Krys and kissing her sensually. He let her legs down and she stood on tiptoe with her arms coiled around his neck as she kissed him back. Then he turned them so she could get warmed under the hot water.

Rick squirted some shampoo onto his hand and washed Krys' hair for her, the gesture sweet, sexy and intimate. He rinsed her hair and applied a generous dollop of conditioner to her long mane, then took his turn to wash the remnants of the food fight from his own hair.

He took a bath sponge, lathered it up with lightly scented suds and washed Krys' body. After he rinsed her, he squeezed more shower gel onto the sponge for himself, but Krys intercepted, taking the sponge and washing Rick as sensuously as he'd washed her.

When they were both clean and all the bubbles were washed down the drain, Rick turned off the faucet and grabbed two fluffy bath towels from the pile beside the tub. He slung one around his hips and stepped over the edge of the tub onto the bath mat. He gave Krys his hand and helped her step over the rim of the tub onto the mat where he wrapped her in the towel and lifted her in his arms, kissing her sweetly.

Rick carried Krys to his bed and laid her down gently. He climbed on top of her and eased himself between the cradle of her legs while she held on to his shoulders. They were face to face and she had an odd look that Rick couldn't figure out. "What's on your mind, Princess?"

"I'm just overwhelmed with everything that's happened to me this weekend and you're so... so..." she started, unable to continue as her voice cracked.

"I'm so..." he prompted.

"Handsome, erotic, sexy, seductive, addictive..." she admitted, blushing.

Rick was thrilled at her word choices in describing him and it puffed him up, inspiring him to prove every single one of them to her. "Well, that's certainly encouraging," he smirked sexily.

He rolled them side to side, whipping off both of their towels and flinging them onto the floor. Then he resettled between her thighs, nuzzling her neck and kissing her sensuously.

His hand slid down Krys' belly to her wet heat and he slipped a finger inside, massaging her sweet spot with his thumb. Then he began licking a path down her body headed for paradise.

By the time he kissed his way down her belly, Krys was close to erupting, so Rick threw her legs apart and dove in, replacing his fingers with his tongue and continued until she writhed her release.

He crawled up her body as it was still spasming from her orgasm and plunged his hard cock deep into her slick center in one smooth stroke, pulling out slowly then pushing back in just as slowly. Krys grabbed Rick's hips and bucked hers up to meet him halfway as he drove into her, moving faster at Krys' demand.

After several minutes of aggressive thrusting, Rick groaned his release just as Krys began spasming for the second time. He collapsed on top of her and she revelled in his weight, feeling warm and loved...

Loved?

After only two days?

She let that thought go, not wanting anything that heavy laying on her mind in the afterglow of phenomenal sex with her Rick...

My Rick?

Well, I guess he is now, after all this...

"Rick, I have to go to school tomorrow, so I can't stay the night, as much as I want to," Krys began.

"I have school, too," Rick admitted.

"You do?" she replied, shocked.

"Yeah, I'm in grad school. After I got my Bachelor's Degree in Psychology, I decided I wanted to go further. I had really good grades in University, so I got accepted right away to take my Master's Degree. Once I'm finished, I'll be able to practise as a Clinical Psychologist specializing in Child Stress and Trauma," he concluded.

"Wow..." was all Krys could say as Rick grinned at her and leaned down to kiss her again, their tongues tangling. Then she stiffened up and froze in the middle of winning that particular round of tongue wars. "We didn't use a condom," she said in a whisper.

Rick's grin faded to a thoughtful look. "Are you on the Pill?" he said hopefully.

"Yes, but still..." she began.

"Krys, I have to get regular medical check-ups for school and I was just given a clean bill of health earlier this month. And contrary to rumours about musicians being sexual deviants, I haven't been with nearly as many women as Alex and Diego have," Rick told her.

"Well, that's good to know," Krys said slowly.

"I'm a one-woman guy and when I'm with a woman, it tends to stick for a long time. In fact, it's been a few months since I was even with another woman," Rick told her, hoping to quell her rising panic.

"I don't know what to say to that," she breathed, feeling her panic subsiding.

"Just know that once I spotted you, I gave up other women, hoping that I'd get a chance to have you as mine," he replied, kissing her nose, then rubbing along side it lightly with his own.

Krys was stunned at such a romantic revelation. Realizing that Rick was still on top of her AND still inside her, she gifted him with a breathtakingly beautiful smile and pulled him down to kiss him.

Rick slid out of her and off to her side, positioning them with her back to his chest so they could cuddle for a while before they had to get up for him to drive Krys home.

After an hour or so, they reluctantly got up and got dressed. Rick gave Krys a pair of sweatpants and a hoodie, both overly large on her, because her clothes were still hopelessly wet.

When they got to her house and she exited his car, she leaned back in and smiled sweetly at him, saying, "When do you want to..." she started, but he cut her off.

"Tomorrow evening, if you're free," he asked.

"I think that will work," she answered back as they leaned towards each other for one last kiss.

Krys smiled as she made her way to the back door of the house with her bundle of wet clothing in her arms. It was late, nearly eleven PM, but she had prepared her bag for school before she left in the afternoon, anticipating being out late.

Krys' mother, Lily, met her inside the back door and gave her the once-over, taking in what her daughter was dressed in, her eyebrows raised. "Kryssie, would you mind explaining to me your clothing situation?" Lily asked, taking the wet bundle of clothes from her daughter and eyeing the larger, obviously male clothing she was wearing.

"We got into a food fight," Krys admitted, giggling at the memory of all the food hanging off everyone's faces and splattered all over the deck.

Lily grinned, then got serious. "That wasn't Darryl who dropped you off. Did something happen that you want to tell me about?" she asked warmly, placing her arm around her daughter's waist and hugging Krys close to her. Lily was a sprightly, petite 5'2" with brown, bespectacled eyes and short, curly brown hair.

"No. Not tonight..." she started, intending to stop there, but decided to continue. "Actually, that was Rick. He's going to be a fixture in my life from now on and Darryl is... out. That's all I really want to say about it for now, Momma. I need to go to bed and concentrate on school tomorrow, not my mixed-up love life," Krys admitted.

"Okay, my Baby. When you decide that you want to tell me, I'm all ears," Lily told her sad and close-lipped daughter, kissing her cheek.

"Thanks, Momma, I love you," Krys snuggled into her petite mother's embrace, then went to her room and climbed into bed, falling asleep instantly and sleeping the sleep of the well loved.

CHAPTER 17

October 1992 to March 1993
Krys & Rick

Over the next few months, Krys and Rick grew closer, talking every day after their first wild weekend together and spending all their free time with each other. They talked about things in the medical field, music, movies, food, fashion, nothing was off the table. They didn't always agree or see eye to eye on everything, but they respected the other's different opinions and were able to move on amicably.

For her birthday in early November, Rick bought Krys a guitar and began teaching her how to play. He often commented on how she was a fast learner and picked it up easily.

"All those years of piano lessons," she shrugged humbly.

She loved playing her blonde wood, classical nylon string guitar and even started composing short songs, which she hummed along to at first, then started singing lyrics to them that she made up herself.

She didn't know that Rick was listening when she was in her *zone,* playing, humming and singing, but listening he was and he paid attention. He even rigged up a device to record her. He wasn't sure what he was going to do with it, but perhaps one day an opportunity would present itself.

After their first weekend together, they decided that they no longer needed to use condoms since Krys was on the Pill and they were definitely exclusive and monogamous.

Early one Saturday morning in late March, after a particularly vigorous night of sex, Krys woke up in Rick's bed to horrifically painful cramps. She was in the middle of her cycle and wasn't due to start her period for another ten days, but the cramps seized her and she barely made it to the bathroom. When she looked in the bowl after the cramping eased for a moment, she blanched at the amount of bright red blood and clots that she saw.

"Rick," she called to him in a quiet voice. "I need to go to the hospital."

"Why? It's the weekend, no school today," he answered back sleepily.

She cleared her throat and spoke louder. "Because I'm bleeding."

Rick jackknifed out of bed and was in the bathroom beside her in a flash, looking in the bowl. All he saw was a whole lot of fresh blood and a sizable blood clot. "Could this be from what we were doing last night?" he asked. "I didn't think we were any more wild and rough than usual, were we? Was I? OH! Wait a minute, is it your time of the month, maybe?" he rambled.

"No, the timing is all wrong... This is something else..." she strained to talk as another wave of cramping hit her, doubling her over, causing her to drop to her knees and crouch in half, her nose brushing the floor.

Rick was beside himself not knowing what was wrong with Krys and not having any idea what to do to ease her incredible pain.

She was able to unfold herself enough from the floor in between bouts of cramping to climb her way back onto the toilet, gasping in agony as she expelled more blood and clots.

When the pain lessened, Krys lifted her torso up and began rambling off all the possible things that might be wrong with her. Then a look of absolute horror crossed her face, so Rick crouched down and wrapped his arms around her, holding her close while she closed her eyes and started to shake.

"Rick, I think I'm having a miscarriage," Krys whispered, almost inaudibly.

Rick was stunned, then he spoke, his voice low. "But you're on the Pill. I thought you can't get pregnant while you're on the Pill?" he said quietly.

"I was taking antibiotics for bronchitis in January. Antibiotics nullify the potency of birth control pills and I was on them for ten days! Ten days! And we didn't use condoms! OHMYGOD, Rick! How could I have been so careless when I know better?" Krys rasped, her voice hoarse with anxiety, her face tucked into Rick's chest.

She began to cry, quietly and silently, until she could hold back no longer. Wracking sobs burst forth from her chest as she leaned forward and collapsed in Rick's arms.

Once her sobs settled, Rick helped Krys to the sink to get cleaned up, her legs weak, her mind in a flurry. She looked at him in the mirror in thanks, then slid down the wall to the floor with him as he held her close, rocking her gently back and forth, each lost in their own thoughts.

After a time, Krys lifted her head and placed her tear-stained cheek on his chest, her nose turned up to his face. She cleared her throat and said, "I just spotted a bit last month and I was wondering why. I thought maybe it was just the stress of school. It *never* dawned on me that I might be *pregnant!*"

"Do you still want me to take you to the hospital to get checked out?" Rick asked, his voice quiet.

"Yes, I think that would be best," Krys decided.

Krys was right. She DID miscarry, the fetus only seven weeks gestation.

On the way home, Rick asked her, "Where do you want me to take you?"

"What do you mean? Your place," Krys replied, a confused look on her face.

Rick sighed audibly, relief crossing his face. "Okay."

"What's going on in your head, Rick? Do you think I'm mad at you or blame you for this happening? Because I can tell you with absolute certainty, I am NOT in any way upset with you. It's sad and untimely, but I also think it was just not meant to be for us at this point in our lives. Thankfully, it didn't ruin my ability to get pregnant again in the future. Now, let's go home and rest. Diamond Angel is playing tonight and I don't want you to be off your game for your fans," Krys answered.

"Okay, Princess," Rick acquiesced.

Rick thought it was a bit odd that Krys wasn't more broken up about miscarrying their baby, but HE was certainly fucked up about it.

How could you mourn the loss of something you never even knew you had in the first place?

Krys and Rick decided it was best to keep this information to themselves and not tell anyone, not even Natalie and Tony. They needed to process it and come to terms with it first.

And if Krys ever did decide to tell Natalie? That meant Darryl would find out and that was the LAST thing Krys wanted. She was going to carry this to her grave and Darryl would NEVER know...

CHAPTER 18

October 1992 to March 1993
Darryl

In the months since Darryl and Krys split up, Darryl became a different person. He was no longer the carefree, fun-loving guy his friends knew and loved. Most of them knew what had happened to make him so despondent and withdrawn, but none of them knew what to say or do to help him cope and get over losing Krys. He was perfectly content to be miserable and he was making the most of his miserableness.

Darryl's birthday rolled around shortly after New Year's in January and was rather uneventful. He was at another bar called SHENANIGANS with Keith and Jeremy, playing pool.

After a few beers, he picked up another nameless, faceless piece and nailed her in the coat room. No emotion, no feeling, no oral sex, and NEVER any kissing, just straight fucking, him coming in record time and hauling ass away from there as fast as he could. And most importantly, he *ALWAYS* used a condom, without fail. He may be a selfish prick now, but he wasn't a *total* asshole. He didn't care about any of the girls he was systematically banging. He was in it for him and him alone now.

Cynthia, that rancid, fucking bitch, sure did a number on him.

The most unexpected thing about the entire situation was that Darryl delved head first into his schooling and he was doing better than ever. The assignments he created were gaining recognition and more scholarship money was being thrown at him, as well as offers for internships with the possibility of future employment at several architectural firms.

Where his personal life was a shambles, his professional life was shooting into the stratosphere. But he'd give it all up in a heartbeat to rewind a few months, erase everything that happened and have Krys back in his life.

He'd also love to wrap his hands around Cynthia's neck and strangle the life out of her for decimating his life into rubble.

CHAPTER 19

October 1992 to March 1993
Natalie & Tony

The past several months were equally happy and stressful for Natalie.

Happy, because she was with Tony. He was everything she wanted in a man. And the sex? Totally and completely mindblowing...

Stressful, because with Krys and Darryl having split up, Nat spent very little time with either of them anymore. She didn't want to say something out of turn or let something slip to upset either of them.

Natalie caught wind that Darryl was screwing anything in a skirt to cope with his broken heart, something that if Krys knew, it would hurt her immensely. That was one behavior Natalie never thought Darryl would succumb to. But she also never thought in a million lifetimes that things would have gone to shit they way they did between Krys and Darryl.

It was such a damn shame...

And she sure as hell wasn't going to tell Darryl how happy Krys was with Rick. That might possibly be the end of him.

One night, when she and Tony were wrapped in each other's arms after a great night at ILLUSIONS and even greater sex at his house afterwards, they got to talking about him and his job. He wasn't in school, but working as a mechanic until the band took off.

And he was convinced they would...

He could feel it in his bones...

They were so close...

In the meantime, he worked hard, wrote great songs, played a mean guitar and harmonica and along with Rick, co-managed the band. It was just a matter of time before they were seriously noticed and were offered a recording contract that would change their lives and all the people around them.

Tony did have one concern, though.

A big one.

As close as Rick was now with Krys, Tony was starting to get the feeling that when Diamond Angel DID record an album and go on tour, he may have trouble convincing Rick to go away and leave Krys for months at a time. Plus, Rick was in graduate school and nearing completion of his Master's Degree. Tony wasn't sure if Rick was ready to just toss all of that aside for fame and fortune when he was setting himself up for a very good life here with Krys.

They would just have to bide their time and wait and see what the future held for all of them.

CHAPTER 20

April 1993

Krys & Natalie & Diamond Angel

Diamond Angel were playing their usual Friday night gig at ILLUSIONS.

What they didn't know was that there was a scout from Global Music Entertainment watching and listening to them play that night.

Greg Hansen had heard a lot about this local band who had gathered quite the following of die hard, loyal fans, both male and female, and he liked what he was hearing.

A lot.

Greg was 6'2" with salt-and-pepper hair and blue eyes. He was a runner with an athlete's physique. Women loved him, but he only had eyes for his wife, Lorraine. He was also a doting father to his two kids, a boy and a girl.

He had been following Diamond Angel for several months, but wanted to get a better idea of their musical style and stage presence from more than just a few shows. If he was going to guide this band towards *supergroup* status, he had to be sure of every last detail.

I can feel it...
They're going to be huge if I have anything to do with it...

After Diamond Angel finished playing the second of their three sets, Greg confidently approached the table where the five band members were sitting, three of them with beautiful women, the other two holding their beers. "Hello gentlemen, my name is Greg Hansen and I'm a talent scout from Global Music Entertainment," he said, extending his hand and shaking all five of the band members hands, smiling at each in turn as they told him their names.

Tony stood up, pulling Natalie with him. He draped his arm around her shoulders and smiled widely. "Mr Hansen, what can we do for you this fine evening?"

"I've been following your career for the past several months and I have an offer for Diamond Angel. Is there somewhere a little quieter and more private that we can talk?" Greg asked.

"Sure. We can use Mickey's office," Bryan replied, standing with April at his side, holding her hand and leading the way with Tony and Natalie right behind them.

Alex and Diego began vibrating with excitement and got up quickly to follow.

Rick looked at Krys, but all he saw was a blank look on her face. He stood up and offered her his hand, saying to her, "This concerns you too, Krys, I'd like you to be there to see what he has to say."

Krys nodded her head and gave her hand to Rick as they walked towards the office.

Once there, they all crowded in to listen to Greg's pitch. "Firstly, let me tell you, you guys are good, really good, one of the best original bands to come out of this city in a very

IN AND OUT OF LOVE

long time, and I've been doing this for eighteen years. Your sound is classic enough and current enough to span several genres and give a varied sound to an album. This is what I've got to offer Diamond Angel. You have one month to write at least ten songs to be recorded at our studio here in the city. You will be provided with everything you need to record the best album you can, with a generous financial advance and a healthy financial bonus if you finish it early. We'll have an album release party and you'll play the best venue in the city to get you maximum exposure. Then we'll send you on tour, opening for various established rock'n'roll bands throughout North America. Here are copies of the contract for each of you. Take the weekend to think about it and bring along a lawyer of your choice to look over the contracts to ensure that you understand everything and feel comfortable signing on the dotted line. How does Monday morning at ten work for all of you?" he concluded.

The boys of Diamond Angel sat there, poleaxed. To be associated with the likes of Streetheart, Harlequin, The Pumps/Orphan, The Guess Who, Bachman-Turner Overdrive, Burton Cummings, Randy Bachman, Neil Young and Crash Test Dummies was incredibly humbling!

Rick broke out of his daze and spoke up first. "Mr. Hansen, I appreciate your coming to see us, but the timing for me, personally, isn't great. I'm in the final weeks of graduate school and I really don't have a lot of spare time to spend recording an album."

Tony stared at him with his mouth gaping open. "You... ungrateful... selfish... asshole!!" he screeched. "You *know* how long we've been working for this and how much we want this and you're just going to throw it all down the drain for a few more weeks in school? What the fuck is the matter with you? Krys! Talk some sense into him! This is the chance we've been waiting for and busting our asses for!" Tony began, turning to the rest of the guys, continuing, "And he just wants to throw it all away and ruin it for the rest of us!" he huffed, then turned back to face Rick again. "Fuck, man, I thought I knew you, I'm at a loss," he trailed off, shaking his head and looking at the floor, totally disgusted.

Bryan, Alex and Diego just stood there and collectively stared at Rick, not sure if there was anything else to add as they agreed with everything Tony had just said.

In front of the entire audience in Mickey's cramped office, Krys looked at Rick and took his hands in hers. Her blank face was no longer blank. It was filled with emotion as she spoke. "Rick, can I tell you what I think of this situation?"

"Of course, Kryssie. You know I'll always listen to you," Rick replied as Tony snorted angrily.

"Okay, then. Please think carefully about what you may be giving up if you do not take this incredibly generous and exciting opportunity you're being given. You may have only a few weeks left of school, but can you really give all of this up without at least trying to negotiate with the record label to accommodate completing both? We all know that school and the band are equally important to you and you shouldn't have to compromise one for the other," she said.

Rick looked at Krys and said slowly, "Yeah, you're right, they are."

Then she turned to Greg. "Mr. Hansen, would it be negotiable for Rick to have the time he needs to finish his schooling AND record the album? I believe it would provide him with the motivation and incentive to do his part in making the best Diamond Angel record possible."

Greg looked at Krys and grinned as she dazzled him with her polite, respectful request. "I don't think that would be a problem. We can discuss all of these details on Monday morning."

"Alright, so that's settled. It will be discussed with both parties satisfied in the end. My second point is that this is a once in a lifetime opportunity that very few people get. Don't throw it away because of school, me, or anything else. Make it work. If this is something that you want, take it with both hands and run with it. Make your parents, and me, proud. You have it in you, I know you do. You're so talented, all of you. It would be an absolute shame to forsake it by not taking this good fortune and sharing it with the musical world by watching it grow into something simply amazing," she concluded, her eyes dark with emotion.

Rick just stood there and stared at Krys. School was just an excuse. He was already finished his thesis and had a couple of weeks free until he had to present it. Recording an album would only enhance his excitement for that day and certainly motivate him to write some spectacular songs. He wanted this so badly he could taste it, but in getting what he'd always wanted, he was terrified to lose Krys, the love of his life, because of it.

But she had faith in him, all of them. That was the one factor that pushed him off the fence. Now that he had her blessing, he was going to make his other dream come true. "Mr Hansen, you've got yourself a deal," Rick said slowly, smiling at Krys, then at Greg, dropping Krys' hands and shaking Greg's in agreement.

Tony's head shot up and his look of disgust morphed into one of absolute euphoria.

Rick turned to Tony and explained, "You gotta understand, Tony, I have a lot riding on this decision and I can't take any part of it lightly. I have to consider all of my options and choose the best course for my life and my woman. Krys is right. I DO want this and I know how much it means to all of us. We've been working towards this for a long time and I would be the biggest asshole of all time if I fucked it up for us. Now, let's shake on this and go kick the audience's asses with our last set, okay?"

They shook hands, clapped each other on the back in a quick man-hug and started laughing together, the realization of getting a record deal beginning to sink in. Bryan, Alex and Diego joined them in a football huddle and they all giggled like little boys.

Greg observed them, a smile playing across his lips.

These boys have GOT IT and I can't wait to launch them onto the rest of the world!

When they were able to settle themselves down, all the men filed out one by one – Diamond Angel back to the stage and Greg back to the bar.

April went to the ladies' room.

Natalie stood quietly in the background for the entire meeting watching the events unfold, especially Krys' reaction. She wasn't surprised at what Krys had said, because she knew it was how she felt. "Nice job, Ms Negotiator."

"I know how important this is and I don't want them to miss their chance," Krys answered, but her voice betrayed her feelings.

"And?" Nat pressed.

"I have to be honest, Nat. I have a feeling down to my soul, that not only are they going to hit it big, but we're going to lose them. As much as I love being Rick's girlfriend, I don't know if I'm going to be able to handle him being on the road, touring for months on end and fending off all those aggressive groupies. I'm still in school and I can't put that aside to go on tour with him. I want this so much for them, but I feel like Rick is going to have to make a choice and I'm going to be the one losing out in the end," Krys admitted sadly.

This took Natalie back a step. "Wow, you've really thought about this a lot, haven't you?" Natalie hadn't stopped to think of things in those terms and had to admit, Krys made a lot of sense. Krys and Rick were so close, moving ahead together with their lives and careers, now this once-in-a-lifetime opportunity comes along and throws a huge wrench into their future.

On the other side of the situation, Natalie and Tony were close and had a great relationship, but she still had a ways to go in school before she was finished. For Natalie, University was over for the semester in April and she was done until September, so if she wanted to take some time off to go on tour with Diamond Angel over the summer months, she could. But the hospital-based nursing school Krys went to was set up much differently. She went to school for eight hours a day, five days a week, for ten-and-a-half months straight, with only a six week break in the summer, so taking off for any length of time was basically impossible.

"Yes, I have. It's been bouncing through my mind for a while, now," Krys admitted.

Is this the beginning of the end for Rick and me?

April came back into the office and saw the looks on both Krys and Nat's faces. "Are you two okay? Krys, you look like you're about to cry," April said, staring at Krys' sad face.

Nat spoke up for them both. "We're just thinking about how all of our lives are going to change in the next few months."

"Yeah, it's a huge step our guys are taking, but they've worked hard to get here. I'm proud of them and happy for them. I've been working for a couple of years in the entertainment business and I may be able to get a job behind the scenes and go on tour with them," April told them.

"Wow! That'd be great for you and Bryan!" Nat exclaimed.

"Yeah, it will be. We've been together for nearly three years, so I'm pretty confident that we'll stay as solid as we are now. And with us being on the tour together, we don't have to worry about being separated. Is that what you're both concerned about?" April replied sympathetically.

"Yes," Krys answered simply.

"Kind of," Nat admitted.

"It will be tough, but your guys are completely head over heels for the both of you, so I don't think you'll have any issues," April smiled.

"How do you know that?" Krys asked.

April continued to smile warmly as she explained, "Krys, do you *see* how Rick looks at you? He's always got a look of such love and devotion in his eyes. I've NEVER seen him like this before. EVER. We grew up together and went to the same schools all the way from kindergarten to high school. He had a steady girlfriend for a while and he was devoted to her, but nowhere near as much as he is to you. His sun seems to rise and set by you," she concluded.

"I'm... Uh... Wow..." Krys stammered.

April hugged Krys and simply said, "Yeah."

Natalie sighed sweetly, "Awe."

"And you, Natalie," April grinned, turning towards her. "I've known Tony the same length of time and I've never seen him like this with a girl before, either. He had a steady girlfriend for a time in high school and when they split up after graduation, he bounced from girl to girl, but you are the one he's chosen to keep in his life. I'm blown away at how committed he is to you."

Natalie just stood there, her face transfixed in a happy grin as she stared into space.

April smiled to herself, hoping that her pep talk did the job to help the girls feel a little less stressed about the adventure their boys were going to be embarking on soon. Besides, if she did get a job with the company and was able to go on tour with Diamond Angel, she'd keep her eyes on Rick and Tony for them. She honestly liked these two girls and saw how good they were for the boys. Rick and Tony were like brothers to her and she wanted to see them continue to be as happy as they were with these lovely ladies.

Nat snapped out of her reverie. "Okay ladies, let's get out there and cheer on our guys, huh? Then I'm sure we'll ALL have some celebrating to do after the bar's closed, right?" Nat elbowed April in the ribs and play-punched Krys in the shoulder.

The girls left the office and wound their way back to the bar to watch their guys on the stage, relishing these last few weeks of privacy and anonymity, for their lives were all about to change immensely.

CHAPTER 21

April 1993

Natalie & Tony

After the last set was played and ILLUSIONS was locked up, Diamond Angel and their women went back to their house and sat around the living room in stunned silence.

After a while, Krys spoke up to the band. "If you like the idea, my brother Vince is a lawyer and I could ask him to look over your contract on Monday morning."

Tony scanned the guys and they all nodded in agreement. "That would be excellent! Thank you, Krys!" Tony said as he jumped out of his seat, picked her up and twirled her around in a huge bear hug.

Krys broke into a huge smile. "I'm just happy that I can contribute to the excitement."

Tony put her down and held out his hand for Natalie. "Time to go celebrate in private, Strawberry. See you guys in the morning." He took Natalie by the hand and they ran down the stairs to Tony's basement bedroom. He slammed the door shut and began whipping off his clothes, encouraging Natalie to do the same. "I can't wait to get inside you," he breathed, stripping at warp speed.

"Then what are you waiting for?" Natalie asked, her voice husky as she tore off her clothes.

She smiled and grabbed for Tony's shoulders once they were both naked. He wrapped his hands around Nat's ass, lifted her legs up, swung them around his hips and backed her back against the wall. While he was looking into her eyes and she was staring back into his, he slowly slid inside her, then started his ritual of plunging his tongue in her mouth with each thrust of his cock.

Natalie held on, loving Tony's strength and endurance, closing her eyes to savor the feeling. It didn't take long before they both exploded in an orgasmic frenzy.

As their post-orgasm quivers stopped, he pulled out, dropped her legs to the floor and turned them, walking her backwards towards the bed. They fell onto it with him on top of her, then they rolled to their sides and just stared at each other, huge smiles gracing their faces.

"It's finally happening for us," Tony said, slightly out of breath. He picked up the remote for his stereo and pushed a few buttons. One of their favorite sexy rock'n'roll ballads flooded the room at a low volume, Journey's "Lovin' Touchin' Squeezin'".

"I'm really excited for all of you! I hope I can come and visit you once in a while," Nat said, hoping she wasn't being presumptuous.

Tony's smile got even bigger. "Really? You'll do that? Come visit me on the road? It's going to be so exciting, but I know I'm going to miss you every day until I get to see you in person."

Natalie smiled carnally. "Let's stop talking. You have better things to do with your mouth," she murmured as Van Halen's "Black And Blue" began playing.

Tony got her message and, indeed, used his mouth for better things.

CHAPTER 22

April 1993

Krys & Rick

Alex and Diego looked at each other as Tony dragged Natalie off to his basement domain. Each of them had picked up a girl at the bar and were itching to get their catches horizontal.

"Well, we're off to find out if I can make my gal see stars," Alex declared. He deftly slid her off his lap and onto her feet as he got up off the couch, hung his arm around her shoulders and whispered something into her ear, making her bite her lip and smile wickedly as he led her to his room, shutting the door. Within a few minutes, all the rest of them could hear was Italian ballads on Alex's stereo.

"*Ay Carumba*, I can't be outdone by that *gringo*! *Chica*, how about you and I go and see if we can make the Earth move better than Alex and his lady?" Diego crooned to the gal tucked in beside him on the chair in the corner. Her eyes sparkled with excitement as she licked her lips in anticipation. She knew all about Diego and his stellar reputation, so she knew what kind of a good time she was in for. They took off to his room and he slammed his door with his foot. Within moments the remaining group could hear Spanish ballads on Diego's stereo.

Next up was Bryan and April. They looked at Rick and Krys, then at each other, saying in unison, "We're going, see you tomorrow."

Rick got up from his chair and pulled Bryan aside as April went over to Krys. "I don't know what April said to Krys earlier, but please give her a huge *thank you* from me. Krys seems a lot more relaxed about things now," Rick said, exhaling in appreciation and relief.

"No problem. April was just giving Krys some peace of mind about what to expect in the coming months. It's going to be tough on all of us, but I think we'll get through it with few battle scars," Bryan noted.

They did the usual male hug-with-one-arm-and-back-slap-with-the-other, then let go and smiled at each other with brotherly affection.

April and Krys hugged and kissed each other's cheeks, then the couples reformed to go their separate ways for the remainder of the night.

Bryan and April went to Bryan's room to pick up his overnight bag, then left for her apartment. No one could blame them for taking refuge there every weekend when the house was full of couples in various forms of constant undress and sexual activity!

This left Rick and Krys alone in the living room, listening to the various sounds of music and other liveliness coming from the two bedrooms on the main floor and the bedroom in the basement. He gathered her in his arms and kissed her softly, rubbing his nose along side hers, his eyes closed. "Thank you for everything you said tonight to everyone, Princess. It means the world to me that you support the band, me, and us. I just... Wow, I'm just so happy and relieved," he admitted.

"I wouldn't have said those things if I didn't mean them, Rick. I will miss you terribly when you go on tour. And once school is finished for the summer, I hope I can sneak away for an illicit weekend with you somewhere," Krys said, her lips tipping up in a sexy grin.

Rick kissed her upturned, delectable lips and grinned back at her. "I'm going to make sure of that! I already miss you and we haven't even gone into the studio yet!"

"So let's go make some of our own music together, shall we?" Krys suggested as she licked his ear and kissed his jaw.

Rick shivered from the sheer pleasure of Krys kissing him. He bent down to kiss her throat as his hands trailed down her back to her ass and cupped it, grinding it to his pelvis.

Krys moaned and grabbed onto Rick even harder, her nails digging into his shoulders. She slid them around to his back and pulled him even closer, making Rick groan with lust.

"Okay, enough of this out here or I'll be forced rip your clothes off and take you right here on the couch," Rick warned, making Krys smile and bite her lip in excitement.

They loosened their grip on each other and walked, hand in hand, to the door leading to his attic bedroom space. He kicked the door closed as they ran up the stairs, laughing at each other's impatience to get naked and celebrate. When they reached Rick's space, he turned on his stereo to play tunes for him and Krys to get naked to. "Feel Like Makin' Love" by Bad Company began playing softly in the background, setting the mood.

While he was doing this, Krys stood behind him with her hands around his waist, fiddling with the button fly on his leather pants. She undid it quickly, yanked his Jimi Hendrix t-shirt up and over his head, tossed it in the corner, then dragged his black leather pants down his long legs.

Krys turned him around and dropped to her knees, still fully clothed, while Rick stood there fully naked. She grasped his cock in both hands and proceeded to give him one of the best blow jobs he'd ever had. She rasped her tongue up and down his length, dragging her teeth lightly along the way, cupping his balls with just enough pressure to make him tingle with carnal lust.

Rick could barely keep his balance. His head was thrown back and his eyes were closed as he grabbed onto the stereo stand to keep upright while she pleasured him into absolute euphoria.

Just before his cock was about to detonate, Rick pushed Krys away and grabbed her hands, standing her up with him. He kissed both her palms, then lifted her arms up, pulled her flimsy top over her head, tossed it across the room and watched as it landed on top of his t-shirt.

His hands returned to Krys' soft skin and undid the top button on her jeans. He slid the zipper down and grabbed the waistband, inching it slowly over her ass and down her legs to the floor, letting it puddle at her feet. He crouched and helped her out of each leg, even though he still had his own pants down around his own ankles from when she was blowing him.

Rick grinned at that visual while he got Krys fully naked, then stood up and kicked off his remaining clothing as he pushed her back onto the bed and crawled on top of her, smiling seductively.

"Let the celebration continue," Rick growled, leaning down to ravish Krys with sensual kisses all over her neck and breasts with the intent on nibbling and licking his way down to her sweet spot to feast on paradise.

Krys decided it was time to turn the tables on this episode and take control.

She kept firm hold on Rick, slid her foot up and pushed, flipping them so she was on top with her knees on either side of his hips and her forearms resting on his chest. She tenderly took his face in her hands and kissed him sweetly once, twice, then a third time, her tongue softly probing his mouth each time. Then she let go and slid off him to the side, moving her body up the bed while gently prodding him to move down the bed.

To Rick's great delight, Krys positioned herself so that she was kneeling over his face, her wet core suspended above his mouth and her face inches from his cock. He clutched onto her ass, pulled her greedily to his mouth and began his intended feast in a position they had not tried before.

Krys gasped at the rush of pleasure from this position and could barely concentrate on continuing her ravishing of Rick's cock, so it didn't take long before she was writhing in ecstasy. She reached a mindblowing orgasm, then Rick's lips and tongue worked her up into a frenzied second orgasm that rode on the heels of the first one. He kept his mouth on her, wrapped his arms around her hips and held onto her securely, not letting let her go until he felt her spasms ease and her body liquefy in his arms.

Once she relaxed, he knew he could let himself go and have his own release. Her talented mouth and tongue led the way to a magnificent orgasm that seemed to go on and on. Krys held on and refused to remove her mouth from around Rick's cock until she drained him dry.

When they both finished their releases, Rick let go of Krys and she slid off him, righting herself and crawling on top of him. She crossed her arms on his chest and propped up her chin on her hands, smiling smugly. "I think that position is a winner, don't you?" Krys drawled.

"Top five, I think," Rick answered.

Krys smiled and reached up to kiss him as she snaked her hand down to stroke his cock. To her great surprise, he was already getting hard again. "Seriously? Already?"

"What can I say? You do that to me," he said, groaning in appreciation. He leaned up to kiss her again, their tongues entwined.

Krys moved back on top of Rick and sat up, her hand still wrapped around him. She slid his now rock-hard cock inside her and slowly began moving up and down. Rick's hands grasped her hips and guided their motion, picking up the pace to match their rhythm to the tune now playing on the stereo, Led Zeppelin's "Whole Lotta Love".

By the middle of the next song, "Let's Put The X In Sex" by KISS, Krys had her third orgasm of the evening and Rick was gearing up for his second. Before he was ready to let loose, he flipped them so he was on top and began thrusting deeply into her, his forearms braced on either side of her on the bed, her knees tight against his hips.

By the end of the following song, Whitesnake's "Slow And Easy", Rick grunted his release into Krys, kissing her through her fourth orgasm as he pulsated inside her. Then and only then did both of them feel spent, satiated and completely drained of all bodily fluids, and every last ounce of energy.

Rick pulled out and groaned in gluttonous satisfaction as he positioned Krys with her back to his chest, draping his arm over her waist and clutching her breast in his hand.

Krys nestled into Rick's groin, expecting to feel him getting hard yet again, but he growled softly in her ear, "Don't expect anything more from my dick for a while, Princess. You've wrung it dry for now. I need to sleep and recover from you ravishing me."

She giggled softly, then sighed contentedly as she pulled his arms tighter around herself, their hands laced together. She stared up at the ceiling, feeling Rick relax into sleep, his breathing slow and rhythmic, as she wondered about their future.

After some time, she drifted off into a deep sleep wrapped in Rick's arms, feeling peaceful and satisfied.

CHAPTER 22

April 1993

Diamond Angel

Diamond Angel met with Krys' lawyer-brother Vince, at eight AM on Monday morning in his downtown office. Vince was 5'10" with ash blond hair and hazel eyes.

"Well gentlemen, I've gone over this contract with a fine-toothed comb and I've found nothing wrong with it. In fact, it looks pretty spectacular for all parties concerned," he smiled warmly at the five band members gathered around his desk.

The collective sigh of relief and excitement permeated the room.

Right before the strike of the hour, they all went together to the Global Music Entertainment offices on a higher floor in the same building for their ten AM meeting. There they met with Greg and were walked through the office to meet their new boss.

"Diamond Angel, welcome to the Global Music Entertainment family. I'm Vanessa Wilson, President and CEO of the company, and your new boss. I'm looking forward to a very long and happy relationship with all of you," she said as she rose from behind her desk and walked around it, reaching out to each of the guys to shake their hands, smiling warmly and greeting them by name. Vanessa was a petite 5'3" with white blonde hair pulled severely back into an elegant chignon, and icy blue eyes. She wore a navy business suit with a white silk blouse and matching white silk pocket square. She also wore sensible, three inch navy leather pumps that showed off her shapely legs from beneath her skirt. Vanessa was married to her second husband, Zachary, and had three kids, all girls, and five grandchildren, all boys.

Standing behind Vanessa's desk to the right was a big man, standing at 6'4" with closely cropped white hair, steel gray eyes and the physique of a linebacker. "Hello gentlemen. My name is Brad Walsh and I'm the Vice President of Global Music Entertainment. I'm very glad to meet all of you and I echo Vanessa's sentiment. I'm also looking forward to a long and prosperous relationship with you." Brad was married to a firecracker named Deanna and was still devoted to her after more than thirty years and four children together, three boys and one girl.

Vanessa and Brad shook hands with Vince, inquired about his credentials, then escorted him and the band across the way into the conference room so they could sit comfortably and discuss their contract to mutual satisfaction.

In the conference room was a man sitting to the right of the head of the table. His name was Frank and he was appointed by Vanessa as the new manager for Diamond Angel. Tony and Rick had been doing a good job of managing themselves when they were a local, popular bar band, but now that stardom was going to be hitting them like a runaway freight train, they were going to need someone experienced who knew how to handle the ins-and-outs of a recording and touring rock'n'roll band.

Frank was that guy. He had been in the business for over thirty years and had managed some of the most successful bands that ever came out of Winnipeg. Frank was 6'3" with dark brown skin, black eyes, bald and built like a wrestler. He was currently married to his fourth wife and had several children with each of his three former wives. He may have been a failure at being a husband, but he more than made up for it with being a stellar band manager.

Frank stood up, smiled a brilliant white smile and introduced himself to the band, shaking their hands just as Vanessa and Brad had. "Gentlemen, welcome. I'm Frank Blackwell and I'm your manager. Get ready for your lives to change. Let's get comfortable and start talkin', yeah?"

"Okay gentlemen, let's talk about the terms of your contract, what you like, what you don't like, and how we can come up with something mutually beneficial to all of us. Vince, what do you think about..." Vanessa opened, directing her look towards him, launching into full-on discussion mode.

After two hours of discussion, Diamond Angel walked out of the office with the deal of the century, an unprecedented feat for a brand new band who hadn't even recorded an album yet.

Both Vanessa and Brad saw something simply extraordinary in the five young guys in their conference room. They also patted themselves on their backs for having hired Greg to be GME's talent scout because he sure as hell hit the jackpot.

Frank spent the afternoon getting everything set up for Diamond Angel to begin recording their debut album. At four PM, he called the band's house and when Tony answered,

Frank gave him all the details they needed to know for their first recording session.

Tony relayed all the info to the guys as they sat around the kitchen table having celebratory shots of their favorite whiskey, their collective excitement palpable in the air.

Holy shit, it's really happening...
Everything is going to change for us now...

CHAPTER 23

April 1993

Diamond Angel

Diamond Angel went into River City Recording Studio the very next day. Since they had already written many songs together over the past several years, all they had to do was choose the ten best songs to record that would flow together to make the most incredible Diamond Angel debut record album, which they simply titled "Diamond Angel".

Over the next three weeks, they recorded eight original hard rocking anthems, two love songs, one cover song and one instrumental piece.

The original songs were titled – "The Weekend Comes To This Town", "An Angel's Smile", "Half Way There", "Can't Start A Fire Without A Spark", "Steel Horse", "Out On The Run, Under The Gun", "It Comes Down To Me And You" and "This Is My Hometown".

The love songs were titled – "Nothing Without Love" and "Together Forever".

The cover song they decided on was Bon Jovi's "In And Out Of Love". Diamond Angel always played that song every weekend at ILLUSIONS, bringing the house down every time without fail, so there was no question that this would be the cover song they would record and include on their album.

The instrumental piece was a solitary offering by Rick that he titled "Princess". It was Krys humming softly and playing the guitar that Rick had bought her for her birthday. He laid down a complementary track of his own voice humming in harmony with her, doing so in private with their mixing engineer, Phil. Phil Westwood was a lean 5'11" with electric blue eyes covered by wire-rimmed glasses and steel gray hair scraped back into a ponytail.

Rick didn't want any outside influence for his special dedication to his Princess, because he wanted to surprise the guys with it. He also intended to surprise Krys with her very own copy, once the guys heard it. He couldn't wait to play it for her...

When it was finally ready to unveil to the rest of the band, Rick sprung it on them at the end of a long session during their third week of recording. "Guys, I know it's been a tiring day, but I have something I'd like you to listen to," Rick told them after they finished recording their last song.

He took off his guitar and placed it in a stand, then went to the mixing booth and sat down beside Phil. He turned to Rick and smiled as he leaned back in his chair, lacing his hands behind his head, waiting to see the boys' reaction at what they were about to listen to. He already knew it was simply breathtaking.

"Are you ready?" Rick asked through the microphone. He pushed a few buttons and moved a few levers, then the most beautiful melody began playing through the speakers.

Soft strumming on an acoustic guitar led to a gorgeous voice humming along with it.

Tony dropped the guitar pick in his hand and looked up into the booth directly at Rick, his face blank.

Bryan had been fiddling with his keyboard, but stopped and stared at a spot on the wall, his eyes closed and his lips tipped up at the corners, his head bobbing gently along with the music.

Alex unplugged his bass and took it off, laying it across his lap, swaying slightly side to side in time to the soothing sound of the music.

Diego simply let his arms hang at his sides, his drum sticks laying across his snare drum as he let the music envelop him and carry him away.

When the one minute, forty-five second song was finished, Rick let the silence coming from the recording area wash over him. He knew they had a total winner with this piece. It was a simple song with a beautiful melody. His intention was for it to be the lead in for "Together Forever", similar to Heart's amazing acoustic guitar intro titled "Silver Wheels", played by the incredible Nancy Wilson, just before she kicked it into the stratosphere with the opening bars of "Crazy On You".

Rick waited for the guys to say something, but they seemed too stunned to talk. "Guys? What do you think about this instrumental being the lead-in for "Together Forever"?" Rick asked over the mic, already knowing their answers by their collective reactions.

Diego broke out of his reverie first. "That was the most gorgeous piece of music I've ever heard! Where did it come from? And I absolutely agree. That should be the lead-in for "Together"."

"That's my Kryssie. I bought her an acoustic guitar for her birthday and taught her how to play. When she began playing on her own, I started recording her. She has no idea," Rick smiled smugly, shrugging his shoulders at his sneakiness.

"That girl has some serious talent!" Bryan said, exhaling and shaking his head to bring him back to ground level. "I'm in. Totally excellent lead-in for "Together"."

Alex still had his eyes closed and was still swaying to the music, now playing in his head.

Tony walked by him and cuffed him lightly across the back of his head, laughing. "Wake up, Al, the song's over."

"No, it's not. I'm never going to quit hearing it playing in my head. That was just... magical," he breathed dreamily.

"You like the idea of it leading in "Together"?" Tony asked him.

"One hundred percent! No question there," Alex agreed excitedly, snapping out of his dream-like trance.

"Then it's unanimous because I agree, too," Tony added.

Tony kept walking until he got to the mixing booth door, walked through it and slapped Rick on the back in brotherly accord. "Rick, you sneaky sonofabitch! Brilliant move! She really doesn't know you recorded her?"

"Nope, not yet. I'm going to play it for her tonight, now that you guys have finally heard it. And I'd like to dedicate it to her on our album, if you guys are okay with that," Rick concluded.

They all looked at each other and agreed in unison, "Absolutely!"

Rick couldn't wait to play "Princess" for his Princess...

CHAPTER 24

April 1993
Krys & Rick

Diamond Angel needed just one more week to put the finishing touches on the album and it would be ready to be released to the masses.

The album cover art was a close-up photograph taken by Alex of a tiny Christmas angel made out of crystal that looked like diamonds twinkling from the lighting behind it.

Their manager Frank had already secured them their first opening gigs on tour with Bon Jovi, Def Leppard, Guns N' Roses, Aerosmith and Motley Crue, with dates starting in the New Year opening for ZZ Top, KISS and The Rolling Stones!!

"Holy shit! I can't believe it, somebody pinch me! On second thought, *don't!* I don't *ever* want to wake up from feeling this happy!" Bryan said excitedly when they found out how they would be spending the next year of their lives.

It was certainly a great way to start their weekend!

In the meantime, Diamond Angel was going to keep playing at ILLUSIONS until they left on tour, which was just a few short weeks away.

Rick was overloaded with things to do before leaving, the first thing on his list being presenting his thesis. As much as he wanted it and had worked his ass off for it, getting his Master's Degree was starting to slip in importance to him now that the band had gotten a record deal, recorded an album and were about to go on tour. But, he'd come too far to give up and back out now. Even more, the thought of leaving Krys behind felt like pure acid in his gut. He'd have to find a way to cope that wouldn't be destructive to either of them.

All of the boys were in their own worlds as they drove back to their house to enjoy some down time before heading out to ILLUSIONS to play their usual Friday night gig.

Rick was up in his attic space at his desk when the door to his room opened and closed softly. Then he heard light footsteps on the stairs headed up towards him. He saw Krys hit the top step, smiling happily. He got up off his chair, met her half-way and gathered her in his arms, dipping her backward for a deep kiss.

"Wow! What was that for?" Krys asked, breathless.

"Because I'm in an exceptionally good mood tonight," he replied.

"Oh? Why is that?" she asked.

"Come over here and sit, I want to play you something we're putting on our album," he replied, taking her by the hand and leading her to the corner where the stereo system was set up. He slipped in a compact disc and pressed *PLAY.*

The sound of an acoustic guitar filled Krys' ears and she closed her eyes, scrunching her face as she recognized the tune, trying to place where she had heard it because it sounded *so familiar* to her. Then the lovely sound of a female voice humming joined in, then a male voice humming in harmony added a layer of depth and beauty to it.

She suddenly snapped her eyes open when she finally identified that it was HER!

SHE was playing the guitar and SHE was humming!

But who was the male voice humming with her?

How was this even possible?

"Rick! That's ME! How did you do this?" Krys asked, in total shock.

"Simple. Once you started making up your own songs, I started recording you," he admitted.

Krys was stunned. "You did? Why? I'm not a singer or a songwriter and I only learned how to play the guitar a few months ago!"

"That may be, but you're a natural at it. Your voice is clear and strong, and you have a feather-light touch on the fret board," Rick explained.

Krys was still in shock. "Thank you, Rick! That means everything to me, coming from you."

"No need to thank me for your own talent, Kryssie," Rick replied.

"One thing I'm curious about, who's humming the harmony with me?" Krys asked.

"That's me. I added my voice to give it a bit of texture. Do you like how it sounds?" Rick said, suddenly feeling nervous of her answer.

Krys looked at Rick, her eyes shining with tears. "It's the most beautiful sound I've ever heard, you and me humming together."

Rick was relieved that Krys liked it. "I played this for the guys today and it's going to be the lead-in for one of the love songs that Tony and I wrote for the album. I've titled it "Princess", after you."

Krys was dumbstruck. "Are you serious?"

"Yup. You're being credited for it and it's being dedicated to you," he revealed, smiling proudly.

Krys was speechless as tears formed in her eyes and slid slowly down her cheeks. She fell into Rick's arms and hugged him tightly, overwhelmed by emotion.

At the same time, Krys' mind was in turmoil. She had come to deeply love this man in her arms, and in just over a week, he was leaving for a new adventure without her, one that could never include her.

Krys couldn't let herself fall apart. She was going to miss him so much, her heart ached. But she had to put it out of her head for the next week and try to enjoy her remaining time with Rick.

CHAPTER 25

April 1993 to May 1993
Krys & Rick & Diamond Angel

On April 27, Rick presented his thesis and was granted his Master's Degree in Psychology. He was on top of the world and celebrated privately with Krys that night, taking her to the Revolving Restaurant in the oldest, most lavish, ornate hotel in the city, the Hotel Fort Garry.

After their exquisite dinner, he took her for a carriage ride through the historical district of the city. They ended their evening making love all night in one of the luxurious, opulent suites at the hotel. It was undoubtedly the most romantic time Rick and Krys had ever spent together. It went off without a hitch, a night for them to remember and cherish in the days to come.

On May 1, Diamond Angel's debut, self-titled album was released.

The record company threw a huge release party that night at the Winnipeg Convention Center, where Diamond Angel played their first official concert as a signed band to their adoring fans, old and new. Also in attendance were *the big three* rock'n'roll radio stations in the city that would be playing their music in the coming months – 92CITI FM, Q94 FM and Power97 FM.

The album was a smash hit.

On May 10, Diamond Angel left on tour.

CHAPTER 26

March 1993 to May 1993
Darryl

Darryl became trapped into a mindnumbing routine of his own making. He would go to school during the day, then to his evening job, and on weekends he would meet his friends at ILLUSIONS to play pool while trolling for an easy lay.

He honestly thought that once Diamond Angel left on tour, Krys would come back to him.

How wrong he was...

Krys refused to give him the time of day whenever she saw him. She turned in the other direction and ignored him as if he were invisible.

Keith and Jeremy were worried about him. Oddly, since Darryl's love life got so heinously messed up, theirs had improved considerably.

Keith found himself head over heels for a business school major. Olivia was a curvy 5'4" with dark brown, shoulder-length curls and dark brown eyes.

Jeremy met Alyssa not long after Keith and Olivia met. She was tall and lean at 5'9" with straight, light brown hair cut in a bob to her chin, with light blue eyes. She worked as a paralegal.

Darryl was equally happy and jealous as hell of his two best friends because he'd had an incredible woman in his life, the woman he wanted to marry and have children with, and because of that destructive psychotic bitch Cynthia, he lost everything.

Speak of the devil...

Darryl scowled as he saw the devil incarnate herself saunter through the doors into ILLUSIONS. He swiftly approached Cynthia with a menacing frown on his face, pulled her into the shadows and growled at her, "You... fucking... BITCH!"

There were so many people who hated her, Cynthia wasn't sure who had her arm in a vice grip until she was facing the Greek God himself. "OH! Darryl! You sexy thing! How have you been? I've missed you!" she cooed.

Darryl was barely able to control his fury at her absolutely absurd behavior. "Are you fucking crazy? I hate you! You ruined my life!" he seethed.

"Darryl, don't you see? I *saved* you! You would've been miserable if you stayed with Miss Vanilla. You're much better off without *her* dragging you down. Now, what's been keeping you? I've been waiting for you for *months*!" Cynthia responded.

"Are you fucking serious? Or are you just insane?!" he yelled at her.

"I know what I like and I don't stop until I get it," she responded simply.

Darryl slapped his forehead with his open palm and shut his eyes. "You are unfuckingbelievable."

"Now Darryl, wait until after we've had mindblowing sex to say that," she suggested as she moved into his personal space and tried to cuddle into his embrace.

He moved back away from her with his hands in front of him, pushing her away. "Stay away from me, you fucking lunatic!" he yelled, turned around and began to walk away.

Cynthia hooked her finger into the belt loop at the back of Darryl's jeans. He stopped walking when he felt the tug, reached back and removed her hand. Then he turned around slowly and got right in her face, saying very quietly and very scarily, "I told you to stay away from me. Let go, or you will regret it."

Cynthia was crazy, but she wasn't stupid, so she let go and backed off as Darryl asked. She would bide her time and wait for him to come to her. "You'll change your mind," she singsonged.

"Not if you were the last female on Earth," he fired back and walked away.

CHAPTER 27

May 1993
Natalie & Darryl

The rest of the night went by in a blur for Darryl. He began drinking heavily and woke up in a strange bed in the morning, not sure where he was or how he got there. He opened his eyes in absolute horror to find Cynthia smiling her psychotic smile at him. Grabbing his clothes and yanking them on, he ground out, "What the *fuck*? How did I end up here, with *YOU*?!"

Cynthia patiently explained. "After you yelled at me, I backed off as you asked. Then you started drinking pretty heavily and when I walked past you to go to the ladies' room, you grabbed me, laid a huge kiss on me and dragged me out of there, insisting I take you home and let you fuck me properly. Which we did. Magnificently. And here we are," she summed up.

Darryl was gobsmacked. He vowed to give up drinking and got the hell out of there. As soon as he got home, he had a shower hot enough to scald the skin right off his body, then called Keith and Jeremy and was absolutely *mortified* with what they told him.

Cynthia HAD told him the truth.

He DID grab her after getting blindingly drunk...

He DID kiss her of his own accord...

And he DID leave the bar with her, with the intent to fuck her...

Keith and Jeremy told him they had both tried to stop him, but Darryl wouldn't listen to them. He insisted on leaving with Cynthia and what happened after that, they didn't know.

He sat outside in the sunshine that afternoon and thought about how seriously fucked up his life was.

The sliding door opened and Natalie came out, pulled up a lounge chair and sat beside him. "Darryl, if you don't stop screwing so many chicks, your dick is going to fall off," Nat nudged him, smiling sadly at her big brother.

"I can't help it, Nat. I just miss Krys so much and I know I'll never get her back. Nothing matters to me anymore. I really thought that when *they* left town, she'd come back to me..." he trailed off, looking sad and hopeless.

"There's so much more to it than that, dear brother," Natalie admitted.

Darryl turned to face his sister. "What, Natalie? What is '*so much more*? If I even have the smallest chance to get her back, please tell me how I can do it. I'm so lost without her."

"There is nothing I can say to help you, except for this, and it's gonna hurt. She's *happy* with him, Darryl. He makes her *happy*. Please, for your own sake, let her go. Be glad that she's with someone who treats her well. She wishes that for you. Please, return the favor," she said sadly.

Darryl sat there, completely at a loss. "She's happy?"

"Yes, she is," Natalie confirmed.

"Does she love him?" Darryl asked quietly.

"I think so," she replied slowly, continuing as she stood up, "Darryl, you're my brother and I love you. I want you to find some peace and happiness, but you will not find it pining for Krys. Please, just accept that she is with someone else and move on."

Darryl's face fell and he stared into the yard. "She's really out of my life, isn't she?"

"Yes, Darryl, she is," Natalie replied sadly.

Natalie leaned down and gave her brokenhearted brother a quick hug, then went back inside the house to her room. She flopped onto her bed and stared at the ceiling, wondering what the fuck was going to happen to her brother if he didn't start dealing with losing Krys.

CHAPTER 28

May 1993

Krys & Natalie

A little while later, Natalie got up and called Krys. "Whatcha up to, Kryssie? Wanna go clubbing tonight? Maybe we can switch it up and go to SHENANIGANS for a change?" she suggested.

"Maybe... I need a night out. Rick's been gone for two weeks already," Krys lamented.

"I know. I miss Tony, too. I'm trying to keep myself busy so I don't obsess about missing him, but I need to get out and have some fun! Let's get dressed up, drink and dance, and have a good time!" Nat exclaimed.

"Okay, let's go to SHENANIGANS and see if we can live up to its name, huh?" Krys said, warming to the idea.

CHAPTER 29

May 1993

Krys & Natalie & Darryl

Krys and Natalie went to SHENANIGANS that night not knowing that Darryl was there, too. And the kicker was that Darryl wasn't alone – he was with *CYNTHIA*, of all people!

Natalie zeroed in on her brother and grabbed his arm, turning him roughly away from Cynthia to face her and hissed, "Darryl!! What the hell are you doing with *HER*? Have you lost what's left of your mind?"

"Hi Nat. No, I haven't. I actually feel clearheaded for the first time in months. I paid attention and listened to what you said to me today and I decided that you were right. I have to quit feeling sorry for myself and stop wanting something I'll never have, so I'm going to give it a shot with Cynthia. She's had a crush on me for a long time, so why not give her what she wants? Makes sense to me. If you'll excuse me, I'm going to get us a couple of beers, then we're going to play some pool," he said as he deftly removed Nat's hand from his arm and walked to the bar, slinging his arm around Cynthia's shoulders on the way.

Cynthia looked up at him adoringly and wrapped her arm around his waist in a possessive hold. She reached up and linked her hand with his dangling around her shoulders.

"Holy shit! I'm in the fucking Twilight Zone!" Natalie exclaimed to the air around her.

Krys came back from getting their drinks and stood beside Nat, her mouth gaping open and her eyes wide with disbelief as she stammered, "What the... I... What the hell did I just see?"

Nat's voice was dead. "He's with *her* now, effective today."

Krys felt her heart shatter into a million pieces all over again. She couldn't wait for school to be done in another month, then she could take off and visit Rick, wherever he was. She *hated* being separated from him.

And now seeing Darryl with *HER?* Pure torture...

Krys and Natalie left SHENANIGANS and went home, deep thoughts swirling in their heads about Darryl and the bombshell he just dropped.

CHAPTER 30

July 1993
Krys & Rick

A couple of days after school ended, Krys received a registered letter in the mail. In it was a plane ticket from Vanessa Wilson and a hand written note from Vanessa, herself, that read:

> *Hi Krysten, pack a bag and go visit your man in Vancouver. He's missing you a lot and this is a surprise for his birthday from me that I'm SURE will perk him up! Enjoy your time together!*
>
> *Vanessa*

Krys couldn't believe how amazing Vanessa was! She did what the note suggested – she packed a bag and flew to Vancouver to visit her man. Diamond Angel had a few days free since they were in between tours, so they were going to take some time off to enjoy all that Vancouver had to offer.

Frank picked Krys up at the airport. When he saw her, he pulled her into a big hug, smiling warmly. "It's really good to see you, Krys. When Vanessa suggested this, I agreed immediately! I give her daily reports on how things are going with the guys and she was instrumental in engineering this trip for you and Rick to see each other. She's such a softie when it comes to romance," he said with laughter in his voice.

"I'm so grateful to you both! It's been really hard being at home while Rick is away on tour. I miss him so much," she said as they walked out of the airport to the waiting limousine.

They drove to the luxurious Four Seasons Hotel in downtown Vancouver and Frank managed to deliver Krys secretly to Rick's room. "The band is out today at Little Mountain Sound Recording Studio and are due back in about an hour, so that should give you enough time to unpack and freshen up for your man, yeah? If you two want, you can join all of us for dinner tonight at eight PM in the restaurant unless you're *too busy*, then don't worry about it," Frank nudged her in the ribs and winked lewdly, making her laugh.

Frank left her alone in Rick's room and she got busy unpacking her bag. When she was done, she wandered around the suite, inspecting the opulence and looking out the window to admire the view. She couldn't help herself and rummaged through Rick's t-shirts, holding one to her nose and smelling his scent on it.

A short time later the door opened and she heard Rick talking, his back to the room. She smiled, happy tears forming in her eyes at the sound of his sexy voice in person. "Yeah, I'll see you guys at eight. I'm going to have a shower and I have to write down those lyrics for that song we were talking about, before I forget them. Later, guys," he said.

Rick turned with his head down and was about to take a step into his room when he spotted a pair of lovely, high-heeled, dark brown leather sandals attached to the loveliest legs he'd ever seen. His eyes travelled up to view a short, turquoise sundress on a gorgeous, curvy body he knew well, to meet the loveliest sapphire blue eyes he'd ever seen, misted with tears. His Princess was standing in his hotel room, clutching his favorite Led Zeppelin t-shirt in her hands and trembling as she stared at him with excitement on her face.

Rick couldn't believe his eyes...

Krys is ACTUALLY HERE WITH ME!!!

They moved towards each other at the same time, Krys still clutching Rick's shirt. She couldn't seem to let it go.

They collided against each other, kissing each other all over their faces, hugging each other fiercely, both of them mumbling *"I missed you so much"* in between kisses.

It wasn't long before hands began roaming and clothing was pulled at in a frenzy. Rick unbuttoned his jeans and yanked them down past his hips as Krys pulled up the hem of her sundress and jumped up into his arms. She wrapped her legs around his waist as he held her up by her ass, having already taken off her panties in anticipation of greeting him just this way.

Rick backed Krys against the wall, slowly thrusting into her as he kissed her. Soon they both orgasmed, his face buried in her neck, smelling her scent. He lifted his head and grinned, "I like the way you say hello to me, Princess. Wanna show me again how much you missed me?"

He was still hard and still inside her.

"You betcha!" Krys said, a sexy smile on her lips.

He moved them away from the wall and sat on the side of the bed, Krys' legs still wrapped around him. She swept off her sundress and tore off her bra, but left her sandals on.

Rick let go of her and leaned back, tearing off his shirt while Krys shifted her legs to straddle him. She lowered herself down to kiss him as he gripped her hips, moving her along his cock until the frenzied passion returned and the sweet lovemaking flew out the window.

Krys pushed up so her hands were on his chest and moved faster, grinding her pelvis into his until she collapsed on him, having her second orgasm within minutes. Rick came again right after, having grasped her around her back with one arm and her waist with the other, holding her close and pushing his pelvis up as far as he could.

He was *still hard* and *still inside* her.

Rick lifted Krys off him, removed her sandals and tucked her under the covers, then stood and got rid of the rest of his clothing. He crawled onto the bed, growling, "Ready for round three?"

Krys chuckled softly, glancing down at his still-hard cock then back up to his face. "Absolutely."

Rick pulled the covers back and gently dropped himself onto Krys, covering her with his body. He slid into her wetness while pulling her right leg up and over his shoulder so he could thrust in as deep as possible. She planted her other foot on the bed, thrusting her hips up at him.

Krys sighed contently and tried to close her eyes, but Rick wouldn't let her. "Gimme those beautiful blues, Princess," he said, his voice thick with lust.

He started pumping in and out of her, kissing her face and neck, his breathing becoming more labored as he felt orgasm number three rocketing up his dick. As Rick started pulsating into her, he could feel Krys contracting around him with her third orgasm, finally draining him.

He pulled out gently, leaned to the side and lowered her leg, then moved back over her and kissed her deeply, their arms wrapped around each other. "I love you, Krys," Rick said, full of emotion.

Krys felt an avalanche of happiness overcome her. "I love you, too, Rick," she answered, tightening her arms around him and pulling him even closer to her, kissing him sweetly.

Rick felt unbelievable happiness wash over him. He lifted his upper body off Krys and planted his forearms on either side of her head, holding her face in his hands and brushing her hair away so he could stare at her loveliness.

Krys looked at Rick, feeling overwhelmed with emotion, smiling happily at their mutual revelation.

After a few minutes, Rick turned his head and glanced over at the clock – it read 4:07PM. "Do you want to go down for dinner with everyone this evening? Or do you want me to order room service instead?" he asked Krys.

"I want to stay up here, remain very naked with you and take advantage of every space in this suite," she answered, a sexy glint sparkling in her eye as she grinned at him.

"Room service it is," he rumbled sexily. He dropped onto his side, tucking her back to his chest and draping his arm across her waist, pulling her close to him.

Krys yawned and settled into Rick's embrace, revelling in the happiness she felt at being with her man, having been ravished by him and being told that he loves her.

CHAPTER 31

July 1993

Krys & Rick

They slept for just under two hours. Krys woke up and turned in Rick's arms to face him, kissing his jaw and sliding her arms around him as he gathered her close to him. "I seem to recall you telling Tony, just before you walked in and saw me, that you were going to have a shower," Krys said innocently.

Rick grinned wickedly. "I'm feeling pretty dirty right about now. Wanna help me get clean?" he said as he kissed her neck.

They got out of bed and walked with their arms around each other to the bathroom where Rick leaned in to turn on the spray in the walk-in shower, never losing physical contact with each other.

Once the water temperature was just right, Rick backed in, pulling Krys with him. He ran his hands up and down her body under the warm water, then washed her long locks as he'd done countless times before.

When Rick was done rinsing the bubbles out of her hair, Krys gently pushed down on his shoulders for him to sit on the shower seat. She dropped to her knees, wrapped her lips around his still-hard cock and grabbed hold of his balls, moving her mouth up and down, bringing him to a swift orgasm.

Rick lifted Krys up to stand in front of him, placing her foot on the bench beside him so his face was in line with her pelvis. Then he grabbed her ass, pulled her close and dove in, licking and sucking at her nerve bundle until she trembled through a fantastic orgasm and her legs turned to jelly.

Keeping a firm grip on her, Rick leaned back against the wall of the shower and lowered Krys down on top of his hard cock, guiding her in and out, up and down. They started laughing at the way their hands kept sliding all over each other, so it took a little longer for them to orgasm together this time, but they did and it was tremendously satisfying.

Rick lifted Krys off him, setting her on her feet along side himself. They turned to the spray to rinse themselves, then got out and wrapped each other in large, fluffy towels.

Rick called down and ordered a variety of food from room service as Krys snuggled into him. She burrowed her hand under his towel and grabbed hold of his semi-hard cock, making him grin. "You can hang on to my dick all you like, Princess, but it doesn't change the fact that I'm hungry and I need to eat to get back some of the strength that you've zapped out of me."

Krys looked lustfully at him. "I don't want what you've got here to go to waste. What position are we going to try next?"

Rick looked up at the ceiling and tapped his chin with his forefinger, pondering her question. "We've got just enough time for a quickie on the desk before room service gets here," he suggested, walking her backwards towards the desk in question.

"You're on," she said as she whipped off her towel and draped herself on her back over the desk, hanging on with both hands to the edge for traction.

Rick's mouth curved into a mischievous smile as he dropped his towel and pounced on Krys. He wrapped her legs around his hips and thrust his cock into her while his thumb found her sweet spot, swirling in circles before they both shuddered to a satisfying finish with minutes to spare before the room service was delivered. They kissed passionately, giggling at their insatiable lust.

Krys found two bathrobes hanging on the back of the bathroom door. She handed one to Rick while she wrapped herself in the other as the knock came at the door and the room service trolley was wheeled in.

As soon as the door closed, they devoured the entire contents of all the room service trays, then settled in to watch a little TV and rest up from their incredible sex-a-thon.

A short time later, they were both asleep, cuddled with each other on the bed with contented, exhausted and sated smiles on both their faces.

CHAPTER 32

July 1993
Krys & Rick

The next day, July 11, was Rick's birthday, so he and Krys spent the entire day naked in each other's arms, continuing their sex-a-thon from the previous evening. Krys was surprised that either of them could move by the time they had to get ready for their special evening out!

A huge party was organized by the record company and attended by all kinds of musicians from the industry, with a special part of the evening dedicated to celebrating Rick's birthday.

The rest of Diamond Angel had no idea Krys had flown in as special birthday surprise for Rick. Frank was able to keep that little nugget under wraps, knowing what bigmouths those guys were. When Rick showed up to the party with Krys on his arm, Tony, Bryan, Diego and Alex all shouted out happy greetings to her, hugging her in turn and slapping Rick on the back.

"NOW we know why you didn't come down for dinner last night! Frank said some urgent family matter came up that you had to deal with and you weren't going to be able to make it," Tony laughed.

"Yeah, something came up, repeatedly," Rick quipped, grinning from ear to ear.

Krys punched him lightly on his arm, smiling shyly. "I'm sure Tony doesn't need to be informed of what we've been up to."

"He's just feeling sorry for himself that Natalie isn't here to do the same things with him that you and I have been doing," Rick said, gloating.

"It's hard being without her," Tony admitted, looking mournfully at the floor. "Would you tell her that I'm behaving myself and I hope she's able to get out to see me soon? I miss her," he asked Krys.

"I'll be happy to deliver that message to her for you," she replied.

April was also there as she had gotten a job working behind the scenes. She was happy to see Krys and they embraced warmly. "I'm so glad you're here! Rick has been mooning around here like a lovesick puppy, missing you. And for you to be here for his birthday is so fantastic!"

Krys replied, "It's been hard being away from Rick, but being here with him now has made the time apart melt away. How are you liking your job?"

Krys and April chatted for a while until it was time for everyone to sing Happy Birthday to Rick as the chef wheeled out a huge birthday cake.

The party went into the wee hours of the morning, but Krys and Rick didn't stay until the bitter end like the others did. They stayed just long enough to be seen, make the rounds and have something to eat and drink. They took off back to their room shortly after midnight where they got naked and resumed their sex-a-thon, finally falling asleep totally spent and exhausted.

CHAPTER 33

July 1993
Krys & Rick

The day after Rick's birthday was a free day that Krys and Rick spent together at Stanley Park and the Vancouver Aquarium, then went browsing around the shops at Granville Island. They ended their day together by going for a late dinner at a fantastic Italian restaurant in Gastown, just the two of them.

Instead of having wild jungle sex when they returned to their hotel room, Rick made slow, sweet, leisurely love to Krys and they drifted off to sleep afterwards, happily snuggled together in each other's arms.

CHAPTER 34

July 1993
Krys & Rick

All too soon, their time together was over and Krys was in the limo with Rick, heading to the airport to catch her flight home. She was checked in, but was dragging her feet to go through security. "I don't want to go. I don't want to leave you," Krys said quietly, her voice tremulous.

Rick pulled her to him and hugged her close, staying silent because if he dared speak, he would just end up blubbering like a fool. When he was able to control himself, all he could mutter into her hair was, "I love you, Kryssie, so much. I'll be home before you know it."

That just made Krys cry harder. "I love you, too, Rick, so much," she responded, clutching him as close to her as she could.

When they finally let go of each other, Krys walked slowly to the security line, wiping her eyes and sniffing back more tears. Once she was through, she turned to look at Rick one last time before she had to go to her gate.

He dipped his chin and winked at her.

Krys blew him a kiss from her fingertips, then rounded the corner out of sight.

When she boarded her flight, she put in her earbuds, turned on her music, closed her eyes and slept the entire way home, her face wet with tears, already missing him.

CHAPTER 35

July 1993
Krys & Natalie

Natalie picked Krys up from the airport.

"Kryssie!! How was everything? I missed you!" Natalie cried as she threw herself at Krys when she came through the arrivals gate, hugging her fiercely.

"It was exactly what I needed," Krys sighed. "But now that I'm home, it feels like it never happened. By the way, Tony misses you. LOTS. He asked me to tell you he's behaving and wants to know when you'll be able to fly out to see him."

"I already have Vanessa and Frank working on it. I didn't want to go at the same time as you because it would have been too much with both of us there. I'm going in a few weeks when they have another stretch of days off in San Francisco," Nat said, her eyes shining with excitement. "Now let's get out of here so you can tell me all about what you did, *outside* of the hotel room!"

They drove home and Krys regaled Nat with tales of what she and Rick did when they weren't wearing each other out inside their hotel room. Talking with Natalie always made

Krys feel better and she was in a good mood when they pulled up in front of her house on their street.

As the girls got out of Nat's car, they saw Darryl getting into his LeSabre. He paused when he noticed them and nodded his head once, then climbed in, turned the car on and took off.

"He looks good. I guess he's happy with *her*," Krys said sadly.

Natalie positively *pounced* on that comment! "No, Krys, he's not. He's hurting. He's been hurting for the last ten months. My brother is a shell of what he was and he's filling his emptiness with *her*. He doesn't feel he deserves any better because of what happened between them. I've kept my silence like he asked me to and because you've never asked about him."

"Asking about him is just too painful, Nat. I'm with Rick and I'm happy. He told me he loves me and I told him I love him. We're together and totally committed to each other. I'm sorry Darryl is hurting, but it doesn't change what happened between him and I. Now, let's drop this convo and go do something fun, okay?" Krys replied, firmly closing the door on THAT subject.

Natalie just stared at her and kept her thoughts to herself.

They told each other they love each other?
SHIT...

CHAPTER 36

July 1993
Natalie & Tony

Tony met Natalie at the airport in San Francisco holding a sign with her nickname on it, *Strawberry*, wearing ripped jeans and an Aerosmith t-shirt, a limo driver's cap perched on his head and a huge smile that lit up his whole face.

When Nat saw him, she ran for him and jumped into his arms, knocking the cap off his head and kissing him passionately.

He dropped the sign as he caught her. "Happy to see me, huh?" he asked in between kisses.

"You have no idea!" she replied, kissing him again.

In the back of the limo, Nat crawled onto Tony's lap, straddling him. He unzipped his jeans to release his cock for her while she hiked up her dress to her waist, pushing her panties aside. She raised herself up, grabbed his cock and plunged him smoothly into her excited wetness, his hands gripping her hips. She rode him all the way to the Fairmont Hotel, grinding each other towards a fantastic, long-overdue, mutually satisfying orgasm just before pulling up to the front of the hotel.

They spent the rest of the day together, naked, smiling, happy and completely satisfied.

The next day they spent together sightseeing, exploring Alcatraz, laughing while trying to walk up crooked Lombard Street and exploring Pier 39, revelling in each other's company.

They had dinner together with the band, then moved the party atmosphere into the bar where they drank and laughed with some of the crew from the tour.

Diamond Angel was cultivating quite the following of fans as their popularity steadily grew. Each of the guys had their own groupies, but so far, only Diego and Alex had been acting on all the attention.

And how...

Bryan had April with him, so he was completely uninterested, while Tony and Rick had steady girls and were staying faithful to them.

When Nat got a look at Rick, she leaned over to Tony and whispered, "Tony, what's wrong with Rick? He's so quiet and withdrawn! Is he not well?"

"Not really, Strawberry. He's missing Krys like crazy. Ever since she surprised him for his birthday in Vancouver and they spent those few days together, he's been moping around like a lost puppy. He pulls it together for the concerts and is totally brilliant onstage, but outside of that he's absolutely miserable. This separation is not good for him. I'm worried he might do something stupid to fuck everything up, for him and for all of us," Tony admitted.

"Tony, I'm so sorry you're having to deal with this! I wish there was something I could do, but Krys isn't faring much better. I've never seen her so down in the dumps as she's been since she got home from Vancouver! And it doesn't help that Darryl is now hot and heavy with Cynthia. I just don't know what to say to her or do for her," Natalie confessed.

"There's nothing that either of us can say or do for them. They're going to have to figure things out for themselves. In the meantime, let's concentrate on ourselves and have a great time together!" Tony said, pulling her close and kissing her temple, his hands roaming over her body.

Natalie agreed, wrapped her arms around Tony as they did just that.

CHAPTER 37

July 1993
Krys & Natalie

Natalie flew home a couple of days later in a great mood.

Krys picked her up at the airport and they did a role reversal of a few weeks prior when she came home from Vancouver. "Nat! I missed you! How was San Francisco? How are the guys? Is Rick okay? I miss him so much..." Krys trailed off, falling back into her melancholy.

Natalie ignored Krys' sadness for a moment and focused on the good parts of her trip. "We had a blast! I love San Francisco. And the band is doing *so well*! They're gaining popularity and their album is selling out everywhere."

"That's great news," Krys admitted, but her sad voice wasn't convincing.

They drove home, Natalie chatting excitedly along the way. "Their next set of days off will be in New York at the end of August! Isn't that exciting Kryssie? Why don't we try to go together then to see them! Wouldn't that be excellent?"

Krys perked up at that suggestion. "Yeah, I like that idea."

Things will be different once we see each other in New York...

CHAPTER 38

August 1993
Krys & Rick & Natalie & Tony

Krys and Natalie boarded their plane bound for New York to spend a few days with Rick and Tony during their time off. When they arrived, the girls were met by their guys, smiles on all their faces.

Natalie did a repeat of her previous arrival and jumped right into Tony's waiting embrace, smothering each other with kisses.

Krys walked into Rick's arms and hugged him tightly, burying her face in his neck and snuggling into him. Rick wrapped his arms around Krys and pulled her in as close as he could, resting his cheek on her head. They pulled back and looked at each other, then looked over at Nat and Tony all over each other. Smiling at the sight, they leaned towards each other for a slow, sweet kiss.

They rode to the Waldorf-Astoria Hotel in separate limousines, each couple adjusting their clothing as they got out from having had sex in the back seat. Then both couples disappeared into their rooms until morning.

But their reunions couldn't have been more different from each other.

Where Nat and Tony were all over each other, Krys and Rick behaved more sedately.

When they got into their room, Rick grasped her gently by her arms, looked into her eyes and asked, "Kryssie, what's up? Aren't you happy to see me? Because I sure as hell am glad to see you! I've missed you so much."

"Yeah, I am. I've missed you, too," she said as she kissed him.

"Then why aren't we all over each other like Natalie and Tony? Like we were the last time we saw each other? It's all I can think of every day, missing you and wanting to have you with me, getting naked and doing all kinds of sexy things with you," he replied, smiling at her.

She warmed to the topic, wiping the sadness off her face and smiling back at him. "Well then, let's get naked and do sexy things together."

So they did.

CHAPTER 39

August 1993

Krys & Rick & Natalie & Tony

Their few days in New York flew by, as expected. The foursome went sightseeing together to Central Park, Times Square and the Empire State Building, and indulged in a couple of Broadway shows in the evenings. The girls went shopping to Macy's, Saks Fifth Avenue and Tiffany & Co., while the guys took in a New York Yankees vs. Toronto Blue Jays game at Yankee Stadium.

Then it was time to go home, but this time, their goodbyes couldn't have been more different.

Where Natalie and Tony were wrapped around each other, Krys and Rick were stiff and awkward.

After checking in at the airport, Krys had huge tears coursing down her cheeks as she looked sadly at Rick and said, "Rick, this... What we're doing... isn't working. I'm going back to school next week, so it's going to be a while until I can come and see you again. I love you so, so much, but... I can't do this anymore. I hate being away from you and this separation is killing me. I know how important this tour is to you and I don't want to hold you back, so... I need to... let you go."

Rick stood there, stunned, his face blank. "Don't I get a say in this?"

"I don't see how you are happy with our situation, either. What other option do we have?" Krys challenged.

"Stay together and make it work, like people who love each other do," Rick responded.

"I've thought of every angle how to make it work and nothing stands out. Please don't make this any harder than it has to be," Krys said, her heart breaking.

She tried to move away from him, but Rick wrapped his arms around her and kissed her with everything he had, trying to change her mind. Then he looked into her eyes and said quietly, "I'll never give up on us, Krys. I will always love you and I will always be there for you. Take the time you need to figure things out and know that I'll be waiting for you."

"Rick, please don't... Just... let me go," Krys pleaded.

"I can't do that, Princess. We're worth it," Rick answered.

"You have to. I've agonized over this and I can see no other way," Krys said as her voice broke.

Rick was crestfallen, like she'd shot him through the heart.

Krys stood still for a moment, absorbing Rick's shattered expression, the expression she was responsible for putting there. Then she turned and walked briskly to the security gate, disappearing through to the other side, not even waiting for Natalie.

Rick watched her walk away from him with a look of wretched devastation on his face, then collected himself and walked out of the airport to the limo and waited for Tony.

Natalie and Tony witnessed the entire scene, knowing they had their work cut out for them.

He kissed her one more time before letting her go, "'Bye, Strawberry. We'll talk soon, okay?"

"Okay. Go take care of him. He's going to need you," Natalie said, smiling sadly, then turned to go through the security gate to catch up to Krys.

Tony walked out of the airport to the limo, climbed in and they took off. "I'm so sorry, man."

"This isn't the end. Far from it," Rick said, a steely determination in his eyes.

"Rick, I heard her suitcase say goodbye. You have to let her go as she asked you to," Tony urged.

Rick looked at Tony, ready to argue, but instead exhaled a ragged breath. "You're right. Why didn't I see this coming? Fuck, Tony! Why didn't I see the signs?"

"Because you love her. It's harder for those we love and have to leave behind, Rick. Natalie and I are having a tough time, too," Tony commiserated.

"Yeah, but she's not breaking up with you because of this separation," Rick replied.

"No, she's not," Tony agreed, as the limo slid through traffic back to their hotel.

CHAPTER 40

September 1993

Krys & Darryl

Krys had been back in nursing school for a week when she came home from school on Friday afternoon and found Darryl sitting on her front steps.

"Darryl! What are you doing here?" she asked, completely surprised.

"Nat let it slip that you and your guy split up. For what it's worth, Krys, I wanted to tell you, in person, that I'm sorry you're hurting. Honestly, I am," Darryl told her.

"Thank you," she replied quietly, looking down and frowning, her lip threatening to quiver.

He got up from the front step, walked towards her and pulled her gently into his arms, giving her a light hug and a kiss on her forehead.

Krys was taken by surprise at the sweet gesture and sagged into his embrace. She dropped her bag and slid her arms around his waist, snuggling close to him, letting the sadness in her heart seep out and the warmth from Darryl seep in.

They stood there, silently wrapped in each other's arms, then they both pushed back and just looked at each other for a moment.

Krys could feel the emotional pull of wanting to lean in and kiss Darryl, but instead blurted, "Things going well with Cynthia?" As soon as the words left her mouth, she felt like the world's biggest bitch.

Darryl took a moment to form his answer carefully. "Not really. In fact, I broke things off with her." What he did NOT reveal was that as soon as he got it out of Natalie that Krys was the one who dumped Rick, he called Cynthia and dumped her ass over the phone. It was a bit of a dick move, but their relationship had been anything but civilized.

"You did? Why?" she asked.

"Because I just wasn't feeling it with her. She just... It just wasn't working out," he admitted, almost saying out loud *because she isn't you.*

"Oh. I'm sorry, Darryl," she answered simply, then realized they were still standing there in each other's arms.

And it felt good...

Really good...

"Hey, how about you and me and Nat go to ILLUSIONS tonight? Keith and Jeremy will be there with their girlfriends and there are some new local bands playing. Interested?" Darryl suggested, changing the subject and smiling at Krys, hoping that he could convince her to come out with them.

"I could do with a night out. And I haven't been to ILLUSIONS in a while," she said, continuing, "Are you headed home? Can you tell Nat to come by later so she can help me get ready?"

"Yeah, I'll tell her. Are you okay with me driving? I promise I'll be a good boy and keep my hands to myself," he teased as he winked at her.

That brought out a small smile in Krys, remembering when he used to drive with one hand so he could hold hers in his other. "I think I can handle that," she replied, blushing.

Darryl noticed, remembering her shyness and how she blushed when he flirted with her before they started dating.

There she is...

My Kryssie is still in there...

They let go of each other and Darryl gave her his arm like a gentleman, walking her to the back door. He practically floated home down the back lane, smiling all the way and feeling the first ray of hope in almost a year.

CHAPTER 41

September 1993

Krys & Natalie & Darryl

Natalie showed up at Krys' house that evening, her eyes wild with enthusiasm. "Kryssie! I'm so excited that we're going to ILLUSIONS! I have a feeling it's going to be a phenomenal night!"

"I'm looking forward to it, too," Krys agreed, grinning.

They got down to beautifying themselves and when they were ready, Nat called Darryl to fire up the LeSabre. As he held the door open for them, Darryl gave Natalie a look that said, *get in the back or you're walking,* so she did, conspiring with him to ensure that Krys sat in the front.

As Krys took her seat beside Darryl, it evoked the earlier memories of her and Darryl holding hands while he was driving.

Krys had to admit, it felt *really* good to be back in this seat...

They got to the bar and went in, finding Keith and Jeremy with their girlfriends deep in a game of darts. Darryl had his arms draped around both Krys and Nat's shoulders, smiling smugly at his buddies as they raised their eyebrows into their hairlines. Darryl introduced Olivia and Alyssa to Krys, since Nat already knew them, then he went to the bar.

While he was waiting for Chuck to pour their drinks, Keith and Jeremy flanked him on either side.

"What's the deal, dude?" Jeremy asked, a confused look on his face.

"Yeah, are we in an alternate universe?" Keith added.

Darryl turned his back to the bar and answered, "Krys dumped *him,* so I dumped Cynthia, and now I'm going to get Krys back. Mark my words, gentlemen, I've got a shot and I'm taking it. We were always meant to be together and this time it's going to be for good."

Keith and Jeremy leaned forward and looked at each other around Darryl. They smirked, high-fived each other and patted him on the back in congratulations.

"I can't wait to see how this turns out," Jeremy said, rubbing his hands together in anticipation.

"Me either. You bumping things into high gear, D?" Keith asked, grinning.

"Yup. Hyperspeed," he replied, turning back to collect the drinks for his sister, himself and the love of his life.

CHAPTER 42

September 1993
Krys & Natalie & Darryl

The night flew by in a blur of laughter as the bunch of them played some pool, drank some booze, listened to some great music and had a truly enjoyable time.

Krys spent most of her time fielding Darryl's flirty behavior. He was as affectionate and humorous as ever, but with a slightly harder edge now.

And she liked that...

Natalie watched as her brother and her best friend interacted like old times, feeling a ray of happiness at what she could see was already starting to regrow between them. As much as she liked Rick, Nat felt that Krys and Darryl belonged together

By the end of the night, Krys ended up absolutely hammered and Darryl was more than willing to step in and take care of her. He picked her up like a groom holds his bride, carried her to the car and drove them to Krys' house.

When they got there, Natalie knocked on the door and explained to Krys' mom why Darryl had Krys cradled in his arms. "Hi, Mrs H. Krys got a little drunk tonight, but we made sure to bring her home safely," she said, smirking.

"I see that. Darryl, would you stay with her for a while to make sure she doesn't get sick or need anything?" Lily asked, smiling.

"I sure can, Mrs H," Darryl smiled back, happy to oblige as he carried Krys down the stairs to her basement bedroom.

Lily and Nat followed Darryl downstairs and saw that he had placed Krys on her bed, still clothed, but had removed her shoes and covered her with her favorite throw blanket.

"I can see that my Baby is in good hands, so if you both will excuse me, I'm off to bed. If she needs me, Darryl, please don't hesitate to call for me. Good night, all," she said as she placed her hand on Darryl's arm in a gesture of appreciation, smiled warmly at him and Natalie, then went upstairs.

When they heard the sliding pocket door close at the top of the stairs, Natalie pulled her brother aside, saying softly, "Don't fuck things up tonight, Darryl. Take things slow with her. She's still hurting, so please don't take advantage of her vulnerability."

Darryl held his sister by the shoulders and said, "You know I would never do that and I certainly will not force her to do anything she's not ready for, or doesn't want to do."

Nat replied, "Good. Now win her heart back and never let it go." She stood on tip toe and kissed her brother's cheek, then left him alone with Krys, who was passed out in her bed.

I hope this is the start of something wonderful for them!
They both deserve a second chance to make things right...

Darryl closed the bedroom door, toed off his shoes and got into bed beside Krys. He lay on his back, contemplating this turn of events.

Could this be it?
Could this be the start of us again?
I love her so much...

Initially, Krys had her back to Darryl, but soon turned and snuggled into him, curling her arm over his abdomen as she slid her knee between his legs. Her cheek rested on his chest and she sighed in complete contentment, all while asleep.

With a small smile on her face, Krys exhaled a contented, "Darryl..."

Darryl closed his eyes and gathered Krys close, feeling that with the way she breathed his name like that, she had just brought him back to life.

CHAPTER 43

September 1993

Krys & Darryl

Krys woke up a while later and looked at her bedside clock – it read 3:38AM. She noticed that she was wrapped around a man and that man was *Darryl*! She smiled happily at being back in his arms where she had always felt safe and loved.

She reached up and kissed him softly on his lips, believing him still asleep as she said quietly, "Thank you for tonight. I needed a good night out and you gave that to me without pushing me for anything I'm not ready for."

She wasn't expecting any response, but Darryl squeezed her gently and whispered, "You're welcome, Kryssie."

They shifted so they lay on their sides facing each other, their hands entwined together between them.

"Darryl…" Krys started, but Darryl stopped her.

"Krys, don't say anything. Let's just enjoy this moment and we can talk later, okay?" Darryl suggested.

"Okay," Krys agreed.

Soon their eyes closed and they slept, cuddled together like a couple in love.

CHAPTER 44

September 1993
Krys & Darryl

In the morning, Krys awoke alone in her bed, her mouth dry and her head pounding. As she crawled out of bed, she noticed Darryl had left her a note on her desk that read:

Good Morning Kryssie,

I really enjoyed our night out and especially our time together afterwards. If you want to hang out or talk, I'll be at home all day today.

D

Krys smiled when she read the note, her headache instantly clearing, and took the invitation at face value. After lunch, she walked down the back lane into Darryl's back yard, wearing pink shorts, a white tank top and flip flops. She saw him laying shirtless on a lounge chair, wearing navy swim trunks. He was drinking a beer and reading an architecture magazine.

"Homework?" she said as she sauntered up the deck stairs. She flipped up her sunglasses into her messy ponytail, pulled up another lounge chair and sat down, smiling at him.

Darryl was overjoyed that Krys was there with him, but kept his cool. "Nope, not homework. A potential employment opportunity," he replied.

"Oh? School going that well?" she asked.

"Yup. I'm at the top of my class and I've already got a few firms interested in hiring me after I graduate next May," Darryl replied humbly.

"Wow! That's fantastic! I'm so excited for you!" Krys exclaimed, thinking that she sounded like a proud girlfriend...

Darryl smiled and offered her a drink from the cooler beside him.

She took a bottle of water, cracked it open and took a sip as Darryl watched her while taking a swig of his own cold beer.

They eased into small talk, getting comfortable with each other, and ended up spending the entire afternoon outside talking, laughing and enjoying each other's company. The only thing Krys didn't mention was how much she loved being back in his arms last night...

And missed it...

CHAPTER 45

October 1993

Krys & Darryl

Since their night at ILLUSIONS and the next afternoon in Darryl's back yard, Krys and Darryl began spending most of their free time together. Krys suggested one warm Sunday evening that they take a drive out to the Half Moon Drive-In in Selkirk for ice cream.

After they made their choices, they sat side by side on a picnic bench, licking their ice cream cones. She had Butterscotch Ripple and he had Rocky Road.

"Darryl, can we talk?" Krys asked as she looked out at the water lazily sliding by in the Red River.

"Sure. About what?" Darryl replied.

"What happened between us," she answered, turning to face him.

"Okay," he said slowly. "Where do you want to start?"

"I'm sorry. For the way I acted and for the way I *reacted*, going out and getting together with someone else the day we broke up. I'm sorry for not letting you explain or listen to your apology, because all I could process was that you had sex with someone else, not the awful circumstances around it," she blurted, leaning into his side and grabbing his arm, her eyes watery with tears and regret.

Darryl pulled his arm out of her grasp and wrapped it around her, cuddling her close to his side. "Kryssie, I'm sorry, too. I'm sorry for getting so obliterated that I didn't realize what I was doing and what was happening until it was too late. And I'm *most* sorry that I hooked up with her after the fact. What a nightmarish mistake *that* was," he shuddered.

Krys continued, "I know that what you did wasn't cheating. You were deceived and I should have trusted you. I can't ever apologize enough for that lack of faith in you," Krys sniffed as she burrowed into Darryl's side.

"I was there that night, at ILLUSIONS, Krys. I saw you flirting with him and I saw you leave with him. It tore my heart out to see you with him, but I understand why you did what you did, since I ended up doing the same thing, myself," Darryl confessed.

Krys looked up at him, hearing the hurt in his voice as he stared straight ahead at the water. "Darryl, do you think we can get past all this and put it behind us?" she asked.

"I really want that, Kryssie. I've missed not having you in my life," Darryl looked back at her and smiled.

"I have to make sure that I listen when you need to explain something important to me. I need to work on that," Krys admitted.

"And I have a bit of a hare-trigger temper that I need to work on," Darryl added.

"So, are we square now? Can we start fresh?" she asked, hugging him close to her.

"Yeah, I think we can," he replied, kissing her cheek.

Krys paused before she spoke next, then whispered, "I loved him, Darryl. Not the way I love you, but I did love him, and that's been really hard for me to get over. I broke up with him because I couldn't see our situation working out. And because of you... I couldn't get you out of my head, or my heart..."

Darryl smiled at what Krys said, not sure if she realized what she just admitted. "You still love me?"

Krys blinked, smiled shyly and confessed, "Yeah."

Holy shit!

She still loves me!

"Okay, good," Darryl said as he winked at her.

"*'Okay, good'*?" Krys repeated, her eyebrows raised in question.

"Yup. Let's drive home and I'll let you hold my hand," he teased.

"You will? Now my life is complete," she answered sarcastically, lightly punching him in the arm.

I still love him and now he knows...

They finished their ice cream cones and drove home the long way, holding hands.

CHAPTER 46

November 7, 1993

Krys & Darryl

The night before Krys' twentieth birthday, Darryl gave her a gift he knew she was going to love. They were sitting together on the couch in her basement watching Sixteen Candles on TV when he gave her the small box, noting that she looked both excited and apprehensive.

"What's this? You didn't have to get me anything," she said shyly.

"I know I didn't have to, Kryssie. I wanted to," he replied, looking at her with a sparkle in his eyes.

She opened the royal blue velvet lid and her mouth dropped open. Inside was nestled a fourteen karat gold box chain, on which hung a large oval sapphire with diamonds surrounding it, set in yellow gold. "Darryl!" she gasped as she stared at the gorgeous piece of jewellery in her hand.

Darryl smiled triumphantly at Krys' reaction as he took the box from her hand and gently removed the necklace from its white satin nest. He turned her around so she was facing away from him and had her hold up her hair. He struggled to resist the urge to kiss her neck as he did up the clasp, then turned her back around to face him again. "Beautiful," he said, referring to the jewellery, *and* the neck it was around.

Krys got up and went to the mirror in her bedroom to see it on herself. She was so overwhelmed at his generosity, she didn't notice Darryl behind her until she felt his warm body at her back.

"Do you like it?" he asked, grinning smugly. He knew damn well she loved it...

She gave him a dazzling smile that took his breath away. "It's... It's..." was all she could utter.

"I'll take that as a yes," he grinned.

Krys looked at him in the mirror and breathed, "I love it. Thank you so very much. But, why?"

Darryl revealed what was in his heart. "Why? Because it's your birthday. And because I love you, Krys. I never stopped loving you, even though we've been apart for the last year. These past couple of months spending time with you again has reignited the fire in my soul for you. I want you back in my life again, Krys. You are *The One*. You always have been and you always will be. We belong together and we belong to each other," he concluded.

Krys turned around to face him, tears of joy in her eyes at his heartfelt words. "I love you, too, Darryl. You're *The One* for me, too. You always have been and you always will be," she repeated.

They pulled each other close and their lips fused together in a fiery inferno of emotion.

Darryl tore his lips away from hers and asked smugly, "So? Are you and I back together?"

"Absolutely!" she cried as she threw her arms around his neck and hugged him tightly.

Since her parents were out for the evening, they took advantage of the empty house. Krys shut her bedroom door with her foot and smiled seductively at Darryl. "I think we need to make it official," she murmured in his ear, then nipped his jaw with her teeth.

Darryl growled in anticipation and tried to control his sheer excitement at what was about to happen between the two of them. It had been *so long* since he'd held his Kryssie in his arms and kissed her, feeling her body against his. He was consumed completely by his love for her.

He wanted to take his time and savor every moment of their long-awaited reunion, so Darryl slowly began undressing Krys. He pulled her tank top over her head while he kissed and licked a delightfully wet trail from her belly up to her mouth, stopping to pay homage to her bared breasts.

After licking his way up from her chest to her lips, he plunged his tongue back into her mouth and kissed her passionately. While he was driving up her desire with his tongue play, his thumbs hooked into the waistband of her yoga pants and swept them down her lovely legs, taking her satin panties with them. She stepped out of them and Darryl carefully nudged them out of the way so he wouldn't lose contact with Krys' lips.

All she had left on were the diamond stud earrings she always wore and the sapphire pendant and gold chain that Darryl had just given her this evening.

She wore no rings on her fingers...

Yet...

Krys reached between them and unbuttoned Darryl's shirt, running her fingers over his chest hair that she loved so much. Darryl shucked off his shirt, then returned his hands to her face, keeping them out of her way so she had full control of removing the rest of his clothes.

Krys unbuckled his belt and undid the button on his jeans, then slid them down his legs, pausing to grasp onto his rock-hard cock and give it an *I-missed-you* squeeze. She pulled his jeans off and moved them aside.

Finally, they were both naked, facing each other.

Krys thought it would feel awkward standing nude in front of Darryl again after so long, but it wasn't. It was erotic and familiar and she couldn't wait to get her hands on the rest of him.

Darryl was beside himself with joy that they had finally gotten to this point. "I love you, Kryssie," was all he could manage to say.

"I love you, Darryl," Krys answered, her voice tremulous with emotion and excitement.

They moved slowly into the other's embrace and began kissing sweetly, their arms wrapped around each other, feeling the other with sensitive fingertips.

Darryl walked Krys backwards until she hit the bed and in a fluid movement, they crawled together onto it, keeping their lips attached in their steamy kiss.

Krys lay on her back while Darryl propped himself up on his forearms on either side of her. She raised her knees and wrapped them around his hips so she could cradle him between her legs.

Darryl's cock was as hard as granite, but he paused before sinking into her. He slid one hand down between Krys' thighs and felt her slipperiness. He zeroed in on her sweet spot with his thumb and slid one finger inside her, thrusting gently as he lowered his lips, pulsing his tongue into her mouth.

Krys was engrossed with sensation. While Darryl was revving her up, she grabbed hold of his cock and slid her hand up and down, rubbing the tip with her thumb.

Darryl groaned and tried to pull away from her, afraid he would blow too soon and totally fuck up their long-awaited reunion.

Krys chuckled softly as she let go of his swollen cock, aching to have him inside her again after so long without him.

Darryl moved his hand slowly up her body, pausing to knead one breast while he bent to suckle the other. He licked his way back up to her face and resumed kissing her, then paused again, this time with the head of his cock at her opening. His eyes locked on hers as she gazed at him with absolute love and devotion, then he reared back and plunged in all the way.

Krys moaned in sheer pleasure and arched her back, taking him even deeper. They stayed bound together that way for a moment, eyes locked, lips touching, the sacredness of their union and the bounty of feelings between them overwhelming.

When Darryl finally began moving his hips, Krys matched him thrust for thrust. The burn began slowly building in both their bodies, preparing them for a volcanic eruption of epic proportions. After a few minutes of slow-and-sweet lovemaking, carnal lust took over and Darryl's thrusts grew deeper and more passionate.

When the burn was at the tip of his dick, Darryl slowed down and began grinding into Krys to indicate that he was close to exploding.

In response, she tilted her pelvis and took him in as deep as she could, bringing on her orgasm like a strike of lightning. She began convulsing around his cock, draining his orgasm right out of him and wringing them both completely dry.

Darryl sagged onto Krys, both of them panting. She revelled in his weight and the scent of him as she buried her nose in his neck. Then she started laughing softly, making him frown at her.

"What's so funny?" he asked, staring down at her and scowling.

"I was just thinking of the first time we had sex and how good I thought it was. And it *was,* back then, when we were both pretty green. But this? I couldn't have imagined this any other way for our *second* first time together. It was... perfect," Krys admitted.

Darryl puffed out his chest and felt like crowing from the rooftops. "Now *that's* what I wanna hear," he said, leaning down and kissing her lovingly.

They stayed connected for a while longer, then Darryl pulled out gently and got off the bed, taking Krys with him. They weren't sure when her parents would be home, so they got dressed and resumed their previous cuddling on the couch, sly smiles on their faces when Lily and Jack came home and asked them what they did that evening.

Krys showed her mother the necklace that Darryl gave her and Lily clapped her hands together. "Oh Kryssie, it's absolutely lovely! But Darryl, isn't it a little extravagant?" she asked.

Krys and Darryl stood together with their arms wrapped around each other and revealed their news. "Momma, we're back together," Krys said, beaming from ear to ear, cuddling into Darryl's warm embrace.

At that, Lily whooped for joy, waving her fists in the air, a huge smile on her face as tears formed in her eyes. "Oh Yay! Yippee! My prayers have been answered!"

Krys started laughing. "You've been praying for Darryl and I to get back together?"

"Absolutely! You two are part of each other, like your father and I are. It's been plain for anyone who has eyes to see that you two belong together," Lily smiled, her eyes tearing up, reaching for Jack as he wound his arms around her.

"See Krys? That's what I said to you, remember?" Darryl added smugly as he held her close, kissing her temple.

"Yes, I remember," Krys admitted.

Jack, standing at 6' with a salt'n'pepper brush cut and wire glasses covering his brown eyes, moved out of Lily's embrace and slapped Darryl on the back, saying with an equally smug grin, "About time you two made things right."

Darryl answered, "Yes, it is, Mr H," as he squeezed Krys closer to him.

CHAPTER 47

November 8, 1993

Krys & Natalie

When Natalie came over the next morning to wish her best friend *Happy Birthday*, she saw Krys sitting at the table in her kitchen with a huge smile on her face, her hand toying with something dangling around her neck.

"Happy Birthday, Kryssie!! Hey! Is this what your parents gave you for your birthday? It's beautiful!" Nat exclaimed, gently holding the beautiful sapphire pendant between her fingers.

"No, my boyfriend gave it to me," Krys said as she looked up, smiling dreamily.

Natalie was convinced that Krys had lost her damn mind. "Uh, boyfriend?"

Krys looked directly at her and replied, "Yes, my boyfriend. *Your brother*!"

Natalie's eyes bugged out of her head and her mouth fell open. Then she grabbed Krys and hugged her. "OHMYGAWD!!! AREYOUSERIOUS???" she cried.

"Yup!" Krys said happily.

"Tell me what happened!" Nat exclaimed. "I want details!!"

"Last night, Darryl came over and totally surprised me with this beautiful necklace! And he said the most loving things to me, Nat! You have to have noticed the way we've been behaving around each other since September, haven't you? We hashed things out a few weeks ago, so getting back together was inevitable," Krys said, smiling shyly.

"Yeah, I've noticed. I was wondering how long it would take YOU to notice and do something about it!" she laughed.

"Timing is everything, isn't it? As much as I HATE what we've both been through this past year, I have no regrets about it. Being with Rick was truly wonderful," Krys paused and reflected on her time with him, then continued, "and I will always cherish that and hold it dear in my heart... But Darryl and I... *WE* belong together" Krys finished, smiling serenely.

Natalie positively beamed when she heard the love in Krys' voice directed towards her brother. "I'm so glad to hear you say that, Krys! Darryl loves you so much!"

Krys decided it was time to switch gears. "When was the last time you saw Tony? I don't know how do you do it, Nat. I hated every minute of being separated from Rick."

"What we do just works for us. We talk on the phone every few days and with the way my classes are set up, I'm able to get away every now and again so we can spend a few days together. In fact, I *did* sneak away for a couple days in mid-October to Chicago to see him," Nat started.

"Wait, wait, wait," Krys interrupted. "*That's* where you went? You told me you went down to Minneapolis for the weekend to go shopping with Charlotte! Why didn't you tell me?"

"Because me seeing Tony meant I'd be seeing Rick, too. I didn't want to hurt you by bringing it up because I could see things were going well between you and Darryl, and I didn't want to crush that," Nat explained.

Krys settled herself. "Oh... Thank you for that."

She was about to ask Natalie how Rick was doing when Lily and Jack came into the kitchen singing *Happy Birthday* and carrying a cake lit with twenty candles.

"Happy Birthday, my Baby! Your father and I hope you have a wonderful day today!" Lily said, hugging Krys tightly.

"Happy Birthday, Caboose," Jack said as he kissed Krys on the top of her head.

Darryl came in behind Jack, smiled lovingly at the birthday girl and said, "Happy Birthday, Kryssie."

Krys zeroed in on his dimples and forgot all about Rick...

CHAPTER 48

December 7, 1993
Natalie & Tony

In early December, Natalie flew to New Orleans to visit Tony for her birthday. Tony surprised her with a road trip in a silver 1970 Corvette Stingray to Oak Alley Plantation for a private tour, followed by an authentically prepared southern feast of Cajun and Creole favorites.

As the sun was setting, they drove back to the Four Points Sheraton Hotel in the French Quarter on Bourbon Street for their usual I-missed-you-like-crazy sex-a-thon. They started making out in the elevator, unable to resist the urge and having no restraint against their feelings towards one another. As they stumbled their way into their suite, they began frantically tearing off each other's clothes, trying to get naked as fast as possible.

In a sexual haven't-see-you-in-three-months frenzy, Tony took Natalie while standing up against the wall facing each other, then he turned her so both of them were facing the wall, then he turned her back around, picked her up and carried her to the bed where he was on top, then they rolled and she was on top, and finally he was behind her with her on her knees when they both orgasmed and collapsed against each other with huge, satisfied smiles on their faces.

Once they were totally sated and almost ready to fall asleep, Natalie told Tony about Krys and Darryl getting back together and how happy Krys was.

Tony was both happy and sad to hear this news.

Happy, because he genuinely liked Krys and wished her nothing but happiness. He knew she had hated being separated from Rick and couldn't cope with them being apart, no matter how much they loved each other. He also knew of her history with Darryl and had to agree that they were much better suited for each other.

And sad, because he saw how crushed Krys was to break things off with Rick, who was a shattered mess in the weeks after she dropped that bomb on him, and continued to be.

Since their split, Rick had taken to the rock'n'roll lifestyle, drinking to excess and getting laid as much as his dick would let him. With all the groupies hanging around, it was easy for him to take his pick and indulge himself.

Because of that, Tony and all the guys were worried about him. Rick was still brilliant on stage, no matter what turmoil his personal life was in, but Tony was afraid that Rick might do something stupid and unfixable because he couldn't cope with the break up of his relationship with Krys. He couldn't even fathom what something stupid and unfixable could be and that scared him even more.

But right now, it was all about him and Natalie, so he pushed those haunting thoughts out of his head and concentrated on his birthday girl snuggled up to him in bed.

Over the next few days, they kept busy wandering up and down the shops on Bourbon Street, took a bayou swamp boat tour, went for a stroll through St Louis Cemetery and a paid a visit to Marie Laveau's Voodoo shop. They ate at Antoine's, Brennan's and Cafe Du Monde, indulging in muffalettas, po-boys and as many beignets as they could eat.

Then, as always and all too soon, their time together came to an end and Natalie was on a plane back home to her life, away from Tony.

CHAPTER 49

August 1993 to December 1993
Rick

The past few months without Krys in his life were the worst Rick had ever experienced. Even though he was hanging on by a thread emotionally, he refused to let his personal life interfere with his professional one. They played to sold-out crowds everywhere they went and he gave it his all, each and every night.

Where Rick was a social drinker before, not one to indulge too much, now he was never seen without a whiskey bottle grasped in his hand.

And the groupies he so consciously avoided when he had Krys in his life? Now they were hanging off him, two to three deep.

But ONLY blondes...

He NEVER strayed from blonde...

And the blonde hair HAD to be long...

Rick was now competing with Alex and Diego to see who could screw the most girls in each city. Both of them were still horndogs, but now that Rick threw himself into the mix, pickin's were slim, even with Rick only going for blondes.

Bryan had tried to talk to him and even sent April to talk to him to see if she could try to pull Rick out of his black depression over losing Krys.

Nothing worked.

Frank tried to talk to him, but Rick told him to mind his own business and to keep his nose out of Rick's private life. He said that he was delivering a stellar show every night to the crowds so he was keeping his end of the contract and what he did on his own time was nobody's business but his. Frank talked with Tony, Bryan, Diego and Alex about Rick's situation and tried to figure out a way to help him, but they all came up empty.

"With his Psychology background, you'd think he'd know how to cope with this and help himself, not drink himself into a stupor every day and screw himself into an early grave," Tony said, exasperated and sad to see what Rick was doing to himself.

Tony had his back to the door of the room, so he didn't notice when Rick walked up silently behind him and cuffed him across the back of the head with his free hand. In the other hand was his trusty bottle of whiskey, the cap off and a few swigs already taken from it.

It was ten in the morning.

"You asshole! Do you think it's been easy for me being without Krys? I knew, *I knew,* when we signed those contracts and our lives changed in that instant, that I'd have to give her up at some point. I just didn't think it was going to be so soon, after what she and I had been through together already," Rick yelled, turning away and taking a big swig of whiskey, his eyes watery with grief.

The room got silent as the guys tried to put themselves in his position.

One by one, they all went to him to give him their support.

Tony was first. "Rick, I'm sorry you're hurting, but the way you're coping isn't helping you get over her, is it? We're all worried about you! We know how much you loved her, it was plain as day to all of us. But she made her choice and you need to accept that and move on. Find another woman to love, one who will be better able to accept your career choice."

Bryan was next. "Rick, pour your feelings into your music. You are a brilliant musician and songwriter. Put the bottle down and start writing for our next album. I'm telling you, it will help."

"It's easy for you to say, Bryan, you have your woman with you," Rick moaned.

"You're right, I do. So I'm the last person who should be saying anything to you, but Krys has moved on and you need to find a way to accept that, so you can move on, too," he replied.

Bryan moved over and Diego moved in, clapped one hand on Rick's neck and grabbed onto his shoulder with his other, looking him straight in the eye. "*Mi hermano*, she is a lovely woman and was admittedly perfect for *you*, but *not* for this lifestyle. I'm sorry things ended the way they did for you both. Please, take what we are saying to you as brotherly love. We care."

Alex shoved Diego out of the way with his usual piss-and-vinegar energy and barged in, his bull-in-a-china-shop moves incongruous for a guy of his size. "Dude, it totally fucking sucks that you lost her, but you can't let that shit rule you. Mourn your loss and get the fuck on with your life. You will not always feel this shitty because you don't have her anymore. You WILL find someone else to love," Alex pronounced.

Out of all what the guys said to Rick, what Alex just said to him resonated the most and he almost grinned. "Where did you get that shit from?"

"Your psychology textbooks. What do you think I'm always doing in my room, jerking off? That's some interesting stuff you studied. I read and learned," Alex shrugged his shoulders.

That actually made Rick smile. "You're always full of surprises, Al."

Feeling a little better about things and knowing that the guys had his back, Rick was able to let go of a little bit of his sadness. He dropped the bottle of whiskey and picked up his guitar, played a few notes and hummed something to himself.

I can do this...

If she can move on, so can I...

CHAPTER 50

January 1994

Krys & Darryl

Christmas came and went with Krys and Darryl firmly back together and happier than ever. All of their family and friends noticed a huge difference in both of them, as the light in their eyes that had died when they split was now burning brighter than before.

Darryl's twenty-second birthday was on January 8 and he was *really* looking forward to this one. Last year's birthday was shitty because he didn't have Krys in his life. But now? His life was shaping up quite nicely.

Krys surprised him with a vintage Rolex watch she found at an estate sale and had it engraved:

Together for all time...D&K

He was completely speechless as he never expected such an extravagant gift from her.

Darryl and Natalie's parents, Audrey and Owen, were away for the month on vacation in Hawaii, so the siblings had the house to themselves. Darryl booted Natalie out for the weekend because he had plans for him and Krys that did NOT involve his sister, in *any* capacity. She packed a bag and happily went to stay with her friend Charlotte until she got the *all clear* to return home.

Since his birthday landed on a Saturday, Darryl and Krys went out celebrating with their friends to ILLUSIONS, as usual, on Friday and Saturday nights. After a hot-and-heavy weekend of wild jungle sex to celebrate his birthday, Darryl surprised Krys by making dinner for them on Sunday night. He was no slouch in the kitchen, his mother having taught him and Natalie how to cook.

When Krys arrived, Darryl was waiting at the door for her. She found the lights turned down low and heard music playing softly to complete the ambience. The Honeydrippers were crooning "Sea Of Love", setting the tone of the evening.

"Wow," she breathed, taking it all in. "You've been busy," she smiled, feeling tingly with excitement.

"Nah," Darryl grinned, down-playing the romantic mood he created for them.

Then Krys noticed what Darryl was wearing – a dark gray suit with a bright white button-down shirt, a pale gray and navy striped tie, a pale gray pocket square and shiny black dress shoes. She could smell his aftershave she loved so much. "You're so handsome," Krys said appreciatively.

Darryl had requested that Krys dress up. He helped her remove her deep blue peacoat to reveal a navy linen dress with a deep scoop neckline and cap sleeves, the hemline at her knees with a small slit up the back. Her legs were encased in sheer black stockings and on her feet were shiny black stilettos.

She kept her hair down in long, soft waves, wearing only her diamond studs in her ears and her sapphire pendant around her neck. She did her makeup with a romantic hand of soft pink lips and cheeks with natural eyes. She also wore her vanilla perfume oil that always drove Darryl out of his mind with lust.

"You look gorgeous, Kryssie. You really take my breath away," Darryl said as he wrapped his arms around her and kissed her softly.

"Thank you. But it's not a chore for me to dress up for you," Krys replied, hugging him back.

Darryl tucked Krys into his side and spanned his hand across in front of them, surveying the dining room. "I wanted to do something different tonight, something I've never done for us before. What do you think, so far?" he asked, his lips tipped up in a smug grin. He had set the dining room table using his mother's china and silverware, poured chilled champagne into beautiful crystal stemware and even set a bouquet of white and pink carnations, Krys' favorite flowers, in a crystal vase on the table with a pair of beeswax taper candles in crystal candle holders.

"So far? Ten out of ten. But the real test will be what you made for dinner," she joked as they moved towards the table, knowing how good he was in the kitchen.

"I think you'll be pleasantly surprised. How does filet mignon with sauteed mushrooms and grilled asparagus sound to you?" Darryl knew that Krys hated potatoes and he wasn't too fond of them either. "And for dessert... Well, I'll keep that a surprise for now."

"Mmm, that all sounds so decadent!" Krys exclaimed.

"Then by all means, let's eat, shall we?" Darryl answered.

He led Krys to her chair and held it out for her. She settled in, then Darryl went to the kitchen to retrieve the feast he had made for them. He served Krys before serving himself, treating her like the special guest she was. They sat opposite each other at the table and devoured everything, feeding each other, enjoying the different tastes and textures.

After Darryl cleared away the dishes, refusing Krys' offer to help, he brought a covered dessert plate to the table and placed it in front of her. Then he pressed *PLAY* on the CD player and Paul McCartney's "Maybe I'm Amazed" began serenading them quietly in the background. He turned her chair so she was facing him and dropped to one knee in front of her, taking both of her hands in both of his, smiling lovingly at her.

Krys blanched at his position...

On one knee...

OHMYGOD!!!

IS HE DOING WHAT I THINK HE'S DOING???

Darryl's hands were shaking slightly as he began speaking, his voice slightly tremulous as the words registered in her mind. "Kryssie, I love you. I've loved you my whole life. Since we've gotten back together, I'm the happiest I've ever been. I want to continue feeling this way for the rest of my life and I will, if you say yes..." Darryl paused, turned to the table and lifted the lid off the dessert plate.

In the middle of the plate was a small, white leather box, opened to reveal the most beautiful diamond engagement ring Krys had ever seen, tucked into white velvet. It was an exquisite setting, the center cushion-cut diamond surrounded by two levels of tinier diamonds set in white gold, the yellow gold double band set with pave diamonds half way down each side.

Krys' eyes widened in shock and she breathed out a simple, "OH!"

Darryl took the ring box off the plate and held it up for her to see, his nerves on red alert. "Krysten, will you marry me?" he asked as he took her left hand in his and waited for her answer before he dared to slip the ring on her finger.

Her mouth opened and closed, then slowly spread into a dazzling smile as she rasped out an emotionally throaty, "YES!"

Krys threw her arms around Darryl and launched herself into his arms, knocking him off balance and falling on top of him onto the floor, crying and laughing at the same time. Darryl lay on his back with Krys on top of him in his arms, the ring box still open and clutched in his hand.

She said YES!!!

He gently pushed her off him and righted them so they were sitting on the floor facing each other. Darryl took the ring out of the box and held her left hand up between them. He slipped it on her ring finger and she stretched her hand out, admiring its beauty. She was delightfully surprised at how perfect the ring was that he chose for her as it was exactly her taste and exactly what she would have chosen for herself.

"Do you like it?" Darryl asked again, knowing that she loved it, but wanted to hear her say it.

Krys looked at Darryl with pure love in her eyes as she gushed, "I absolutely do! How? When?" she stammered.

Darryl smiled angelically and replied, "How did I know what kind of ring you'd like? I've always paid attention to your jewellery style because I knew that one day I was going to give you an engagement ring. And when did I buy it? The day after your birthday when we were officially back together. I've just been waiting for the right time to give it to you."

Krys was absolutely speechless. Darryl had put so much thought into this and planned it down to the last detail because he had absolute confidence that it would go off without a hitch and that she would say yes. That was when the tears started. "All this, for us," she whispered.

"All this, for us," Darryl repeated, pulling her into his embrace and holding her while she cried tears of joy. "Now can we get up off the floor? I'd like to dance with you," he said, his voice thick with emotion.

Darryl got up first, then offered Krys his hand and pulled her up to stand with him. He walked with her to the stereo and pressed *PLAY*. Then he moved them to the middle of the living room, wrapped his arms around her and pulled her close as Krys wound her arms around him.

"Dream Come True" by Frozen Ghost began playing and that brought out a fresh round of tears from Krys, the lyrics exactly how she and Darryl felt about each other. It was her favorite love song of all time. She had mentioned countless times since the very first time she heard it that this was the song she wanted played for the first dance between her and her groom at her wedding one day.

And Darryl remembered.

They swayed together to the beautiful song with Krys' face tucked into Darryl's neck. When the song ended, Krys pulled away thinking that was it, but Darryl held her firmly to him and whispered, "Wait…"

"Could I Have This Dance" by Anne Murray began playing next. It was her second favorite love song and Darryl remembered that, too.

Krys was overwhelmed by emotion.

"Do you want to go tell your parents now?" Darryl asked her.

"I think my Mom might explode with excitement," Krys giggled.

"Then let's go and make her evening," he replied, moving to the table to blow out the candles and collect their coats while Krys went to the bathroom to repair her makeup.

"What about your parents? Don't you want to call them in Hawaii and tell them? I doubt they'd want to wait until they come home to hear news like this, would they?" Krys asked.

Darryl replied, smirking, "They already know. I told them I was doing this before they left last week. They're really excited for us."

"You were so sure I'd say yes?" Krys questioned, grinning.

"Absolutely," he answered, kissing her.

They walked hand in hand down the street to Krys' house, smiling lovingly at each other as they crunched through the snow together.

Lily and Jack were sitting in their matching recliners in the living room, eating popcorn and laughing at the British comedy they were watching on TV.

"Mom, Darryl and I have something to tell you," Krys squeaked out, fresh tears welling in her eyes.

Lily looked at her daughter, *her Baby*, got up and walked towards them with a look of excited jubilation on her face.

It can only be one thing...

Krys held out her left hand to her mother and said nothing, letting the ring speak for itself, her face split in two by an enormous smile.

Lily grasped Krys' hand gently in both of her smaller ones and stared at the beautiful diamond ring, tears raining down her face. She gathered her only daughter in her arms and they cried happy tears together, leaving the men to glance conspiratorially at each other.

Darryl had asked Jack's permission for Krys' hand in marriage back in November on the evening they'd announced that they had gotten back together.

Lily let go of Krys and reached up to hold her beloved daughter's happy face in her hands for a moment before gently tugging her down and kissing her forehead. "I'm so, so happy for you both. Thank you, Darryl, for being so good to our daughter and making her so very happy," Lily said, taking one of her hands from Krys' face and placing it on Darryl's cheek.

Jack got up from his leather chair and came over to his wife, daughter and soon-to-be-son-in-law, holding out his hand to Darryl to shake and accept the news. "Welcome to our family, Darryl," he said, winking.

Lily's expression turned to ecstatic delight as a thought occurred to her. "Now we get to plan your wedding! Oh Kryssie, this is so wonderful! Let's get started!" She pulled Jack by the hand into the kitchen and sat him at the table. She got all of them pads of paper and pens, sat down beside Jack and started writing. She chattered about the food, the caterer, the flowers, when to reserve the church, the music, the photographer, the wedding cake, the wedding favors, all the things that were involved with planning a wedding.

Jack looked to the ceiling and rolled his eyes while shaking his head, making Krys laugh.

Krys sat on Darryl's lap and they grinned at each other, enjoying Lily's excitement while snickering at Jack's gloom at the financial implications of paying for his daughter's wedding.

Darryl felt like he won the lottery and in a way he had, hadn't he? He had gambled and won Krys' hand AND her heart.

CHAPTER 51

January 1994
Krys & Natalie

After school the next day, Natalie ran into Krys' bedroom screaming her head off in excitement. "KRYSSIEEEEEEEE!!!!!!!! OHMIGOD!!! LEMME SEE THE RIIIIIIING!!!" Natalie screeched, grabbing Krys' hand and holding it up to her face, looking at it from all angles.

Krys just smiled. "I take it Darryl told you?"

"He sure did!" Nat answered breathlessly. "So? Have you set a date yet? Who are you having in your wedding party? What kind of wedding gown are you going to wear? What about the music? The food? The flowers? The photographer? The DJ?" Nat started in on her usual avalanche of questions.

"Stop right there, Nat," Krys said, laughing at Natalie's intense excitement. "We JUST got engaged last night. We haven't gotten that far with any plans yet, but as my Maid of Honor, you will be privy to all the details," Krys confirmed.

Nat squealed in delight. "I'm your Maid of Honor? Frigging awesome!!!"

"Of course! Who else would I have?" Krys asked, smiling.

They just stood there looking at each other, then collapsed into each other's arms and hugged, letting the tears of happiness slide down their cheeks.

"I'm so happy, Nat. I didn't think we'd ever get back here. Darryl is the love of my life," Krys whispered in Nat's ear.

"I'm glad to hear that, Krys, so glad," Nat whispered back.

Now that the world is right again, I hope things stay as happy as they are!

CHAPTER 52

January 1994 to June 1994
Natalie & Tony

Natalie told Tony about Krys and Darryl's engagement when she talked to him on the phone later that day. "Tony, PLEASE don't tell Rick! It's going to hurt him a lot, knowing how quick this happened between them. He's a good guy and I don't want to see him hurt any more than he already has been," Nat pleaded.

"No problem, Strawberry. Actually, he's been coping a bit better since we had it out with him last month and he seems to be snapping out of his dumpy mood. He's been writing some great songs for our next album and they're sounding totally incredible so far," Tony told her, continuing. "He's also eased up on the boozing and womanizing. But enough about him. When are you coming out to see me again? I miss you."

"I'm glad to hear that about Rick. I miss you, too. I'm going to try for Valentines Day, if Vanessa and Brad can swing it, or maybe for your birthday in March? Depends on school," Nat answered.

"We'll make it happen, one way or another," Tony declared.

Tony's declaration yielded results. Natalie was able to fly out to see him in Las Vegas for a whirlwind three days over Valentine's Day in mid-February, then again in early March for his birthday in Toronto. By the time April and May rolled around, Natalie was finished with school for the year and she was able to fly out a couple more times to Miami and Phoenix.

Since January, it was getting harder for Natalie and Tony to remain inconspicuous when she flew out to visit him. They had such a large and ever-growing following of fans that Tony started wearing different sorts of odd costumes. This was the only way he and Natalie could get out and see some of the sights without getting totally mobbed. They made a running joke out of it, laughing and waiting to see if they were noticed and how long it took for people to figure out who was under the bizarre get-ups they came up with.

With Natalie being home in Winnipeg and Tony jet-setting all over North America, they somehow managed to stay monogamous and committed to each other. Natalie wasn't exactly sure how they made it work, but they did.

As things stood now, they had been together for more than a year and a half and she was happy with how things were at this moment in time. When she was done school in a year, and if they were still together, then maybe she'd rethink their situation.

But until then? She was going to enjoy the ride.

CHAPTER 53

January 1994 to June 1994
Rick

After Rick was blindsided and set upon by the guys and Frank about his behavior and how worried they were about him, he rethought how he was living his life.

He *had* to stop pining for Krys because nothing was going to bring her back to him.

Ever.

He dialed back on his drinking and cut way down on the number of groupies he slept with, but he would still only screw chicks with long blonde hair...

Baby steps and all...

Putting his psychology studies into practice, he started writing out his feelings to cope with his profound loss. This was when his creative juices began overflowing. He was writing some of the best material of his life and couldn't wait to start recording it. He played a few samples to the guys and they totally loved it.

Whenever Natalie would fly in to visit Tony, Rick would say a quick *'Hey, how's it going?'* then steer clear of her, for fear he would succumb to the devil on his shoulder and ask about Krys. As much as he wanted to know about her and if she was happy, he didn't want to sabotage himself and all the progress he'd been making and be more the fool.

One morning in late March, Rick woke up feeling unsettled. He couldn't put his finger on it until he looked at the date.

March 25.

One year ago today, Krys miscarried their baby that she didn't even know she was pregnant with.

Rick had never told a soul. He and Krys decided that they were going to keep this tragic loss to themselves, and he had.

He wondered for a moment if she had, too...

Thinking about their baby, Rick picked up his guitar and composed the sweetest, most beautiful instrumental piece he'd ever created, but decided to keep it to himself. No one would ever get to hear the heartbreak and utter despair that the piece evoked in him. It was haunting, beautiful, and profoundly tragic, and he never played it again.

As April rolled into May, then freight-trained into June, Rick caught himself thinking about Krys on her graduation day from nursing school. He so wanted to be there with her to celebrate such a wonderful accomplishment as she had been there for him when he was granted his Master's Degree the year before. He thought about flying home to surprise her, then decided that was a move that would only cause both of them great pain.

Instead, that day he composed an acoustic love song, recorded it and dedicated to her. He titled it "Forever And A Day" and sang it himself. His voice was deeper and raspier than Tony's, totally suited for the style of song. He played it for the band and they loved it, knowing it was him and Krys written all over it.

In another month and a half on the road, and after more than a year away, Diamond Angel would finally be going home...

Maybe he would take a chance and go see Krys...

Maybe Natalie would bring her to their concert in Winnipeg on the last night of their tour...

Maybe Krys would still be single and missing him...

CHAPTER 54

May 1994 to June 1994
Krys & Darryl & Lily & Jack

At the end of May, Darryl graduated at the top of his class from the University of Manitoba with his Bachelor's Degree in Architecture. He was offered an incredible position at a very prominent Architecture firm in the city, the same firm he had taken his practical training at, where they absolutely loved his innovative ideas. With the offer of employment came a huge signing bonus, so after discussing it with Krys, he moved into an apartment on the first of June and she would move in after they got married.

Things were moving so fast and smoothly in their lives, Krys was waiting for the axe to fall.

But there wasn't one.

With plans firmly underway for their wedding on July 10, and her own graduation only weeks away at the end of June, Krys' life kicked into high gear.

However, there was a shadow cast over Lily and Jack with all this talk of family gathering for Krys' upcoming nuptials...

Lily and Jack had been happily married since November 10, 1956. They had five kids in the first eight years they were married – four sons and one daughter – Dean, Vince, James, Michael, all about a year apart in age, and Marie, who came along four years later. Krys was born nine years after Marie, a planned, final addition to the family.

The Harris Family lived a charmed life for twenty years, then things slowly started to unravel and deteriorate.

Dean was a model son, got good grades, held down a part-time job and generally behaved as the typical responsible oldest child.

Vince, as the second born, was similar to Dean as he got good grades and had a part-time job. He also had a steady girlfriend and a car he loved to drive and tinker with.

Michael was the youngest of the boys and a mischief-maker, but he was so charming that most of the time his misgivings were forgiven.

James and Marie – they were another story.

James was the quintessential third son and middle child. He fooled around in school, got into trouble a lot and ended up, more often than not, in detention. Everyone could see the direction his life was going to go if things didn't change.

Marie was the baby of the family and the only girl for a long time before Krys came along. She idolized James and followed him around everywhere, copying everything he said, did, wore, ate, drank, everything.

James and Marie became the hellions of the family, especially once Marie turned twelve and James was seventeen, becoming more defiant towards Lily and Jack. They were always causing problems and creating terrible drama for them, in turn pissing off their brothers with their shitty antics.

When James decided to start smoking, Marie decided to start smoking.

When James decided to start drinking, Marie decided to start drinking.

When James decided to start doing drugs, Marie decided to start doing drugs.

Things were reaching a fever pitch when James began going out partying on weekends, taking Marie with him. They would often roll in on Sunday afternoon after being gone since Friday evening and nothing Lily and Jack could say or do could control either of their wayward children. They tried everything the counsellors suggested, short of locking them up in juvenile delinquent detention.

Things kept progressing negatively until a horrific tragedy occurred that made the entire family implode.

For the life of them, Lily and Jack just could not figure out where they went so wrong in their raising of six such different children, two of them being such bad seeds and causing such emotional trauma to their family.

Jack was a decorated, highly respected Staff Sargent in the Royal Canadian Mounted Police. He swallowed his humiliation and asked his co-workers at the RCMP detachment he worked at in Headingley to help him, once and for all, to wrangle his two errant offspring, who were out on another weekend bender.

The Mounties found out about a huge bush party happening that evening and Jack was fairly sure that's where his two delinquent children were going to be. Lily wanted to go with him, but he flatly refused, not wanting his beloved wife to see what horrible things he was likely going to be witnessing.

Jack took a few plainclothes mounted policemen with him both for moral support and *just in case*. When he arrived at the location, he got out of his family car, wincing at what he was seeing.

His twenty-two-year-old son was snorting cocaine off the bare stomach of the local tramp, a bottle of scotch clutched loosely in his hands, a drunk and drugged-out smile on his face.

Jack looked in the other direction to find the scene even more devastating. His seventeen-year-old daughter was laying on the hood of a sports car in a state of near undress, smoking a joint, a bottle of rye tipped into her open mouth and a lascivious look on her face as she swallowed the contents, several boys surrounding her cheering her on, their hands all over her.

Jack was stunned into silence and immobility. He could almost feel his heart shattering into a billion pieces.

One of the boys attempting to debauch his daughter saw Jack and screeched, "COOOOOOOOPS!!!"

Everybody scattered to the four winds.

James caught sight of what was going on with his sister and jumped up, ran over to her, grabbed her hand and dove into his vintage 1969 Camaro, taking off at top speed away from the scene of the debauchery, not realizing it was his father and that he'd seen them. They were both carrying their nearly empty liquor bottles and neither of them had the wherewithal to do up their seat belts.

This kick-started Jack and his comrades into action. He got into his car and began the chase. His son was certainly not fit to drive and his daughter was busy laughing, drunk and high, not caring what the outcome of this exciting adventure would be, as usual.

James and Marie sped along the gravel road going nearly twice the speed safe to drive on gravel, kicking up rocks and dust behind them.

Jack could barely see to keep up with them.

James hit a dip in the road, or perhaps it was just his drunken, drugged-out haze making him drive in an erratic, unpredictable pattern, and he lost control of the car. He spun out in the middle of the road, flew through the air and landed head-first into the ditch, hitting it perpendicular to the soggy, wet ground beneath them.

Jack slammed on his breaks and leapt out of his car with his eyes bulging out of his head, not believing what he had just seen. He was about to run into the ditch to rescue his two children when the car ignited, blowing up in a gigantic volcanic fireball, the flames accentuated by the liquor that had spilled all over the inside of the car from the opened bottles James and Marie had been swigging from.

NNOOOOOO!!!!!!!!

My children!!

Jack stood there, stunned, the pain of what he just witnessed happen to two of his children piercing through his heart, right into his soul. The plainclothes Mounties arrived in time to observe the fireball explode, holding Jack up as he crumpled under the weight of despair and devastation, their eyes not believing what they saw, either.

He was driven home by one of his officers and was met at the door by Lily. Jack took her by the hand, led her to the kitchen table and sat her down. He held her hands in his and told her what had occurred with their two errant children just a few short moments before.

At first, Lily was frozen into silence. Then it hit her that two of her children had just been incinerated and her husband had actually borne witness to it. She began shaking, then opened her mouth and let out a primal scream of such anguish, it threatened to shatter all the windows in the house.

Jack gathered Lily in his arms and he broke down crying with her as they collapsed to the kitchen floor. They stayed clutched together for a long time, their other three sons and their remaining daughter joining their huddled, grieving parents in a heap on the floor.

The next few days were a blur, as Lily and Jack were nearly catatonic in the wake of destruction that had cleaved their family apart. And because of how James and Marie had died, there weren't any bodies to bury, nothing but ash...

Dean, Vince and Michael were twenty-four, twenty-three and twenty-one, respectively. Their thoughts on the situation were not what would normally be expected. The loss of their calamity-causing siblings who had been tearing their family apart for years, making their Mother cry incessantly and their Father age prematurely, made them collectively sigh with relief.

Krys was only eight years old and didn't really understand what was going on. All she knew was that James and Marie were gone and not coming back.

The years began to slide by and the tragedy that ripped the Harris Family into scraggly pieces slowly began to mend and heal itself. Dean, Vince and Michael had all moved out and gotten married within a few short years after the incident and began having their own families, leaving Krys as the only child left at home from age twelve. Jack and Lily doted on her, took her on vacations with them all over the world and spoiled her, nicknaming her their *Golden Child* – their model, well behaved daughter.

And now she was getting married and leaving the nest that Jack and Lily had made so warm, so loving and so comfortable for her since that tragedy when she was eight years old...

CHAPTER 55

June 1994

Krys

Krys' graduation from nursing school was held on June 23. She graduated with honors and was offered a full-time position in the Labor & Delivery Unit where she did her last clinical practicum. She was overjoyed and felt so incredibly blessed, but at the same time, she had worked really hard for the career she had wanted since she was a child.

Once the festivities of her graduation were over, there were only eighteen days until her wedding to Darryl on July 10, and there was so much left to do!

Krys didn't know how she was going to finish it all…

CHAPTER 56

July 10, 1994

Krys & Darryl

Krys woke up on the morning of her wedding to Darryl in a haze of ecstatic happiness. She looked at herself in the mirror and smiled radiantly at her reflection.

I'm getting married today!

She opened her bedroom door to go to her bathroom and start getting ready for her big day, but was roadblocked. Darryl was standing there, a small box in his hand and a deep pink rose in his teeth.

"DARRYL! What are you doing here? You're not supposed to see me before the ceremony! It's *bad luck*!" Krys shrieked and tried to slam the door, but Darryl stuck his foot in the way.

He pushed it open and handed the rose to her, then gathered her in his arms and laughed as she struggled in his grasp. "Good morning, my beautiful wife-to-be. I'm pretty certain we've already had all the bad luck we're going to have, so I think we're safe."

Krys had no argument for that so she stopped struggling, softened her face and gave him a dazzling smile. "Okay, husband-to-be, you've got a point there. But why are you here?"

"Because I want to give you your wedding present before you walk down the aisle to me," he smiled and placed a small royal blue velvet jewellery box into her hands.

Krys stared at the box, smiling. "You spoil me too much."

"Yes, I do. Open it," he said, a look of happy anticipation on his face.

She did and her jaw dropped open. Inside on a bed of white satin were a pair of sapphire drop earrings surrounded by diamonds, set in yellow gold.

"They're so beautiful! And they match my necklace! Thank you!" she cried as she hugged him.

"Will you wear them today?" he asked.

"I sure will! I'm wearing the necklace as my *something blue* and now I can wear the matching earrings with it! You take the cake, you really do. How did I get so lucky?" she beamed.

"I think we both dipped into that pool. Now gimme a quick kiss and I'll disappear," he grinned.

"Wait a minute. I have something for you, too," Krys said, grinning shyly. She turned to her dresser, picked up a large wooden box and handed it to him.

Darryl sat back down on the edge of her bed and admired the intricate scroll work on the hinged lid. He opened it and investigated the contents – a crystal decanter, a stainless steel beer stein engraved with his name in Old English script, a monogrammed handkerchief, a personalized pocketknife and gold cuff links engraved with Darryl and Krys' initials entwined together. He took out and inspected each item.

"Wow, Krys... I'm speechless," Darryl said softly, staring down at the cuff links in his hands.

"Will you wear them today?" she asked as he looked up at her, smiling.

"Of course I will. These are the most thoughtful things you've ever given me, Krys. Thank you. I love each and every one of them," he said, his voice low and full of emotion.

"I'm so glad! I chose things that I thought would be meaningful to you," she replied.

Darryl stood up, placed the wooden box and its contents down on the bed and pulled Krys into his embrace. "*You* are the most meaningful to me," he said and leaned in to kiss her.

They stood together with their arms around each other, smiling excitedly as Krys whispered, "We're getting married today!"

"We sure are!" Darryl whispered back. He kissed her once more, then picked up the wooden box and winked at her as he slipped out of her room.

Krys was floating on a cloud, wondering what other wonderful things were in store for her today...

CHAPTER 57

July 10, 1994
Krys & Lily & Jack

Natalie came over later in the morning, after Krys had showered and set her hair in curlers. They were sitting at the kitchen table talking about where Krys and Darryl were going on their honeymoon when Lily and Jack came into the kitchen together.

"Krysten, your father and I have a little something for you," Lily said, tears welling in her eyes.

"Mom, don't cry! You'll make *me* cry!" Krys said, her voice tremulous.

"Lily, just give it to her already," Jack said over the sniffing of his wife and daughter.

Lily sat beside Krys and gave her another royal blue velvet box that looked just like the one Darryl gave her only a few hours ago.

Krys' eyes bugged out. "Today sure is my day for getting jewellery!"

"What are you talking about?" Lily asked.

"Darryl showed up here early this morning and gave me the matching earrings to the necklace he gave me for my birthday. He asked me to wear them today," Krys answered.

The look on Lily's face was one of pure horror. "He saw you today before the ceremony? That's bad luck!" she shrieked.

Krys laughed at her mother's response which was identical to what hers had been. "I said the same thing! But he reminded me that we've had our quota of bad luck and only good things are ahead for us. Then he gave me the earrings, I gave him his wedding gift, he kissed me, then he left, all within ten minutes."

"Smart boy," Jack muttered under his breath, making Krys laugh.

"Open this and see what's inside," Lily said excitedly, recovering from her fit.

Krys opened the lid to find a sapphire and diamond ring set in yellow gold, nestled in white satin, the match to the necklace and earrings Darryl had given her. Her mouth fell open as her Mother pulled the ring out of the box and placed it on Krys' right hand ring finger. "Mom! Dad! Really?"

"We asked Darryl if it would be okay with him if we bought you the ring to give you today so you could wear the matched set as your *something blue*," Jack finally said, as Lily was too busy crying her eyes out.

Krys just sat there, dumbfounded. Then she squeaked out, tears flowing, "This is all too much! I'm getting everything I ever wanted and I can't handle it!"

"The day isn't over yet, Blondie!" Nat chimed in.

That just brought the waterworks on full blast between Krys and Lily as Jack looked to the ceiling and prayed for strength to get through the rest of the day. "I have to go with Owen to get the other surprise," he said, mostly to himself, then leaned over to kiss his girls on their foreheads and got the hell out of the estrogen-filled room.

CHAPTER 58

July 10, 1994

Krys

Krys' bridesmaids Corrine, Daphne and Heather came over a while later, dressed in their royal blue bridesmaid dresses – a sleeveless, fitted, V-neck sheath, the hem just past the knees with a modest slit up the back, worn with white leather sandals. They each carried a bouquet of yellow carnations wrapped with white satin ribbon.

Natalie wore the same dress and shoes as the girls, but she carried a bouquet of pink carnations to indicate her role as Maid of Honor.

All four girls wore crystal drop earrings with matching necklaces that Krys gave them as bridesmaid gifts, just before she closed herself away to get dressed and finish her hair and makeup.

A short time later, Krys emerged from her Mother's sitting room into the kitchen. "I'm ready..." she called, her voice strong and clear.

The room went silent at her stunning beauty.

Krys looked like a fairy tale princess in her ballgown-style wedding dress. The gown was white satin with sheer, fluttery cap sleeves, a sweetheart neckline in the front and a deep scoop in the back. It had crystal beadwork on the bodice, trailing down the front towards the bottom hem of the full skirt with a short train at the back.

She wore her Mother's crystal tiara with her hair in long, soft waves, bangs sideswept, the sides up and back from her face to show off her sapphire earrings and necklace. Her veil fell to her hips, framing her face with crystal beading along the edge. Her makeup was fresh and natural, but her lips were a bright, bold pink.

Her fingernails were painted an iridescent pink and her toes were a deep, electric blue. On her feet, Krys wore strappy white sandals with crystal beading accents. She had a pair of more comfortable blue sneakers to wear later on at the reception.

The collective gasps from her mother, her maid of honor and her three bridesmaids nearly undid her.

"Well, how do I look?" she asked, radiating a smile of pure joy as she picked up her bridal bouquet, a mix of white, pink and yellow roses wrapped with two dainty lace handkerchiefs, one from each of her deceased grandmothers.

Lily was dressed in a beaded, champagne, Mother-of-the-Bride cocktail-length dress. She blotted her eyes with a tissue and refrained from hugging her baby, not wanting to crease or stain Krys' wedding gown. "My Baby… is getting married…" was all she could say as she sniffed back tears.

"Momma," Krys said, her voice shaky.

"Krys, you are simply stunning!" Natalie said, smiling excitedly. "I can't believe in a few hours we're *finally* going to be related! Darryl is going to *lose his mind* when he sees you!"

"That's the point!" Krys winked at Nat.

"So, what do you have for *old, new, borrowed* and *blue*?" Daphne asked.

"*Old* are the lace handkerchiefs from both my grandmothers wrapped around my bouquet, *new* is my wedding gown with some really sexy lingerie underneath," she began, smiling cheekily as she continued, "*Borrowed* is my crystal tiara that Mom wore for her wedding to Dad, and *blue* is my sapphire necklace, earrings and ring set," she finished, flashing her right hand at the girls.

Sam, the wedding photographer, arrived and began taking the usual pre-wedding pictures of all the ladies. "I've just come from your groom's home down the street and I must tell you Krys, he's over-the-moon excited to marry you! I got some fantastic pictures of him with his groomsmen that I think you'll have a good laugh at," Sam revealed, laughing.

Krys smiled. "I can't wait to marry him, either! Now let's get some fun pictures of us girls!"

CHAPTER 59

July 10, 1994

Darryl

The groom and his groomsmen were dressed in their wedding finery. Darryl wore a black tuxedo with a white vest and long white tie with a white rose in his lapel, the cuff links Krys had given him that morning and the Rolex she had given him for his birthday.

Keith was his Best Man and his groomsmen were Jeremy, Patrick and Gavin. They each wore the same black tuxedo, but their vests and ties were royal blue to match Krys' bridesmaids.

Keith had a pink carnation in his lapel to match Natalie's bouquet, and Jeremy, Patrick and Gavin had yellow carnations in their lapels to match Corrine, Daphne and Heather's bouquets.

Darryl gave his groomsmen engraved flasks with two shot glasses in a leather case as well as a bottle of their favorite liquor for the flasks. He hugged his buddies in that manly way men do, shaking hands and pulling into the other's embrace for a quick back-pound-and-release.

Sam, the wedding photographer, arrived as Darryl was handing out the gifts to his groomsmen and began taking spontaneous snapshots. He got the usual posed pics, then he told them to act casual. He watched as the five grown men, one of them about to get married, began acting like prepubescent boys.

Sam got pics of them being goofy, gross, funny, immature and totally ridiculous.

He captured it all.

"So Darryl, you're the lucky man today," Sam said as he stopped to change the film in his camera.

"You bet I am! I can't wait to marry Krys. She's the best thing that ever happened to me," Darryl said, beaming.

"Awww," was the collective from Keith, Jeremy, Patrick and Gavin as they batted their eyes at him.

"She is, you clowns, and you all know it. I hope all of you are lucky enough to find a woman who fits you like Krys fits me. Are we done with the pictures?" Darryl asked impatiently.

"Yes, Darryl. I'm heading over to Krys' right now. See you at the church at three," Sam replied, packing up his photo bag and walking out the back door.

Darryl looked at the Rolex watch Krys gave him for his birthday and grinned, saying softly under his breath to himself, "Two more hours and she'll be my wife..."

CHAPTER 60

July 10, 1994

Krys & Jack

As Krys and her bridesmaids were finishing with the pre-ceremony pictures, they heard a honk from the street.

"Oh! That must be your Father!" Lily said, snapping out of her emotional roller coaster ride.

Everybody went to the front door and stood in the landing together, looking at Jack sitting behind the wheel of a gorgeous, shiny white classic automobile.

"What kind of car is that?" Krys asked, grinning excitedly.

"It is a 1955 Chevy Bel Air. It was the car he had when we got married. Your father is neither an emotional nor sentimental man, Krysten, but he wanted to contribute something other than *just the bills* for his daughter's wedding and this is it. Completely knocked me off my feet when he came up with the idea!" Lily told her daughter.

Krys teared up again, hoping she wasn't messing up her makeup.

Jack got out of the car, walked up to the front door and paused when he saw his youngest child in her bridal gown.

"My daughter, you are..." he began and for the first time in Krys' life, her father didn't have a joke ready for the occasion. He was truly tongue-tied, his eyes misting over at her incandescent beauty as he continued, "... a true beauty, just like your mother was on our wedding day," he finished, swiping at his eyes.

"Thank you, Daddy," Krys murmured, hugging her father as Jack kissed his daughter's forehead.

This sent Lily into another fit of emotional tears, through which she said, "Jack, you better go get dressed. We're leaving for the church in ten minutes."

CHAPTER 61

July 10, 1994

Krys & Jack

And in ten minutes, they did. Lily, Corrine, Daphne and Heather rode ahead in a white limo to the church while Natalie followed, driving the Bel Air with Jack and Krys in the back.

As they arrived at the church, Jack held Krys' hand firmly in his and pulled his daughter close to him, speaking quietly and full of emotion. "You are my only daughter, Krysten. It means everything to me that I've been given the gift of walking you down the aisle today to the man you've chosen for your husband. I love you, my Caboose, and I'm so very proud of the woman you've become. Your mother and I wish nothing but happiness and everlasting love between you and Darryl, like what she and I have had all these years we've been together," Jack said, his voice slightly tremulous as he kissed her hand and smiled at his daughter.

"Daddy..." was all Krys could utter, her emotions in hyperdrive.

Jack cleared his throat and said, his voice stronger, "Now, let's go get you married!"

CHAPTER 62

July 10, 1994

Krys & Darryl

Krys walked down the aisle on her father's arm to the traditional Wedding March Processional of "Here Comes The Bride", barely able to hold back her tears of joy.

When Darryl saw her, his knees turned to jelly. "I... She's..." was all he could utter.

Keith leaned over and whispered, "She's gorgeous, man. Just... Wow!"

Once Jack and Krys arrived at the end of the aisle, Jack turned to face his daughter and lifted her veil to give her one last kiss on her cheek. Then he shook Darryl's hand and gave his only daughter to the man she chose to marry, his expression solemn.

Jack took his seat beside Lily with Krys' brothers, their wives and children all in attendance in the rows behind them – Dean and his wife, Lori, with their daughter, Natasha; Vince and his wife, Kim, with their daughter, Amanda, and son, Scott; and Michael and his wife, Maureen, with their daughters, Alicia and Kaitlyn.

Krys and Darryl said their vows to each other in front of their family and friends, then exchanged wedding rings. Hers was a custom diamond and yellow gold band designed to fit with her engagement ring and his was a wide matte yellow gold band. Then they signed the register and were pronounced *Husband And Wife* to loud clapping from the congregation at the announcement.

Darryl was itching to kiss Krys when Father Currie said those six all-important words every groom can't wait to hear, "You may now kiss your Bride!"

He leaned in close, wrapped his arms loosely around his bride and kissed her chastely on her lips. They had talked about how they were going to kiss at the conclusion of their wedding ceremony without being disrespectful to the religious establishment they were in, but Krys decided at the last minute to surprise Darryl. As she kissed him back, she wound her arms around his neck and slipped her tongue into his mouth, to his delight. He lost all control, pulled her in closer to him and deepened the kiss as everyone whistled and clapped.

They pulled apart after a few more kisses and smiled at each other, not caring in the least that they made a spectacle of themselves, in church, at their own wedding. They turned together and walked back down the aisle to the traditional Wedding March Recessional, ready to greet their family and friends at the back of the church.

After much hearty congratulations from their guests, Darryl and Krys got into the Bel Air. They took off to Assiniboine Park for wedding pictures with their wedding party and families.

"Kryssie, you absolutely take my breath away. I've never seen you look more beautiful," Darryl said quietly in her ear as he kissed her temple.

"And you've never looked more handsome," Krys replied, turning her head and capturing Darryl's mouth for a deep kiss. She had to fix her messed-up lipstick before they got out for their outdoor wedding photos.

After the pictures were finished, it was time for the wedding reception. A luxurious buffet dinner for their one hundred and twenty guests awaited them at the Hotel Fort Garry.

Next came the toasts to the Bride and Groom, then it was time for the First Dance for the newly wedded couple.

Darryl stood up and held out his hand. Krys placed her hand in his and rose to stand with him. He led her out to the dance floor where he twirled her around before pulling her close to him.

The opening bars of "Dream Come True" by Frozen Ghost began playing, bringing tears of absolute elation to Krys' eyes. Darryl held her close and sang the words quietly to her as they danced, swaying together while the words of the song registered between them. Krys snuggled in close to Darryl, so happy and eternally grateful that they found their way back to each other to make it to this moment.

The next song that Darryl specifically requested the DJ play was "Could I Have This Dance" by Anne Murray. Krys was absolutely beside herself with joy.

As "Could I Have This Dance" finished, Darryl glanced in surprise at Krys when the next song began, Bryan Adams' "Heaven". It was Darryl's favorite love song, one he never told any of his friends he liked for fear of being mercilessly teased to death as a sap, but Krys knew. She just grinned cheekily and pulled him close to her, kissing his jaw and singing softly to him.

Just when Darryl thought things couldn't get any sweeter, Captain & Tenille started singing "Love Will Keep Us Together" as Krys winked at him. It was his other favorite love song that he would never admit to either, but Krys knew, and requested the DJ play it for them. They laughed and sang to each other as he twirled her around the dance floor, the two of them focused completely on each other.

Until the next set of songs.

Just because Krys hadn't been emotional enough that day, the music changed and the DJ asked Jack to join Krys on the dance floor for the traditional Father-Daughter dance.

"Daddy's Little Girl" by Al Martino started playing and Darryl handed Krys to Jack. Krys was tearful as she clung to her father while he led her around the dance floor, one hand at her back and the other holding her hand in his old-world-courtly-style she loved so much.

Lily stood at the edge of the dance floor, flanked by her three sons Dean, Vince and Michael. She watched her daughter and her husband dance together, feeling utter happiness at witnessing this joyous moment.

Darryl stood between his parents, placed his arm around his mother and held her close. His father clapped a hand on his son's shoulder and squeezed proudly. Darryl choked up, watching how happy Krys was and how happy he was that they made it to this day.

When the Father-Daughter dance finished, Krys and Jack left the dance floor.

Darryl took his mother by the hand and led her to the dance floor for their Mother-Son dance as "Simple Man" by Lynyrd Skynyrd played just for them. Darryl had to hold back tears of his own as Audrey began to sniffle and her breath hitched in her throat.

As the last few bars of the song faded out, Darryl led Audrey off the dance floor back to his father Owen, then left them to rejoin Krys.

Then the DJ changed the mood, playing more upbeat, classic wedding reception songs that people got up out of their chairs to dance – Boney M's "Rasputin", The Village People's "YMCA" and the classically silly "Bird Dance", to name a few.

By this time, Krys had shed her veil and sandals and changed into her blue sneakers for the rest of the evening. Darryl took off his tuxedo jacket and vest, loosened his tie, unbuttoned the top couple of buttons and rolled up his sleeves, pocketing his cuff links to keep them safe.

Now that the emotional part of the reception was concluded, it was time to cut the wedding cake. Darryl daintily fed Krys a tiny piece of cake to avoid messing up her face and her dress. He knew if he pulled what some grooms do and smash cake in her face, he would be sleeping on the couch in their suite instead of having wild wedding night sex with her, and likely for a long time afterwards! Krys thanked Darryl for being a gentlemen with the cake by feeding him a small piece, then kissing him, licking icing from his lips and giving his ass a squeeze as she winked at him.

Next up was the throwing of the bouquet and the tossing of the garter. Krys' friend Colleen caught the bouquet and Darryl's friend Doug caught the garter.

Then the reception really got underway with everyone, at one point or another, getting up to dance, drink and mingle.

It was one of the best wedding receptions Krys and Darryl's guests had ever attended and would be talked about for many years to come.

CHAPTER 63

July 10, 1994

Natalie

Natalie left the ballroom to find the ladies' room. She literally bumped into a very handsome gentleman in a dark gray suit as he was leaving the men's room.

"Oh! I'm so sorry!" Nat and Mr Handsome said at the same time, clutching each other by the arms to steady themselves. They both smiled and chuckled, eyes looking up and down, checking the other out.

Natalie couldn't help herself. Mr Handsome was 6' tall with short, dark brown hair, hazel eyes and a well-built physique. He had a sexy smile which took her breath away.

He offered her his hand. "Hi. I'm Ed. Which wedding are you here for?" he asked, his voice pleasing to her ears.

"I'm Natalie. Mine is the Harris/Sheridan wedding. The groom is my brother. You?" she asked politely.

"My cousin, Valerie. She married her childhood sweetheart, Malcolm. I'm happy for them, but all that happiness can be a bit... stifling. I needed a breather," Ed admitted.

"Yeah, I get that. I feel the same way. My boyfriend isn't here and all the happy-happy is getting to me a bit today, too," Natalie also admitted.

"Oh? Where is he?" Ed asked.

"On tour. He's in a band," Nat replied casually.

"Anyone I know?" Ed wondered.

"Diamond Angel. He's the lead singer," Nat answered, her eyes sparkling at just the thought of Tony.

"Oh yeah. I saw them play here before they hit it big last year. They're pretty good," Ed responded.

Natalie smiled proudly, then asked, "What about you? Do you have a lady?"

Ed replied, "No. Our break-up is still a bit fresh."

"Oh, I'm sorry. I didn't mean to be insensitive," Nat said, feeling terrible.

"You aren't. We just weren't going the same direction anymore. It's hard to be at a wedding seeing all that love and happiness when it's something I want for myself," Ed explained.

Natalie looked pensive for a moment, but shook those thoughts from her head. "So, Ed, what do you do for a living?" Nat asked, wanting to steer the conversation away from relationships.

"I'm a contractor. I build and renovate houses – electrical, plumbing, you name it, I do it," he answered. "What about you?"

"I'm at the University of Winnipeg taking Education. Another year of school and I'll graduate with my Bachelor of Education and I'll be able to teach elementary school kids. Get 'em while they're young and mold their minds," Nat said, grinning. "I started out wanting to teach high school kids, but their hormones are just too rampant for me to wrangle."

"Oh yeah? My sister is at U of W taking Education, too. Maybe you know her? Nancy Graham?" Ed told her.

"I know Nancy! We've got a few classes together! What a small world," Nat said.

They chatted a little longer, finding out they knew some of the same people and ran in some of the same social circles. Then they went their separate ways, back to the weddings they belonged to.

CHAPTER 64

July 10, 1994
Krys & Darryl

At one o'clock in the morning when their wedding reception was officially over, Krys and Darryl finally departed the ballroom to begin their wedding night together. They were staying in the Honeymoon Suite at the hotel, so they took the elevator reserved for guests of the special suites.

As they exited the elevator, Darryl picked Krys up and carried her to the door and over the threshold into their suite, marvelling at how romantic the staff had made it look for them. There was a mass of candles in various sizes flickering soft light throughout the entire suite while romantic instrumental music played softly in the background.

While still holding Krys in his arms, Darryl walked to the bedroom and paused at the doorway so he and Krys could take in the sight ahead of them. There were red rose petals all over the bed, more flickering candles scattered throughout the room and a bucket with chilled champagne on one of the bedside night tables. On the other were two crystal champagne flutes engraved with "Bride" on one and "Groom" on the other.

Krys was overwhelmed at the attention to romantic detail throughout the suite.

Darryl walked to the bed, leaned into the mattress with his knee and placed Krys gently in the middle of the king-sized bed, her ballgown-style wedding dress fanning out around her. He lay down beside her and they turned their heads to gaze at each other for a moment, exhausted, but elated.

"So, Mrs Sheridan, what would you like to do?" Darryl asked, kissing his wife lightly on her lips.

"Hmm, Mr Sheridan, with it being our wedding night, I'm thinking I'd like you to ravish me," Krys purred seductively to her husband.

Darryl smiled and rolled off the bed, pulling Krys with him. They stood together and began kissing while undressing each other, letting the slow burn gather heat.

Darryl had already shucked off his tuxedo jacket, vest and tie, but left it up to Krys to unbutton his shirt and trousers. She kissed his throat and licked his jaw as she slid the zipper down, pushing his pants over his hips so they could drop to the floor. She grabbed his hard erection, straining through the thin material of his black silk boxer-briefs and gave it an appreciative squeeze. Darryl groaned, closing his eyes in sweet anticipation. Krys pulled the waistband of his boxers down his legs and he stepped out of them, kicking them aside.

Now it was his turn.

Darryl was glad that Krys' wedding gown had a short zipper and not a million little buttons that would have taken days to undo. Once he helped her out of it and laid it carefully aside, Krys was left wearing the sexy white satin and lace bra-and-panty set she bought especially for this night. He undid the clasp and peeled the bra off her slowly, keeping eye contact with her. Then he knelt down and hooked his thumbs into the thin strings at her hips. He tugged the panties down her long legs, savoring her soft skin as he kissed a trail back up to her mouth.

Finally, they were both gloriously naked.

Krys crawled backwards onto the bed, laying down on the rose petals with her bare skin. Starting at her ankles and kissing his way up her legs, Darryl stopped to devour her wet heat with this mouth and tongue, delivering one hell of a powerful orgasm to her. Then he moved up her torso to pay homage to her breasts, suckling each nipple as if he was indulging in the most decadent thing he'd ever had in his mouth.

He licked and nibbled his way up to her mouth, then kissed her voraciously, his hand finding her tender core. He stroked her sensitive nerve bundle with his thumb and slid two fingers inside her to prepare her for the invasion of his rock-hard erection.

Krys reached between them and grabbed his cock, sliding her hand up and down with one hand while lightly squeezing his balls with the other.

Darryl let out a groan of intense pleasure and removed his hand, settling himself between her legs and replacing his fingers with his cock. He pulled her knees up on either side of his hips and began slowly and rhythmically thrusting in and out of her as they kissed each other softly.

They orgasmed together, riding a wave of pure pleasure.

It was sweet, romantic and exactly how Krys had imagined her wedding night would be. They had the rest of their lives to have raunchy jungle sex. Besides, they were somewhat tired after the exciting, emotional day they'd had.

Darryl pulled out gently and moved off to Krys' side, turning her so they lay face to face. "How was that for ravishing you on our wedding night, Mrs Sheridan?" he inquired of his wife.

"Very well done, Mr Sheridan. I give it a ten out of ten," she giggled, sighing in satisfaction.

They cuddled for a short time, then settled into a comfortable position wrapped around each other and fell asleep.

Bliss...

Pure bliss...

CHAPTER 65

July 1994 to August 1994
Krys & Darryl

Krys and Darryl went to Europe for a three-week honeymoon. They flew to London and spent a few days there before flying to Paris and taking the Eurorail throughout France, Belgium, Holland, Germany, Switzerland, Austria and finishing in Italy, finally returning home on July 31.

On August 1, Krys packed up all her things, to her parents' sadness, and moved into Darryl's apartment, now *their* apartment.

They had been home only a week when Nat came screaming over to the apartment late one afternoon. "KRYS!!! Tony's coming hooooome!!!!!!!! Diamond Angel is playing their last night on tour HERE at the Winnipeg Arena!! And they're *headlining!!* Can you believe it?? August 10 is only two days away! Tony sent me two all-access backstage passes and front row tickets for us! I'm so damn excited! I CANNOT WAIT!!"

Krys was silently digesting this news when Darryl walked in the door from work. He kissed her and smiled at Natalie, asking her, "Hey Nat, what's got you so fired up?"

"Oh, nothing, just my boyfriend is coming home after being away for *fifteen months*!" Nat started talking in a normal volume and ended screeching in excitement. "And he's sent me and Krys tickets and backstage passes for their concert in *two days*!!"

Darryl stiffened for a moment, then remembered that Krys was married to HIM, not the other guy. "Are you gonna go?" Darryl turned and asked his wife, his expression neutral.

"I don't know..." Krys started.

"OF COURSE WE ARE!!!" Nat yelled excitedly, then calmed herself and took Krys by the shoulders and said seriously, "Krys, I know things didn't work out between you and Rick and I'm sorry about that, but I'm not sorry that you married my brother. You get along with everyone in Diamond Angel and they would all love to see you again. They all know how uncomfortable it will be for you to be around Rick and no one will leave you alone with him. *Please* come with me!" Nat pleaded, swinging her eyes towards her brother for his support.

Krys also looked towards Darryl, waiting to see what he had to say.

I DO want to go, for no other reason than to see all the other guys...

But I don't want to tempt fate...

He gently shifted Natalie out of the way, placing his hands on Krys' shoulders just as his sister had. "Kryssie, I love you and I trust you. I know that you love me and you would never do anything to mess up what we have together. I also know you loved *him* for a time and that it was hard for you to let go of and get over. That being said, if all those people you used to know would like to see you, don't let one person's attendance ruin that for you. Like Natalie said, you won't be left alone with him. Go and have a good time, then come home and tell me all about it while I kiss you all over," Darryl declared, smiling at her.

"Really?" Krys answered in a small voice, looking up at her husband.

"Yes. I can see that you're torn. You want to see everyone, even *him*. Go. Do it for yourself and maybe seeing him will put some of your guilt and sadness to rest," Darryl concluded.

Krys' eyes welled with tears. "You are the very best man I have ever known." Her voice shook as she threw herself into his arms and hugged her amazing husband tightly.

CHAPTER 66

August 10, 1994
Natalie & Tony

Natalie was wearing a turquoise bikini, stretched out on a lounge chair in the back yard when the gate opened and she heard someone coming towards her. Her eyes were closed as she sat facing the sun, her sunglasses on her face and her hair up in a messy topknot, a glass of iced tea on her side table with a magazine waiting to be read. "Hey Krys, how's it going?" Nat said, her eyes still closed.

"Much better now that I see you right in front of me and hear your sexy voice in person," was the reply, but that voice was NOT Krys!

Natalie jumped up, knocking off her sunglasses. Her mouth hung open with a scream of exuberance stuck in her throat. Then her lips morphed into a beautiful smile and she squealed, leaping towards Tony and nearly knocking him backwards off the deck.

He caught her, hugged her close and buried his nose in her hair. "Fuck, Strawberry, I haven't seen you in so long!" Tony breathed.

Nat was crying tears of joy. "Tony! I missed you so much! But I wasn't expecting to see you until tonight! Don't you have lots to do to get ready, being the headliner?"

"Not really. I told Frank that we all had to have some private time with our families today so that when we're all together this evening, it isn't a total emotional cry-fest," he laughed.

"Smart thinking! Now let's go to your place! We have some missed time together to start making up for!" Nat grinned sexily.

"I was hoping you'd say that," he winked.

CHAPTER 67

August 10, 1994
Natalie & Tony

They tumbled through the door to his bedroom in the midst of tearing each other's clothes off.

Natalie's bikini was tied at her neck, back and both hips, so all Tony needed to do was pull the ties and she was delectably naked.

Tony was wearing a fashionably torn Diamond Angel concert t-shirt and denim cut-offs. Nat grabbed each side of the shirt at the collar and completed the rip so it was hanging open like a vest and pushed it off his shoulders. Then she unzipped his cut-offs and yanked them down his legs to the floor so he could kick them off.

Hands and mouths went everywhere.

Standing face to face, Tony grabbed Natalie and crushed her to him. He wrapped one hand around her hair and burrowed the other between them down to her aching wetness. He zeroed in on her with his thumb and circled her sensitive spot, swirling her to a toe-curling orgasm, kissing her the entire time.

IN AND OUT OF LOVE

All Natalie could do was hold on and hope she didn't crumple into a puddle of liquefied bones from the sheer pleasure of being naked with Tony again as he lay her onto the bed, kissing his way down her body. He grasped onto one breast with one hand while the other moved back between her legs and his mouth latched onto the other breast.

After orgasm number two ripped through her, Natalie tried to push against Tony to flip him beneath her. However, she was unsuccessful because he was far from done with her.

With no words spoken between them, Tony kept up his pursuit of giving Natalie as many orgasms as he could before he felt good and ready for his turn. He slithered down her body and buried his face in her drenched heat, his hands cupping her ass while his tongue lapped up the two orgasms he'd already given her, gearing her up for a third.

He was totally insatiable.

Natalie was nearly out of her mind from the intense pleasure Tony was giving her. She was hoping she would have enough energy left to give some back to him, but at the rate they were going, she was going to be a boneless heap before long.

Once orgasm number three erupted from her, Tony looked up with a greedy, satisfied grin on his face. He crawled his way up her body, licking a wet path all the way to her mouth while Natalie just lay there, breathless. She tried to open her mouth to say something, but Tony stuck his tongue in and silenced her, thrusting his cock into her at the same time. Nat was so overwhelmed with sensation, she was building up to orgasm number four in no time. Tony began moving faster, his own breathing increasing in tempo.

Just as Nat was about to come again, Tony pulled out abruptly and flipped her over. He knelt behind her, pulled her hips up and drilled into her repeatedly as deep as he could. He slammed into her one final time, groaning loudly in carnal satisfaction as he pulsated deep inside her, setting off Nat's fourth and last orgasm. Only after the spasms ebbed did Tony let Nat's hips go and lay her down, collapsing on top of her back.

Nat's head was turned to the side and Tony leaned over to kiss her, saying softly, "You were about to say something earlier?"

Nat smiled back. "I was? I can't remember. But that's one hell of a way to say hello."

Tony slid off her back and shifted them so they were laying face to face. "I missed you, Strawberry. I'm glad I'm finally home so I can fuck you in my own bed," he said contentedly.

Natalie kissed him and snuggled into his arms, falling asleep with her man by her side.

CHAPTER 68

August 10, 1994
Natalie & Tony

A couple of hours later, Tony was in a dead sleep when he felt a set of incredibly talented lips kissing their way down his hairy chest all the way to his dick. He grinned lazily, knowing what Natalie was about to do.

He had managed, just barely, to remain faithful to her. Tony was in love with Natalie, but having women endlessly throwing themselves at him was getting harder and harder to resist as Diamond Angel's success grew. He became adept at deftly removing the multiples of women from around himself and directing them to Diego and Alex instead. Rick had screwed around for a while after he and Krys had split, but after the intervention Diamond Angel and Frank orchestrated for him, he reigned things in and wasn't such a horndog anymore. He focused on making music and because of his musical brilliance, they were going to have an absolute blockbuster for a second album.

Nat ran her tongue up and down his shaft, rimming the head with her lips and licking the tip. Using her hands, she grasped the base of his cock in one hand and cupped his balls in the other while moving her head up and down, her lips now wrapped around him.

Just before he was about to blow, Tony grabbed Nat under her arms and pulled her up his body, planting her on top of his dick. With his hands on her hips and her hands on his shoulders, he thrust upwards, impaling her.

Nat groaned at the wonderful feeling of fullness inside her, but pouted, "Hey, I wasn't finished yet."

Tony grunted, "I want to come inside you again."

"Oh... okay," she breathed, an erotic feeling of pure lust shooting through her at his words.

Tony enjoyed watching Natalie ride him as he connected with her eyes. "I missed you," he said quietly.

She replied just as quietly, "I missed you, too."

"I love you, Natalie," Tony said, a little louder.

Smiling brightly she replied, "I love you, too, Tony."

At their mutual declaration of love for each other, Tony could feel the burn rocketing up his dick, so he wrapped one hand around Natalie's lower back and moved his other hand between them. Finding her sweet spot, he circled his thumb until she began writhing on top of him. When he felt her spasming around him, he grasped her hips with both hands, grinding his pelvis upwards while holding her down on him. Then he blew his load inside her, just like he wanted to.

He felt on top of the world.

He just had explosive sex with his girl, they told each other that they love each other and tonight his band was headlining the Winnipeg Arena, their home turf.

Life was pretty damn good today.

CHAPTER 69

August 10, 1994
Krys & Rick

Diamond Angel threw a huge pre-concert gathering with their families and close friends at the Winnipeg Arena. The party was in full swing by the time Natalie and Krys arrived.

Tony saw them enter and walked over to them, kissing Nat full on the lips before turning to Krys and pulling her into a huge bear hug. "It's really great to see you, Krys. You look beautiful, as always," Tony told her, then dropped his voice as he spoke softly in her ear. "Marriage to the man you love agrees with you," he said as he pulled away and smiled warmly at her.

"Natalie told you," Krys breathed, her eyes wide.

"She did, but I've kept it to myself. No one else knows, at least not from me," he confirmed.

Just then, Diego, Alex and Bryan came over, grabbed Krys and passed her around for more bear hugs, cheek kisses and *I-missed-you's* all around.

Then Rick walked in and the entire room lapsed into absolute silence. He and Krys hadn't seen each other since they split, nearly a year ago. He walked right up to her, smiled warmly, took her hands in his and said, "Kryssie... it's good to see you."

"Hi Rick. It's good to see you, too," she replied, her voice shaky. The electric current that flew through Krys made her shiver as Rick leaned in and kissed her sweetly on the cheek. She was shocked at how powerfully she reacted to his touch. He held his lips to her cheek just a touch too long, making Krys' eyes flutter closed and her heart race. She opened her eyes and looked at him, willing her heart to calm down.

Rick leaned back and gazed at her, still holding her hands in his. When he brought them up to his lips to kiss them, he paused and looked at her left hand, noticing the engagement ring and wedding ring on her ring finger. "You got married?" he asked, his voice quiet.

"Y-yes, I did... to Darryl..." she stammered.

"When?" he asked, stiffening.

"Last month," she replied.

"*Last month*," he parroted.

Krys steadied her voice. "I'm happy, Rick. I hope you can be happy for me, too."

Rick shook himself out of his stunned stupor and plastered a fake smile on his face. "I can see that. And I do wish for your happiness, Krys." He looked at her beautiful face again, then let go of her hands and moved over to give Natalie a hug and a kiss.

Krys let out a breath and closed her eyes again, glad that she survived the interaction. Maybe now she could relax and enjoy the rest of the evening.

CHAPTER 70

August 10, 1994
Rick & Tony

Rick pulled Tony aside a short time later. "You knew she got married, didn't you, you fucking dickhead, and you never said anything to me!" he hissed.

Tony huffed out a breath and admitted, "Yes, I knew. And no, I didn't tell you because I knew how much it was going to hurt you and I thought it would be better coming directly from her when she was ready to tell you. Look at her, Rick, she's happy. She's married to a good guy, not an asshole, so let it be and don't fuck things up with her, okay?"

"What do you mean by that?" Rick glared back at him.

"Lemme guess. You thought that once she saw you, she'd want to get back together with you, right? Just fall into your arms and you'd sweep her away for a sex-a-thon and everything would just fall back into place, right? I know how your mind works, Rick. She wasn't cut out for this lifestyle. She tried it and couldn't cope with it *then*, so what makes you think she'd be any better with it *now*? We'll only be home for a while, then after the next album comes out, we'll be away on tour again, for who knows how long next time. Can't you see that?" Tony explained.

Rick pressed his lips together in silent agreement. "Yeah, I do. It's just... I still love her."

Tony wasn't without sympathy at his best friend's predicament as he clapped Rick on the shoulder and gave him a brotherly squeeze. "I know you do, but she's not yours anymore. Now that you know, you can move on and find someone who will be able to give you everything you want. She's out there."

Tony moved away and left Rick standing alone with his thoughts.

She may be out there, but where is she and when will I finally find her?

CHAPTER 71

August 10, 1994

Krys & Natalie

"That went better than I expected," Krys admitted to Nat.

"I'm glad, Krys. I know how hard it is for you to see Rick. I can still see a tiny spark in your eyes for him, but don't worry, I'll keep your secret," Nat winked.

Krys just stared at Natalie and whispered, "Is it that obvious? I didn't stop loving him because we split up, Natalie. I'm always going to have a soft spot for him, but I don't want to get his hopes up that he still might have a chance with me, because he doesn't. I'm married to *Darryl* and I love *him*," Krys declared.

"It's obvious to me and you kept your head pretty cool. And I know you love my brother. There's no denying that. Now let's go mingle with everyone else and get ready to rock our asses off!" Nat cried excitedly.

CHAPTER 72

August 10, 1994
Diamond Angel

The two opening acts were local bands hand-picked by Diamond Angel themselves.

The first band, Crakkerjax, was a four-man hard rock/glam metal band that got the crowd fired up with their energetic show and fabulous stage presence. They played for forty-five minutes.

The second band, Moonglow, was an all-girl hard rock band that heightened the excitement even further. The five women put on an amazing show full of sexy lyrics, excellent music and an incredibly dynamic stage show. They played for sixty minutes.

Right on time, the lights went out and the crowd whipped into a frenzy of mass hysteria. Over the speakers a deep voice announced, "Winnipeeeeeg!!! Put your hands together and welcome home our boys, Diamooooond Angeeeeelllll!!!"

Diamond Angel took the stage to thunderous applause of the sold-out arena.

A lone spotlight shone at center stage, illuminating Tony wearing a *Welcome to Winnipeg* t-shirt, tight faded jeans, sneakers and sunglasses, his hair long and wild, with the biggest smile on his face. "Hellooooo Winnipeeeeeg!!! We are HOOOOME!!!!!!!!!!!!" Tony yelled into the microphone.

The spotlight widened to reveal Rick and Diego to his right, with Bryan and Alex to his left.

Rick was wearing his customary black tank top, black leather pants with thick-soled boots, stars on his guitar strap and his now-trademark black cowboy hat.

Bryan wore black jeans and a Winnipeg Jets t-shirt.

Alex wore faded jeans and a Winnipeg Blue Bombers t-shirt.

Diego wore spandex shorts and was bare-chested.

The screams from the crowd got even louder as all five members were showcased by the spotlight.

Tony continued, "I hope you're all ready to rock your asses off, because this is a very special show to us. Not only is it the last show of our first major tour, but it's our first headlining show! We hope you enjoyed Crakkerjax and Moonglow. We hand-picked them ourselves because we see the potential in them, as was seen in us not too long ago, and we wanted to share our good fortune with them."

The crowd squealed their approval.

At this point, Rick, Bryan, Diego and Alex moved to their respective areas of the stage – Rick to Tony's right with his electric guitar, Bryan to the keyboards behind Tony and to the left, Diego to the raised drum kit behind Tony and slightly to the right, with Alex and his bass guitar to Tony's left.

"Now... ARE... YOU... READY... TO... ROOOOOCK???" Tony teased, smiling widely.

Diamond Angel got into position on stage as Tony looked left and right at them, then nodded.

All five of them began singing the opening lyrics to the first song released from their debut album that had shot straight to number one and into the hearts of their fans, "An Angel's Smile".

The crowd roared with absolute adoration.

Rick strummed the first few guitar chords.

Bryan played the first few keyboard notes.

Diego banged out the first few beats on the drums.

Alex tied it all up with the first few notes on the bass guitar.

The crowd went positively nuclear.

Tony moved energetically around the stage, interacting with the crowd and winding them up, holding out the microphone for them to sing with him.

Rick moved to center stage for his guitar solo, blowing everyone away with his talent.

Diego pounded out his drum solo, wowing everyone with how amazing he could play the skins.

Bryan and Alex kept the beat going with the keys and bass, holding on strong and sure.

When they wound down "An Angel's Smile", Tony stopped to talk to the crowd, telling them what inspired the song. Then they launched into "Out On The Run, Under The Gun", "The Weekend Comes To This Town" and "Can't Start A Fire Without A Spark", with Tony telling the crowd about the genesis of each song.

Then they slowed it down with "It Comes Down To Me And You" and "Nothing Without Love" as the women in the crowd swooned over Tony's sexy voice.

When the opening notes began for "Together Forever", Rick looked directly at Krys and gave her a quick, sad smile, then turned back to the crowd, singing the harmony to Tony's lead.

After the sweet love songs, Diamond Angel decided to kick things up a few notches and performed a few of their favorite cover songs, beginning with Bon Jovi's "In And Out Of Love", Def Leppard's "Pour Some Sugar On Me", Guns N' Roses' "Sweet Child Of Mine", Aerosmith's "Dude Looks Like A Lady", Motley Crue's "Kickstart My Heart", Poison's "Nothin' But A Good Time", ZZ Top's "Sharp Dressed Man", KISS' "Rock And Roll All Nite", Heart's "Crazy On You", Pat Benatar's "Hit Me With Your Best Shot" and Van Halen's "Panama".

Tony stopped again to talk to the crowd. "Now that you've heard some tunes of our famous mentors, here's a few of our hometown favorites," he said, swigging from his water bottle.

They played Streetheart's "Snow White", Harlequin's "Innocence" and The Pumps/Orphan's "Success" to rousing excitement and applause for the nods to their hometown musical heroes.

Going back to their favorite cover bands, they played Thin Lizzy's "The Boy Are Back In Town", Led Zeppelin's "Ramble On", AC/DC's "Highway To Hell", The Rolling Stones "Brown Sugar" and "Satisfaction", finally ending with Journey's "Don't Stop Believin'".

At the closing notes, the stage went black and Diamond Angel exited off to the side, listening to the crowd scream their approval, wanting more.

They waited a couple of minutes, then went back out for their encore. They started with the slow keyboard build-up and bass guitar riff opening notes of "Half Way There" which they played an extended version of, to the delight of the crowd. Then they played the instrumental piece "Princess", which led into the fabulously cowboyish "Steel Horse", concluding with "This Is My Hometown".

When the final notes of the last song were played and the house lights went on, Diamond Angel gathered together at the front of the stage with their arms around each other, sweating, smiling and feeling invincible as they collectively yelled out, "THANK YOU, WINNIPEG!!!"

They bowed low, once, twice, three times to the crowd, ever clamoring for more. Then they stood and left the stage, walking back to their dressing room and the after-party waiting for them to celebrate into the wee hours of the morning.

It was the best night of their career, a night they'd never forget.

CHAPTER 73

August 10, 1994
Krys & Natalie

Just before the lights went out, Krys and Natalie headed to their front row seats, their all-access passes dangling between their breasts.

Krys was wearing a hot pink, low-cut tank top with spaghetti straps, dark wash jeans and silver high-heeled sandals.

Natalie wore a short sundress in a bright, leafy green with deep red stilettos.

The crowd parted like the Red Sea as they approached their seats.

When the lights went dark, the crowd went wild. Krys and Nat held each other's hands, smiling at each other in excited anticipation as they heard a voice announce, "Winnipeeeeeg!!! Put your hands together and welcome home our boys, Diamooooond Angeeeeelllll!!!"

Krys and Natalie's seats were situated just slightly to the left of center stage in the front row, directly between Tony and Rick.

"Krys, they've really made it! I'm so excited for them! Look where we are! Can you believe it??" Nat yelled over the noise of the crowd.

"It really is amazing, isn't it?" Krys yelled back, a melancholic smile on her lips.

Diamond Angel certainly didn't disappoint. They all interacted with the crowd, especially Tony, who held out the microphone at times to entice the crowd to sing with him. The stage presence of the band as a whole was truly electrifying.

Tony sang directly to Natalie most of the time, winking at Krys now and again.

Rick sang back-up and harmony, even singing lead on a few songs. He constantly glanced at Krys, but especially as he played "Princess", her creation that they dedicated to her on their album.

Once the concert was over, Krys and Nat wound their way through the crowd of people to the backstage area for the after-party.

They stayed and partied until dawn. It was a night they'd never forget.

CHAPTER 74

August 10, 1994
Krys & Natalie & Diamond Angel

When everyone who was invited to the after-party was admitted backstage and the arena was cleared, the party got started and was in full-swing in no time.

Vanessa, Brad, Greg and Frank were there with their families and other staff from Global Music Entertainment and River City Recording Studios, even Ryan Collins, the band's producer. Ryan was a lean 5'10" with a dirty blonde brush cut, goatee and dark brown eyes.

Food and drink abounded, laughter shook the walls and an impromptu after-concert concert got going when Diego picked up a pair of chopsticks and began banging on the table while Tony pulled a harmonica out of his back pocket.

Rick was never far away from an acoustic guitar, so he grabbed the one beside him, propped it on his lap and began strumming out a fast-paced little ditty.

Alex and Bryan helped out Diego by slapping their hands on their thighs to keep the beat going.

Then Tony and Rick began a verbal banter back and forth, singing about love, fishing and shopping.

It was hilariously ridiculous and made no sense whatsoever.

As always, Rick had rigged up a recording device, convinced that this sort of thing would occur. He said that these were the best times to capture the magic that would make up the best songs for their next album.

And he was right.

Krys got into the musical spirit of the evening and stood beside Rick, smiling in encouragement. This energized him, and when they finished what they christened "The Shopping Song", he handed his guitar to Krys to play and grabbed another one for himself. As he began strumming and singing The Rolling Stones' "Not Fade Away", Krys joined him. It was just the two of them singing and playing as everyone else stopped talking to listen and watch the silent exchange between them.

Sparks...

Flew...

Everywhere...

Natalie and Tony looked at each other, part in awe at the fabulous sound coming from Krys and Rick, but also worry, not wanting to see anything wreck the delicate truce reached between them earlier in the evening.

When Krys and Rick were done their impromptu jam session, they set down their guitars, smiling at the rowdy applause of the group and dispersed among the crowd. However, they ended up meeting in the middle at the bar, trying to shake off the heat flourishing between them.

"You've been keeping up with playing, haven't you?" Rick asked Krys as he gave her a shoulder bump.

"Yeah, I find it a good stress reliever. I really love the sound of acoustic guitar and the nylon strings don't rip my fingertips apart like the steel strings do," she grinned at him.

Just then, Phil and Ryan ambled over to the pair.

"You, darlin', have a gorgeous voice. How'd you like to sing some harmonies and background vocals on the next Diamond Angel record?" Phil asked Krys.

Krys' mouth dropped open. "I'm sorry, *WHAT*?"

"Yeah! You've got a fantastic, clear soprano voice and it sounds so pure and perfect singing with Rick. I want to have both of you in the recording studio to sing more together! And I want to hear you sing with Tony, too. Wow! This next record is going to be infuckingcredible!" Ryan said, rubbing his hands together in absolute glee.

Krys was dumbstruck. "But I'm not a singer! I'm a nurse!"

"I don't care if you're a bullfighter! Your voice is beautiful and complements Rick's perfectly. And this is in a casual, uncontrolled environment. Can you imagine how me and Phil will get you to sound once we get you in the recording studio?" Ryan shot back excitedly as he closed his eyes, smiled widely and mumbled to himself.

Tony joined the conversation, Natalie tucked into his side. "I like the idea. What do you think, Strawberry?"

Natalie considered her response carefully before she spoke. "I think it's a great idea! Krys, you do have a great singing voice and you sound awesome singing with Rick. And I'm sure you'll sound just as great singing with Tony. Why don't you give it a shot? Can't hurt, can it?"

Krys was shocked to a standstill, her mouth opening and closing like a fish out of water, no sound coming out until she finally squeaked, "Sure. I can't see that it would hurt to give it a try."

As Phil and Ryan pulled Tony and Rick aside to plan for the next batch of recording sessions for the new album, Krys dragged Natalie to the corner of the room, her eyes big as saucers. "Natalie! What the hell am I going to tell Darryl? He's NEVER going to agree with me to do this! Absolutely *NEVER*!" Krys panicked.

Natalie smiled her mischievous smile. "He will if you invite him to come and watch from the control booth. He'll see you're there in a strictly professional capacity and when you come back for more sessions, which I'm sure you will, you can enjoy yourself with his blessing. You've been given this opportunity because of your raw, natural talent. It's worth exploring to share with the musical world, dontcha think?"

Krys relaxed a bit at this explanation. "I... guess so..."

That's how Krys came to be a background singer and guest acoustic guitar player on Diamond Angel's second album... with Darryl's blessing.

CHAPTER 75

August 1994 to January 1995
Natalie & Tony

The morning after Diamond Angel's homecoming concert, both the Winnipeg Free Press and the Winnipeg Sun newspapers announced the identical headlines.

> *TRIUMPH FOR HOMETOWN*
> *MUSIC GROUP!!!!!*

This jump-started the band on writing new songs for their next album after they took a few weeks of much needed time off to rest and regroup. They were determined it was going to be bigger and better than their debut, which was a gigantic smash.

Could they top it?

They could and they would.

At the beginning of September, Natalie started back to school for her last year of University, so she and Tony weren't able to see as much of each other as they'd hoped.

"This sucks," Nat complained one Saturday in early October as she and Tony disentangled themselves from each other. They lay on their sides catching their breath after having spent the afternoon naked in bed together. They had sex with him on top and both her legs over his shoulders, her on top straddling and facing him, her on top facing away from him so all he could see was her gorgeous auburn hair and her delectable ass, him behind her with her on her hands and knees, him behind her with her back to his chest and both of them on their knees, and finally facing each other with him on his knees and her back against the headboard. Now it was rest time until the next wave of lust hit and their energy returned, then they would be all over each other again.

"What does?" Tony asked, licking Nat's neck, already raring to go for another round.

"Me busy in school and you busy writing new songs for the new album so we can't spend more time together," she frowned.

"Yeah, it does, but what we're both doing is important. Besides, it's only temporary. You'll be graduating in May and Diamond Angel will be going on tour around then, so you can come with me, if you want to," Tony said, twirling a lock of Nat's auburn waves around his finger.

"Really? You want me to come with you on the next tour?" Natalie perked up.

"Yeah, I do, but only until you get a teaching job," Tony said.

Natalie sighed, "Yeah, I guess. But what if I –"

Tony took her face in his hands, cutting her off in mid-sentence, "Strawberry, you can't put your life on hold for me. And I sure as hell am not going to ask you to do that for us.

You need to make sure you get a job and build that part of your life here for us while I'm away the rest of the time. You're not going to school and busting your ass to be a teacher to drop all of that to be a road wife, however long my music career may last. I want you to have some stability here because that is the one thing I cannot provide for you with the life I've chosen."

"Wow. How long have you been rehearing that speech for?" Natalie frowned again, shifting away.

Tony pulled her back into his embrace. "I haven't rehearsed anything, Natalie. It's the way I feel. And I've been feeling this way and thinking about this for a while. We need to be realistic about our relationship and our future together. Besides, I want to have kids with you one day and I want them to have some semblance of a solid home life. And that is for you to be here with a steady job when I'm away on tour."

Natalie's eyes bugged out at Tony's verbal presentation of their proposed future. "You want… kids… with me?" she squeaked out.

Tony smiled sweetly. "Yeah, I do. Just not any time soon. I don't think either of us are ready for that trip quite yet!"

"That is definitely something we can agree on!" Nat laughed as they began kissing again.

Tony pushed Natalie onto her back and moved on top of her, falling through the split in her thighs and sliding easily into her wet heat. He began rocking in and out, gaining momentum, alternately kissing her and licking her neck, jaw and throat.

Nat's hands slid over Tony's back down to his ass where she grabbed on, thrusting her hips up to meet his. He reached down and pulled up her right leg over his shoulder so he could drive in deeper, increasing both their pleasure until he felt that familiar tingle down his spine, sweeping through his pelvis right down to his balls.

"Fuck... Strawberry," Tony grunted as he plunged his cock all the way to his balls, at the same time feeling Nat convulse around him, sending him off the deep end into orgasmic delight.

"Tony..." Nat moaned as she felt Tony empty himself inside her.

He pulled out and flopped beside her onto his stomach, a satisfied smile spread across his face. "Love you, Natalie," he said, finally exhausted.

"Love you, too, Tony," Nat replied, turning to her side and cuddling into him.

They slept for a short time to reset their energy levels, then awoke again, lust burning in their eyes as they stared at each other. Hands roamed, kisses were exchanged and soon they were wrapped up in each other for another round of their sex-a-thon.

CHAPTER 76

August 1994 to January 1995
Krys & Darryl

Krys and Darryl got into a regular routine of him working daytime hours and her working shift work. It was tough, but they figured it out together to make it work.

They celebrated their birthdays in November and January, respectively, as Christmas came and went in between with the usual fanfare.

Then in mid-January after Darryl's birthday, Krys went into the recording studio to sing and play guitar with Diamond Angel on their new album, with Darryl's blessing.

"Are you SURE you don't mind me doing this? Because if you do, I won't do it," Krys asked, feeling torn in half.

"Yes, Krys. I can see how excited you are about it and I won't stand in your way," Darryl told her, kissing her forehead and hugging her close.

"You don't mind that I'll be spending time with Rick?" she pressed.

"You're not going to be naked with him, are you?" Darryl replied, hiding a grin.

Krys pulled back and slapped him on the arm. "Absolutely NOT! This is strictly business!"

Darryl was taken aback at her vehemence on the subject. "Krys, why are you so sensitive about this? Is it because... you still have feelings for him?" Darryl asked hesitantly, his voice quiet.

Krys blanched at the words said out loud by her husband. "I... No... Yes... No, I do not..." she fumbled.

Darryl stiffened slightly. "Well, which is it? Yes or no?"

Krys took a deep breath and tried to make sense of her conflicted feelings. "Firstly, I love YOU and *ONLY YOU*. Let me make that clear as glass. But I *did* love him once and seeing him again last August for the first time since we split was difficult for me. I no longer love him the way I once did, but I do have some latent feelings for him. And I'm trying to be respectful of your feelings towards him," Krys explained, feeling frustrated.

Darryl smiled, pulled her back into his arms, kissed her deeply and said, "Thank you for being honest with me and asking me to come with you. But just to make things clear as glass on my end, I love you and I trust you absolutely. I always have and I always will." He was proud of his talented wife and was interested in what the recording process was all about. He was also appreciative when she had come home after the concert back in August and told him immediately about this golden opportunity. He was especially humbled that she had fretted about how he would take it.

And maybe just a tiny bit smug...

Now it was time for Krys to have that golden opportunity come to fruition as they drove to River City Recording Studios for her very first professional recording session with Diamond Angel.

CHAPTER 77

January 1995
Krys & Darryl & Diamond Angel

Darryl remained quietly observant in the control booth beside Phil, not wanting to get in the way. He just wanted to experience the creative process and to make sure Krys' former lover kept his hands, and everything else, to himself...

Krys was a natural as she sat on a stool with headphones on and an acoustic guitar in her lap. Her clear, melodious voice blended well with both Tony's and Rick's voices as she sang harmony on several of the new tracks.

Diamond Angel had written about thirty songs, enough for a double album.

Of the ten songs the guys chose, eight of them were hard driving rockers and mid-tempo songs, titled – "Ready, Willing And Able", "Your Kiss Is The Drug", "Made To Be Your Man", "Til Kingdom Come", "Here I Come, Baby", "Cold Is The Night", "Only If You Have To" and "Tell The Boys I'm On My Way".

The two love songs were titled – "Living On Love" and "These Five Words".

Rick was still not completely over his split with Krys. Seeing her last August at Diamond Angel's headlining final concert brought up a lot of his feelings for her and he was pretty damn sure that she had felt *something* for him that night, too. Using that is his inspiration, he poured out his heart and soul into the songs on the new album.

He knew that even if Krys did have the tiniest scrap of affection for him, she would never act on it now that she was happily married to Darryl, and especially since he was sitting not ten feet away from her in the control booth. So, Rick was destined to adore Krys from afar and behave himself around her if he wanted to be in her life, in any capacity.

The final song on the album was called "Shopping For Love" and it was a sharpened-up version of the impromptu acoustic, silly ditty "The Shopping Song" that Tony and Rick played at their after-concert party. It was played in a fast strumming tempo with Rick on acoustic guitar and Tony on harmonica, bantering the lyrics back and forth. Diego used a fan brush on the snare drum, Alex played the bass line on another acoustic guitar and Bryan tied it all together by slapping out a rhythm on his thighs.

Their first session went very well, Krys' additional acoustic rhythm guitar added depth to a few of the songs and her clear soprano voice harmonized beautifully with both Tony and Rick's deeper voices.

At the end of the day, Tony went to Krys and gave her a bone-crushing hug. "Krys! That was magnificent! Your voice is absolutely beautiful and your subtle acoustic guitar is superb! Can't wait for the next session with you!" Tony beamed, kissing her cheek in a brotherly way.

Rick came and stood next to her while she was still sitting on the stool. He hugged her close to his side with one arm while holding his electric guitar in the other. "Kryssie, just... Wow! Thank you for doing this with us. It's working out even better than I thought it would. Really looking forward to our next session together," he said, smiling at her.

As he moved away, she saw a line up of Alex, Diego and Bryan waiting to shower her with their collective praise.

Darryl watched it all, and when they were driving home later on, he said, "Those guys really love you a lot. All of them."

Krys sighed in contentment. "Yeah, I know. And I love all of them, too. This was really fun today and I'm so glad you were there to see how it all works. I'm feeling a lot less anxious about the next session. Rick and I are going to be singing a duet cover version of "It's Only Love" and before today, I wasn't sure how that was going to go, but now I know it's going to be just fine."

"You know this, how?" Darryl inquired.

"Because I don't feel anything more for Rick than I do for any of the other guys," Krys smiled at her husband.

Darryl smiled back and reached for her hand as he drove, lacing their fingers together and kissing the back of her hand. "Let's get home quick. I have the sudden urge to make mad, passionate love to my wife," he murmured.

"Why not just pull over into that empty parking lot and we can have sex in the car?" Krys suggested innocently.

Darryl's eyebrows lifted up and his mouth broke into a sexy smile that lit up his whole face. "As you wish, my little sex kitten," he replied as he turned into the deserted parking lot, parked the car, then pulled Krys into his lap.

Since it was January, he left the car running with the heat on full blast. Krys straddled Darryl and kissed him deeply, holding his face in her hands while his hands roamed her back under her layers.

"Kryssie," Darryl mumbled in between kisses, "This may not have been the best idea. We're both wearing too many clothes and it's damn cold, even with the heat blasting in here."

Krys started giggling. "Yeah, you're right. Let's just go home. We can get naked there instead and not worry about getting frostbite on our asses or anything else important!"

She slid off Darryl's lap back into her seat and they drove home quickly, running up the stairs to their apartment. Once inside, they stripped off their clothes, leaving a trail from the door all the way to the bed and fell onto it, side by side, giggling like children.

"Maybe let's leave the car sex for the summer when it's warm outside and we're both wearing less clothing?" Krys continued to giggle.

"Agreed," Darryl said, turning Krys so she was underneath him.

He leaned down to kiss her, his passion for her flaring as his kisses became more heated, drawing her in and encouraging her to respond as passionately as him.

She reached up to kiss him back and felt an incredibly powerful bolt of lust streak through her body as she stared at his handsome face, his bulky muscles holding her with equal strength and tenderness. "I love you, so much," she whispered softly.

"I know you do," Darryl whispered back, kissing her behind her ear. "I love you, too, Kryssie, so much..." he declared as he thrust himself into her, groaning in carnal ecstasy.

They clutched at each other, hanging on, thrusting, kissing, licking, teasing, gorging themselves on each other, smiling lovingly at each other, until finally Darryl plunged in one final time and came so hard he saw stars, which kicked off Krys' electrifying orgasm.

When he collapsed on top of her, she lifted her foot, planted it on the bed and rolled them so she was on top, straddling him. They lay chest to chest, still connected. He was still semi-hard and still inside her as she began sliding herself up and down his chest, his arms wrapped around her, holding her to him as he helped her move.

They kissed sweetly, allowing the heat to build between them again, then Krys pushed up to her hands, planting them on Darryl's chest and began riding him. It didn't take long before he grabbed onto her hips and began impaling her on him, their sexual hunger for each other about to explode again. Krys could feel the throbbing low in her belly and was pretty sure that this one was going to be a heart-stopper.

As the sensation intensified, she closed her eyes and bit her lip in anticipation. Darryl watched the expression on her face change from happy excitement to carnal lust as he pleasured her with his body. He held Krys as she writhed on top of him, reaching orgasmic euphoria together.

When they were finally zapped of energy, Krys pulled herself off him, his spent cock sliding out of her and landing on his belly with a wet slap, making them both giggle. Krys felt loose-limbed like a rag doll as Darryl pulled her down beside him, cuddled her close and kissed her cheek, ultimately satisfied.

"Kryssie?" Darryl started to say, unsure of how she was going to take what he said next.

"Mmm?" she replied sleepily as she closed her eyes, snuggling into his side and settling in for a nap after such strenuous exercise.

"Let's... have a baby..." he began.

Krys slowly opened her eyes and stared at her husband. "What? Where did that idea come from?"

"I'm just really happy with our life together and that's the next logical step for us to take, isn't it?" Darryl answered.

Krys sat up and leaned one hand in the bed, the other draping the sheet over her breasts. Taking a deep breath, she said, "I absolutely want to have babies with you, Darryl, but not just yet. Everything with us moved at lightning speed when we got back together and I'd like for it to be just the two of us for a while before we begin the next generation. Besides, it's only been six months since we finished school, started working and got married! Plus, we're living in this apartment, which is enough for us, but I would rather be settled into a house when we bring our first baby home."

Darryl thought about her explanation and he agreed. "You're right, Krys. Your points are all valid and make sense."

She dropped the sheet and caressed his face with her hand as she asked, "What brought this on?"

Darryl replied, "I don't really know. I just love you and we have such a strong connection with each other, I get a bit overwhelmed sometimes at how happy I am that I have you in my life. And the thought of a mini-you or mini-me wandering around sounds like Heaven on Earth to me," he finished, grinning at her.

Krys' eyes widened and her eyebrows raised up to her hairline. "Isn't that more what a girl says to her guy? When did we have a role-reversal here?" she grinned back, leaning down to kiss him.

"Ha ha, very funny, Miss Comedienne," Darryl smirked as he pulled her back down on top of him, wrapped his arms around her and cuddled her to him.

"Well, I think we've settled that topic of conversation for the next while, right?" Krys asked, snuggling into his arms.

"Yeah, I'm good. Now let's get something to eat. You've depleted me of all my energy. If you want me to fuck you some more, I need to fill up my reserves," Darryl joked as he got out of bed, threw on a pair of sweatpants and helped Krys into her robe.

"Ha ha. Then you better eat a lot," Krys retorted.

They walked with their arms around each other into their kitchen and raided the fridge, laughing and kissing each other, happy and content. They fed each other from the leftovers in the fridge, then went back to bed. They continued their raunchy fuck-a-thon for a while longer until they were both completely exhausted, contentedly falling asleep in each other's arms.

CHAPTER 78

February 1995
Krys & Rick

By late February, Diamond Angel had only one song left to record for their album. It was their cover version of the best rock'n'roll duet ever recorded, titled "It's Only Love", originally sung by Canadian treasure Bryan Adams and the unstoppable Tina Turner. This song was going to be sung by Rick and Krys and they planned to blow everybody away.

Krys made sure that Darryl wasn't in the studio with them the day they recorded it because she didn't need the added pressure of him there making her nervous. It was going to be tough enough for her to sing it in the first place with her not being a singer, never mind singing it with Rick. But sing it she would, and it was going to be nothing short of spectacular, if she had anything to do with it.

She shelved her usual melodious voice and sang Tina's part with a gritty growl that surprised her. She honestly didn't know she had it in her to sing like that! Her gritty voice was the perfect complement to Rick's lower register and gravelly rasp.

They started out standing on opposite sides of the recording studio, but after several warm-up takes that just weren't cutting it, Phil blurted out, "Krys, you're supposed to be singing a sexy duet with a sexy guy you totally wanna fuck. Can you make all of us believe it? Right now you look like you want to bolt out of here and never look back. If the listener thinks you're not into it, they won't be, either."

Krys broke out into a cold sweat, dropped the microphone and closed her eyes as she began to shake and hyperventilate.

Rick crossed the studio in a few strides and caught her just before she hit the floor. "Phil, can we clear the room for a bit? This is a lot for Krys to take in. You know that we have a history and that she's married, right? You complete asshole," Rick gritted between clenched teeth.

"Shit, yeah, sorry about that. I forgot," Phil said, suitably chastised.

As the control room and studio space cleared out, Rick sat Krys in a chair and stood at her side, rubbing circles on her back to help calm and ground her.

She looked up at him, tears glistening in her eyes. "Thank you, Rick. I really didn't think it was going to be so hard for me to sing with you. It's just bringing up so many memories for me..."

"It's not easy for me either. You're married, Princess. *Married...* To someone else... Do you know how hard it is for me to keep my hands to myself when all I wanna do is wrap my arms around you and kiss you breathless?" Rick said, leaning down and speaking softly into Krys' ear.

This made Krys sniff back a sob as her shoulders hunched into herself. "Yes, I know how hard it must be for you," she replied.

Rick moved around so he was in front of her, dropped to his haunches and took her hands in his. "Kryssie, are you sure you still want to do this?" he asked.

"Yes, Rick, I'm sure. I just need a minute to compose myself, okay?" Krys replied.

He moved his hands to either side of her face and looked into her eyes. "You're going to be great. Just imagine you're singing to your... husband. That should help you focus." Rick smiled at Krys, let go of her face, stood up and moved back over to his guitars.

It took everything he had not pull her into his arms and kiss her...

Krys stared at him as he retreated, picked up his favorite amplified acoustic guitar and began playing "Princess" for her. She leaned back into the chair and closed her eyes again, allowing the deep, soulful sound of the song she had composed, but Rick perfected, to wash over her. Then she finally began to relax and a small smile played around her lips.

When he finished playing, Rick asked her, "Better?"

Krys opened her eyes and got up out of the chair, went to Rick and hugged him lightly, whispering, "Thank you, Rick. I'm alright now."

Rick hugged her back and kissed the top of her head, resting his cheek where he kissed her. "You're welcome, Kryssie. I'm glad I could help you."

Krys broke the hug and went back to her music stand where she left the lyrics and her headphones. She made sure everything was where she wanted it, then went to the door and opened it, calling out, "Okay guys, we're all good in here now. Let's do this!"

The guys filed back in to their respective spots in the studio and control booth, resuming their previous positions.

Rick threw his guitar strap over his head, fitted his sunburst Fender Stratocaster to his body and began playing random notes, flexing his fingers and practising the song.

Krys watched him play, his eyes closed in concentration.

He really was a brilliant guitarist...

Rick looked over at her and murmured, "You're going to be fabulous. Just take a deep breath and everything will be fine, okay?"

She nodded and put her headphones on. Then she took a deep breath, held it and blew it out slowly. "Okay Phil, I'm ready to sing the shit out of this song," Krys said, readying herself.

"Good! Let's get this recorded in one take, huh?" he said, rubbing his hands together in anticipation of something spectacular.

Diamond Angel played the song and Rick and Krys sang it.

And it was magnificent.

CHAPTER 79

February 1995
Diamond Angel

"It's Only Love" was recorded in one take, minimally mixed, finished, and ready for the album by the end of the work day.

Over the next couple of weeks, Phil and Ryan were completely blown away with what the boys in Diamond Angel had created as they mixed the album. This record was even more inspiring and incredible than their first album.

It was destined to be a gigantic hit.

And it was.

CHAPTER 80

March 1995

Natalie & Tony

Natalie and Tony celebrated Tony's birthday on March 2 as expected – holed up in his bedroom all day, totally naked.

As he collapsed on top of her, Tony barely had the strength to pull out of her because she had worn him completely out.

Natalie was a true sex goddess!

He rolled off her, pulled her back to his chest and kissed her neck as he snuggled in and promptly fell asleep.

Nat grinned, let the happiness she felt overcome her and fell asleep, too.

CHAPTER 81

March 1995

Natalie & Tony

Natalie awoke a while later and went to the bathroom to relieve herself. As she was washing her hands at the sink, Tony snuck in behind her and wound his arms around her belly, rocking his hard cock against her ass cheek.

They were both naked.

She looked at him in the mirror and smiled greedily, licking her lips. He snaked one hand down between her legs and found that she was wet and ready for him. He brought his other hand back around from her belly to grasp his hard cock. He rocked back on his heels, aimed and plunged into her wet heat as she tipped her hips back to gain maximum penetration.

They both groaned, keeping their eyes locked on each other in the mirror. He rhythmically pushed in and pulled out, standing behind her while she stood with her legs apart, leaning forward and gripping the counter top. As they both came close to climaxing, Tony grabbed Nat's hips and slammed in one last time, pouring himself into her and blasting her off into one hell of a powerful orgasm.

Nat dropped her head down when he pulled out of her, then looked up to find Tony's head tilted back to the ceiling, a sexy smile on his lips. "Isn't your dick tired yet?" she asked playfully.

Tony tipped his face down to look at her in the mirror, then glanced down at his half-hard dick and replied, "Nope. Now I'm dirty and need a shower. And I need you to wash me," he added matter-of-factly.

"That would be my pleasure, Birthday Boy," Nat agreed readily.

They moved into the shower, pulled the curtain and started the water, constantly touching and kissing. They washed each other's hair and when Nat began soaping Tony's chest, he grabbed the washcloth out of her hands, dropped it behind him, pulled her close and kissed her deeply. Nat lifted one leg and wrapped it around Tony's hips, then grabbed her ass and brought up the other leg, sliding into her at the same time. She held onto his shoulders as he pumped her on and off his cock to a quick and satisfying orgasm for them both.

Neither of them said a word.

They resumed washing each other and got out of the shower as the water started to cool off. Wrapped in fluffy towels, they made their way back to Tony's bedroom and fell back onto the bed, kissing each other softly and sweetly.

"I'm going to miss this," Tony said, his voice sad.

Natalie silently agreed and hugged him close instead.

Me too, more than you'll ever know...

CHAPTER 82

March 1995

Natalie

Diamond Angel's second studio album was titled "River City Angels" and was released in mid-March to huge fanfare, rocketing to the tops of all the music charts.

Their second tour was gearing up to begin towards the end of April, but this time Diamond Angel were the headliners. They were going to tour internationally throughout North America, Europe, Japan and Australia, and they were going to be gone for eighteen months.

Eighteen months...

This was a lot for Natalie to take in as she was getting ready to graduate from University in May. She wondered if Tony was even going to be able to be there for her important day. She was also wondering, like Krys initially did with Rick, if she was going to be able to handle Tony being away for such a long time.

She hated that she was beginning to doubt their future. That being said, she did NOT doubt Tony's love for her. That was never in question.

But *eighteen months* away?
She was seriously going to have to think about this…

CHAPTER 83

April 1995
Natalie & Tony

The end of April came quickly and Natalie only had a few days left with Tony before Diamond Angel left on tour...

For eighteen months...

They were at George's Burgers, a local hole-in-the-wall burger joint that Tony loved, celebrating the end of Nat's exams and upcoming graduation. They were sitting at a table slightly removed from the rest of the patrons, lingering over a pile of french fries doused in vinegar and sprinkled with salt, the way both of them liked it. Their hands were linked together as they played with each other's fingers.

Tony was the first to speak. "Strawberry, when do you think you'll be able to join me on tour? We leave in a few days and I know you're busy right now with graduation plans."

"I've been meaning to talk to you about that," Nat started, pulling her hands away from him.

"You're not coming with me, are you?" Tony said sadly.

"No, I'm not," Natalie replied quietly.

"What are we doing?" Tony asked.

"I think we're letting each other go," Natalie responded, her eyes tearing up and her voice tremulous.

"Let's not do this here. Come on, I know a better place we can go," Tony said as he stood up and pulled Nat with him out the door to his car.

They drove to Assiniboine Park and parked along side the English Garden, awash with beautiful spring blooms that smelled simply amazing. They got out and walked through the garden until they reached a bench that was hidden by the flowers, then sat facing each other.

"Natalie, I love you and I have for a long time. I want a future with you, but I've felt you pulling away from me this last little while and I think I know why. I'm going on tour, far away this time, and I'll be missing everything here for the next year and a half. And now you don't think you're cut out for this kind of life, do you?" Tony guessed.

Natalie started tearing up again before she answered. "Tony, I love you so much, but you're right. I don't think I can be away from you for so long, waiting for the next time I can fly out to spend a few precious days with you. And with you going overseas, a few days isn't going to be enough. It was okay on the last tour, but I just can't go through that again and again, year after year. That's not the kind of life I want. I want you in my life, but having you comes at a price I'm just not able to pay. It's not fair to either of us because I can't come with you and you can't stay. You'll be busy and I don't want to get in the way." Nat dropped her head and began crying.

Tony pulled her close and tucked her head under his chin as he looked up to the bright blue evening sky, tears in his own eyes. "So... we're... ending us?" he confirmed, his voice hoarse.

Natalie burrowed closer into Tony's arms and hung on as tightly as she could, saying quietly, "Yes..."

When the sun started to go down and the air began to cool, Tony and Natalie broke apart, still holding each other's hands, tears falling down both their cheeks.

"I'll take you home now, Strawberry," Tony said quietly.

"Okay," Natalie nodded, her voice thick from crying.

When they got to Nat's house, Tony shifted the car into park, letting the engine idle as he turned to face her. "I will love you, always, forever..." he said as his voice cracked. He reached forward and kissed Natalie softly, his eyes closed, tears coursing down his face.

Natalie squeaked out, "I will love you, forever, always..." Then quick as a shot, she bolted from the car and ran towards the house, not looking back as tears flooded her cheeks.

CHAPTER 84

April 1995

Tony

Tony drove away slowly, hoping that he could steer the car safely. He had a hard time seeing carefully with all the tears pouring out of his eyes.

When he arrived home, he shuffled through the front door with his head hung low.

Rick was sitting on the couch while Diego had claimed the recliner. They were watching Beverly Hills Cop and laughing their asses off.

As usual, Bryan was out with April.

"Whoa, *mi hermano*, you look like shit! What the fuck happened between you and your girl?" Diego asked.

Rick looked over and caught Tony's defeated expression. "I can guess. You two split, didn't you?"

Tony nodded miserably.

Just then, Alex stumbled into the room smelling of cheap perfume. "Can you guys turn that shit down? It's screwing with me trying to screw!" Then he looked at Tony and his facial expression of annoyance changed to soft concern. "Hey T, where's Natalie?"

Tony shook his head slowly back and forth and wandered into the kitchen. He grabbed a beer from the fridge, came back and settled onto the couch beside Rick to watch the movie and hopefully take his mind off Natalie.

Alex watched Tony try to focus on the TV, then turned on his heel and left the room. A few moments later, the guys saw him escort the girl he'd been screwing out to her car. He came back in, nabbed himself a beer and a bag of chips, then got comfy on the couch between Tony and Rick.

They continued to watch the movie and soon they were all laughing, even Tony.

After what Rick went through in the aftermath of his break-up with Krys, they all hoped they weren't in for a repeat performance.

They weren't.

Tony's split with Natalie wasn't mentioned again.

CHAPTER 85

April 1995

Natalie

When Natalie burst through the back door, she bolted to the phone. "Kryssie, can you come over? I need you!" she blurted, crying.

Within fifteen minutes, Krys was sitting on the couch with her arms around Nat, holding her and letting her cry. "I'm so sorry it had to come to this for you and Tony," Krys whispered softly to her, tears falling down both their cheeks.

Natalie lifted her puffy face with her red, swollen eyes, looked at Krys and said sadly, "Kryssie, I'm so sorry I wasn't more supportive of you when you went through this with Rick. I was selfish and just wanted you back together with Darryl. I didn't think of how in love you were with Rick and how hard it was for you to do what you did and let him go. Now I totally get it. And it fucking sucks!"

"Natalie, don't beat yourself up over that. Things worked out how they were meant to for me and they will for you, too. Keep the faith that this sadness will pass in time and you'll have a reason to smile again, like I did," Krys said soothingly.

Krys was right.
Soon, Natalie did have a reason to smile.
His name was Ed Graham.

CHAPTER 86

May 1995
Natalie

In May, Natalie graduated from the University of Winnipeg with her Bachelor of Education Degree.

After Convocation, Krys and Darryl, with his parents Audrey and Owen, met Natalie outside for pictures and a street party thrown by the University. It had been about two weeks since Diamond Angel left on tour and Natalie was keeping busy with her graduation festivities so she didn't have to think about Tony and how much she missed him.

Natalie and her school friend Nancy wound their way through the crowd to where Krys, Darryl, Audrey and Owen were standing with Nancy's parents, Carol and Shaun, stopping for pictures along the way with other graduates in their caps and gowns. They were posing together for a few snaps when Nat spotted a handsome man in a light blue button down shirt and tailored khaki pants carrying a bouquet of flowers, headed towards Nancy.

Nancy's face lit up and she squealed in excitement, launching herself at him and throwing her arms around his neck. "Eddie! You made it! I'm so happy!" Nancy cried.

"How could I miss my little sister's University graduation?" Ed smiled back, kissing his sister on her cheek. "Sorry it took so long for me to get over here. I got held up talking with a few people I know." Then he noticed Natalie, turned to her and said warmly, "Well hello, we meet again."

Natalie felt a quiver in her belly as Ed recognized her. She recalled meeting him the night of Krys and Darryl's wedding reception the previous summer. She smiled back at him, "So we do."

"Congratulations... Natalie?" Ed said, saying her name slowly with an upturned lilt to his voice, hoping he remembered her name correctly.

"Yes, it's Natalie. Good memory!" Nat laughed appreciatively and asked, "Ed, right?"

"You got it," he replied, smiling at her.

Krys watched the flirtation between the two and nosed her way in, holding out her hand to shake Ed's. "Hi, I'm Krys, Natalie's sister-in-law. So, when did you two meet?" she asked bluntly.

Ed took Krys' hand and shook it in a friendly manner, explaining simply, "We literally ran into each other outside the bathroom at your wedding reception last summer."

Krys' eyes sparkled in delight. "Oh! How sweet!"

"Yes, it was," Ed replied, looking at Natalie as he spoke, letting go of Krys' hand.

Natalie blushed and smiled back at him, feeling the butterflies in her belly again.

When the street party began winding down, Ed pulled Natalie aside. "I don't mean to be intrusive, but are you still with your boyfriend? I don't see him here," he asked respectfully.

Nat's face clouded over briefly at the mention of her now-former love. "No, he's not here. We aren't together anymore," she admitted sadly.

Ed's face softened as he replied, "I'm sorry to hear that. Was it recent that you split up?"

"Yeah, only a couple of weeks ago, just before they left on tour for the next eighteen months," Nat answered.

"Wow, this feels like a role reversal of our conversation last summer," Ed noted. "But, if you don't feel like I'm being a callous asshole, I'd like to tell you something, Natalie. I've been thinking about you since we ran into each other at the hotel last year and I can't get you out of my mind. Would you allow me to take you out for dinner?"

Natalie's jaw dropped and she smiled excitedly at him. "I'd love that!"

"I'm going to need your number," Ed said as he pulled a pen out of his pocket and a business card out of his wallet, scratching out her number as she rattled it off to him. Then he pulled out another card, wrote on the back and handed it to her. "Here's my business card. My personal number is on the back."

Nat took it from him, glanced at it, then tucked it in her pocket, grinning.

"I need to get back to my sister or she may accuse me of trolling for a date instead of celebrating her graduation with her," he joked, then added, "Let me know when you're free for dinner, okay?"

Natalie blurted out in response, "I'm free tomorrow night."

Ed smiled and replied, "As a matter of fact, so am I. I'll call you later this evening, say around nine? Will you be home from your festivities by then?"

Nat answered, "You betcha!"

"Then we'll talk tonight," Ed winked at her and returned to his family.

Krys moved close to Natalie as she saw Ed departing and said, "So, what's up with Mr Handsome?"

"He wants to take me out for dinner tomorrow night!" Nat breathed excitedly.

Krys smiled and clapped her hands together. "Oh Nat! I'm so excited for you! He seems like a really great guy! And wow, he really suits his nickname, too!"

"Yeah, he does..." Nat trailed off.

CHAPTER 87

May 1995
Natalie & Ed

Ed kept his word and phoned Natalie at precisely nine that evening, so they made plans to go for dinner the following night.

When the next night rolled around, Ed showed up at her door at exactly six o'clock. He was wearing a casual button-down shirt in classic white with the collar opened a few buttons, dark wash denims, casual shoes and a light gray sport coat that showed off his tanned skin, hazel eyes and short, dark brown hair rather appealingly.

Natalie decided to wear a spaghetti strap sundress that came to mid-calf in a bold floral pattern that accentuated her deep brown eyes and auburn hair. She added dark brown leather sandals and a pale green wrap. In her small brown leather purse she tucked her lipstick, wallet and keys.

When Ed saw her he exclaimed, "Wow, Natalie. You're absolutely gorgeous."

Nat smiled back and did a twirl for him. "Thank you, Ed."

He took her elbow and walked her to his car, a brand new Lexus in a muted silver exterior with a cream leather interior.

"Business is good?" Nat asked, staring at the vehicle.

"Pretty good. I can't complain," Ed agreed, chuckling.

He took her to Rae & Jerry's Steak House, a Winnipeg staple, where they dined on steak and lobster with grilled mushrooms, a bottle of red wine, and for dessert, bread pudding with vanilla sauce.

Ed was sincere, open, honest, genuine and a joy to be around as they talked about all kinds of things, getting to know each other.

After dinner, he paid the bill, tipping well.

As they were leaving, Ed asked Natalie, "Is there anywhere else you'd like to go?"

"How about your place?" she replied boldly.

Ed raised his eyebrows in surprise, his lips forming an attractive smile. "Sure."

Natalie smiled back at him, her heart beating wildly in her chest.

When they got to Ed's house, he parked in the driveway at the side of his bungalow and gave her a quick tour once they got inside. "It's small, but it's all mine," he said confidently. "It's enough until I get married, then I'll need something bigger. I do want to have kids somewhere down the road."

Natalie was taken aback at how candid Ed was about his life and what he wanted for his future. "You sure know what you want, don't you?" she commented, suitably impressed.

"Yes, I do. I also know what I *don't* want, which makes knowing what I *do* want that much easier to look for... and find," he admitted, looking directly at her.

Natalie blushed as Ed moved closer to her, pulling her into his embrace. She looked up at him and asked, "Are you always this direct?"

He grinned as he said, "Yup."

She smiled back, her voice slightly husky. "Good to know."

They leaned towards each other and their lips met in a soft, sweet kiss as their arms wrapped around each other tightly.

He pulled away and said, "Natalie, I would really like to take this further tonight, but I also want to take this past tonight. Is this something that interests you?"

Nat opened her mouth, closed it and opened it again a few more times before she formulated what she wanted to say. "Yes. This, and you, really interest me. But seeing as I've just gotten out of a long term relationship and I'm still working through it, I need to take wherever we're headed slow to start. Are you okay with that?" she countered.

"Yep. I can do that for us," he replied.

A shiver of excitement rippled through Natalie as those words rolled off Ed's tongue.

'I can do that for US'...

Ed kissed her again, pulling her close to him. She let herself feel happiness and excitement from Ed's kisses and relaxed in his embrace, winding her arms around him a little tighter.

He liked that she was getting more into their kiss, but was reluctant to do anything to ruin their budding relationship. "Natalie, maybe I should take you home. If you stay and we continue doing what we're doing, neither of us will be able to walk by the morning," Ed grinned.

"Oh! Um, okay," Nat blushed at what he was inferring.

When Ed pulled up to Natalie's house, he leaned over and kissed her again, saying, "Can I see you tomorrow? I can pick you up around six and we can go out for dinner, then talk a bit more. Sound good to you?"

"That sounds great. See you tomorrow at six," Natalie confirmed, then got out of the car and floated into her house.

Ed watched her and made sure she was in her house before driving away, being the gentleman he was.

They both had the same thought at the same time...
WOW!
I think I just hit the relationship jackpot!

CHAPTER 88

June 1995

Natalie & Ed

Ed's twenty-seventh birthday was on June 17. He and Natalie had been seeing each other since the day after her graduation and they were taking things slowly, out of respect for Natalie's prior relationship status. But for Ed's birthday, Nat had *big plans* for what she wanted to do for him...

And to him...

Ed had been behaving like a perfect gentleman since they started dating. As much as Natalie appreciated him giving her space to grieve her broken relationship with Tony, she was ready to move on and start giving him her full attention. He made no bones about the fact that he was extremely attracted to her and would like to move things along further, so Nat decided that *tonight* was going to be the night.

Natalie wanted to treat Ed to an evening on her as he'd been footing the bill every time they went out. He made good money and enjoyed spending it on her and spoiling her, seeing her face light up and shine just for him. But this time, she wanted to take the reins.

Ed picked her up at seven that evening wearing a dark gray suit, light pink button down shirt and a deep burgundy tie. He had never looked more handsome and Natalie had a hard time keeping her hands to herself and her thoughts out of the gutter.

Nat decided to wear a dark metallic green, scoop neck sheath dress with sheer tulip sleeves and a hem that came just below her knees, snakeskin stilettos and a black crocodile handbag. She topped it with a delicate ivory lace wrap.

Ed whistled when he saw Natalie and she smiled happily. He took her hand and kissed the back of it, then pulled her into his embrace, dipped her back over his arm and laid a fantastic, open-mouthed kiss on her, right in the front door of her parent's house.

When Ed lifted her back up, he noticed a small travel bag by her shoes. Grinning, he nodded to it and asked, "What's this all about?"

"I thought I'd stay the night with you and I'll need a few things," Nat replied, noting his grin and feeling quite satisfied at his expression.

Ed picked up the bag in one hand and placed his other at the small of her back, leading Natalie to his Lexus. He tossed her bag in the trunk and they took off, Nat informing him of their dinner reservations for eight PM at the Velvet Glove in the Westin Hotel.

Dinner was absolutely delicious. Ed dined on grilled pork chops, Nat chose glazed salmon and for dessert, they shared creme brulee.

After dessert, they moved to the lounge area where they indulged in snifters of Grand Marnier while sitting in high backed chairs by the fireplace.

They began chatting casually, then the conversation took a distinctly sensual turn, thanks to Natalie. She leaned over to face Ed after taking a sip of her Grand Marnier and whispered, "If you want to know where I see us going from here, may I suggest we swiftly finish these marvellous snifters, then you can take us back to your place and I can show you what I'm referring to."

Ed downed the rest of his snifter in one gulp as Natalie daintily finished hers.

She had already taken care of the bill, so Ed helped her out of her chair and grabbed her hand, hauling her out of the lounge at top speed to the front of the hotel where the valet retrieved his car. After a quick drive back to his place, Ed pulled his Lexus into the garage and led Natalie into the house through the back door. Barely saying a word, he pulled her into his arms and crushed her to him, groaning as he kissed her, tasting the orange liqueur on her lips and tongue.

Natalie let Ed ravish her for a time, then she firmly got back in the driver's seat. She pushed him away, smiling at his still-puckered lips as he tried to keep kissing her. "Uh-uh, this is the other part of my present to you."

She turned and sashayed away from him into the living room, closed the draperies on the front window, then turned back and led him to the sofa. She pushed him down onto the middle cushion, giving him her back as she turned on the stereo.

Joe Cocker's "You Can Leave Your Hat On" began rasping out of the speakers, a sinful coincidence, as Nat began twitching her hips and smiling suggestively at Ed. He leaned back into the cushions, loosened his tie, undid the top buttons of his shirt and watched her show of burlesque, just for him.

Happy Birthday to me!

Natalie kept her back to him as she peeled off her dress to the beat of the music, then bent at the waist with her ass up in the air. She turned her face, smiling and mouthing the words to him. Ed sat up a whole lot straighter and pulled the tie out from his collar altogether, throwing it over the arm of the sofa, his eyes never leaving her.

She flung her dress at him and it landed partly on his shoulder and partly hanging off his ear. He pulled it off and draped it over his tie, then shrugged his suit jacket off and tossed it over the back of the sofa.

"You Can Leave Your Hat On" ended and segued into The Rolling Stones' "Honky Tonk Woman".

Natalie turned around and faced Ed, watching him watching her as he undid the buttons at his wrists and the rest of the buttons on the front of his shirt, pulling the tails out of his pants. His light pink shirt was now hanging open, his chest covered in dark hair that appealed to Natalie, making her eyes dilate with lust.

She smiled seductively, enjoying what her show was doing to him. Nat could just imagine what was going on behind the zipper of those suit trousers...

Ed leaned forward with his elbows on his knees, his eyes locked with hers. She undid the clasp at her back and slowly pulled the straps of her hot pink satin and black lace bra down her arms. She stood directly in front of him, her legs apart with her arm straight out, dangling her bra off her forefinger in his face. He took it between two fingers and dropped it onto the coffee table.

Ed grabbed Natalie by the hips and pulled her towards him, his face right in line with her hot pink satin and black lace panties. Nuzzling her belly with his nose and mouth, Nat let her head drop back a bit, wetness seeping out of her and onto the satin between her legs. Ed caught on to her distraction and before she knew what was happening, he bit the top edge of her panties and tugged them down her legs to mid-thigh, where they dropped to the floor around her ankles. Shock at such erotic behavior flooded her body and Nat was momentarily frozen to the spot.

Holy shit!

I don't know if I've ever been so turned on before!

She recovered quickly, enough to lift one snakeskin-shod foot, then the other, to toe away her sodden panties. She stood in front of Ed again, her legs spread with her hands on her hips, waiting to see what he would do next.

I do believe I've been ousted out of the driver's seat!

Ed did, in fact, take control. He sat on the edge of the sofa, shucked his shirt off his shoulders, leaned forward and licked at Nat's cleft, groaning at her taste. His hands were braced at his sides, his knuckles white as he gripped the sofa cushions to maintain some semblance of control.

"Holy fuck, I've never tasted anything so fucking sweet," he growled as he raised his hands and pulled her hips to his face again, delving deeper with his tongue.

Natalie felt her orgasm rocketing up her spine as it tackled her from out of nowhere. Never had she had this done to her while she was standing.

Ed held her up as her knees buckled and she started to fall forward, his face still buried between her legs. He chuckled at her loss of leg strength as he pulled his face out of paradise and leaned back against the sofa.

He pulled her onto his lap to straddle him, but Natalie regained control, hovering her lips in front of his. She licked Ed's bottom lip, then slid off to kneel between his thighs.

Maintaining eye contact, she pulled his belt out of the belt loops and dropped it at her side. Then she unbuttoned the top button and slid the zipper down on his pants, pushing down his boxer briefs at the front to get to his erection. Grabbing on, she started running her hand up and down his length, licking her lips to arouse him further.

It worked.

He bucked his hips and she assisted by pulling his pants and boxers down to his ankles. She leaned back onto her haunches, still in her stilettos, and slowly tugged off his dress socks and dress shoes, pushing them aside. Then she yanked off his pants and boxers, tossed them behind her, leaned back in and dove for his hard cock with her hand, admiring his built physique.

He's an Adonis...

She wrapped her hand around the base with one hand, cupped his heavy sac with the other and plunged the tip of his cock between her lips, sliding her teeth and tongue up and down its hard length.

Ed was nearly out of his mind from all the sensation as Natalie tasted and teased him with both her mouth and her hands. He tried to keep his hands off her, but he was no longer in possession of all his faculties. He caught her head in his hands and guided her at the pace he needed to preserve his erection and maximize both their pleasure.

After a few minutes of Nat's talents, Ed began to stiffen and he groaned, encouraging her to pick up the pace of her ministrations to his dick. She did so and he orgasmed in strong spurts down her throat where she lapped up every drop. Ed sagged against the back of the sofa, eyes closed with a smile plastered to his face.

"Happy Birthday, Ed," Nat said, licking her lips.

"Holy fuck, Natalie, you are something else," he panted, out of breath.

"Do you think we're done?" she asked as she bit her bottom lip, her eyebrows raised.

Ed looked down at her, still kneeling between his thighs, still wearing her stilettos and still naked. "Not even close," he growled, pulling her up to straddle his lap, his dick hardening against her belly.

Natalie grabbed hold of his cock and directed it at her core, lowering herself onto it slowly, her eyes closing in ecstasy. Ed grabbed her hips, Nat's hands found his shoulders, and they began moving in a matched rhythm, up and down, in and out. She leaned down to kiss him as he reached up to kiss her back, their tongues entwined, their bodies rubbing together.

Ed took one hand from her hip and grabbed onto her breast, pinching her nipple and twisting gently, just enough for her to gasp in pure pleasure. He broke contact with her mouth to latch onto her other nipple with his teeth and lightly bit, causing another orgasm to explode through Natalie's body.

Ed leaned back into the sofa with both hands on her hips, his own hips jerking up as his second orgasm erupted out of him. Nat leaned back away from him, her hands braced on his knees, allowing deeper penetration. He held her down in place on his cock as the last of the spasms shot through him.

Nat dropped forward and collapsed onto his chest as Ed wrapped his arms around her, kissed her neck, her cheek and finally her mouth, both of them panting and out of breath.

"Natalie, you are..." Ed started to say.

Nat cut him off and finished for him, smirking, "The best?"

Ed smiled and kissed her again. "Absodamnlutely."

She licked a path along his jaw to his ear and whispered, "I'm only getting started."

Ed hadn't withdrawn from inside her, and even though he just had two back-to-back, toe-curling orgasms, Natalie could feel him hardening again.

This is the most erotic sex I've ever had!

I think I've met my sexual match!

Ed stood up, wrapped Nat's legs around his waist and walked through the house into his bedroom. He kicked the door shut and turned them so Natalie's back was to the door. He began pumping slowly in and out of her, kissing her neck while she closed her eyes in ecstasy.

Ed pulled them away from the door, holding Nat by her delectable ass cheeks as he turned to sit on the edge of the bed and lay backwards with her on top of him. She automatically began moving her hips, sliding him in and out of her.

When Nat started to feel the burn again, she slid off Ed's hard cock and crawled to the head of the bed. She grasped the slats of his headboard and tipped her hips up, ready for a different position. Ed smiled sexily as he positioned himself on his knees behind her, grabbed her hips and plunged into her wetness. He began thrusting back and forth as deep as he could go and she thrust her pelvis back as far as she could, meeting him stroke for stroke.

As Ed increased his tempo, Nat took one hand off the slats of the headboard and began caressing herself, matching his thrusting. Before long, Ed grunted and slammed himself in all the way, pouring out his last orgasm into her while Nat pleasured herself to a shuddering climax.

Ed finally pulled out and fell to his side, sweat pouring off him. Natalie let go of the headboard with her remaining hand and collapsed onto her stomach with her head turned towards him, breathing heavily.

They were both totally exhausted and completely sexually sated.

Ed turned onto his back and pulled Natalie partially on top of him, their arms and legs intertwined.

She looked at him with a sparkle in her eyes and winked at him. "So, Birthday Boy, did you like your gift from me? I tried my best to make it memorable," she said huskily.

"You absolutely did. Thank you," he replied, his voice raspy.

"You're welcome. By the way, I'm all tapped out. I got nothin' left," she giggled.

Ed giggled back. "That goes the same for me, Sweetcheeks."

They fell asleep wrapped around each other, shifting slightly throughout the night.

In the morning when they awoke, Natalie had turned to her other side with Ed behind her, one hand on her breast, the other between her legs. He slipped into her wet heat from behind and rocked them slowly and sensuously to a satisfying mutual orgasm before pulling out and getting out of bed to shower together.

Ed dropped Natalie off at home, then drove to work with a huge smile plastered on his face all day. He couldn't stop smiling because they made plans for later that evening, which would likely include more of the same of what they had done together the night before and that morning.

Natalie had the day off, so she called Krys to come over and hang out with her in the back yard since she had the day off, too. Nat told Krys all about her evening with Ed and watched as Krys' face lit up with genuine happiness for her.

"Nat, I'm so happy for you! He seems like a truly good man and I'm glad you've found someone who can give you what you're looking for," Krys smiled warmly.

"Me too, Krys. Do you know how hard it's been for me to watch you and my brother since you got back together, wanting the same thing for myself? I thought I had it with Tony, and for the most part I did, but then his career and mine didn't jive and I just couldn't rectify that. I really like Ed and he's so good to me. In fact, he reminds me a lot of Darryl and how he is with you," Nat revealed.

"Then you got it made, sis-in-law!" Krys laughed.

They spent the rest of the day lounging outside in their bikinis, talking, laughing and feeling totally happy with the men of worth in their lives.

CHAPTER 89

June 1995 to September 1995
Natalie & Ed

During the summer, Natalie applied for several teaching positions at several elementary schools around Winnipeg. Just before the school year started, she received word that she was the successful candidate for a Grade 1 classroom. She was still living at home with her parents until she got a full-time teaching job and now she had one.

Ed was all over that as soon as she told him about her good fortune. "So now that you've gotten a permanent teaching job, what do you think about moving in with me?" he asked. They were sitting at his kitchen table having breakfast together.

"Wh-what?" she stuttered.

"Natalie, we're together all the time. You only go home to sleep on occasion and to change clothes, otherwise you practically live here with me already. Let's just make it official. What do you think about that?" Ed rationalized.

"I... Uh..." she started, then cleared her throat and said, "You have a point," she finished, smiling at him over her mug of Earl Grey tea.

"I have some boxes in the garage that I've been saving for when I asked you. Wanna fill them up today? I've already cleared room for you in my closet and some drawers in my dresser. Plus, there's the spare bedroom we can use to store stuff until we figure out what to do with it," Ed smiled smugly.

"You've thought it all out, haven't you?" Nat grinned.

"Yup," Ed smiled, leaning over to kiss her cheek.

"Then I think the answer is... YES!" Natalie squealed, jumping up into Ed's lap and kissing him.

CHAPTER 90

September 1995
Natalie & Ed

Later that day as they moved in all of Natalie's things, unpacked some stuff and stored other stuff in boxes, Nat thought of how different her life was not quite six months ago.

She called Krys and told her the news, inviting both her and Darryl over that night for a barbecue. She also invited her parents Audrey and Owen, Ed's parents Carol and Shaun, Ed's sister Nancy and her boyfriend Kyle.

It seemed that everyone was happy for the couple and that just made Natalie's day, week, month, year, that she was loved and supported by these important people in her life.

It made all the difference in the world.

CHAPTER 91

December 7, 1995
Natalie & Ed

Ed outdid himself for Natalie's birthday. He threw her a surprise birthday party, enlisting Krys as his partner-in-crime. He got her to take Nat out for the day while he and his sister Nancy decorated the house. His mother Carol picked up the birthday cake and dinner was being catered by the Silver Heights Restaurant in St James, known as *"The Best BBQ Ribs In Winnipeg"*.

Ed and Natalie lived in Charleswood, just around the Perimeter highway from Natalie's parent's home in Westwood. When Natalie moved in, Ed let her decorate how she wanted to because the place needed it and she had a great eye for design. What she ended up doing to spruce their place up made it look a lot better, her *woman's touch* adding some femininity and softness to his otherwise stark, masculine abode.

When Krys brought her home at the appointed time, Natalie was honestly surprised that he managed to pull off such a feat.

"I'm so totally in love with him," Natalie sighed to Krys later that evening, after most of the guests had left.

Krys beamed a huge smile at her. "Nat, do you realize what you just said?"

Nat smiled back softly. "Yeah, I love him."

Ed rounded the corner and heard what Natalie said. He set down his glass of scotch, came to stand in front of her, took her hands in his, looked into her eyes and said, "I love you too, Natalie," then pulled her into his arms and kissed her sweetly.

Darryl came over and hung his arm around Krys' shoulders, asking, "What's going on?"

Krys laid her cheek on Darryl's chest and snuggled into him, replying happily, "They just told each other they love each other."

"You're such a romantic," Darryl teased, kissing her forehead and cuddling her close to him.

"Yup," Krys answered.

After all their guests left, Natalie and Ed showed each other over the next few hours just how much they did, in fact, love each other.

CHAPTER 92

March 1996
Natalie & Ed

Natalie was sitting at the kitchen table one morning in early March in a complete daze.

Ed walked in and saw her sitting there looking natural and beautiful, gazing out the kitchen window at the snow melting on the grass. He reached into his pocket and pulled out the ring box he'd been carrying around for the past several weeks. "Natalie, can I ask you something?" he blurted out before he realized what he was about to do.

Natalie turned her head to him, her eyes unfocused. "What? Oh, sure," she replied, totally not paying attention.

Ed caught onto her odd mood and pulled a chair around to sit in front of her. "Nat, what's up? You look in another world right now," he asked, concern washing over him.

Natalie just stared at him. She wasn't sure she could utter the words she needed to say. "Ed, I... Um..." she started.

"What is it, Nat? You know you can tell me anything. Whatever it is, we'll get through it together," he answered, taking her hands in his and trying to get her to focus on him.

"Ed..." she started, feeling dizzy and flushed.

"Do you want me to go first? I have something to ask you. Maybe that will help you tell me what's on your mind?" he asked.

"Okay," she said quietly.

"Natalie, I love you. I've never been happier in my life since we've been together. This isn't how I expected to do this, but here goes... Will you marry me?" Ed declared, dropping to one knee and opening the ring box to show her the three stone diamond engagement ring in set platinum he chose just for her.

Natalie's eyes finally focused sharply on Ed as he asked her his question, taking in his position on one knee and her hand in his, awaiting her reply. She answered, "I'm... pregnant..."

CHAPTER 93

March 1996
Natalie & Ed

Ed was stunned at Natalie's news. His expression turned from one of hope of her saying *yes* to his question to one of surprised disbelief, then to one of pure jubilation that she just told him she was pregnant with his baby. "Natalie! When did you find out?"

"About ten minutes ago. I missed my period a couple of weeks ago, so I took a pregnancy test this morning and it's positive. I'm pregnant," Natalie said in a monotone voice.

"Aren't you happy about this?" Ed asked.

"I don't know how to feel about it. I certainly wasn't *planning* on getting pregnant! I swear, I did NOT do this on purpose! Please don't hate me!" Nat screeched. She stood up and started freaking out, pacing back and forth across the kitchen floor, her arms wrapped around her middle.

"Natalie! I do *not* hate you! I couldn't be happier!" Ed said, catching her on her next pass-by and holding her close to him.

Nat stilled and looked into his face, searching for... she didn't know what. "You're not angry? You want to stay with me?" she said quietly, almost a whisper.

"Of course I'm not angry! I was just asking you to marry me *before* you blurted out that you're pregnant with our baby! Which, by the way, you still haven't answered me," he added as he smiled and kissed her temple.

Natalie closed her eyes, tears streaking a path down her cheeks as she nestled into his embrace, tucking her face into the collar of his robe. "Yes," was her muffled answer, warmth stealing over her.

Ed lifted her chin with his finger and brought them eye to eye. "What was that? I couldn't understand you," he teased.

Natalie smiled and said clearly, "YES!"

Ed smiled back and crushed her to him, kissing her passionately, then abruptly let her go and turned back to the table where he left the ring box open. He pulled the ring out of its velvet nest and placed it lovingly on her left ring finger. "How do you feel about a very short engagement?" he asked, grinning at her.

"How short are we talking?" she asked.

"How about we get married next weekend?" he replied.

"How about, SURE!" she answered.

CHAPTER 94

March 1996

Krys & Natalie

Natalie was on the phone minutes later telling Krys her doubly exciting news.

Krys squealed in excitement at both parts.

They spent the rest of the day planning Natalie and Ed's expedited wedding and plans to decorate the nursery for the upcoming newest addition to their family.

Life was finally perking up.

CHAPTER 95

March 1996
Krys & Natalie

The following Saturday morning on March 16, Natalie and Ed were married in their living room with a Justice of the Peace and a small gathering of family and friends.

Natalie wore a simple white column dress with cap sleeves and a lace overlay, the hem at mid-calf, her shoes white platform pumps. She wore her auburn hair partly up, partly down in waves and carried a small bunch of daffodils.

Ed wore a dark blue suit with a light blue shirt and a dark blue tie with tiny white polka dots.

Krys wore a hot pink wrap dress that fell below her knees with short fluttery sleeves and white pumps, a gorgeous complement to Darryl's navy suit and light gray shirt with a navy and gray striped tie.

As the happy couple wandered around their house after the ceremony chatting with their guests, Natalie noticed something odd about Krys, but couldn't quite put her finger on it...

And Darryl was acting weird, too...

Then Natalie noticed that Krys wasn't drinking champagne. Instead, she was drinking a glass of non-alcoholic sparkling grape juice that was offered to those who didn't want to imbibe in alcohol. Nat's eyes grew wide at what that could possibly mean...

Then it hit her and she hurried over to Krys, a huge smile plastered on her face. "OHMYGOD KRYSSIE!!!" Nat blurted, her eyes bugging out in absolute excitement. "Why aren't *YOU* drinking champagne? I know why *I'M* not drinking champagne!"

Krys' eyes narrowed as she hissed, "*Keep your voice down!*" She clapped her hand over Nat's mouth and rushed her into the spare bedroom that was cleared out to become the nursery for Nat and Ed's impending bundle of joy in the fall. Krys kept her hand over Nat's mouth as she gritted out, "If I remove my hand, are you going to keep quiet?"

Nat nodded her head up and down to indicate that *yes, she would keep her big, loud trap shut.*

Krys peeled her fingers away, one at a time, until her hand was totally removed from Nat's mouth.

Nat kept her word, but asked again in an excitable stage whisper, "Kryssie, why aren't you drinking champagne with me? Is it because *you're pregnant, too*?!"

Krys closed her eyes and nodded affirmatively, saying softly, "Yes."

Nat nearly whooped with joy, but caught Krys' unhappiness at her impending motherhood. "Krys, what's up? Why aren't you happy about being pregnant?" Natalie asked, confused.

"I'm more terrified than anything, but Darryl is over the moon. He can't stop smiling and puffing up his chest like a gorilla. It's embarrassing," Krys said, agitated, pacing the room while cradling her still-flat belly.

"Kryssie, what's the matter? When did you find out? And why are you so freaked out?" Natalie questioned.

"We found out yesterday," Krys started, but hedged in continuing.

"Krys, what aren't you telling me?" Nat urged.

Krys looked like she was about to vomit from the strain of whatever secret she was keeping inside her. "This isn't my first pregnancy," she whispered so quietly, Natalie almost couldn't hear her.

Natalie stood there, her mouth gaping open. "Um, what?" was all she could say to THAT bombshell.

"Darryl doesn't know! He can *NEVER KNOW*!!! Promise me, Natalie, on the life of the baby you carry, right now, that YOU WILL NEVER TELL HIM!!!" Krys said frantically.

"I promise. But can you tell *me* what happened?" Nat said in a small voice, horrible scenarios of Krys being forced against her will by some heathen brute flashing through her mind.

Whoa, this is huuuge... I can't even begin to imagine what she's going to tell me...

Krys took a deep breath, sat down on the futon with Natalie beside her and told her everything. "I got pregnant last year when I was with Rick. It was totally unplanned and I miscarried at seven weeks. If Darryl *ever* finds out that I was *pregnant with Rick's baby* and that I never told him about it or what happened, that would be it for us, Nat. He would divorce me in a heartbeat. PLEASE, Natalie, DON'T tell him! I'm so scared that I'm going to miscarry again like I did the first time. Rick and I had some pretty energetic sex the night it happened, but I don't think that's what caused it. In all likelihood, I'll never know..." she trailed off, looking more freaked out than Nat had ever seen her.

"Thank you for confiding in me, Kryssie. And I promise on the life on my baby that I will keep your secret, always," Natalie declared.

Krys sighed in relief, sagging against Natalie's strength. Then she pulled back and smiled softly as she said, "I hope our babies are girls and they grow up together to be best friends, like us."

Natalie threw her arms back around Krys and hugged her close again, saying with happiness in her voice, "I have no doubt they will."

CHAPTER 96

April 1996 to September 1996
Krys & Darryl

Natalie and Ed went on a short honeymoon to Las Vegas, then came home to get down to the business of being newlyweds and expecting their first baby together.

Krys and Darryl were also preparing for their impending arrival around the same time.

Krys and Natalie spent the spring, summer and early autumn comparing belly sizes, ankle sizes and food cravings, went nursery shopping together, went to their doctor appointments together and even house-hunted together, as Krys was hell-bent on getting out of the apartment before her baby was born.

Darryl and Ed would just shake their heads, grin conspiratorially at each other and go back to watching sports on the TV when their wives got carried away with one of the above topics of conversation.

One Friday morning in late September on Krys' day off, Darryl woke up early and left their bed without her even realizing it. He got dressed silently and prayed she wouldn't wake up.

She didn't even stir.

He returned an hour later and crawled back in bed beside her. Krys turned to face him and snuggled into his arms, not having the faintest clue that he had been gone. Darryl kissed her sweetly, enticing her to wake up.

Krys smiled in her sleep, then slowly opened her eyes. "Good morning, Daddy. Your baby is already kicking up a storm in my tummy," she grinned, cradling her big belly full of baby.

"Good morning, Mommy. Wanna rock the kid back to sleep with me?" Darryl waggled his eyebrows at her, moving his hands over her much bigger breasts and giving them a gentle squeeze.

"I AM feeling kind of frisky and I really like the way you say good morning to me," Krys admitted. She kissed him, slipping her tongue in his mouth as she coiled her arms around his neck.

Darryl rolled to his back and helped Krys climb onto him so she could straddle his thighs, a hungry look on her beautiful face. She wore a short nightie, never wore panties to bed and he usually slept naked, so it didn't take long after he slid his hand between them and circled Krys' sweet spot that she shuddered to a quick and satisfying climax.

As Darryl was pleasuring her, Krys had his cock in her hand. She slid it up and down his shaft, feeling him twitch in anticipation. While she was still in the throes of her orgasmic high, she guided his cock to her opening and slowly lowered herself onto him. She groaned in sweet ecstasy at how good he felt and how smoothly she slid down right to the base.

It was truly amazing how sexually heightened she felt since being pregnant.

Darryl grabbed onto her hips and lifted his knees to give her back a bit more support while Krys held onto her eight-months-pregnant belly, thrusting until he brought them both to a satisfying orgasm.

They had been enjoying a very active sex life since they got past the twelve-week mark. Prior to that, when Krys found out she was pregnant at five weeks along, she had been in a closed off, tumultuous emotional state that Darryl couldn't break through. No matter what he said or did, Krys was shut down and stayed that way towards him until the magical twelfth week.

Magical, indeed!

That day, she came home from her doctor appointment after work and attacked him in the kitchen, pulling off her scrub pants, yanking down his jeans, wrapping her legs around his waist and sinking his cock into her while he held her up with her back against the fridge.

He had been so hard and so starved for her over the previous seven weeks that he came after only a few thrusts. She just laughed and kissed him sensually, having had her orgasm after the second thrust. She was so hypersensitive being pregnant, it didn't take more than that for her to get off.

Darryl couldn't have been happier. Non-Pregnant Krys was a sexual powerhouse, matching his sex drive perfectly, but Pregnant Krys was over-the-top horny, even more than he was! Every chance she got, she was on him like an animal in heat, always running her hands all over him, grabbing his ass, kissing him more than usual and grabbing his dick, trying to get his pants off so they could have sex.

He wondered how things were going to go after she had the baby...

Would she still want to have sex with him?

Was she going to put a padlock on it and that would be it?

Would she ever let him touch her again?

He shook his head to clear those shitty thoughts away and just enjoyed the feel of being inside her, her on top of him pregnant with their baby and having fantastic sex together.

Krys raised herself off Darryl and he slid out, still semi-hard. She lay down on her left side and snuggled back into him, reaching back and pulling his hand around her to cradle her belly, linking their fingers. Darryl took advantage of the position and slid into her slick wetness from behind her, pumping in and out of her slowly, kissing her neck.

After they both crested over a rolling wave of an orgasm, Darryl pulled out of her and said huskily, "Kryssie, I have a house for us to look at today. We need to be there around ten o'clock, okay? I really hope you like it..."

"Have you seen it already?" she asked sleepily.

"You could say that," he said to himself. Darryl was glad she was facing away from him so she couldn't see the enormous grin splitting his face in half. "Oh yeah, I drove past it the other day. I think it's perfect for us, but you need to see it to give your seal of approval," he said convincingly.

After cuddling for a while and caressing Krys' belly, they got up, showered together and got dressed, eating a quick breakfast before driving to the house Darryl was so excited to show Krys. It was situated in the newer part of Tuxedo that was being developed.

Krys' mouth dropped open as they parked in the driveway. "Darryl, it's *beautiful*! It's *exactly* what you and I have discussed! Let's go inside. I wanna see!" Krys exclaimed.

Darryl kept his mouth clamped firmly shut for fear of spoiling the surprise he was about to lay on her. He pulled a set of keys out of his pocket and put the key into the front door lock. Turning the key, Darryl's heart was in his throat as the door opened to reveal the glory of the interior to Krys for the very first time. "After you, Kryssie."

He stepped aside to let Krys step over the threshold and as she entered the front foyer she looked around, her eyes wide open in ecstasy. She noticed *everything* – the paint, the flooring, the woodwork, the lighting, the curved staircase, the windows, the direction the house faced, every last detail. "Darryl! This is *exactly* what we want! EXACTLY!!! Right down to the furniture we looked at, absolutely EVERYTHING!" she shouted in excitement.

She wandered around the completely furnished first floor, looking into an office, powder room and mud room to the right of the front door by the garage entrance. Across the foyer was the living room and dining room and to the back of the house was the huge kitchen, complete with an island and large folding patio doors to the deck and a large back yard.

"Wanna go upstairs and see the bedrooms?" he asked, feeling less stressed now that she was inside and her reaction was so positive.

She LOVES it!

"You betcha!" she said as she walked through the kitchen to the stairs. She grabbed hold of the banister with one hand, her huge belly with the other, and walked slowly up the curved staircase. She ran her hand lovingly over the gleaming dark wood as she climbed stair by stair until she reached the top, Darryl right behind her.

She looked into three bedrooms and noted that they were empty, but painted in neutral colors. The main bathroom was decorated exactly how she would have decorated it.

Then they came to the double doors that opened to the master bedroom suite.

"Allow me, Mrs Sheridan," Darryl said as he swept the doors open inwards.

Krys looked inside to see the most beautiful bedroom suite, the one she'd had her eye on for months, with the bedding she'd picked out, the paint and carpet exactly what she would have chosen. It had a large ensuite with a dual vanity, free-standing soaker tub and a separate walk-in shower. Beside the ensuite was a walk-in closet that was large enough to hold both hers and Darryl's substantial wardrobes.

As Krys walked through the closet, she noticed that some of the clothing on the hangers looked very familiar... "Darryl, why are some of *our* clothes in this closet?" Krys asked, truly perturbed.

Darryl just smiled, reached into his pocket and pulled out another set of keys, jangling them at her. "Because this is *our closet*," he said as he handed the keys to her. "And because this is *our house*."

She took the keys gingerly in her hands and stared at him, then her mouth curved into a beautiful smile. "Are... you... serious?"

"Yes," he replied simply.

Krys just stood there, poleaxed. "When? How? Why?" she stammered.

He answered her, grinning. "I bought the lot just after we got married with a great bonus I got at work, designed the house to our specifications like we discussed and started building it in March, just after you told me you were pregnant. I even hired Natalie's Ed as our contractor. He's really good at what he does, by the way. Then, painstakingly, I took detailed notes every time we talked about our future house, went house hunting or went shopping, and systematically bought all the things we decided on. I have to admit, I *did* have a little help getting it all done in time for you and I to pack up our few remaining things and move in... TODAY!" he finished.

Huge tears slid down her cheeks as she stared at her incredible husband. "I just cannot believe you pulled this off!" Krys said, her voice tremulous.

"I sure did!" Darryl said proudly.

"Without letting me in on anything?" she added.

"Kryssie, we DID discuss everything! I wanted it to be a surprise for you. You were so freaked out when you found out you were pregnant and had such a shitty time of it those first few months that I needed to do *something* to cope with you shutting me out. I thought this would be something constructive..." he trailed off, not happy with the direction this conversation was going.

"I was really awful to you, wasn't I?" Krys asked, her voice a whisper.

"Kind of, but I get it. It's you who has to be pregnant, not me. I tried to be loving and supportive, but you did a fantastic job of keeping me at arms' length from you. So I poured my heart and soul into this house. For us. I hoped your mood wouldn't last, and thankfully, it didn't. I really didn't plan on keeping this from you for the entire time, but by the time you and I were on good footing again, it just seemed like something really wonderful I could do for you, since you were giving me the most amazing gift of all," Darryl admitted, holding out his arms for her to come to him.

Krys did and he pulled her right into him. "You really did listen when I was talking about all the things I wanted in a house, everything we talked about together, the colors, the finishes, every last detail," she said, truly amazed.

"Of course I did. Are you shocked about that?" Darryl asked, amused.

Krys pulled back, smiled adoringly at him and replied, "Yes and no. You just keep surprising me."

"I left one room for us to decorate together, or you can do it all on your own, whichever you prefer, since I did the rest of the house – the nursery," Darryl told her.

"I've already bought the crib and a few other things," Krys said, grinning.

"I know. They're in the garage, ready to be brought up once you pick out the paint color you want," he grinned back.

Krys just couldn't believe how on top of everything Darryl was! "How are you two steps ahead of me every time?" she asked, shaking her head.

"Your mother and my sister. Need I say more?" he laughed, kissing her forehead.

"Seriously? I'm impressed they could keep a secret like this!" Krys laughed.

"Me, too!" Darryl said, then continued, "Plus, I had a little help from a couple of the interior designers at work who are, right now, at our apartment packing up the rest of our things."

"They're packing our things?" Krys looked mildly uncomfortable.

"Yep. It's mostly our clothes and some other stuff that's easy to just dump into boxes. Haven't you noticed the amount of stuff we have in the apartment slowly dwindling down lately? I've been packing a few boxes here and there and moving them over here for the past few weeks when you were at work on evening shift. In my line of work, all of this was easy to do. And I got nearly everything wholesale and cut deals and called in favors all over the place. Plus, I picked up a few more contracts and got another couple of bonuses. We're rolling in it, Kryssie! And now, in another six weeks or so, we'll be able to bring our baby home, *here,* to *our house,*" Darryl said smugly.

Krys stammered, "I... I just cannot believe all you've done... for us..."

"Kryssie, you're giving us a baby, I'm giving us a home. Let's call it square and celebrate!" Darryl smiled, hugging her close.

"Deal," Krys said, hugging her incredible husband back.

At noon, a small U-Haul moving truck arrived with the interior designers who packed up their apartment. They got right to unloading and unpacking the rest of Krys and Darryl's things. Krys was on cloud nine, flitting all around the house, helping to unpack and directing where things should go.

Both of their families came by in the evening for a celebratory barbecue.

When they finally collapsed into their new bed, under their new bedding, in their new bedroom, in their new house that night, Krys and Darryl faced each other and held hands, giggling joyfully until they fell asleep.

CHAPTER 97

March 1996 to October 1996
Natalie & Ed

When Natalie and Ed returned from Las Vegas, Nat got busy with Krys talking all things baby. As spring moved into summer and summer turned into autumn, Natalie was having the time of her life with keeping the details of her brother's private project from Krys. She couldn't wait until it was ready to be revealed near the end of September.

The moment Krys called her, hyper and squealing, Natalie knew Darryl showed her the house he had designed and built for them. Her brother had moved up a few notches in her good books for hiring Ed, giving his already booming business a boost.

Win-win all around!

Natalie did not go back to work when the school year started on September 1. Instead, she started her maternity leave since she was due by the middle of October.

Now it was late October.

Natalie awoke early in the morning on October 26 feeling energetic. She climbed out of bed and stretched, then leaned over to kiss Ed. As she did so, she felt a horribly painful cramp low in her belly that extended all the way around to her lower back that caused her to gasp in pain.

Ed's eyes flew open. "WHAT? Is it time??" he screeched, jack-knifing out of bed.

Natalie had both hands under her belly, holding it in place while she breathed through the painful cramping. "Call Krys," she whispered.

Ed did so, panicking while he waited for her to answer the phone. "Krys!!! It's Ed! Natalie might be in labor!!! How do we know?!" he yelled.

"Ed, tell me what's happening and I'll direct you what to do," Krys said calmly.

Ed relayed what was happening, so Krys directed him to pack Natalie up and get to the hospital, especially as Nat was already two weeks overdue.

After fifteen hours of labor, Natalie and Ed's daughter Carly was born just before ten o'clock that evening. Ed was beside Natalie the entire time, holding her hand and helping her focus and breathe.

Krys had also been with them the entire time. Now huge herself and on maternity leave for the past couple of weeks, she was exhausted, so she sat down to rest.

Darryl arrived shortly after the baby was born and stopped to kiss Krys on the forehead, then went to Natalie to have a brother-sister bonding moment.

As Darryl and Natalie hugged and talked quietly, Ed brought the baby to Krys to hold. "Thank you for being here with us today, Krys. It means the world to us. And thank you for keeping me calm on the phone this morning. I'm sorry I had to call you and wake you up," he said apologetically.

"You're so very welcome! I'm just happy to have been a part of things and that everything turned out so well!" Krys replied, looking down at the cute little bundle in her arms.

"You'll be here soon, won't you? You're due in a few days, right?" Ed inquired.

"Yeah, November 1 is when I'm due, but it's quite uncommon for first time pregnancies to deliver on their due date, but we'll see, won't we?" Krys grinned.

Ed stared down at his child, a soft smile on his lips as he walked over to Natalie in the hospital bed. "Look at what we made, Sweetcheeks," he declared.

Natalie smiled back, absolutely glowing. "I know! She's so cute!"

"Does it make you want one, Darryl?" Krys joked.

He looked over at his pregnant wife and replied, "Sure does."

CHAPTER 98

October 31, 1996

Krys & Darryl

Krys sat in her rocking chair in the nursery while Darryl finished handing out Halloween candy to the last few kids around eight o'clock in the evening. She had been having lower back pain and some mild contractions for the past five days since Natalie had given birth to Carly, but was otherwise totally convinced that she was NOT going to deliver on her due date.

She was wrong...

When Darryl got to the door of the nursery, he stood there for a few minutes watching Krys rock slowly back and forth. Her arms were wrapped protectively around her belly, her eyes were closed and she was humming softly. He moved towards her and knelt down in front of her, placing his hands on her thighs. She opened her eyes and smiled tiredly at him.

"What were you humming? I can't place it," Darryl asked.

"Oh, just a lullaby I made up," Krys replied. What she did NOT tell him was that it was "Princess", the instrumental song that she had created and played acoustic guitar on, the song that Rick included on Diamond Angel's first album.

Just then, her serene smile turned to a frown as a very bad cramp, make that *contraction*, hit her. She shut her eyes tightly and tried to breathe through it.

Darryl surged forward as Krys surged backwards in her chair, gritting her teeth through the pain. "Krys! What is it?!"

"Get my bag and let's go... it's showtime..." Krys grunted through the pain.

Thankfully, he didn't panic and got them safely to the hospital. Krys was taken directly into a delivery room with Darryl by her side.

It took several more hours until their daughter Julie came into the world at just after five in the morning on November 1, her due date.

Krys' parents came by in the morning after breakfast to see their newest granddaughter.

Lily made a huge fuss, as was expected. "It's altogether different when your own daughter has a baby. As much as I love my daughter-in-laws, I can't get as close to them as I can with you," she said, dissolving into tears of pure joy. She cuddled the baby and cooed at her, then wrapped her arm around Krys, hugged her close and whispered, "My Baby had a baby..."

Jack leaned over Krys in her hospital bed, kissed her forehead and smiled thoughtfully as he held the baby. "She looks like you when you were born, Caboose."

Krys closed her eyes and let the overwhelming love and emotion surround her.

Darryl's parents arrived next, excited to hold Baby Julie.

Audrey snuggled the baby and exclaimed, "A Girl! With Natalie having a girl, I'm going to have the most fun shopping for cute little dresses and such! I can't wait to get to the mall!"

Owen gently took the baby from his wife, looked at the tiny bundle in his arms and said, "She's a looker, that's for sure!"

What made Krys tear up the most was watching Darryl take their newborn daughter into his arms and cuddle her close, keeping her safe and secure next to his heart. He stood with her near the window and spoke in a quiet, low voice to their baby, every now and then looking over at Krys and grinning at her, his face shining with love and joy.

She was so blessed...

CHAPTER 99

December 1996

Natalie

The morning papers carried a very interesting front page headline two days before Christmas.

> *Tony DiAngelo, Lead Singer Of Winnipeg Band Diamond Angel, Marries High School Girlfriend Debra Hurney In Private Las Vegas Ceremony At The Little Chapel Of Love By An Elvis Impersonator*

Natalie closed the paper and felt a twinge of sadness as she called her best friend. "Kryssie, did you see the paper this morning?"

"Yeah, are you okay?" Krys asked sympathetically.

"I am, mostly. I would be an idiot not to be when I love Ed, am married to him and have his baby," Natalie rationalized.

"Yes, but you wanted this with Tony at one point, right?" Krys said quietly.

"I did," Nat agreed. "But I'm more than happy with the direction my life has gone. Ed is so good to me and such a fantastic father to Carly. I have no regrets at the way my life has turned out."

Ed walked into the kitchen cuddling Carly and smiled at Natalie. "Good to know," he said as he bent and kissed her cheek.

Natalie smiled at her husband and daughter, sighing contentedly.

CHAPTER 100

June 1997

Natalie

Natalie opened the morning papers to find another headline screaming at her.

> *Hometown Music Maker Tony DiAngelo And Wife Announce The Birth Of Their First Child Together, A Baby Girl Named Sabrina*

Natalie knew she shouldn't be upset, but finding out that Tony was first a husband, and now a father, upset her more than she cared to admit.

This time, it was Krys who called Natalie. "Nat, I just read it," she said empathetically.

"Yeah, I did, too. Kryssie, why does it feel weird? You and I are both married to other men, have their babies and are blissfully happy with them. WHY is it weird?" Natalie asked.

"I don't know. Maybe because at one time *WE* were going to be their wives and mothers of their babies? That's all I got," Krys answered.

"I suppose so," Nat replied, feeling pensive.

"Life sure does goes on, doesn't it?" Krys concluded.

She had no idea how true that would ring over the next bunch of years...

And headlines...

CHAPTER 101

December 1998

Krys

The same day Krys found out she was expecting hers and Darryl's second baby was the day the next headline grabbed her attention and actually made her cry.

> *Rick Sutherland, Lead Guitarist For Winnipeg Rock And Roll Band Diamond Angel Surprises Fans With Marriage Announcement To Local Photographer, Holly Lockhart*

Krys was sitting at the kitchen table with two-year-old Julie eating cereal in her high chair when Darryl walked in. He was holding something in his hand and smiling excitedly until he saw her face. "Kryssie, what's wrong? Why are you crying?" he asked as his huge smile turned into a frown, concerned at the mournful look on her face.

"It's nothing..." she lied.

"It is absolutely NOT nothing when you look like that! What's wrong?" he repeated.

"This…" she answered as she slowly opened the paper and showed him the headline, tears streaking down her cheeks.

His face softened as he wrapped his arms around her, kissing her cheek. "I'm sorry that his getting married hurts you Kryssie, but you had to expect this sooner or later. After all, *you* are married to *me* and we have a child together… and apparently another one on the way?" he said, letting go of her and waving the pregnancy test stick around in the air, his frown receding back into his previous huge smile.

Krys was momentarily speechless at Darryl's announcement. "Aren't I supposed to be the one who tells you this news?" she said, wiping her tears away and looking up at him.

"Yes. Why didn't you?" he asked, softly.

"I was getting ready to when the paper caught my eye. I'm sorry I wrecked this moment for us," Krys answered, her voice warbly, her gazed locked onto the floor.

Darryl pulled her back into his embrace and said quietly, "You didn't ruin anything. I know seeing anything written about him still sets you off and this one is a particularly hard blow to deal with. But can we put that aside and concentrate on the fact that you're pregnant again with our baby and I'm over the moon about it?"

Krys looked back up at him, smiled and reached up to kiss his lips, saying softly, "You're so good to me, Darryl. What did I do to deserve you?"

"Everything, Krys. Everything…" he responded, kissing her back.

CHAPTER 102

May 1999
Krys & Darryl

Krys and Darryl became parents for the second time on May 16 when their son Lucas was born.

Darryl was feeling quite smug at having a baby boy. He held up the tiny, squirming bundle to his face and stood at the window of their hospital room looking out into the morning light, murmuring incomprehensible words to him like he had when Julie was born.

Krys smiled tiredly and cuddled her daughter as she watched her husband bond sweetly with their son.

This is what I've always wanted...
A devoted husband to me and father to our children...
My life is so good, I'm so happy...

Darryl returned to Krys' hospital bed, climbed in beside her, wrapped his free arm around her and placed their newborn in her arms. He reached for Julie and cuddled her close, talking quietly to her about being a big sister and what her new responsibilities were going to be.

We're so blessed...

CHAPTER 103

August 1999

Natalie

Another announcement in the papers.

Diamond Angel Frontman Tony DiAngelo And Wife Welcome Second Child, A Boy Named Jonah

This set Natalie off since she and Ed were having trouble trying to get pregnant again. She couldn't understand why, since they had absolutely no problem the first time. And with Krys and Darryl having their second baby only a few months ago, it felt like fate was slapping her in the face. They were trying everything short of hormone shots, which was next on her list if nature didn't hurry it up and bless them with another baby.

She just hoped that she would conceive soon...

CHAPTER 104

February 2000
Krys & Darryl

Darryl came home from work on a Friday afternoon in late February, bursting at the seams with news he couldn't wait to tell his wife. "Krys!! Where are you?" he called from the front door, tossing his coat over the bench and kicking off his wet shoes.

"In the nursery with the kids," she called back.

Darryl took the curved stairs two at a time and bounded into the nursery as Krys finished diapering Lucas. Julie was sitting on the floor playing with blocks. He leaned down, picked his daughter up and swung her around, smiling joyously. He cuddled her close and kissed her soft, little girl cheek.

"What has got you so fired up?" Krys asked, smiling at her husband's obvious happiness. She tossed the diabolical diaper into the garbage, picked up Lucas and gave Darryl his son to cuddle. She went to the bathroom to wash her hands, then came back to the nursery to focus on Darryl's news.

He moved in close to Krys and whispered excitedly in her ear, "I... Made... Partner..."

Krys' mouth dropped open as she threw her arms around Darryl, Julie and Lucas, kissing him and jumping up and down in excitement and pride. "OHMIGOD! Darryl! That's incredible!" Suddenly, she let go and dashed to the phone. "Mom? Are you and Dad busy this evening? No? How would you like to have your delightful grandchildren for a sleepover?" Krys said, looking over her shoulder at Darryl, winking and biting her lip in sweet anticipation.

Darryl mouthed, "You are the best wife, EVER!"

Krys smiled back at him, then turned back to the phone. "You will? THANK YOU!! You're the best GrandMommy and GrandDaddy, EVER! Darryl will drop them off in about a half hour, okay? Love you so much! Bye!"

Krys and Darryl tag-teamed, with Darryl dressing the kids in their winter clothing while Krys packed their backpacks.

Darryl delivered their children to Lily and Jack and was back within the hour to find Krys posed seductively in their bed. There was an open bottle of Tequila on his nightstand and a tray on her nightstand that held a basket of strawberries and a bowl of whipped cream. She was leaning back provocatively into the pillows wearing a short, blood red satin nightie with black lace trim. She held her head in one hand while the other traced the delicate lace trim at the bottom hem, her legs bent at the knees. Darryl could see she wore nothing underneath the nightie...

"Congratulations, my most deserving husband. Now come and get your reward for a job well done," she purred seductively.

Darryl whipped off his clothes so fast he nearly strangled himself with his tie. He kept eye contact with Krys as he crawled up to her from the foot of the bed until he met her mouth and kissed her with wild abandon.

They spent the rest of the night naked together, relishing the alone time since they now had two kids and time like this was sparse and indeed precious.

We are so blessed...

CHAPTER 105

October 2000

Krys

Krys opened the morning papers to see the front page headline blaring at her.

> *It's A Girl! Diamond Angel Lead Guitarist Rick Sutherland And Wife Holly Welcome Daughter Anya*

She went numb, dropped the paper, closed her eyes and wept. Thankfully, Darryl had already left for work, so he wasn't there to witness her meltdown. Before she realized it, strong arms were around her and she was pulled into an embrace by Natalie.

"Oh Nat! I'm so glad you're here! How did you know I'd react like this?" Krys asked, her nose plugged and her voice nasal.

Nat smiled back sadly, "Because I know you and anything to do with Rick still hurts you."

"Why, Nat? *Why* does Rick still affect me like this when I'm so happily married to Darryl and I have two beautiful children with him?" Krys questioned, weeping loudly.

"It's the same for me and Tony. Maybe it's because it was simply our circumstances that led to our break-ups and nothing more sinister like infidelity? We still loved our guys and only split up with them because of our situations, not because we stopped loving them. That's all I can think of that makes any sort of sense to me," Nat explained.

Krys nodded her agreement. "That does make sense, but were you coming over here for another reason anyway?"

"Yup! I want to tell you something wonderful!" Nat said, pulling back from Krys, positively beaming at her.

Krys blew her nose and looked at Natalie's shining face, her expression turning from one of sorrow to inquisitiveness. "Oh? What could possibly..." Krys started, then it dawned on her. "OHMIGOD, NAT!! REALLY??"

Natalie's relieved smile was truly radiant. "More like *finally*! I'm due in May! Ed is absolutely beside himself!" she laughed happily as they hugged each other in exuberance of Natalie's long awaited news.

CHAPTER 106

April 2001
Natalie

And another headline appeared in the morning papers on April 11.

> *Diamond Angel Lead Singer Tony DiAngelo*
> *And Wife Debra Welcome Their Third Child,*
> *Son Joshua*

As Natalie read the headline, she felt a huge twinge in her enormous belly, then a hard cramp and a gush down her legs. "OH SHIT!! ED!! LET'S GOOOO!!" she screeched.

Ed rounded the corner, Carly at his heels. "What's the matter?" he said, then noticed the look on Nat's face and the wet mess on the floor beneath her feet. "OH SHIT!!" he yelled as he scooped Carly up and grabbed Nat's bag from the front hall closet.

They made it to the hospital quickly and Natalie was whisked away to the delivery room while Ed met Krys at the nurses' station. He handed Carly to her, asked her to call his parents to come to the hospital and dashed to the delivery room to be at Natalie's side.

Several hours later, Ed walked out of the delivery room with his arm slung around Krys' shoulders. They walked towards the waiting area where they saw Ed's parents Carol and Shaun, his sister Nancy, Natalie's parents Audrey and Owen, and Darryl with Julie, Lucas and Carly.

Ed was positively electric from head to toe, bursting with absolute joy at the news he was about to drop on his loved ones. "It's a BOY!! And a BOY!!" his excitement palpable as he yelled out, "WE HAVE TWINS!!"

Gasps went around the room at the news of the double surprise.

Carol and Audrey covered their mouths with their hands and began to weep tears of unbelievable joy while Shaun and Owen went to Ed and shook his hand, patting him on the back in fatherly congratulations. Nancy joined in and hugged her big brother, tears of delight in her eyes.

Krys went to Darryl and hugged him in exhausted happiness. "Did you know?" he asked, grinning and hugging her back.

"Nope! They didn't either!" Krys laughed.

Ed made the rounds getting hugs and hearty congratulations from his family, then they all filed into the delivery room and saw Natalie cuddling the two tiny bundles.

"Everyone, meet Andrew and Robert," Nat said proudly.

Ed sat on the bed beside her as Carly climbed up onto his lap. "They're fraternal, so hopefully we'll have an easy time telling them apart," he smirked.

Everyone gathered around to *ooh* and *aah* at the tiny babies and investigate all the differences between the two.

Later on, after everyone left, Natalie and Krys spoke quietly while the newborns snoozed in their bassinets. "You weren't due for another six weeks, Nat. What did it?" Krys asked.

"You mean, what did I read in the paper this morning that sent me into early labor?" Nat answered.

"I thought so," Krys replied.

"Do you realize that Tony and I both had a girl first and two boys after? Is that a cruel cosmic joke or what?" Nat griped.

"I don't know, but your twin boys are healthy and well, so let's just concentrate on that and try to put other stuff out of our heads, okay?" Krys suggested.

"You're right, Krys. We are blessed, all of us, aren't we?" Nat agreed.

CHAPTER 107

September 2002

Krys & Darryl

Darryl was at Krys' side holding her hand on September 12 when she gave a final push and their daughter Kayla was born.

Shortly after, their families piled into the delivery room to congratulate the happy, exhausted mother and ecstatic father.

Natalie stayed behind after the crowd left and sat on the edge of the bed beside Krys. "So, three kids, huh?" she grinned.

"Haha, funny coming from you, fellow mother-of-three," Krys joked.

"Do you think you're finished?" Nat asked.

Krys didn't hesitate to answer, "Absolutely. No more. We're done. What about you and Ed?"

"Not sure yet," Nat smiled.

"Are you pregnant again?" Krys eyes widened.

"No, but we're not ruling out having one more down the road," Nat admitted.

They looked at Krys' newborn daughter and sighed, happy and content with their lives and the journeys they were on, side by side as best friends.

CHAPTER 108

July 2005
Natalie

And yet another headline hit the front page.

> *One More Time! Tony DiAngelo And Wife Debra Welcome Their Fourth Child, A Son, Rodney, To Their Growing Brood*

When Natalie read the headline that morning, she barely flinched. It had been just over ten years since she and Tony had split, married other people and had children with said spouses.

Maybe time DID heal all wounds...

CHAPTER 109

August 2008
Natalie

Krys was working an evening shift on August 21 when she got the call that a special patient was coming in to deliver.

Natalie arrived not long after, clutching her belly and breathing through a strong contraction as Ed helped her into a wheelchair.

Krys beamed from ear to ear and launched into action as she followed them. "When did your contractions start?"

"About two... hours ago... Get me... into a room... QUICK! This kid's... coming... NOW!" Nat gritted as another contraction hit her.

Not fifteen minutes later, at just after six in the evening, Natalie gave birth to her and Ed's third son, a boy they named Nicholas.

Krys sat in a chair beside Nat's bed cuddling the baby and asked her with a cheeky grin, "So, are you done now?"

Natalie smiled, looked over at Ed and replied, "Yes. Ed's getting snipped next week."

Ed grinned, "Sure am. Four of these rug rats is enough! We already had to move into a bigger house after the twins were born and I don't want to do that again!"

"I agree. Plus the house you and Darryl built for us is perfect. I love it, and you," Natalie gushed.

Ed hugged Natalie close and whispered in her ear, "Thank you. I love you, too."

Natalie slept that night, feeling content and one hundred percent secure in her marriage, for the very first time.

CHAPTER 110

March 2011

Krys

Krys wasn't sure how she made it home in one piece on Monday after work.

Darryl, Julie, Lucas and Kayla greeted her with the usual hugs and kisses and happy yelling when she walked in the door.

"So, didja get it?" Darryl asked.

Krys' face broke into a victorious smile and she yelled out, "YES!" as she threw her arms out to the ceiling and twirled around in circles in the middle of their kitchen.

"Yay Mommy!" their three kids chorused.

"I'm so proud of you, Kryssie! You're going to make an excellent Manager. You've been working there for almost fifteen years and you know everything there is to know about labor and delivery," Darryl said as he crushed her to him and kissed her.

She was so, so blessed...

CHAPTER 111

May 2011

Natalie

Natalie picked up the phone on May 19 not expecting the news she received from the other end.

When the person finished telling her what she needed to be told, she dropped the phone and collapsed to the floor, devastated and catatonic. She didn't think she would even be able to cry and that's all she wanted to do, from now until her last breath.

When Ed had left for work that morning, he kissed her on the lips in his usual way – wet, deep and with promise for more to come when he got home from work that day.

But now, that wasn't going to happen.

Ever again.

Ed had been electrocuted to death on a job site less than an hour ago.

CHAPTER 112

April 2013

Krys & Natalie

The past two years since Ed's horrific and untimely death had been brutally difficult for Natalie. She was a widowed mother with four kids. Her parents Audrey and Owen, Ed's parents Carol and Shaun, Ed's sister Nancy, and Krys and Darryl helped out a lot, but all Natalie wanted was to turn back the hands of time and have her husband back.

Due to circumstances beyond her control, she lost the two men she'd loved. To say she was permanently pissed off was the understatement of the millennium, so when she opened the paper one morning in April, she scowled bitterly when she saw the headline.

> *Sad News For Fans Of Homegrown Rock And Roll Band Diamond Angel – Rick Sutherland And Wife Holly Divorce, Share Custody Of Twelve-Year-Old Daughter Anya*

She closed the papers and shut her eyes, let her head fall back and exhaled an exhausted sigh. Natalie was pretty sure that any minute now, Krys would be calling or coming over to discuss this latest bit of news with her.

That was one thing Natalie *was* happy about. Krys never let Natalie's being widowed and all the horrid shit that went along with that life-altering event change how she behaved towards her. She kept saying and doing the same things the same way around her and her kids. Krys wanted Nat to have some semblance of normalcy, if not for her kids, then at least a tiny slice for Natalie herself.

And right on cue, Krys came flying through the back door, her eyes wide.

"NAT! Can you believe the headline this morning? I... I'm... I just can't believe it!!" she stuttered.

Natalie welcomed the break from her monotonous sadness. She knew that Krys had followed Diamond Angel's explosively popular career over the past twenty years, especially anything to do with Rick. "Kryssie, why are you so upset at Rick's getting divorced? It has nothing to do with you, does it?" Nat asked innocently.

Krys' eyes opened wide and her mouth dropped open. "Natalie! How can you say such a thing! You know it does NOT! I haven't seen Rick in years!" she screeched with indignation.

"Don't get your panties in a wad, I'm not implying anything. I just wondered why you're so fired up about something that has nothing to do with you, is all," Nat explained.

"I can't help it. I thought that when Rick got married, he would make sure it was forever. He talked that way enough when we were together," Krys revealed.

"Well, shit happens, doesn't it?" Nat frowned. "Life throws us shitty fucking curve balls that completely decimate families and rip apart the hearts and souls of the wives left behind who were entirely in love with their husbands. I'm sorry that Rick's life hasn't turned out how he wanted, but his spouse is still alive. Mine is not."

"Natalie, I'm so sorry," Krys said quietly, getting up and walking to the back door.

"You don't have to leave, Krys. I'm not mad at you. I'm just having a bad day, today. I miss him... Both of them..." Nat said, then she broke down and wept.

Krys went to Natalie, wrapped her arms around her, hugged her close and cried with her.

CHAPTER 113

July 9, 2014

Krys & Darryl

The day before Krys and Darryl's twentieth wedding anniversary was a day Krys would never forget. She arrived home from work and walked into the house from the garage to whispers and giggles from her daughters, Julie and Kayla.

"She's home, Dad! Turn it on!" she heard her son Lucas call out to Darryl.

The house flooded with Eddie Money singing "Two Tickets To Paradise".

Darryl rounded the corner from the living room where the mammoth stereo system was blasting out one of Krys' favorite songs, waving some sort of paper at her.

She smiled happily, took the papers from her husband and kissed him while looking at a pair of airline tickets. Her mouth dropped open and the coincidence of the particular song blasting on the stereo was put into perfect perspective. "Darryl... what are these?" Krys asked slowly, her face in shock.

"Exactly what Eddie Money says they are – two tickets to paradise, with paradise being Tahiti, somewhere you and I have talked about going for a very long time," Darryl said smugly.

"Are you serious?" Krys asked, totally shocked, an enormous smile spreading across her face.

"Yup! Happy Anniversary, Kryssie!" Darryl answered, pulling her close and kissing her. "And here's the best part! You don't even have to pack because the girls already did that for you! And by the way, we DO leave tonight," he said as he dipped her back and kissed her passionately.

When Darryl lifted her back up, a flurry of questions started pouring out of Krys' mouth. "What about the kids? What about your work? What about MY work?" she rambled.

Darryl responded swiftly. "Our kids will be taken care of between our parents and Natalie, I can take off whenever I want since I'm a partner and I already fixed it with your boss a while ago. Now go upstairs and get ready. We leave for the airport in a little over an hour."

Krys just stood there, absolutely stunned. Darryl turned her towards the curved staircase and gave her a little push in the small of her back to get her going. She walked up the stairs with Julie and Kayla trailing her, chatting about all the sexy stuff they packed for Krys to wear. She was astounded that her husband and children were able to do all of this without letting anything slip to her.

Their flight to Vancouver left at seven in the evening and their connecting flight to Tahiti left at ten that same evening. Darryl had splurged for First Class tickets and at one point during their overnight flight, he and Krys became members of the elite Mile High Club, adjusting their clothes and giggling at not getting caught as they returned to their seats.

They landed in Tahiti on the morning of their anniversary and were whisked by private motorcar to their glass floored, overwater villa facing the dolphin lagoon where they enjoyed luxurious privacy for the next two weeks. They swam in the lagoon among the playful dolphins, turtles and other marine life, kayaked, paddleboarded, snorkelled and even learned to scuba dive.

Their meals were brought to them every day by canoe and fresh exotic flowers were placed in crystal vases throughout their suite every morning.

Krys and Darryl made use of all the square footage they had, making love in the whirlpool tub, in the shower, in the oversized king size bed, and even on the glass floor as tropical fish swam by underneath them. They also had a private shower outside on the private deck, where they had sex under the warm rainwater shower head each time after swimming in the lagoon.

Being away from their kids, their jobs and all responsibility made Krys and Darryl feel like teenagers again, just being together and having as much sex as they possibly could, everywhere they could. It was truly the most magnificent way they could have spent their twentieth wedding anniversary.

All too soon, it was time for them pierce the bubble and go home to their kids, their jobs and reality.

CHAPTER 114

September 19, 2014

Krys & Darryl

Krys pulled her SUV into the garage and dragged her exhausted body into the house. She settled in the living room on the couch, put her feet up and closed her eyes, hoping to catch a quick nap before the kids and Darryl got home. She got maybe ten minutes of shut-eye before the front door opened and her three noisy offspring bounded in, dumped their bags and ran to her as she lounged on the couch.

"Hi Mom, here's the mail," Lucas said, delivering the pile of post to her.

"Hey! Look at this! It's from... DIAMOND ANGEL!!! OHMIGOD!!! MOM!!! OPEN IT!!!" Julie squealed, her eyes growing like saucers with each word.

Julie looked exactly like Krys, so much so that they were often mistaken for twins. She was the same height, had the same long blonde hair and the same body shape, except Krys was curvier. The only difference was that Julie's eyes were a shade lighter than Krys' sapphire blue eyes.

Krys opened her eyes and looked at the envelope addressed to her. She was silent as she ripped the end open, tipped it upside down and investigated the contents. Out fell front row tickets and all-access pre-show get-together and post-show backstage passes for her, Julie, Lucas and Kayla for that night's final show of Diamond Angel's exceptionally popular, sold-out world tour. Also included was a note inviting them for dinner prior to the pre-show get-together, hand written in Rick's script.

Julie screamed at the top of her lungs, squeezed her eyes shut and dropped into a half squat, curling her fists to her chest. "YESSSSS!!!!!!!! MOM, WE HAVE TO GO!!!!!!!! PLEEEEEASE SAY YES!!!!!!!! OHMIGAWD!!!!!!!! I HAVE TO CALL CARLY!!!!!!!!!" She whipped out her cell phone from her back pocket and connected with her cousin, squealing with excitement.

Lucas glanced at the tickets and passes, shrugging his shoulders in feigned disinterest. "Cool. Are we gonna go?"

Krys looked at her handsome son, a carbon copy of his father, and replied, "Sure, if you want to, or you can stay home and entertain your Dad."

"No! I wanna go!" Lucas shouted, blushing at his girly excitement, making Krys laugh.

"Daddy's not gonna go?" Kayla asked.

Krys smiled wryly as she answered, "No, KayKay. Daddy's not a fan of Diamond Angel."

Just then, Darryl came in from the garage door and asked, "Hi my gorgeous wife and beautiful children, what's up for the weekend?"

Lucas pointed at the bunch of papers in Krys' lap. "Lookit what Mom got in the mail today!"

Darryl walked over, bent down and kissed Krys, then glanced down. He stood up, stared at the tickets and passes, asking calmly, "Are you going?"

Krys wasn't sure what to make of Darryl's icy tone of voice, so she answered carefully, "Yeah, the kids want to go, so I'll take them."

"Well then, maybe I'll see what Keith and Jeremy are up to. It's been a while since we've gotten together, just us guys," Darryl said as he pulled out his cell and texted his buddies.

The scream of delight that came from Julie's bedroom confirmed what Krys was thinking. "Hmm, I suspect that Natalie got a similar envelope in the mail today."

Krys' cell phone rang, the screen indicating it was Natalie, at the same time Julie came bounding down the stairs with her cell phone glued to her ear, talking excitedly to Carly.

"Hey Kryssie," Nat said, her voice smug.

"Hey Nat. Did you get a particular envelope in the mail today?" Krys asked.

"I sure did. Are we all going?" Nat replied.

"Yup. Except Darryl. He's going out with Keith and Jeremy," Krys answered.

Humor filled Nat's voice as she asked, "What color is his face right now?"

Krys laughed and replied, "Normal. Not green or red, like you're thinking. Did you get a handwritten note about dinner?"

"Yup. Tony's handwriting is still the same. We better get a move on if we're going to get there on time. Meet you there?" Nat said.

"Wait a minute, yours was written by Tony? Mine was written by Rick," Krys said out loud, making Darryl twist his head towards her and scowl.

Nat laughed loudly. "Oh boy, what the hell are we getting ourselves into tonight?!"

"Nothing crazy. Just a night out with some old friends and introducing our kids to their favorite band, who we happen to know," Krys answered as she stared directly at Darryl.

"Krys, I really need this night out. I'm so excited!" Nat admitted.

"I am, too. Go get ready and we'll meet you there?" Krys replied.

"You betcha! See you soon!" Nat said, hanging up.

Krys got up off the couch and corralled her children into her arms as she spoke. "Listen up, my three lovely children. We are going out for dinner with Diamond Angel, then to the venue for the pre-show get-together, then to the concert, to which we have front row seats, then after the concert to the post-show party. Now go get ready. We leave in one hour."

Lucas and Kayla smiled ecstatically at each other, then ran to their bedrooms to get ready for the night of their lives to end all nights.

Julie looked like she had died and gone to heaven. "Mom, you are the best, most amazing, coolest and most wonderfully fantastic Mom in the *entire Universe*!!! This has made my entire life!!! I LOVE Diamond Angel SO MUCH!!! Rick is my FAVORITE!!! And I get to meet him tonight, all because of YOU!!!" she squealed, launching herself at Krys and hugging her so hard she nearly squeezed the breath right out of her mother.

IN AND OUT OF LOVE

Darryl narrowed his eyes and waited to discuss their daughter's fascination/obsession with Rick until Julie left the room. "Krys, do you think it's wise to take our kids tonight? Especially Julie?" he asked, his voice deep and low.

"What do you mean?" she asked back.

"Julie is seventeen and is the *spitting image of you*. There are times even *I* can't tell you apart. And you're going to introduce her to her favorite band, her favorite member of that band *who you used to be involved with,* and who is single. Do you see where I'm going with this?" Darryl answered, gritting his teeth, trying to control his temper.

"What are you implying? Rick is a moral man, Darryl. So what if Julie looks just like me? And so what if Rick is single? It's not like he's going to go after our daughter because he can't have me. Get a grip!" Krys said as she got up from the couch and headed up to her bedroom to get ready.

Darryl was hot on her heels, closing the double doors to their bedroom behind them. Then he followed Krys into their closet and stared at his wife, who was still so obviously clueless about Rick. "Krys, just stay close to her, okay? Don't let her out of your sight. I lost you to him once and I'm NOT going to lose our daughter to him, too," Darryl pleaded.

Krys turned and looked Darryl in the eye, dropping the jeans she had in her hands. She walked over to him and placed her hands on his shoulders. He left his arms dangling at his sides, a dark scowl on his normally handsome face. "Darryl, our daughter is just a star-struck teenager looking forward to meeting her favorite band. And she has a boyfriend! Remember Liam? Now trust her and trust me. Go have a great guys' night out with your buddies and wish us a fabulous night out with our friends," Krys said, kissing Darryl on his cool, firmly-pressed-together lips, hoping to snap him out of his ridiculous freak-out.

She pressed herself close, trying to get him to lift his arms to wrap around her, hoping her breasts pushed up against his chest and her belly pushed against his dick would incite him to respond to her.

She was not disappointed.

Darryl weakened and wrapped his arms around Krys, softening his lips as she continued to kiss him. The passion they had for each other intensified as they stood in their walk-in closet and kissed lustfully, their three kids only steps away.

Once Krys was sure Darryl had calmed himself from his emotional meltdown, she pulled back, smiled at him and daintily licked his jaw up to his ear where she whispered, "I'll drop off our kids with Natalie after the party tonight, so you and I can pick up where we have to leave off now. But let me give you a preview of what to expect later," Krys said as she reached down between them and grasped Darryl's hardening cock, rubbing her hand up and down the front of his jeans.

He groaned, wanting more, as always, when it came to Krys. "Got time for a quickie before you leave me for the night?" he asked, he growled as he grabbed her ass and ground his pelvis into hers, making her breath hitch in her throat.

Krys laughed quietly, "I wish I did, Darryl. Just keep this feeling in mind and know that I'll finish when I see you tonight. Now let me get ready. I'm looking forward to seeing the rest of the guys after such a long time."

She disentangled herself from Darryl's embrace, turned back to the dark wash jeans she was going to wear and picked out a sexy, sleeveless, V-neck white silk blouse with a rich jewel-tone design.

Darryl stood back and watched Krys choose out her outfit thoughtfully, wondering who she was dressing up for more, him or her former lover, then shook that shitty thought right out of his head. He turned to leave so he could text Keith and Jeremy back about their evening out and hopefully deflate the raging hard-on Krys had given him...

Krys left her hair long and wild, added her sapphire jewellery and grabbed her small brown leather purse that went with her high-heeled brown leather ankle boots. Finishing her look with a sleek, dark brown leather jacket, she was ready.

Underneath her outfit she wore a white satin bra-and-panty set with royal blue lace trim that she chose especially for Darryl, quite certain that he was going to enjoy peeling it off her later. Just the thought of that made her shiver with ecstasy.

She went into her bathroom to darken her eye makeup and added deep pink lips.

When she came out of bathroom, their bedroom doors were open and she could hear Darryl talking with the kids. She went down the stairs to the kitchen where she heard all the noise coming from and was met with a chorus of sexy whistles.

"Wow, Mom! You're gorgeous!" Lucas said, proud of his mother's beauty.

Kayla ran to Krys, hugged her tight and said, "Mommy, you're so beautiful, I wanna look just like you and Julie!" Kayla didn't have far to go on that since she already did look a lot like Krys, but her blonde hair was more golden and she had Darryl's ocean green eyes.

Julie was busy on the phone, telling her boyfriend Liam about her plans for the evening. He seemed disinterested at being dumped in favor of a Rock Star...

"Thank you, my darlings. Let's go!" Krys smiled at her brood and ushered them out to her SUV.

Darryl followed behind, stopping her once the kids had gotten in and closed the doors, before she could get behind the wheel. "You do look gorgeous, Krys, you always do. Text me now and again and I'll do the same, okay? I love you," he said, pulling her close and kissing her jaw.

"Thank you, and I will. Stop worrying and go have a great night with the guys. I'll see you later, and I love you, too," she said, kissing him sweetly on his lips and breaking the embrace. She got in her driver's seat and backed out of the driveway, blowing kisses to Darryl as their kids waved at him. She hoped that their excitement would rub off onto him and improve his mood.

Things are so good between Darryl and me...

I just hope Rick doesn't pull something tonight and start a shit storm between us...

CHAPTER 115

September 19, 2014
Krys & Natalie & Diamond Angel

Krys drove to DJay's, a long-standing St James favorite, where Diamond Angel had commandeered the entire restaurant. She met up with Natalie in the parking lot with her kids Carly, Andrew, Robert and Nicholas.

Natalie was wearing dark wash denims, topped with a sparkly, deep green tank top and lots of silver jewellery, black stilettos, a black leather biker jacket and a tiny black leather purse. She fluffed out her wild auburn hair and did her face in vampy, gorgeous makeup.

"Nat! Holy shit! You look fantastic!" Krys smiled happily, glad to see Natalie shining with happiness after the last few years of misery and heartbreak.

"You look pretty good yourself, Kryssie," Nat smiled back, linking their arms.

They strode through the doors together, their gaggle of offspring trailing behind them with their collective mouths hanging open at seeing their mothers walk and talk in such a sassy, sexy way.

As they entered the restaurant, Tony and Rick were waiting to welcome them.

"Hi Krys! It's so great to see you!" Tony smiled happily and grabbed her in a bear hug.

"Hi Tony, it has been a long time," Krys murmured, hugging him back.

Rick took Nat by the hand and pulled her into his embrace. "Nice to see you, Natalie. I'm really sorry about your husband," he said quietly into her ear.

Natalie stiffened up for only a second, then relaxed into Rick's arms. "Thank you, Rick. It's been hard, but I'm a survivor," Nat responded.

Then it was time for the switch...

Tony let go of Krys and turned to Natalie. "Strawberry, it's good to see you," he said as he cautiously pulled Nat into a loose hug.

She hugged him back, melting at his use of the nickname he used to call her. "It feels good to be seen," she whispered into his ear.

Tony tightened his embrace around Natalie and they stood together tuning everyone else out.

Krys and Rick stood apart watching Natalie and Tony, knowing it was now their turn...

Rick turned to Krys with a warm smile on his face as he moved in front of her. "Kryssie, you look gorgeous, as always. It's really good to see you after so long," he murmured, holding out his arms, hoping that she would accept his greeting.

To his delight, Krys stepped into his embrace and looked up at his face, her lips parted. She placed her hands on his shoulders as he wrapped his arms around her back and she gazed at him with a soft look in her eyes, making his heart pound in his chest with excitement.

She still feels the same, after all these years...

"Hi Rick," was all she could utter softly, her breath caught in her throat as Rick gently tightened his arms around her. She turned her head to lay her ear on his chest so she could smell Rick's scent, took a deep breath and snuggled closer, her eyes closed.

He still feels the same, after all these years...

Rick closed his eyes and rested his cheek on top of Krys' head as he exhaled, joyous that he was holding his Princess again.

A collective sigh went around the room at the intense sweetness they were witnessing.

Both couples pulled away, then introductions were made between Tony and Rick and all of the teenagers – Lucas, Andrew, Robert and Nicholas, then Kayla, and finally, Julie and Carly.

Julie and Carly were floating on clouds of teenage lust as they got to meet their rock'n'roll idols.

"Rick, this is my daughter, Julie," Krys said as she hung her arm around her doppelganger.

Julie was star-struck for a split second, then did Krys proud and dazzled Rick with a beautifully warm smile as she said, "Hi Rick! It's so damn cool meeting you!"

Rick responded by staring at her, his eyes volleying back and forth between Krys and Julie. His expression shifted from a serene smile at just having held his Princess in his arms again after so many years, to utter shock at seeing her twin. "Kryssie, this is your *daughter*?" he asked, ignoring Julie for a moment.

"Yep. Uncanny, huh?" Krys said proudly.

"You can say that again," Rick murmured, then snapped out of it and held out his hand to shake Julie's, but decided to pull her in for a hug instead. "I'm glad to meet you, Julie."

The look of surprise and jubilation on her face said it all.

She was in lust...

Rick pulled Krys back into his embrace and hugged them both, feeling bizarre at holding these two gorgeous women in his arms.

Tony broke up the intensity, saying, "Okay ladies, the rest of the guys are waiting to see you and meet your kids. Let's go!"

He led the group around the corner into the restaurant to find Bryan, Alex and Diego with drinks in hand, impatiently waiting. The huge smiles on their faces was wonderful to see, making Krys relax as she ran to Bryan right away while Alex and Diego crushed Natalie between them from either side. More introductions were made, then everyone sat down to eat.

Dinner was a loud and raucous affair, nearly ending in a food fight. Krys and Natalie looked at each other, ready to bolt from the table if that happened as they remembered the last time they got into a food fight with these guys, so many years ago...

Julie and Carly were in another stratosphere, thrilled to be sitting beside Rick and Tony, their crushes.

So far, so good...
But the night is young...

CHAPTER 116

September 19, 2014

Darryl

While Krys and Natalie were out for the evening, Darryl hooked up with his buddies Keith and Jeremy. They hadn't been out for a boys' night in a long time, so when Darryl texted them, the guys jumped at the chance. They met at Hy's Steakhouse for dinner first, then for old times sake they went to ILLUSIONS to play pool, listen to the band play onstage and drink cheap beer.

When they walked in the door, Bon Jovi's "Lay Your Hands On Me" was blasting out of the speakers. They wound their way through the crowd of people to get their beers and noticed a familiar face tending the bar.

"Chuck! You *still* work here?" Keith said, shocked at seeing the guy behind the counter.

"Yup. I'm half owner now. Mickey needed someone he could trust as his partner in the business to keep things on the up and up and he thought I would be a good choice, which I am," he replied, ever humble.

"Good for you. You deserve a reward after putting up with his ass all these years!" Jeremy joked.

Darryl grinned in agreement and took a swig of his beer, then turned his head to look towards the pool tables. Their favorite one on the far end was free and the table closest to the doorway was busy with a game in progress.

Then his eyes swung to the middle table...

He could not believe his eyes when he saw who was draped over the arm of some drunk, oblivious, twenty-something guy, struggling to focus on aiming his pool cue, but failing miserably.

Cynthia... Fucking... Rockford...

"What the fuck did I do to deserve this shit tonight?" Darryl muttered to himself.

Keith and Jeremy turned their heads and saw who he was looking at, then looked up to the ceiling and prayed for the floor to open up and swallow her whole.

No such luck...

Just then, Mickey waddled around the corner from his office. Darryl stared, barely recognizing him. Mickey had gained a significant amount of weight over the last twenty-odd years and now was about as round as he was tall. "Boys! To what do I owe the pleasure?" he wheezed. "Haven't seen you in my fine establishment in many a year! Darryl, are you still married to that hot little blonde number, what was her name... uh, Krysten? What a delectable piece of ass she –" he started, but couldn't finish what he was saying because Darryl had him by the throat and pushed up against the wall.

"Do NOT speak that way about my woman. Ever," Darryl snarled.

At the melee, heads turned and to Darryl's horror, Cynthia disentangled herself from her drunken boytoy and sauntered over to stand right beside him. She looked terrible – scrawny, wrinkly and haggard.

"Darryl! Have you finally come to your senses and are here to take me home with you?" she chuckled drunkenly, laying her bony hand on his bicep.

Darryl recoiled at the stench of stale, unwashed body wafting from her. He would love to have zapped her with a witty one-liner, but she just wasn't worth it.

She never had been.

"Get away from me," was all Darryl could grit out.

Keith and Jeremy flanked him and stared at her, daring her to make another move or say something else stupid.

She didn't.

"Suit yourself..." she mumbled, turned and wandered back to the middle pool table, draping herself back over the drunk, oblivious guy.

Darryl removed his hand from Mickey's throat and let him down.

Mickey began coughing, sputtering and bitching about lawsuits.

"You aren't going to do a damn thing to me, Mickey. As I figure it, you still owe me for nearly ruining my life years ago and I don't feel like you're quite done paying yet," Darryl growled at him.

Mickey was still a weasel with no backbone, so of course he backed right down as he always had during any confrontation. "Sorry, sorry. Yeah, I should know better than to say something like that around you..." he trailed off, holding his throat and coughing as he wandered back to his office, still muttering to himself.

The music changed and Blondie began belting out "One Way Or Another".

"Let's just go play some pool, okay boys?" Keith suggested.

"Yeah, I'm gonna whip both yer asses," Jeremy joked, smirking because he had always been terrible at pool and still was.

"Rack 'em up. I gotta text Krys," Darryl said, pulling his cell out of his pocket and blasting off a quick text to his wife.

"Miss you... Having a good time with the guys. How's your night going?"

CHAPTER 117

September 19, 2014

Krys

After dinner, the rowdy and excited group left for the Bell MTS Place, affectionately nicknamed "The Phone Booth", for the pre-concert get-together. Tony, Natalie, Carly, Rick, Krys and Julie got into one stretch limo SUV and Bryan, Alex, Diego, Andrew, Robert, Nicholas, Lucas and Kayla got into the other.

When they arrived at the party room at the arena, Krys and Natalie were surprised to see who was waiting there for them...

Tony's wife, Debra, and their four kids, Sabrina, Jonah, Joshua and Rodney.

Rick's ex-wife, Holly, and their daughter, Anya.

Bryan's wife, April, and their three kids, twins Grace and Cameron, and daughter Tracy.

Diego's third wife, Margarita, and their son, Lorenzo.

There was no one there on behalf of Alex since he never had gotten married and didn't have any kids... that he knew of...

The introductions were made between all and the party launched into full swing.

Holly tentatively moved to stand beside Krys, looked her in the eyes and took a deep breath before speaking. "Krysten, it's nice to meet you in person. Rick has always talked about you so I feel like I know you. I can see why he fell in love with you and why it's been so hard for anyone else to get into his heart. I managed to get in there a little bit, but certainly not as deep as you did."

"Oh wow, Holly. That's a lot to take in since we *just* met," Krys replied.

"My apologies, I didn't mean to come on so strong and make you uncomfortable. It's just a bit overwhelming for me to meet the woman who Rick's talked about so much all these years," Holly admitted.

"Holly, what are you trying to say?" Krys asked, feeling queasy.

"I tried, Krys, but I could never live up to you, any part of you, and what you had with Rick. Part of why we divorced was because Rick has never been able to get you completely out of his head or his heart. Even now, I see how he's looking at you from across the room. I thought I would be enough for him, that I'd be the woman who would heal his heart. But as much as I tried, that just never happened. I'm seeing someone now who doesn't have the same kind of history with his previous love and I'm finally happy," Holly revealed, a sad inflection to her voice.

Krys looked at Holly and felt her stomach lurch as she replied quietly, "Holly, Rick and I were over a very long time ago. Yes, we were very close for a time, but for many reasons we just couldn't work and I married someone else, someone I am *still* married to. He's the same wonderful man whom

I've been completely in love with since the first time I laid eyes on him, before I ever knew Rick. And yes, it was hard for me to get over Rick, but I did, with the love of a good man, my husband. I'm so sorry that you didn't find what you wanted with Rick. I wished for that for him, that he would find someone to feel about, the way I feel about my husband. But I'm glad you have that now with your new man. I'd really like to be on good terms with you, if that's possible."

Holly looked Krys in the eyes and smiled a small smile. "I'd like that."

They clinked glasses as a tentative friendship was reached between the two women.

And as she started to relax, Krys forgot all about texting Darryl.

CHAPTER 118

September 19, 2014

Julie

Across the room, Julie was talking to Rick about writing and playing music. She was as gifted with instruments as Krys was, learning to play the guitar and piano from a very young age after listening to her mother play.

Julie tried to capture Rick's attention, but his eyes kept drifting towards Krys. Even though Julie had a boyfriend, she'd had a mammoth crush on Rick for the past several years, a crush that had only grown with time. Surprisingly, it didn't lessen when she found out that her mother and Rick were once a hot and heavy item.

And now that she'd finally met him...

And since she looked exactly like her mother...

Julie dialed up her flirting a few notches and moved closer to Rick, making sure that some part of her was touching some part of him at all times – her arm, her elbow, her hand, some sort of constant contact.

She flipped her hair, so like her mother's.

She fluttered her eyelashes, just like her mother.

She smiled her sweet, sexy smile, exactly like her mother.

But she wasn't getting anywhere because Rick was totally focused on Krys.

Dammit...

She was going to have to change her tactics.

Thankfully, her mother didn't seem interested in rekindling her previous relationship with Rick. Julie knew how in love her Mom was with her Dad, so maybe she stood a chance after all...

CHAPTER 119

September 19, 2014
Natalie & Tony

While Debra was busy reigning in their kids, Tony spent his time talking with Natalie. "Strawberry, I was really sad to hear what happened to your husband. I can't imagine..." he started.

Natalie's eyes clouded over as she replied, "Thank you, Tony. It's been really hard for me. He was a great man and I loved him with everything I had. A part of me died when he did."

Tony placed his arm around her shoulders, pulled her to his side and kissed her temple. Natalie let herself be hugged close by him, remembering how good it felt to be in his arms and how happy she had been with him.

Tony took a breath and blew it out through pursed lips before he spoke again. "Do you have anyone else in your life now? It must be tough being a single mother and raising four kids."

"No, I don't have the time. My brood keeps me busy, but I have a lot of help. Both mine and Ed's families are involved with the kids, but Krys and Darryl do the most for me. They take the kids now and again for the day and overnight sometimes, so I can have some *me* time," Natalie replied.

"So, no one special?" Tony repeated, giving her a squeeze around the shoulders.

"No, Tony, no one special. Where are you going with this?" Nat asked as she turned to him, his arm dropping off her shoulder to hang down by his side.

"Just asking, is all," he hedged.

"No, Tony, you're not *'just asking'*. You're asking for a reason, so spit it out, wouldja?" Nat said, slightly narrowing her eyes at him.

"Debra and I are splitting up," he began.

"What does this have to do with me not seeing anyone?" Nat pressed, sensing where he was heading with his line of questioning.

Tony leaned in so close, his lips brushed the hair beside her ear. "I still... love you."

Natalie stiffened, her mouth set in a thin line of disbelief. "You did not just say that to me with your wife not ten feet away from us!" Nat hissed, looking at him with disgust.

"Debra was my high school girlfriend, Natalie. I've known her for a very long time and I can tell when she's not happy. Neither of us are," Tony began.

"So what are you suggesting?" Nat asked.

Tony ignored her question and continued, "We've been separated for most of our marriage because of my career and we've grown apart because of it. She wants a man at home with her every night and I haven't been that for her. She's a good woman and I want her to find someone who can give her all I never could, what I always wanted to give to you. Remember?" Tony confessed.

Natalie began shaking. "Tony..." she said, closing her eyes.

"You don't have to decide anything right now. Just think about it and we can talk soon. But know this, Strawberry. Not a day has gone by in the past twenty years that I haven't thought of you, missed you and loved you," Tony declared.

He gave her a quick kiss on her cheek and left her side, going back over to where Rick and Julie were standing and talking. He hung his arm around Carly's shoulders and began talking with her, like a protective father might...

"Shit..." Nat breathed.

CHAPTER 120

September 19, 2014
Krys & Rick & Diamond Angel

"WINNIPEEEEEG!!!!!!!! It's time to welcome our boys hooooome!!!!!! As their final concert in their world tour, they've saved their best for last, their hoooome tooooown!!!!!!!!! Put your hands together and make some nooooise for... DIAMOOOOOND ANGEEELLLLL!!!!!!!!!!!!!!" the announcer yelled through the microphone.

Diamond Angel did not have an opening act. They had showcased local groups who had won "Battle of the Bands" in each city they played at throughout their tour, but they wanted nothing to take away from the hype and excitement of playing their final concert on home turf.

They went on stage at eight o'clock and were going to play until they were shut down, a "thank you" to the city that birthed the band and launched their careers.

The lights went out and the crowd went collectively insane.

The opening beats of "Ready, Willing And Able" began and a spotlight came on to highlight Diego on the drums.

A few strategic notes from Rick's guitar reverberated throughout the arena.

Alex's bass guitar held a steady, low, rumbling note.

Bryan's keyboards played in complement to Rick's guitar and Alex's bass.

All of them were now spotlit.

Except Tony.

He was nowhere to be seen...

Yet...

He started talking through the beginning of the song in a low pitched voice, not the words to the song that they recorded, but a heartfelt message from him and the band to the audience. "Winnipeg, we are so happy to be home and playing here for you tonight! Tonight is for our families, who have missed us over the past twenty years, for our friends, who have seen little of us during this incredible ride, and for you, our fans, some of you who have been with us since the first notes were played between us on stage at ILLUSIONS. Now, is everybody ready to ROCK???" Tony ended with his voice raised in excitement.

The din of the crowd was as loud as a 747 jet plane rumbling down the runway. The Bell MTS Place was filled to overcapacity at 17,500 fans, the largest crowd ever gathered for a concert there.

Tony began speaking the opening words of the song, but remained unseen.

Then, with a huge explosion, he was catapulted through a hole in the stage floor and onto the stage, the spotlights now illuminating all five members of Diamond Angel.

Krys, Natalie, Julie, Carly and the rest of their kids were front row center for the entire spectacle.

Diamond Angel played all of their hits from all ten of their studio albums from the past twenty-three years and were on stage for nearly four hours. Between Tony and Rick, they spent most of their attention singing various verses and choruses to either Natalie or Krys, seeing as most of Diamond Angel's songs were written about the two of them.

About two and half hours in, it came time to slow things down, so Rick stepped up to the microphone at center stage and looked straight down at Krys.

Wearing his trademark black cowboy hat, Rick dipped it at her in a gentlemanly gesture and smiled his dimply smile at her as he spoke to the crowd. "Many years ago, we recorded a song with a very special friend of the band. She's here tonight, right in front of me, as a matter of fact. I wonder if she'd agree to come up on stage and help me play it, this beautiful song she wrote and recorded with me all those years ago?"

The crowd went wild as Krys stood frozen to the spot, absolutely mortified.

Natalie turned to her, shook her out of her trance and shouted above the noise of the crowd, "Go, Krys! Do it!"

Rick and Tony both held their hands out to her in encouragement.

All she could hear was a bass drum beat and a deep voice chanting, "*Krys! Krys! Krys!*" coming from Diego. Then Alex and Bryan joined in and soon the entire arena was chanting her name.

She had no choice but to go and join them on stage, totally blindsided. Closing her eyes and exhaling in defeat, she just nodded her head in acceptance of the invitation. A huge, burly security guard lifted Krys into his arms and carried her to the stage where he reached up and planted her on the stage, boots first. Rick took one hand and Tony took her other, pulling her up until she was standing facing the back of the stage. They turned her around towards the crowd where she looked out among flashes of light, deafened by screams of excitement.

Then Krys looked down at Julie and saw the look of excited disbelief on her daughter's face. Julie smiled encouragingly at Krys and any backed-into-a-corner feeling she had simply vanished.

A roadie came up to her and handed her an amplified acoustic guitar while Rick got her settled on a bar stool with a microphone in front of her. He sat on his own bar stool that he placed beside her and was handed his own personalized, amplified acoustic double-neck guitar. He adjusted his microphone and settled himself into position to play as Tony moved off to the side where Bryan, Alex and Diego were standing, ready to give his voice a rest.

Then all the lights went out, except for one spotlight directed at Krys and Rick.

"Hi there. I'm Krys," she said into the microphone and strummed a D chord.

The crowd screamed their approval.

Rick spoke up while Krys acclimated herself, never having been on a stage before. "I have to tell you, I totally surprised Krys with this, as you can probably tell by her reaction. The song we're about to play is called "Princess" and I recorded her playing it without her knowledge. I just thought she had a beautiful, melodic voice and the music she created with that acoustic guitar I gave her would be a crime not to share with the music world."

As the crowd roared their excitement, Rick turned to Krys and winked at her. Then he smiled at her, his dimples and the cleft in his chin that she had always loved giving her strength to play. "Are you ready, Princess?" he said quietly while covering the microphone.

"Ready as I'll ever be," Krys replied, smiling sweetly at him, rocking him to his core.

I cannot believe Rick did this!

She closed her eyes and started strumming, remembering how to play the melody she'd created all those years ago. Even though she always hummed it out loud, she had never played it on guitar since the day Rick sneakily recorded her playing in his bedroom when they were together. The fretwork came back to her as soon as Rick started playing with her and she began humming softly into the microphone.

The song that should only have lasted one minute and forty-five seconds stretched into almost four minutes long. The crowd was beside themselves witnessing the beauty of the music created and played between two such talented people who so obviously cared about each other.

When they finished playing, Krys and Rick stood up from their bar stools, handed off their guitars to the roadies and wound their arms around each other in a warm, celebratory hug.

They received a standing ovation that lasted nearly ten minutes.

Before Rick let Krys go, he leaned down and kissed her cheek, then whispered in her ear, "I still love you, Princess. Never stopped, always will…"

Krys pulled away, staring at him as he led her to the edge of the stage and handed her to the huge, burly security guard who carried her safely back to her family in the front row.

He still loves me?

After all these years and everything we went through?

Natalie saw her face and immediately asked, "What did Rick say to you?"

Krys was dazed and couldn't respond. She was too busy reeling from what Rick had just confessed to her.

As the crowd began to settle down from beholding such an incredibly intimate concert moment, the rest of Diamond Angel came back on stage and launched into the most spectacular version of "Steel Horse", then kept playing for another hour and a half until nearly midnight.

Their encores were "Your Kiss Is The Drug", "An Angel's Smile" and they finished with the most hard rocking version of "Half Way There" they'd ever played.

When they finished playing the last notes of their last song, Diamond Angel came to the front of the stage and stood with their arms around each other's shoulders and waists, bowed to the crowd and blew out kisses from their hands.

Rick, Alex and Tony threw out guitar picks.

Diego threw out drum sticks.

Bryan threw out Diamond Angel concert t-shirts.

Then the lights came on and the concert was officially over.

Now it was time to *really* party!

CHAPTER 121

September 19, 2014

Krys & Darryl

Once everyone was backstage for the after-concert party, they all descended on Krys, complimenting her on her voice, her guitar playing and her good nature in going up on stage with no warning to play "Princess" with Rick. She was still stunned at what he whispered to her before she left the stage, but buried her reaction and accepted all compliments with grace and humility.

Then Julie got a hold of her mother. "MOM! I'm just... speechless! YOU are the one who created "Princess"? I had no idea! Why didn't you ever tell us? You were just so wonderful! I recorded it and sent it to Dad! I can't wait to see what he thinks of it!"

Krys was rooted to the spot with a combination of fear and fury. "Why did you do that, Julie? You know your Dad won't appreciate it," she hissed at her daughter.

Julie recoiled at her mother's anger and stammered, "I... I thought he'd be proud of you, like... like all of us are..."

Krys stepped back and closed her eyes, feeling like a total bitch. It was what Rick said to her that had her emotions in a total fluster and she was taking it out on her daughter. "I'm so sorry, JuJu, I'm still in shock that it even happened! It was just so unexpected," she said softly as she pulled her daughter into her arms, hugged her close and kissed her forehead.

Natalie and Carly joined the Mother-Daughter lovefest and burrowed into the hug, talking about the rest of the concert and what an amazing night it was.

Thankfully, there was no further drama or bombs dropped from either Rick or Tony as the party wound down around two in the morning. Many hugs and kisses were given and received among the group, phone numbers exchanged and plans formulated among the younger members of the crowd to start forging friendships.

Now that the tour was officially over, Diamond Angel was taking some time off to rest and regroup for the next several months. They had more than earned it.

Krys and Nat rounded up all their kids and drove to Natalie's house where Krys dropped off her three, then hightailed it home to Darryl. Thanks to Julie's innocent text message video, Krys was sure she was going to walk into a volcanic eruption, even though it was nearly three in the morning by the time she drove her SUV into the garage.

As she walked in the door, Krys heard the TV on in the living room. She ventured ahead, unsure of what she was going to find.

Darryl was sitting in the middle of the couch, asleep, with his cell phone in his hand. His head was tilted off to the side, resting on the back of the couch, and his legs were splayed out.

She noticed an opened bottle of whiskey on the coffee table, some poured into a shot glass beside it.

OH SHIT!!!

I completely forgot about texting him tonight!

I'm going to pay for that, too...

She leaned down, hoping that he hadn't drunk himself into oblivion. "Darryl, I'm home..." she whispered in his ear.

He stirred, slowly opened his eyes and turned his head to stare at his beautiful, talented wife. "I see that. Did you have a good time?" he asked, dropping his phone and reaching up for her.

Krys was apprehensive. She was expecting a blowout, but she got sweet and sexy instead, and that freaked her out even more. "Yes, I did. We all did. I suppose you saw the video that Julie sent you?" Krys asked hesitantly.

I'm in for it now...

"Sure did. I had no idea that you created that song. I've heard you hum it often enough over the years, so it was instantly familiar to me, but I didn't know anything else about it. Why didn't you tell me?" he asked her softly.

Krys was taken aback. This was the last thing she expected to be talking about with Darryl. "I guess it just never occurred to me. But, it's been a very prosperous song," she revealed.

"What do you mean?" Darryl furrowed his brow in confusion.

Krys exhaled, sat down across from him on the edge of the coffee table, took a big breath and revealed, "Because I created it and because it was included on Diamond Angel's album giving me credit for it, I've been getting royalty cheques from sales of it for the past twenty years."

Darryl's eyes couldn't have gotten any wider with surprise. "What have you been doing with the money?" he asked, totally blown away by her revelation.

"I've been putting some away for our kids University education, some for our retirement and some here and there on our mortgage, so we can pay it off faster. I also started putting some away for Natalie and Ed's kids for their education after Ed passed away," she admitted.

Darryl's facial expression turned from surprise to absolute adoration. He leaned forward so they were almost forehead to forehead and grabbed Krys' hands, saying, "That is the most selfless thing I've ever heard. You never cease to surprise and amaze me, Kryssie."

Krys exhaled in relief and smiled at her husband. "It was my creation, Darryl. I never expected it to go any farther than me playing it on my guitar for myself. I was shocked when Rick admitted he secretly recorded me and included it on their album. And even more shocked when it became an unexpected sensation. I'm proud of it and I'm glad that I've been able to do what I've done with the money I've earned from it."

"Now tell me about the rest of your night and I'll tell you about mine, since you were too busy to text me like I asked you to," Darryl asked, his voice taking on a slight edge.

Krys pulled back a bit and replied, rather icy, "I AM sorry I forgot to text you, Darryl, but I WAS kind of occupied, as you can see by the video. Did Julie send you just that video? Or did she send you a thousand pictures, too?"

"She sent me a thousand pictures, see?" he replied as he picked up his phone and started scrolling through the, *literally,* thousand pictures Julie had taken and sent to him throughout the entire night.

Krys tightened, hoping that Julie didn't capture any pictures that would incriminate Krys in any way and anger Darryl.

There weren't. She just sent a huge collection of fun photos from an amazing night out, of a large group of friends having the time of their lives.

"So is that what the whiskey is for?" Krys asked, indicating the opened bottle and shot glass.

"It was, but I thought I'd ask you about your night, first, to avoid a knock-down-drag-out fight if there didn't need to be one. Besides, I haven't told you about *my* night, yet..." Darryl hinted, pulling Krys off the coffee table and onto him to straddle his lap.

She tensed, waiting for the axe to fall as she settled her hands on Darryl's shoulders, then took a deep breath, closed her eyes and asked quietly, "And how was your night out with your boys, Darling Husband?"

"I saw Cynthia," was all he said.

Krys' eyes flew open and she tried to push away from Darryl, but he had a tight grip on her hips and held her firmly to him. "Why? Where did you guys go?" she asked, her body tight with tension.

"We met at Hy's Steakhouse for dinner, then went to ILLUSIONS to play pool and drink cheap beer. Chuck is still bartender and now owns half the bar with Mickey, that asshole," Darryl told her.

"What makes Mickey an asshole this time?" she asked.

"Because he was disrespectful to you and we got into a slight scuffle. I held him up by the throat against the wall and that's when she noticed me," Darryl recalled, grinning at his brawny strength and how shit-scared Mickey looked.

"And?" Krys gritted.

"She tried to come on to me, but I blew her off and she went back to the poor unsuspecting young fool she was accosting before she saw me. Keith and Jeremy and I drank cheap beer, I beat both their asses at pool and I came home to wait for you. End of story," he concluded.

"That's it?" Krys questioned disbelievingly.

"That's it. Now we both know about each other's evenings, and we avoided a potential fight in being open and honest with each other. Can we just go to bed now? It's late," he said.

Krys stared at Darryl, feeling like she was in another dimension. "You want to go to bed? To sleep?" she asked, her eyebrows up to her hairline.

"Yeah, I'm tired," he admitted, yawning to make his point.

"You realize we have the house to ourselves, don't you?" Krys pointed out.

"Yes, I realize that. Still doesn't change the fact that I'm tired and need to sleep," he replied.

"Wow... Just, wow..." Krys said as she backed off Darryl's lap and went swiftly up to their bedroom. She ignored him as he followed her up the stairs and into their closet. She changed out of her sexy outfit, even the lingerie she wore *just for him,* and into a vintage, well-worn and very well-loved Bon Jovi concert t-shirt.

She brushed past him and went to the bathroom to wash her face and brush her teeth, holding back tears the entire time.

He followed her in and watched her, silently brushing his teeth beside her.

When she was finished, she padded to her side of the bed, crawled in and pulled the blanket up to her ears. She lay on her side with her back to the middle of the bed, not sure if she wanted to laugh or cry.

What the hell?

Darryl NEVER turns down sex with me!

And we have the house to ourselves so we can get as loud and as wild as we want!

Darryl came to bed and crawled under the covers on his side, cuddling up behind Krys. She felt his hard dick pressed into her lower back as he kissed her cheek.

"What are you doing?" she asked in a monotone voice, nearing tears.

"I want to show you how much I love you. I know we both had emotionally charged evenings, heightened by telling each other about them with brutal honesty. I know we have the house to ourselves. I know you love me. I know we have a solid marriage based on trust and fidelity. And I want to have wild jungle sex with you, like we did on our anniversary a few months ago," Darryl said softly, giving her baby kisses along her cheek as his hand swept slowly up from her hip to her shoulder blade.

Krys closed her eyes and let out a tiny whimper in relief as a few tears seeped from her lids. She turned into Darryl's embrace and kissed him, her lips burning with passion and relief. "I thought..." she started.

"You thought what?" Darryl interrupted gently.

"You never turn down having sex with me and my mind wandered to dark places when you blew me off the way you did. It scared me," Krys admitted.

"Kryssie, I will *never* not want to have sex with you. *Ever.* I just needed to know that you still feel the same way about me as I do about you, after a night like this. You are the love of my life and I love you, with all of me, always. Now, come here so I can ravish you," Darryl explained as he smiled at her and kissed her again, this time more passionately.

No further words were needed as Krys and Darryl reconfirmed their feelings for each other with that searing kiss.

Darryl shifted them, laying Krys flat on her back and deepening the kiss. His hands trailed down her sides and under her t-shirt as he lifted it up and over her head, tossing it over his shoulder to the floor. "That's much better," he said as he reached for Krys' breasts.

Krys' eyes glittered, happy tears continuing to slowly crawl down into her temples as she reached up to kiss Darryl again, not wanting to break contact.

She lifted her leg, hooked it up over Darryl's shoulder and watched his lips break into a smoking-hot smile as his hand crept beneath the covers. He found her wetness and swiped a finger through it, carving a path for two fingers to find their way inside her. He thrust them in and out while his thumb found her nerve bundle, circling just the way he knew she liked it.

Krys was falling down a spiral of growing lust as Darryl began kissing her jaw, trailing his wet tongue down her neck to the base of her throat and dipped his tongue into the groove. Then he licked her jaw back up to her mouth while moving his hand on and in her below the covers.

In response, she grasped his rock-hard cock, moving her hand up and down smoothly as she rode the rising tidal wave of the orgasm Darryl was bringing on for her. He noticed she was getting close, so his tempo increased until she flew apart in an orgasmic frenzy, wrapping her other leg around his hip and grinding herself against his hand.

Darryl moved her hand away from his cock and positioned himself at her entrance, plunging in as Krys was still coming down from her orgasm. After only a few pulses in and out, he came in an explosion inside her, thrusting deep and hard, their heated tongues kissing and licking each other.

He gently lowered her leg from his shoulder and rolled them so she was on top. He wrapped his arms around her, holding them chest to chest as he thrust up from underneath her, still hard. Krys pushed up to a sitting position, her hands gripping his shoulders as she began to ride him, grinding into him. As she did this, Darryl's hand snaked it's way back to her sweet spot and resumed circling with his thumb while the other hand moved to her lower back.

Krys moved one hand down from Darryl's shoulder to feel where they were joined, thrusting in and out. He moved his hand from circling her nerve bundle to join hers between them, setting her off into the stratosphere with another orgasm.

Darryl sat up, moved his hand from between them and wrapped it in her hair, the other remaining at her lower back. He ground her onto him, harder and faster, until he saw stars with his next orgasm while kissing her feverishly.

Krys collapsed on top of Darryl, totally exhausted. Their arms were wrapped around each other, kissing softly and smiling lovingly at each other.

Darryl broke the silence. "Okay, now I'm *really* tired," he chuckled, burying his nose in Krys' throat.

She smiled back and laughed along with him. "Are you now?" she asked huskily.

Darryl pulled his nose out of her throat and looked up at her sparkling eyes. "Aren't you satisfied yet?" he asked, surprise in his voice.

"Kind of, but I still want more," she said, her voice raspy.

"*Kind of*, she says." Darryl laughed as he pulled her off him and sat them both up facing each other.

"What are you doing?" Krys asked, feeling disappointed.

"Don't worry, Kryssie, we're not done yet. I just want to try a different position," he reassured her.

Krys smiled and breathed out a relieved, "Oh good. What's next, Wild Jungle Man?" as she reached for his semi-hard dick and wrapped her hand around it's slickness, sliding up and down to revive it while cupping his balls and gently squeezing.

Darryl rose to his knees with an aroused shudder at her touch, removed her talented hands and turned Krys around so she was on her knees, facing the headboard, with her back to his chest. One hand reached up to hang onto him behind his neck and the other grasped the top edge of headboard to keep her balance.

He moved in and tipped her hips back so he could bury himself in her wetness again, one hand coming around her to grasp her breast, the other back to her hypersensitive sweet spot. Darryl thrust up as Krys pushed back onto him, their mutual heightened sensation climbing even higher at this new angle of penetration.

It didn't take long before their breathing changed and their tempo increased, another tsunami of an orgasm building its way through both of them. When Darryl felt it speeding up his dick, he held Krys to him and felt himself pulsate inside her as she convulsed around him.

Krys revelled in the feeling of being taken and claimed in such a carnal fashion, needing to feel that Darryl still felt that way about her. She sagged back against him, her head lolling back against his neck. Then she turned her head to kiss his jaw and smiled as she said, "Okay, I think I'm satisfied now."

Darryl sagged forward against Krys and grinned back at her as he replied, "Good, because you've drained me dry, Wild Jungle Woman."

He gently pulled out of her and they lay down on their sides, facing each other, to catch their breath. They held hands, reaching in close to kiss and nuzzle each other.

Shortly after, they fell asleep with their hands intertwined, feeling like they took an incredibly difficult test and passed with flying colors.

Which they did.

Bliss...

Pure bliss...

CHAPTER 122

October 2014

Krys & Darryl

Two weeks after the Diamond Angel concert, Krys woke up feeling sick to her stomach. She made it to the bathroom just in time and puked her guts out. "Damn, what a time to be sick. At least the rest of the house is over it so I can be miserable in peace," she griped to herself.

Darryl walked in and wet a washcloth, then knelt down beside her and handed it to her, saying sympathetically, "Your turn?"

"Yeah, I guess so," she replied, slumping over the toilet bowl.

"I'm not surprised. That flu hit us like a ton of bricks and you took care of all of us. I'm surprised at how long it's taken you to get it, though," Darryl said, helping her up.

They stood side by side in front of the mirror and for some strange reason, Krys glanced down at her belly. It protruded just a little bit and that made her do a double-take. Her hand flew to her mouth and her eyes grew wide with horror. "Darryl... I don't think I have the flu..." she whispered, her other hand cradling her belly.

Darryl's eyes widened as he caught on to what she was suggesting. "What are you saying?"

"I'm going to take a pregnancy test..." she answered.

"Aren't you still on the Pill?" he asked.

"I was... But when we went to Tahiti for our anniversary I didn't have my pills, which means I didn't take them the entire time, and we had *A LOT* of sex!" Krys shrieked, her face a mask of absolute terror.

"Holy shit..." Darryl rubbed his hand down his face. "And you haven't taken them since then?"

"No! I was finished that pack before we left and was waiting for a refill. When we got home, we were so wrapped up with the kids and everything else, I just *forgot*! How could I *forget* about something *so important?!* We're *too old* to be having another baby!!!" Krys cried hysterically.

Darryl pulled her into his arms and held her as Krys trembled. "Kryssie, it's not like we're teenagers and this is going to ruin our lives. We're happily married with three great kids. This is definitely an unexpected surprise for both of us, but we'll deal with this together like we always have," Darryl declared, feeling grounded in spite of the incredible bombshell he and Krys had just uncovered.

"How can you be so calm about this? I'm *freaked way the fuck out*!" Krys whispered, clutching onto Darryl, her eyes wild with anxiety.

"Because I love you and this kid was definitely made out of love, planned or not. Kinda makes me wanna beat my fists against my chest, that I can still knock up my woman," Darryl laughed.

"How can you joke about this, Darryl? I'M PROBABLY PREGNANT!!!" Krys cried as she struggled in his arms, tears escaping her eyes and falling down her cheeks.

"Kryssie, seriously, it's not the end of the world. You're healthy and so am I. We have a beautiful home, three healthy kids and money in the bank. We're going to be fine. This is not as bad as you think it is," Darryl laughed as he hugged her close, tucking her face in his neck.

"So you're not angry?" she said in a tiny voice into his throat.

"No! How can I be? We had lots of fantastic sex and made another baby. It happens sometimes. It's not quite where we expected to be at this point in our lives, but it's not the end of the world, either," he pointed out, kissing her cheek.

"You are something else, you know that?" Krys told him softly, the tension in her body easing.

"Yeah, I know. You tell me often enough," he said as he smiled smugly, cuddling her close to him.

"We're having another baby..." Krys and Darryl murmured together.

Actually, he DID have an ulterior motive for being so happy about this unexpected pregnancy...

Maybe now Rick will stay away from Krys and lay my fear of losing her to him to rest...

CHAPTER 123

October 2014
Krys & Natalie

"ARE YOU SERIOUS??" Natalie screeched into the phone. "YOU'RE PREGNANT???"

Now that it was confirmed and she was used to the idea, Krys sighed in acceptance, "Yup. I'm about twelve weeks along and due around mid-March. Now Darryl and I have to sit the kids down after school and tell them. Mr Potent practically floated out of here this morning when he left for work. It was disgraceful," Krys smiled at the memory.

"Mr Potent!" Natalie snorted, then asked, "Can I tell Tony?"

Natalie and Tony had rekindled their love the day after the Diamond Angel concert, realizing that they just couldn't be apart anymore, even after spouses, children and more than twenty years of separation. Nat had told Krys of Tony's declaration of love for her and his impending divorce, then Krys had told Nat what Rick said to her after they had finished playing "Princess".

What a turn of events, for both of us!

"Not yet. Let Darryl and I break the news to our kids first. But if you slip, Tony has to promise NOT to tell Rick. I want to tell him myself. His daughter Anya and our Kayla have become pretty good friends, and Holly and I are on good terms. How weird is that?" Krys told her.

"Kinda weird. Tony and Debra are keeping their separation civil and amicable for their kids sake, for my kids, and to keep me out of it, even though she knows that he and I are back together. But I feel bad, Krys. I was so in love with Ed, so happy with him and then so devastated after he died," Natalie's voice cracked, but she powered through. "I'm happy with Tony. I was so tired of being sad and moping around. I feel reborn being back in his arms and his bed again. Then I look at my kids with Ed and I feel like I'm cheating on his memory," Nat confessed.

"Natalie, you've been widowed for a few years and you're still young. You shouldn't be expected to stay single with as much love as you have to give. And with Tony already being separated from his wife *before* you reconnected, getting back together with him shouldn't make you feel bad. It happened the way it was supposed to. Just grab it with both hands and hold on for one hell of a ride," Krys encouraged.

"You're right. I just needed to hear someone else say that," she replied.

"Anytime. I can hear the kids and Darryl downstairs, so I gotta go and potentially ruin their lives now," Krys said sarcastically, hanging up and getting off her bed, unsure of how this news bomb was going to be received by her three kids.

CHAPTER 124

October 2014

Krys & Darryl

Krys barely made it two steps away from the bed after hanging up with Natalie when she saw Darryl smiling smugly at her in the doorway.

"Did you see your doctor today?" he asked as he walked towards her.

"Yes," she answered as she backed away from him until the backs of her legs hit the mattress.

"And is it confirmed?" he asked, reaching her and wrapping his arms around her, pulling her close.

"Yes," she repeated as Darryl kissed her softly on her lips. He stopped abruptly, pulled his face back and stared at her for a moment before bursting out laughing.

"What's so funny?" Krys asked, annoyed.

"You were already pregnant the night of the concert!" he blurted.

Krys recoiled, utterly mortified. "I was, wasn't I?"

"And then we had wild jungle sex that night and I thought wouldn't that be hilarious if I got you pregnant!" Darryl started laughing.

Krys had to admit, it was a *tiny bit funny* and she started to laugh with him. "You've got a twisted sense of humor, you know that?"

"Sure do!" he said as he laughed even harder. Then Darryl squeezed Krys gently around her waist and asked, "Ready to tell our kids our news?"

"Yeah, let's go," she said, kissing him.

CHAPTER 125

October 2014

Krys & Darryl & Julie & Lucas & Kayla

"YOU'RE HAVING A BABY? THAT'S SO AWESOME!" Kayla screeched.

Lucas' reaction was more laid back. "Cool. Hope it's a boy to balance things out around here."

They stood side by side in their living room, Darryl's arm around her shoulders and Krys' arm around his waist, united in sharing their happy news with their children.

Julie's face was impassive until her lips bloomed into a smile and she threw herself at her parents, hugging them happily. "That's such fabulous news! I'm so excited!"

As their brood of three wandered off in different directions, Krys said, totally surprised, "That went better than I expected."

"Hmm, I was pretty sure at least Julie, or even Lucas, was going to go down the *'Ew, Mom and Dad had sex'* route. Then I'd have to pull Lucas aside and explain to him the joys of sex and you'd have to do that with Julie and Kayla, in your delicate condition," Darryl said as he dissolved into fits of laughter.

"Guess who's not getting laid until after this baby is born… and maybe not even then," Krys threatened, throwing Darryl's arm off her as she walked into the kitchen and opened the fridge.

Darryl feigned terror. "No! Say it isn't so!" he gasped in horror as he fell onto the couch, laughing his ass off.

"Yeah, Darryl, laugh now, but when you cuddle up to me in bed tonight expecting to get some, you'll be disappointed," Krys muttered.

Darryl got up off the couch, still laughing, and came up behind Krys, now standing at the sink, washing vegetables. He hugged her, kissed her neck and said, "What if I accost you in the bathroom and take you when you're brushing your teeth?"

"Then you'll get a face full of toothpaste foam," she replied brusquely.

"Come on, Kryssie, what's with the prude bit? We had lots of sex when you were pregnant with our other kids, so what's the big deal with this one?" Darryl said as he rocked against her.

"When we were having our other kids, they were all young and didn't know what sex was. Now they all do, and the thought of them knowing we do it and how good it is kinda skeeves me out," Krys shuddered, staring out the kitchen window into the back yard.

This sent Darryl into even more peals of laughter. "Kryssie, if our kids end up having even *half* as good a sex life as we have, they'll be blissfully happy their entire lives!"

"Stop talking about our kids having sex!" Krys shouted as she plugged her ears.

Darryl let go of Krys and hung onto the counter, doubled over, he was laughing so hard.

Lucas came into the kitchen, opened the fridge and asked, "What's Dad laughing at?"

Krys answered in a disgusted tone, "You and your sister's future sex lives."

Lucas slammed the fridge door, looked over at Darryl wiping tears from his eyes and said, "Dad, seriously?" then walked out of the kitchen with an appalled look on his face.

Darryl was nearly on his knees laughing as Krys fired at him, "Way to go, Darryl, you've managed to creep out our son."

"Oh no! Does that mean I don't have to have *The Talk* with him after all because he's too grossed out?" he said as he started laughing again.

Krys rolled her eyes at him. "Can we stop talking about this now? I don't want the girls to come in and be emotionally scarred by all this sex talk and creep them out, too!" Krys scowled as Darryl laughed even harder.

"Okay... sure. What... were we... talking about... before?" Darryl said in between breaths as he tried to stop laughing.

"We were talking about me and this pregnancy. I'm forty, Darryl. I'm in good shape, but am I going to be able to take off all the baby weight this time? It's going to be a lot harder and what if I gain a lot more because I'm older? What if I don't lose any of it? What if you don't find me attractive anymore after this baby is born?" Krys said, tears forming in her eyes.

Darryl stopped laughing and his face became serious as he said, his voice low and soothing, "Krysten, you're just as beautiful as the day I married you. You were beautiful when you were pregnant with our other three children and I was all over you after you gave birth to them, so what makes you think you'll be any different to me this time around? I'll be more than happy to help you work off the baby weight with lots of sex, like we did with our other kids, and I don't see that changing unless there's a medical reason for us not to. Plus, you work out every day and are already in great shape going into this pregnancy, so please, stop worrying and let me kiss my gorgeous, pregnant wife, okay?" Darryl reassured her.

"Okay," Krys said quietly, allowing Darryl to come back to her and kiss her sweetly. She moved into his embrace and tried to let his positive vibes leech into her, but she just couldn't shake this horrible feeling of foreboding...

CHAPTER 126

October 2014

Krys & Darryl

A week after finding out that she was, indeed, pregnant again, Krys and Darryl decided to spend Friday evening at home watching TV, cuddled together on the couch. Their kids were out with various friends for the evening – Julie with Carly, Lucas with his friends from hockey and Kayla at a sleepover with some of her school friends.

Krys heard a car pull up to their house and automatically assumed it was Natalie and Tony coming by for the evening as they had planned.

Then the doorbell rang.

Krys started to get up to answer the door, but Darryl stopped her. "Don't get up. Nat always rings twice and walks in. It's not her. I'll get rid of whoever it is."

"Okay, thank you," Krys said as she lay back and stretched out on the couch. Then she heard raised voices, so she got up to investigate. What she saw when she reached the door turned her blood to ice.

Darryl and Rick were standing face to face, snarling at each other like wild animals.

Krys saw Rick's face over Darryl's shoulder. The look on it was pained and miserable.

"Princess, you're pregnant?" Rick whimpered when he saw her.

Krys stood rooted to the spot, unable to move.

Darryl whirled around and snapped, "Stay back, Krys. He has no right to be here."

Krys didn't appreciate Darryl's domineering tone and glared at him, saying angrily as she moved between them, "You will not dictate who I can and cannot speak to. Let me deal with this."

"Princess..." Rick started to say.

Krys cut him off, exasperated. "Rick, drop the *'Princess'* bit, okay? I was that to you once, but I haven't been in a long time. What are you doing here? Natalie and Tony are coming over and I don't need any drama from you," she demanded.

Rick looked like she just pierced his heart. "Kryssie, you're pregnant," he repeated mournfully.

"Yes, I am. How did you find out?" Krys snapped, losing her patience.

"Your Kayla told my Anya," Rick admitted sadly.

"Shit," Krys said through clenched teeth.

As Krys and Rick were having their showdown in Krys and Darryl's front foyer with the door wide open, Natalie and Tony turned into the driveway. They saw Rick's black BMW SUV parked on the street in front of the house and immediately sensed trouble. Natalie leapt out of her black Jeep Grand

Cherokee and ran to the front door, skidding as she heard the conversation in progress.

"Kryssie, you're having another baby... with him," Rick said, sadly.

"Well, of course it's *with him*! Darryl's my husband! Who else would it be?" Krys said angrily, feeling her blood pressure rising.

"It could have been ours... Remember?" Rick divulged.

Krys blanched and her step faltered as she whispered, "Why are you bringing this up right now? In my home? In front of my husband?"

Darryl caught her around the waist and demanded, "What is he talking about, Krys?"

Krys had always hoped and prayed that her first pregnancy, the one NOT with Darryl, but with Rick, would *never* be brought up again in her lifetime.

How wrong she was...

Tony came up behind Natalie and caught the last bit of the conversation, then took control of the situation that was fast spiralling out of control. "Okay everyone, let's move this into the house behind closed doors. The neighbors don't need to hear this," he said as he stepped between them, Rick on one side of him, Krys and Darryl on his other side. Tony closed the door and they all stood in the front foyer, the negative air palpable.

"Krys, you better tell me what he's talking about, *right now*," Darryl gritted as he turned to his wife, placed his hands on her shoulders and looked into her eyes expectantly.

"I'll tell him, Krys," Rick started.

Krys screeched, "NO! He's *my* husband. *I'll* tell him."

"Tell me what?" Darryl said, his voice a low, angry rumble.

Rick blurted it out before Krys could pull herself together. "Krys got pregnant with our baby when we were together, but she had a miscarriage."

"RICK!" Krys cried out, fury and terror combining in her blood.

Darryl turned to stone, his voice a lethal whisper. "Is this true?"

His grip tightened so hard on Krys' shoulders that she cried out, "Darryl, let go! You're hurting me!"

Rick moved in and tried to pry Darryl's hands off her, but Darryl shook him off and growled, "Don't you touch me. And don't you *ever* touch my wife or you will regret it."

Krys pleaded, "Rick, back off! This is between Darryl and me."

"Kryssie, you never told him?" Rick paled.

"No, I didn't," she answered.

"Why didn't you?" Darryl asked as he eased his grip on Krys' shoulders.

"Because it happened when we were broken up and had no bearing on you and I," Krys tried to explain.

"But it sure did, didn't it? I remember how freaked out you were well into all three of your pregnancies with our babies, and I could never figure out why or what to say to help you feel better about it. Everything sure makes sense now, though. What a fool you must have thought I was," Darryl shook his head and let his arms fall from her. He grabbed his phone, wallet and keys from the table by the front door and stormed out of the house, taking off in his SUV.

Krys was left with her mouth hanging open, Natalie and Tony standing behind her.

Rick stood with his hands dangling at his sides, clearly feeling horrible. "Kryssie…" he started, but he was interrupted.

"Rick, you need to take off. Go now, before more shit falls out of your mouth that you can't take back," Tony said quietly.

Rick turned to go, but before he took a step, he turned back to Krys and said, "If you need me, call me. I'll be here for you in a flash, Princess," then he walked out the door as Tony closed it behind him.

Krys stood in the middle of her front foyer and wondered who in her lifetime she pissed off so badly to have her life cave in as fantastically as it just had.

CHAPTER 127

October 2014

Darryl

Darryl found himself sitting at the bar in ILLUSIONS, nursing a beer with an empty shot glass of whiskey resting beside his bottle.

Chuck mopped up a spill and asked Darryl, "What's up with you tonight, dude?"

"Nothin' I wanna talk about," Darryl answered, his head hung low.

Darryl couldn't figure out why he chose to go to ILLUSIONS, the scene of several shitty episodes in his life.

Then *she* walked up to him and placed her hand on his arm.

Cynthia... Fucking... Rockford...

"Why is it every time I'm in a bad mood, YOU show up?" Darryl bitched, not shaking her hand off him.

"Because we're meant to be, Darryl. Stop fighting it and just go with the flow, huh? Something keeps bringing you back here and that something is ME. So, wanna get it on, Big Boy?" Cynthia suggested, moving in closer to him.

Darryl looked at her and felt a rush of anger bubble up through him at Krys.

HOW could she have kept such an important thing from me?

She didn't cheat on me, it happened when we were apart...

Thankfully it didn't affect US getting pregnant...

But look how freaked out she was and how it strained our marriage by her shutting me out until she passed a certain point and she let me back in!

All because of the pregnancy she had with HIM that she miscarried!

AND NEVER TOLD ME ABOUT!!!

For the second time in his life, Darryl made a life-altering, soul-destroying decision, one that he could never change or take back.

CHAPTER 128

October 2014

Krys & Darryl

Darryl parked his Lincoln Navigator in the driveway of his house just after seven the next morning. He was hung over and still in a bad mood, but willing to talk things over with Krys. He decided not to tell her that he had just woken up in Cynthia's bed, because if she knew that, she'd throw him out and start divorce proceedings before the door closed on his ass.

He walked in and spotted her asleep on the couch, curled into a ball. She had tissues strewn about her and her face was puffy from having been crying. A lot. He went over to her and shook her gently. "Krys? It's me."

She lifted her lids and a dark, hateful look stole across her heartbroken blue eyes. "Get out. Take your cheating ass and get the fuck out," Krys said, her voice hoarse.

"What are you talking about?" Darryl feigned ignorance to buy some time.

"Look at your text messages, then get out," Krys fired back as she sat up and blew her nose.

Darryl did just that and narrowed his eyes in absolute fury as he saw pictures of himself *in bed with Cynthia*. "What the fuck?" he ground out.

"Get... the... fuck... out..." Krys repeated.

"Krys, you don't understand," he said lamely.

"Are you really going to hand me that line? Get... the fuck... OUT!" she hissed at him. "You can contact your lawyer for visitation with our kids."

Darryl was stunned as he registered what had just come out of her mouth. "Krysten! What are you saying?! We have to talk about this!" Darryl insisted.

"The time for talking was last night before you walked out on me and cheated on me with HER!!! Now GET OUT!!" she shrieked.

"Stop yelling, you'll wake the kids," Darryl said loudly.

"They're not here, so get the hell out of my house!" Krys fired back.

"Krysten! I didn't fuck her! Yes, I saw her at ILLUSIONS and went home with her. And yes, I intended to fuck her, but I couldn't do it. I passed out in her bed and she must have taken those photos with my phone and sent them to you. I'm telling you the truth! Have I ever lied to you?" Darryl explained, desperate for her to believe him.

Krys was thoughtful for a moment, then said, "No, you have never lied to me, but you HAVE revenge-fucked *her* before. Now, *get the fuck out of my house!*" She stomped her way upstairs with Darryl right behind her and slammed their bedroom door in his face.

Then he heard her crying, loud, wracking sobs that made his heart break because they were walking through this nightmare again, something he never thought they'd repeat.

Darryl turned and walked slowly down the stairs and out the front door to his SUV. He phoned Keith and told him what happened.

"Darryl you gotta stop fucking up your life. You have a good woman and yes, she had a devastating thing happen to her with another man, but I think she was right not to tell you, because *look at you*! You've made a fucking mess of things by flying off the handle, *again,* and doing it by involving Cynthia, *AGAIN*! What the hell is the matter with you when it comes to her? Give Krys some time to calm herself, then try talking to her again in a day or so. Since you were truthful with her and did NOT fuck the Skank Queen, then she'll come around. She loves you," Keith laid out for him.

"Okay, I get it. Leave her alone and wait for her to come around," Darryl repeated. He just hoped it wouldn't be too long before that happened.

CHAPTER 129

October 2014

Krys & Natalie

As soon as Krys heard Darryl leave, she called Natalie and told her what happened.

"I cannot believe what I'm hearing," Nat replied. "Do you need me?"

"No, Nat, I need to be alone. Can you keep the kids, though? Thank you for taking them last night. I just can't cope with this and have them here right now," Krys said through fresh tears.

"Of course Krys. Call me later, okay?" Nat said softly.

"I will," Krys promised.

When Krys hung up with Natalie she made a second phone call, one that would have repercussions, the likes of which she would never have thought possible...

CHAPTER 130

October 2014
Krys & Rick

When the doorbell rang just after one in the afternoon, Krys answered it wearing navy yoga pants and a light pink babydoll tee with no makeup, wild hair and bare feet.

She looked beautiful.

Rick drank her in as the door opened and he noticed her blotchy, yet still gorgeous face. "Princess, let me hold you," he said, stepping into the doorway as Krys moved into his arms and collapsed, sobs tearing up through her chest.

"Rick... how *could* he?" Krys wailed into his neck.

"What happened, Krys? Tell me," Rick said, his voice soothing to her ears as it always was.

"Darryl... Cynthia..." she sobbed.

"Did he sleep with her?" he asked carefully.

"He says he didn't and he's never lied to me, but how can I trust him? We've been down this road before with her!" Krys cried.

"Princess, I'm so sorry this is happening to you. You don't deserve to be treated this way. Let me take care of you..." he begged.

Krys was so angry and hurt by Darryl's betrayal, she was going to do the one thing that would be sure to annihilate their marriage.

She was going to let Rick back in her life...

And her bed...

Reaching up to kiss him felt natural to her. Even though she hadn't kissed him in over twenty years, when their lips met, it was like no time had passed at all.

Rick leaned down to capture her lips with his own, his arms winding around her body. He pulled her close and deepened their kiss as she tilted her head to accommodate his mouth on hers.

The passion that was once between them reignited instantly. Krys pulled away from Rick, grabbed his hand and led him upstairs to her bedroom. The thought of sleeping with another man in the bed she shared with her husband hit her for a split second, then she pushed that thought right out of her head.

Rick was overflowing with happiness at getting to be with his Princess again after so long. When he was married to Holly, he liked to lavish her with love and affection, but he always wished in the back of his mind that she was Krys. The day Holly told him she was pregnant, Rick thought about the day that Krys miscarried their baby. After Anya was born and Rick held his daughter for the first time, he looked into her beautiful dark brown eyes, so like his, and wished her mother was Krys.

No love in his life compared to his love for Krys.

When they got to the door of her bedroom, Rick stopped her and asked, "Are you sure you want to do this? There's no going back once I've got you naked in my arms again, Princess."

I want this so much...

My Princess back in my life...

She turned to face him, drew him close into her arms and said clearly, "Yes, Rick. I'm sure."

Am I really going to do this?

If I do, my marriage to Darryl will be over...

He closed the double doors behind him and Krys closed the window coverings until they were cloaked in near darkness. They moved towards each other and began kissing again slowly, the heat building between them.

Krys' hands moved in opposite directions, one hand spearing up through Rick's hair, the other down to feel his hard-on pressing against the front of his jeans.

Rick's hands wound around her, one hand cupping the back of her head, the other pressing the small of her back into his pelvis.

Then the kissing and groping grew more intense. Rick's hands went under Krys' baby tee, pulled it off over her head and dropped it onto the floor. He hooked his thumbs into the waistband of her yoga pants, peeled them down her legs and dropped to his knees, allowing her to step from each pant leg while holding onto his shoulders for balance. He rose up and kissed his way from her lower belly all the way up to her jaw, then pulled her to him and kissed her with fiery passion.

Dazed with long-buried lust, Krys managed to reach her hands under Rick's t-shirt, lift it up over his head and toss it away, joining hers on the floor. She unbuckled his belt, undid the top button and lowered the zipper on his jeans, then slid them down his thighs. As he stepped out of them, she remembered that he never did like wearing anything under his pants...

Rick undid the clasp on Krys' white lace bra, slid it down off her arms and flung it across the room. Then he pushed her back onto the bed, her eyes glittering with desire for him. She was still wearing her white lace bikini panties, but he had plans for those...

Krys moved up to the top of the bed and Rick followed, but he stopped when his face was in line with her panties. He bit the edge and dragged them down her legs, keeping them in his teeth as he pulled them off her heels, one at a time. He crawled back up her body, tickling her with the lace from her panties hanging from his mouth. When he reached her face, he dropped them to the floor and took her mouth with savage lust.

Krys was so turned on by Rick's carnal behavior, she whimpered, "Rick, I need you inside me."

Rick smiled as plunged his tongue into Krys' mouth at the same time plunging his hand between her legs. She was drenched for him. He swiftly removed his hand and replaced it with his hard cock, sinking deep into her slipperiness, all the way to the hilt. He began rocking back and forth, in and out of her, kissing her and savoring her softness, her warmth and her sweet taste.

Krys was feeling a flurry of emotions. She felt so right being with Rick again, but it suddenly hit her, *hard,* what she was doing, and she began to withdraw from Rick.

Rick could feel Krys' mood change, so he eased his thrusting and spoke softly to her, "Kryssie, talk to me. What's wrong?"

"I'm breaking my marriage vows right now," Krys said softly as she started to cry.

"That may be so, but does this also feel right?" Rick asked her.

Krys considered that question and answered thoughtfully, "Yes, it does."

"Then just feel it. Feel it with me and let go. Enjoy how you feel, being loved by me," Rick told her in between kisses and thrusts.

Krys let go a ragged exhale and did just that. She let go of her worries and allowed herself to feel loved by Rick.

Picking up his tempo, Rick brought her legs up around his hips and she wrapped her arms around his back. He leveraged himself on his forearms and knees and pounded into her, trying to wipe away her fears, worries and sadness.

It worked.

When Krys' orgasm tore through her, it was as powerful as it had been when they were together more than twenty years before, causing Rick to erupt into her and groan in ecstatic satisfaction.

They stayed locked together until they both stopped trembling, then he pulled out gently and they lay face to face in each other's arms.

Rick smiled a genuine smile.

I have my Princess back!

Krys smiled a fake smile.

What have I done?

CHAPTER 131

October 2014
Krys & Darryl

On Sunday morning, Darryl pulled up to the house he shared with Krys and noticed a black BMW SUV in the driveway that he didn't recognize.

Whose vehicle is that?
One of her brothers?
I hope Krys is in a better mood today so we can talk...

He let himself in the front door and heard music playing – Bon Jovi's "Born To Be My Baby". As he rounded the corner into the kitchen, his blood turned cold as he saw Rick sitting at the table with Krys in his lap. They were reading the comics in the weekend paper and laughing together. "*What the FUCK is this?*" he thundered.

Krys glanced up, looked him directly in the eye and said, "What are you doing here? I thought you'd be with your girlfriend. You don't belong here anymore. GO."

"Did you fuck him?" Darryl asked through gritted teeth.

Krys replied, "Yes. Several times, as a matter of fact. In our bed, in our bathroom, on the stairs and a few other places that I'm going to have bruises from," she taunted.

Darryl exploded with fury. "*YOU'RE PREGNANT WITH MY BABY!!!*"

"*And you walked out on me!* You've made your decision about me, our marriage and this baby. Now leave. You're putting a damper on our Sunday morning together. You can talk to my lawyer about seeing our kids," Krys said, turning her head and dismissing him.

"Are you for real? Krysten! I told you I did NOT sleep with her!" Darryl yelled.

"That may be true, but you walked out on me and went straight to her, whether you realize it or not. I'm done with this conversation. And you," Krys said, her eyes never leaving the comics in front of her.

"I can't fucking believe this," Darryl snarled as he shook his head, turned on his heel and walked out.

Rick had been silent through the entire exchange between Krys and Darryl, but finally spoke when he heard the front door slam shut. "Princess, are you okay?"

"No, not by a long shot, Rick. But I will be as long as I have you beside me," Krys said, kissing him.

"I'm so sorry it's come to this between you and him. I never wanted to break up your marriage," Rick said apologetically.

"You didn't, Rick. Darryl did by letting his hair-trigger temper run riot, then by walking out on me, all the way to *her*," Krys seethed.

"I'm going to do everything I can to help you get through this, Princess," Rick vowed.

Krys smiled at him, kissed him and said, "I know you will, Rick. You'd never hurt me like that."

"No, I wouldn't," he agreed, smiling to himself as she snuggled deeper into his lap.

I finally have Krys...
She's all mine...
Finally...

CHAPTER 132

October 2014

Darryl

An hour later, Darryl's SUV pulled into the visitor parking lot of an old, dilapidated apartment block. He got out and found himself at the front entrance where he rang the buzzer.

Cynthia let him in the building and pulled him by the collar into her suite when he reached her door. "I knew you couldn't stay away," she cackled.

They fell into bed and Darryl felt nothing as he fucked her. He was numb and she was just a receptacle for his angry dick, a means to an end.

When they were finished, all he said to Cynthia was, "You want me? You got me."

She smirked with satisfaction and mentally rubbed her palms together with pure glee at getting the prize she had coveted for over twenty years.

CHAPTER 133

October 2014
Rick

Darryl called Krys' cell phone a little while later and spoke quickly when she answered. "I wanted to let you know that I just did what you accused me of. I fucked Cynthia, so we're even. How does it feel to know the love of your life just ruined your life, *again*. See you in divorce court," he spit out at her.

Krys didn't utter a word as she hung up the phone, silent tears coursing down her cheeks as Rick held her close and let her cry.

He had heard the one-sided conversation and felt bad for how brokenhearted she was, but he was happy it happened.

Now she was totally his.

This time, for good.

CHAPTER 134

October 2014
Krys & Rick

One week later, Krys stood at the door watching as Rick brought the last of his boxes into the garage from his SUV. He officially moved in as Darryl officially moved out the night before.

Never in her wildest imagination did Krys think her life would be on this trajectory – pregnant with her estranged husband's baby and living with her former-now-current lover.

She just wanted to crawl into a time machine and zap herself back to... she didn't even know when. Her time with Rick had been unforgettable, but Darryl? He was her first love. He was the man she'd loved the most, the fiercest and the longest. Her heart was in utter turmoil and she had to get a hold on it or her pregnancy would be in jeopardy. Suddenly, she felt incredibly protective over her belly and spanned her hands over her tiny baby bump.

Rick came up behind her, wrapped his arms around her and settled his hands over hers. "Are you happy, Krys?" Rick asked.

"Yes, but I'm just thinking about this baby and what the next several months have in store for us," Krys answered, smiling sadly.

"Are you scared?" he asked.

"Very much so. Of a lot of things," she admitted.

Rick turned her in his arms and said, "You have me beside you, Princess. And I will be with you every step of the way."

Krys' smile turned from sad to happy. "I know you will be. And I'm thankful for you," she replied.

"Let's go inside. You're shivering and that can't be good for you or the baby," Rick suggested.

Krys allowed Rick to lead her inside to their bedroom, where he lay her down on the bed, covered her with her favorite throw blanket and closed the blinds. He left her to have a nap in peace and quiet, but she couldn't sleep. She couldn't stop thinking about her marriage being over, being back together with Rick and how conflicted she felt about all of it.

She emerged from her bedroom around four in the afternoon and wandered downstairs to the kitchen to find Rick talking to her kids in a fatherly fashion. They didn't see or hear her, so she was able to listen to the entire conversation while she was tucked out of sight around the corner.

Rick was explaining to them about him moving in, without going into details that they didn't need to know.

Krys rounded the corner as Rick was finishing and smiled at them as she asked, "Hey everyone, what's for supper?"

Rick smiled warmly at Krys and said, "The kids have offered to make supper today. Lucas is barbecuing steak, Kayla made a spinach salad and veggie skewers, and Julie made dessert – lemon meringue pie with a graham cracker crust, your favorite," Rick recited.

Krys' eyes tears up. "You remembered," she whispered.

"Of course. That's something I'd never forget..." he winked at her, remembering what they had done one time, many years ago, with the remaining pie after they had eaten their fill.

Krys also remembered what they did and blushed...

Julie caught the wink and the blush, then huffed out *"Gross"* before turning her back and flouncing out of the room to call Carly and dissect the situation.

Lucas and Kayla went to the living room to watch TV before supper.

"Julie has a huge crush on you, Rick. I think she might be jealous of me," Krys said, concerned.

"Julie isn't you, Krys. YOU are who I want in my life and in my bed," Rick declared, hugging her.

"Good to know," Krys smiled, hugging him back.

CHAPTER 135

October 2014

Darryl

As Darryl packed his things to move out of the house he had designed and built for him and Krys to live in together for the rest of their lives, he felt a knot of disgust and fear slide through him.

Never in his wildest imagination did Darryl think his life would be on this trajectory – his estranged wife pregnant with his baby and living with her former-now-current lover.

Cynthia was nothing like Krys, in *any* way.

Krys was beautiful, Cynthia was not.

Krys was a great cook, Cynthia was not.

Krys was sweet and loving, Cynthia was not.

He left his house key behind in the kitchen counter and moved into Cynthia's small apartment. He unpacked in about ten minutes.

He was numb. He lost his wife and was without his three fantastic children. And he would probably not get much of a chance to know the one on the way.

His life was shit. He had to figure a way out before his anger completely consumed him.

He cracked open a fresh bottle of whiskey, sat down at the kitchen table and started drinking, taking sip after sip as he tried to think of a way to fix this mess. Before he knew it, almost half the bottle was gone.

Cynthia came into the kitchen a while later and found Darryl staring straight ahead, his eyes bloodshot and half closed, a frown on his lips and a furrow in his brow. "Whatcha doin', Stud? Hey! You didn't wait for me to crack that baby open!" she cackled, grabbing the bottle out of Darryl's limp grasp and taking a huge swig.

He looked up and stared at her in disgust and revulsion.

How could I ever have fucked THAT???

He got up from the table and moved to the couch where he lay on his side, covered up with a ratty throw blanket and closed his eyes, praying for a dreamless sleep.

All that filled his head was nightmares.

CHAPTER 136

November 2014

Krys & Julie

The first of November was Julie's eighteenth birthday. It was Saturday and Krys planned dinner with the family before Julie went out with her University friends for the evening.

That morning, Krys woke up earlier than usual and went into Julie's bedroom to watch her oldest child sleep. Before she realized it, her slippered feet carried her to the bed and she crawled under the covers, pulling Julie into her arms and cuddling her lovingly. Tears formed in her eyes and crept down her cheeks as she hummed softly to the Birthday Girl.

"Mom? Why are you crying?" Julie asked sleepily.

Krys stopped humming and smiled at her first-born. "Because, eighteen years ago today, you were born. And the very second I saw you, after the very second I heard you cry, I fell completely in love with you," she whispered.

"Oh Mom," Julie whispered back.

"Your Dad was the first to hold you after you were born, but you were with me from the very beginning. I got to feel you moving and kicking from inside me. No man can ever experience that," Krys said, thinking about Darryl holding their newborn daughter by the window after she was born.

Then Krys started to hum "Princess".

Julie hugged Krys back and started to cry a little, happy to be sharing such a deep emotional experience with her mother. "Mom, are you and Dad ever going to get back together? I can see you're happy enough with Rick, but I see how sad you are, mostly, especially being pregnant with Dad's baby. And Dad is totally miserable without you," Julie confessed.

Krys stiffened at Julie's perception. "I don't think so."

"Why not?" Julie questioned.

"For several reasons, Julie," Krys said, not wanting to get into it with her daughter.

"Can you please tell me so I can understand?" Julie asked.

Krys sighed, then chose what she wanted to say very carefully. "Firstly, there's a lot more to this situation than you and your brother and sister don't know, or will ever know, because it's none of your business to know. Secondly, it's your birthday and we need to think about that instead, okay?" she answered, kissing her daughter's forehead, then crawled out of bed.

"Okay," Julie agreed.

"See you downstairs for your birthday breakfast bash in thirty minutes, okay Birthday Girl?" Krys said, smiling as she closed the door.

Julie got up, got ready and made it down to the kitchen just in time for Krys, Rick, Lucas, Kayla, Lily and Jack to start singing Happy Birthday to her.

"Gramma! Grampa!" Julie squealed when she saw her grandparents, hugging them happily.

"Happy Birthday, Julie, my beautiful granddaughter!" Lily said as she kissed her on her cheek.

"Happy Birthday, my Julie-Girl," Jack said, kissing her other cheek.

The birthday breakfast bash was a delicious success and Julie spent the rest of day on the phone making plans for her birthday evening out with her friends.

She also talked to her dad on the phone in the afternoon and when she asked him the same question she asked her mom in the morning, he answered, "I don't know, JuJu. It's for your Mother and I to figure out, so get it out of your head. Go and have a great time with your friends tonight, okay?"

"Okay, Dad," she replied, trying not to think about the shambles her home life was in and how much more crazy it was going to get.

CHAPTER 137

November 2014
Rick & Julie

Krys was busy making Julie's birthday supper.

Julie was sitting on the sofa beside Rick as he watched Krys whip around the kitchen. "Rick, does it bother you that Mom is gaining weight?" Julie asked.

Rick turned his head towards her and frowned. "Julie, your mother is pregnant. She's supposed to be gaining weight. And she still looks as beautiful as the first time I laid eyes on her. She always will, no matter what size she is, pregnant or not."

"Oh, okay," she said quietly.

Rick turned to face her, placing his hands on her shoulders to get her to pay attention to what he was going to say to her. "Look Julie, I'm with your mother now. I've waited a long time for this and I'm happy. In fact, I'm the happiest I've ever been. I know you're sad that your mom and your dad aren't together, but you need to accept that this is the way things are now. I'm flattered you have a crush on me, but what you want to happen between us will *never* happen. I can tell you that with *absolute certainty*. I love your mother. ONLY her. No one else. So, whatever you got cookin' up in your head, just drop it, okay?" Rick said gravely, hoping she would get the message.

"But –" Julie started, but Rick cut her off.

"No, Julie. You have a boyfriend. He's a nice guy and he's good for you. Not to mention he's the perfect age for you. Listen closely and pay attention to what I'm telling you. *This is never going to happen between us*, got it?" he said, exasperated.

"Got it, Rick," Julie said, crushed.

CHAPTER 138

November 8, 2014
Krys & Rick

Krys' forty-first birthday started with a bang.

Literally.

She woke up with one of Rick's hands between her legs and the other on her breast, rolling her sensitive nipple between his talented fingers. Her back was to his chest and she ground her hips into his pelvis in acknowledgement. Rick replaced his hand with his cock, sliding it into her wetness. He swept his fingers over her skin up to her face, cupping her jaw and turning her head so he could kiss her while he drove into her.

"Happy Birthday, Princess," he sang softly, thrusting in and out of her.

Krys was unable to focus on anything other than the mammoth orgasm building up inside her. Right on cue, she began spasming around Rick, bringing on his orgasm as he pushed all the way into her. She moaned breathlessly, "Oh, Rick..."

Hugging her to him, Rick whispered in her ear, "I love you, Princess."

Krys was floating on a cloud of post-orgasmic bliss and answered, "Love you, too, Rick."

Rick smiled joyously, feeling like he won the biggest lottery in history. He hadn't heard Krys say those words to him in over twenty years and they sounded magnificent!

They stayed locked together for a while, then Rick gently pulled out and turned Krys to face him. "What do you want to do today, other than stay in bed and let me have my way with you?" he asked, kissing her.

"Just that," Krys sighed as she closed her eyes, her lips tipped up at the corners.

Rick lowered his hand and placed it lovingly on her baby bump. She was now about four months into her pregnancy. "How's baby?" he asked, rubbing her belly.

"Baby's good. Baby likes the attention... OH!" Krys' eyes shot open and she smiled radiantly.

"What is it? Is there something wrong?" Rick asked, panicked.

Krys stilled his hand on her belly, placed it into the right position and covered it with her own. "Do you feel that?" she asked, grinning widely.

"I... feel... like, a flutter?" he responded.

Krys breathed happily, "That's Baby moving!"

Rick was dumbstruck with emotion. He had missed most of Holly's pregnancy with Anya, so he was excited to get to experience this one first hand with Krys. Despite the sad fact that he wasn't the biological father, he was going to be a father to this baby in every other way that mattered.

CHAPTER 139

November 2014

Darryl

Darryl's hand hovered over his cell phone. He wanted to call Krys for her birthday.

Ever since he moved out a few weeks ago, his thoughts all revolved around her. But he knew that things between them right now were just too raw and any verbal contact might just blow up into an all-out battle royal.

Still, he was totally lost without her.

Moving in with Cynthia was the biggest mistake he had ever made. She was a slob, loud and irritating as hell. He'd even stopped fucking her just after he moved in, he was so disgusted with himself and how his life was turning out.

Moving back in with his parents or any of his friends, who were all married, was out of the question, so he was stuck where he was. He could move into an apartment, but if he did that, it would seem too permanent. He was still holding on to some scrap of hope that Krys would ask him to come home to her and their kids.

It burned him that Rick was living in their house and sleeping in their bed, taking care of Krys while she was pregnant with Darryl's baby, behaving like it was his own.

He felt like he was at the bottom of a pit with no escape imaginable.

He *had* to find a way to make things right...

CHAPTER 140

December 2014
Krys & Darryl & Natalie & Tony

The week after Natalie's birthday, Tony's divorce was finalized from Debra. It had been amicable and they were just hammering out visitation and financial details.

Tony had moved in with Natalie the very next day.

The day after the papers were signed, Tony slid a two carat, diamond cluster engagement ring onto Natalie's left hand. "Strawberry, I know this is a long time coming, but will you marry me?" Tony asked as he dropped onto one knee.

Natalie threw her arms around Tony's neck and screamed, "YES!!!"

They were married two days before Christmas by a Justice Of The Peace in Natalie and Tony's living room. In attendance were Bryan and Diego with their wives and kids, Alex, both sets of parents, Tony's four kids, Tony's siblings with their families, Krys and her kids, and Darryl, who came alone.

Darryl tried to catch Krys alone, but Rick was always beside her with an arm slung around her shoulders. She studiously ignored him, keeping a protective hold on her now six-months-pregnant belly.

"Fuck it... She's *still married* to *me*..." Darryl murmured under his breath as he walked up to Krys and spoke quietly to her, "You look really good, Krys. Is Baby okay? Are you feeling well?"

As Krys turned her head to him, her smile fell away and was replaced with a broken, sad frown. "I'm fine, so is Baby," she clipped briefly, then turned away from him and reached up to whisper something into Rick's ear.

"Krys, this baby is a part of me, too. I still have rights, despite what's going on between us," he said quietly.

"Then talk to your lawyer and he'll talk to mine. But we are not going to talk about this here, today, *at your sister's wedding*," Krys hissed, without even turning her head.

Darryl took the hint and moved away from her towards his three kids to spend some time with them.

I can't believe what a shit show things are...

How are we ever going to get back to where we were before everything went to hell?

CHAPTER 141

January 8, 2015

Krys & Darryl

One week after New Year's, Darryl celebrated his birthday alone because he was avoiding Cynthia at all costs. Besides, he never told her when his birthday was, anyway.

He went to work that morning and spent a good day there with his business partners and staff, receiving texts from his children, sister, niece and nephews. But he really wanted to see Krys. He texted her and asked if he could drop by after work to see their kids and thankfully, she agreed. That put a spring in his step and got him through the rest of his day.

After work, he drove to the house and parked on the street, like a visitor. That made him burn with anger, but he swallowed it and put on a happy face. After all, he was about to see Krys, and he hadn't seen her since Natalie's wedding. She would be about seven months pregnant now. Her belly would be big, round and totally beautiful, and he wouldn't get near it. Of that, he was sure.

When Krys was pregnant with their three kids, Darryl couldn't keep his hands off her belly, lovingly touching her all the time, putting his ear to her tummy, then being silly and pretending that the baby kicked his cheek away when it was being really active.

He was missing all of this and Rick was getting to have it.

And that burned him the most.

He rang the doorbell and Kayla swung it open, screaming happily as she jumped into his arms. "Daddy! You're here! Happy Birthday!" He caught her and smiled, kissing her cheek and hugging her close.

Lucas and Julie met him at the door, giving him hugs and kisses, too.

Then Krys rounded the corner from the kitchen. She looked gorgeous in a flowing, pale blue chiffon dressing gown and her belly was as big and round and beautiful as he expected for her being in her seventh month.

"Happy Birthday, Darryl. The kids were hoping you'd stay for supper. They made all your favorites, just for you," Krys said softly.

He looked at their kids and his throat got tight.

My kids...

"I'd love to, thank you," he said, his voice heavy with emotion.

They went into the kitchen and ate dinner as a family, eating the food that Julie, Lucas and Kayla had lovingly made for their Dad for his birthday. He wondered where Rick was, but didn't want to ask, lest he materialize out of nowhere.

Krys could read him like a book. She leaned towards him, saying quietly while the kids were clearing the supper dishes and getting ready to bring out his birthday cake, "Rick isn't here. He's staying late at the studio tonight. I know it means a lot to you to spend quality time with your kids and this was the best gift I could think of to give you."

Darryl looked her straight in the eye and replied, "Thank you Krys, it does mean a lot to spend my birthday with my family."

Krys understood what he meant – that she allowed him to spend his birthday with his kids…

And her…

It was tearing her apart to see him looking the way he looked now. He was bloated and not his usual put-together self. His clothes were wrinkled and he hadn't shaved in a few days. He had bags under his eyes and his skin tone was blotchy. She could tell he'd been drowning himself in booze as he had all the tell-tale signs.

How did we get so lost from each other?

Just then, the kids turned the lights down and brought out a birthday cake, lit with forty-three candles.

"Are you serious? All those candles? You're going to burn the house down!" he laughed as his kids sang to him.

When they placed the cake in front of him, he glanced over at Krys, closed his eyes, made his birthday wish and blew out the candles…

I wish for Krys and I find our way back to each other, out of this horrific mess…

They enjoyed birthday cake and he opened several presents from his kids. Then it was time for Darryl to go home to the pathetic apartment he shared with the woman he loathed.

At the door, he said his goodbyes to his children, then he was left standing alone with his wife. "Thank you for tonight, Krys. I really appreciate it," he said, a sad smile on his face.

"The kids wanted to do something nice for you. They love you," she answered. As soon as she stopped talking, she grabbed her belly and grunted.

"What is it?" Darryl said, alarmed.

"Oh, this kid. It's kicking me black and blue," she replied, now holding her belly with both hands.

Darryl grinned as he said, "Remember when you were pregnant with Lucas? He kicked you like that all the time."

Krys swallowed her sadness and decided to give Darryl one more precious gift, one he would likely never get again. "Do you want to feel it kicking? It's really active right right now," she offered.

"Really? Hell, yes!" Darryl responded with enthusiasm.

Krys took Darryl's hand and placed it over her belly where Baby was moving the most. The instant their hands touched, they both felt a jolt of lust scorch through them.

Darryl placed his other hand under her belly to support it, excited to feel their baby moving so energetically. He was thrilled to have his hands on Krys, wherever she would let him touch her.

Their eyes met and they didn't realize it, but they smiled so lovingly at each other, it was like the last few months never happened and they were happily together.

Darryl knelt down and turned his head so his ear was to her belly, his hands supporting the beautiful roundness. He closed his eyes and concentrated on listening to his child in his wife's womb.

Baby kicked under Darryl's cheek and he jerked his head back, a smile on his face as he rubbed the spot where the baby had hoofed him. Krys nearly broke down crying, remembering when he used to do that when she had been pregnant with all three of their kids.

He stood up, took her hands in his, looked into her beautiful blue eyes and said softly, "Thank you Krys. That was... Thank you..." he said gratefully.

Darryl leaned in, placed his hand under her jaw, cupped her face and kissed her cheek. It was sweet, soft, and so full of raw emotion, Krys' knees threatened to collapse underneath her. Her hands slid up Darryl's arms and grasped his shoulders to keep her balance.

He pulled back and smiled a genuinely happy smile at her, something she hadn't seen grace his face in months, then turned to leave.

He didn't look back.

Because if he did, Krys would have seen the tears pouring down Darryl's cheeks.

CHAPTER 142

January 8, 2015

Krys

Krys stood at the door, silent and still. She heard a chorus of sniffs and turned to see her three kids looking at her.

"Mom..." Julie said sweetly as she hugged her mother's side, wiping tears from her eyes.

"That was really cool, you letting Dad have that," Lucas said as he hugged his mother on her other side.

"Yeah, Daddy's so sad all the time. Is he ever gonna come home? I miss him," Kayla said sadly as she hugged her mother from the front.

Julie spoke up, her voice soft and full of care. "Dad is really unhappy, Mom. It's obvious just looking at him how he feels. You made him really happy tonight, letting him come home for dinner and especially letting him touch your belly. I overheard him telling Auntie Nat at her wedding how much he loved doing that just to make you laugh when you were pregnant with us."

Krys' lips turned up at the memory. "He did like doing that. I couldn't get him away from me. He was always rubbing my tummy and talking to you three, telling silly stories and..." Krys' voice hitched as she choked out a sob.

"Mom, he still loves you," Lucas said quietly.

Krys snapped out of her sadness. "I know he does, but it's complicated."

"It doesn't have to be. We know you love Rick and you have a history with him. We also know you still love Dad and have an even longer history with him. And you ARE pregnant with HIS baby. How much more complicated do you need to make it?" Lucas questioned.

"Lucas, you're out of line," Krys warned.

"It's obvious Rick loves you, but he's a rock'n'roller, Mom. I'm sure there are babes lined up as far as the eye can see to get a piece of him. Let him pick one so you can get back together with Dad," Lucas finished.

"That's enough out of all of you. This conversation is over. Head up to your rooms and finish your homework. Rick will be coming home soon and I want to spend some time with him," Krys ordered.

Her kids turned tail and did as their mother bade them.

She was just about to text Rick to come home when he walked through the front door, shaking snow off his boots. He noticed the look on her face and came right to her. "Kryssie, are you okay? What happened? Did Darryl upset you?"

"Oh, I'm fine. I let him touch my belly just before he left and the kids are reading something into it that isn't there," Krys said, blowing off the intensity of the emotion she and Darryl shared.

"You let him touch your belly?" Rick breathed through his nose in anger.

"Rick, he IS the father of this baby," Krys defended her action.

"Yeah, okay, he is. But –" Rick started.

"*But* nothing, Rick. I was in no danger, I can assure you. Now can we drop this and go to bed? I'm wiped out," Krys said.

Rick agreed silently, following her up to their bedroom. "Princess, I just don't like to see you sad and you looked sad when I walked in the door," he told her.

"This is a hard situation for me to deal with, Rick. I love two men, am pregnant with the baby of one while I'm living with the other. Do you think this is easy for me?" Krys admitted.

Rick took Krys into his arms and held her. "No, I don't think this is easy for you," he said softly.

"Let's just go to bed, okay? It's been a long day and this kid has been busy kicking the hell out of my insides," Krys suggested.

"Okay, let's go to bed," Rick agreed.

That night was the first night that they did not make love since Rick moved in with Krys.

CHAPTER 143

January 2015

Darryl

Two weeks after Darryl's birthday, he got slammed with news he never thought he'd hear.

"I'm pregnant!" Cynthia squealed.

CHAPTER 144

March 6, 2015
Darryl

If Darryl thought his life spiralled out of control when Cynthia told him she was pregnant, he wasn't ready for the next spin she put on the situation and he had absolutely no idea how she pulled it off.

Ever since the night of his birthday, Krys had softened towards him. She was agreeable with him coming to the house to spend time with their kids, so he made a point of going there as often as he could. And when he inquired about the baby, she would smile and answer his questions pleasantly and honestly. She even let him touch her belly now and again to feel their baby kick.

But if she found out about Cynthia being pregnant, all that would completely disappear.

He was planning to come by and see the kids after work, so he texted Krys to confirm, but she didn't text him back. That was odd, because she *always* texted him back about their visits.

He left work a little early and drove straight to the house, wanting to see if she was okay or if something was wrong with her, the kids or the baby. When he got there, he rang the doorbell and banged on the door with his fist, calling out to Krys to open it.

The door opened and Rick stood there, his face a black mask of fury. "You have a lot of nerve coming here," he spat.

"What the hell are you talking about?" Darryl demanded.

"I've seen how Krys has softened towards you. She's been happier the past several weeks, letting go of some of the anger and hurt that's been tormenting her since your split, and you were just doing that to butter her up, weren't you, you fucking asshole!" Rick yelled.

"I don't have a damn clue what you're talking about!" Darryl repeated angrily.

"Are you trying to tell me you *didn't* send her divorce papers this morning?" Rick seethed.

Darryl blanched as he gritted out, "I. DID. NO. SUCH. THING."

"The divorce papers on the kitchen counter tell another story. And I can't believe what a tightwad you're being with child support! What the fuck, Darryl? You made those children with her! Don't they deserve to be taken care of in your absence?" Rick fumed.

"Listen up. I DID NOT send Krys divorce papers! I want to see them right now and I want to see Krys," Darryl demanded. Rick stepped aside and Darryl went straight to the kitchen, picked up the papers and studied them. They looked legal and binding. "What the hell is this shit? If I *were* stupid enough to divorce her, I would at least provide for our children, not try to pass off this disrespectful bullshit! *Where is Krys?*" Darryl ranted, a dark fury curling its way through his body.

"She is absolutely devastated and doesn't ever want to see you again. She's close to her due date and she's not had an easy time with this pregnancy," Rick spat.

"What do you mean? She's never indicated anything like that to me," Darryl asked angrily.

"Her blood pressure has been high and she's been spotting because of all the stress," Rick admitted.

"Why didn't she tell me?" Darryl whispered, looking through the patio doors into the back yard.

"Because you were the cause of most of it," Rick told him accusingly.

That last comment made Darryl stiffen. The fucker was probably right...

He looked back to the name of the law firm embossed on the divorce papers – *Williams, Tanner & Faulkner* – the law firm Cynthia worked for as a legal secretary. Could she have gone this far by sending Krys false divorce papers so she could keep him for herself? He really didn't think she was that devious. "I don't fucking believe this," he said, his voice lethally quiet.

"What?" Rick asked, noting the icy change in Darryl's demeanor.

"These papers are false and I know who sent them," Darryl said between clenched teeth, trying to keep his rage under control. He stormed out, carrying the false document with him.

CHAPTER 145

March 6, 2015

Darryl

Twenty minutes later, Darryl stormed into the dumpy apartment he lived in with Cynthia. She was sprawled out on the couch, eating chips from the bag and drinking wine from the bottle, while watching something sordid on the porn channel she subscribed to.

"What the fuck is this?" Darryl exploded when he saw her, taking in the chips, wine and porn.

"Friday night at Cyn's when Darryl is out with his *family*," she said, turning to him and grinning insanely.

A curtain of red fell over his eyes as he waved the papers in her face. "You need to explain these to me, *right now*," Darryl demanded.

Cynthia took a swig of wine and crunched a few more chips before answering. "Oh, those? I thought you needed a little boot in the ass to get going on your divorce from *her* so you can marry *me*. I had one of the lawyers at my work draw them up and I sent them to her this morning. I see she got them. Are they signed yet?" Cynthia said casually. She neglected to tell him that she gave the scumbag lawyer in question, who she was currently sleeping with, a magnificent blow job as payment for expediting the paperwork.

"*Are they signed yet*??? You can't possibly be serious!" Darryl said, totally incredulous.

"Of course I'm serious. I'm pregnant with YOUR baby, Darryl. I want our kid to be legit when it's born, so we need to get married. Or have you forgotten about OUR baby?" Cynthia questioned.

"Are you absolutely insane? I would NEVER marry a psycho skank like you, pregnant or not!" Darryl thundered.

Cynthia looked suitably hurt for a split second, then an evil grin crossed her mouth and she said, "We'll see about that."

"No, we will NOT '*see about that*'. You're certifiable and I'm done with you. I'll be back tomorrow to get my things, so you better be somewhere else!" Darryl roared.

He left without another word and slammed the door behind him, leaving Cynthia sprawled on the couch, eating chips from the bag and drinking wine from the bottle, while watching something sordid on the porn channel.

CHAPTER 146

March 6, 2015

Darryl

Darryl drove to his parent's house and told them everything.

Audrey and Owen sat at their kitchen table with their son and listened to him pour out his heart to them, revealing all the sordid details of his messed up relationship with Cynthia, right down to showing them the falsified divorce papers.

Owen stood up, walked around the table to his son and placed his hand on Darryl's shoulder, giving him a squeeze of support, saying only, "Son."

Audrey leaned across and grasped his hands in hers, looked him in the eyes and said, "Son, we'll help you any way we can. Just get your wife and babies back and everything else will fall into place."

Darryl sagged with relief, knowing his parents had his back. He went to sleep in his old bedroom, in his old bed, and slept fitfully, formulating a plan to get Cynthia, the bane of his existence, out of his life, and Krys, the love of his life, back in.

CHAPTER 147

March 7, 2015

Darryl

Darryl awoke on Saturday morning to a harried knock on his bedroom door. "What?" he called out sleepily.

Audrey's voice was strained as she answered, "Darryl! The police are here to talk to you!"

Darryl sat straight up in bed, rubbing his hands through his hair and down his face. He got out of bed, pulled on a pair of sweatpants and a t-shirt, then followed his mother to the door.

Owen was standing at the front door with a Police Detective and two uniformed police officers, his lips in a thin line of disbelief.

"Are you Mr Darryl Sheridan?" the Detective asked.

"Yes, I am. And you are?" he replied.

"I'm Detective Ian Martin with the Winnipeg Police Service. We went to your registered address and a man named Rick Sutherland told us we might find you here," he said.

"Yeah, I don't live there anymore. What's going on? Why are you here? Is everything alright with my wife? Are my kids okay?" Darryl asked, a feeling of dread creeping up his spine.

Detective Martin answered him with another question. "Where were you last evening between five PM and midnight? Please be as specific as possible."

"I was at my house arguing with my wife's boyfriend after work around six, then I went to my apartment and argued with my girlfriend around seven-thirty. I left there around eight and came here to my parent's house. I spent the next three hours talking to my parents, then I crashed in my old bedroom around eleven. Why? What's all this about? Is Krys okay? What about my kids?" Darryl said, the feeling of dread now crawling up his throat.

Detective Martin was succinct and to the point. "Your wife and kids are fine, but Cynthia Rockford is dead."

Darryl stood rooted to the spot. "What? She's... dead?"

"Yes. Would you please accompany us down to the police station? We have more questions for you," Detective Martin asked politely.

"Yeah, sure," Darryl replied numbly, wondering what fresh hell he was in for next.

CHAPTER 148

March 7, 2015
Darryl

Darryl sat in the police station being grilled by Detective Martin about everything to do with his relationship with Cynthia. He answered all the questions honestly, because he had nothing to hide.

After two hours, Detective Martin arrested Darryl on suspicion of murder because he had a motive and was believed to be the last person to have seen her alive.

They had no other viable suspects.

He was escorted into a holding cell and denied bail.

CHAPTER 149

March 7, 2015

Krys & Natalie

"Krys! Darryl's been arrested!" Natalie screeched over the phone.

"What? Why?" Krys screeched back.

"Cynthia is dead and the cops think Darryl did it! They're saying he had a motive because of the shit she pulled with the divorce papers! OHMIGOD, what a nightmare!!!" Nat yelled.

"Wait, what? Cynthia's *dead*? Natalie, slow down! Tell me what's going on!" Krys requested as Natalie recapped about Darryl and Rick's face-off, Darryl racing off with the false divorce papers to confront Cynthia and ending up at their parent's place. "I just talked to Rick and he never mentioned any of this to me. Wait... The divorce papers are false? Darryl didn't send them?" Krys said softly.

"No, Krys! It was all Cynthia!" Nat confirmed.

"Tell me the rest," Krys said as she focused her attention on what Nat was telling her.

"The police questioned someone in the apartment block who said they heard yelling and some sort of noise, like a fist fight, then they saw a guy running out the back door of the complex, leaving a trail of blood behind," Nat recalled.

"Trail of blood? How was she killed?" Krys asked, unsure if she wanted the answer to that question.

"Strangled and stabbed thirteen times in the abdomen," Nat revealed.

Krys swallowed a gulp of air, feeling queasy. "Was Darryl covered in blood when he got to your parents place?"

"No! He didn't do it, Krys! He was pissed off about the false divorce papers Cynthia sent you! He told Mom and Dad everything," Nat replied.

"So then why did the cops arrest him? Stabbing would have made a hell of a mess. And did the eye witness get a good look at the guy with the blood trail behind him? With Cynthia's history, he could be any one of a number of guys," Krys said disgustedly.

"That I don't know. Please, Krys, you have to go to the jail and talk to the police! And you have to see Darryl. Please! He needs you! I'm telling you, he didn't do it! I know it and you know it, too. He told me and Mom and Dad he didn't and we all believe him!" Nat pleaded.

"Natalie, I have no doubt he's innocent, but what difference would it make for me to go there to see him and talk to the police? What have I got to tell them? That he left me, pregnant, for her? That would give ME motive to want her dead, wouldn't it? I'm nearly nine months pregnant. I've been under enough stress and this pregnancy has been difficult enough," Krys explained.

"Krys, he's still your husband, no matter what shit has happened between the two of you," Natalie said persuasively.

Krys closed her eyes and let out a huge sigh. "Okay, fine, I'll go. But I better not go into premature labor from the added stress of all this," she agreed reluctantly.

CHAPTER 150

March 7, 2015

Krys

"My name is Krysten Sheridan and I'm here to see Detective Martin," she said at the front desk of the police station.

The police officer manning the desk picked up the phone and punched in an extension number. "Detective Martin, Krysten Sheridan is here. Yeah... Okay... Uh-huh... Right. I'll tell her," he said into the phone. "He'll be right out."

A moment later, Detective Martin rounded the corner, his eyes drawn to Krys' huge belly. "Mrs Sheridan, thank you for coming in. If you would come with me, please? I apologize in advance for the questions I need to ask you, since they may cause you undue stress. I can see you're quite near your due date, correct?" he asked as he led them to his office and offered her a seat.

"Yes. I have another couple of weeks to go," Krys answered, sitting down on the hard chair and holding her belly.

"May I ask you what you know about Cynthia Rockford and your husband's relationship?" he began.

"They've known each other a long time. Darryl and I split up in October and he got together with her around then. That's all I really know, or want to know, about it," Krys recalled.

Detective Martin picked up some papers on his desk and shuffled them. "Did you know that Ms. Rockford was ten weeks pregnant? The coroner confirmed that this morning during the autopsy."

The color drained from her face as Krys cradled her belly, completely shocked by this revelation. "What?" she whispered.

Detective Martin continued, "Mr Sheridan says there absolutely no way he is the father because the last time he slept with her was near the end of October and she got pregnant sometime during the latter part of December," Detective Martin revealed.

"He knew about her being pregnant?" Krys asked, her voice now barely audible, the pain of Darryl's deceit slicing through her.

"Yes, he did," Detective Martin confirmed. "We still have to do a DNA test to rule out his paternity. If the test conclusively proves he is not the father, that will let your husband off the hook of that claim. As for the murder charge, he was incredibly angry at Ms Rockford for sending you the false divorce papers and that gave him motive."

Krys felt sick to her stomach. It was all too much to take. "This is just unbelievable," she mumbled, closing her eyes and shaking her head, tears welling up and spilling down her cheeks.

"Would you like to see Mr Sheridan?" Detective Martin asked.

Krys replied, "No. I need to leave. This has been a difficult pregnancy and seeing him just might put me into early labor. But I can tell you one thing for certain. He didn't kill her. Darryl may be a lot of things, but a murderer, under *any* circumstances, he is not. And he would never destroy his relationship with our children by doing something like that."

"Is there anything you'd like me to tell him on your behalf?" Detective Martin offered.

"No. He has parents and a sister he can rely on. I have our three children to look after and a I'll be delivering this baby in a few weeks. That's what I need to concentrate on right now," she answered as she stood up awkwardly. She walked out of the police station, waiting until she got to her SUV to break down and cry.

When the tears stopped flowing, she drove home in a stone cold fury to confront Rick.

What the hell am I going to have to deal with next?

CHAPTER 151

March 7, 2015

Darryl

"Did my wife come?" Darryl asked Detective Martin.

"Yes, she did. She was visibly upset at what I told her. By the way, you're a fool to have let her slip through your fingers," Detective Martin said.

"Yeah, rub more salt in that wound," was all Darryl replied.

"I told her about the pregnancy," Detective Martin told him.

"Fuck... how'd she take *that* news?" Darryl frowned, hating that she was told that way.

"Not great. I thought she might drop the kid right there from the look on her face," Detective Martin admitted.

"Shit... But she knows I'm NOT the father?" Darryl asked.

"I told her the dates didn't match from when you claim to have stopped sleeping with Ms Rockford to when she got pregnant, but we still need to do a DNA test to confirm," Detective Martin answered.

Darryl stuck out his arm. "Do it. Now. I need this cleared up as soon as possible. I want to be there in the delivery room when my wife gives birth to our baby."

Detective Martin felt bad for Darryl and what a shitty situation he was stuck in.

CHAPTER 152

March 7, 2015

Krys & Rick

Amazingly enough, Krys made it home safely. When she walked in the door, she saw Rick slouched on the couch, channel surfing. "Rick, is there something you neglected to tell me when we talked earlier?" she demanded, holding her belly and gritting her teeth in anger.

"I was told by the police to let them talk to you about this situation with the divorce papers. They stopped by here looking for Darryl this morning and I told them he might be at his parent's house. Is there something I'm missing?" Rick asked, confused as to why she was looking angrier than he'd ever seen her.

"There sure as hell is. Darryl's been arrested," Krys started.

"Arrested? For what? Being angry about false divorce papers?" Rick asked.

"No, for killing Cynthia Rockford!" Krys announced disgustedly.

Now it was Rick's turn to bug out his eyes. "Killing... What? Are you kidding me?"

"I couldn't make this shit up if I tried! And get this little nugget – she was PREGNANT and trying to pass it off as Darryl's! According to him, he is absolutely NOT the father, but they need to do a DNA test to prove he's telling the truth," Krys told him, reaching for the counter as a cramp hit her. She doubled over and grabbed her belly, exhaling a ragged breath, her eyes clamped shut in pain. "Rick, I think we need to go to the hospital..." Krys whispered through the contraction.

CHAPTER 153

March 7, 2015

Krys

Krys was wheeled into a delivery room, in the hospital where she worked, to deliver her baby. But things weren't going according to her birthing plan. They were headed in a drastically different direction.

When she was being checked by her doctor, her water broke, blood and fluid gushing out. Her blood pressure began spiking and the fetal monitor was showing that Baby was in distress.

Krys was crying, the stress of the past twenty-four hours compounding on her. "Rick, please call Natalie... and have her call my parents..." she breathed through another painful contraction.

"Krys, we're going to have to do an emergency C-section. Baby is in distress and you're bleeding a lot. Do you consent?" her colleague and friend, Dr Lina Parker, asked.

"Yes... Just don't let anything happen to this baby," Krys ground out, clutching her belly as another cramp gripped her, more blood gushing from between her legs.

Rick was pasty white as he watched what was happening to Krys, totally helpless. He was sitting beside her, letting her crush his left hand in hers as she struggled through the painful contractions.

Dr Parker turned to him and smiled warmly. "Rick, do you want to scrub in with me? You can be in the surgical delivery room with Krys, if you want."

Rick looked at Krys and asked her, "Do you want me in there with you, Princess?"

Krys looked back at him with a pleading look and replied through harsh breaths, "Yes... I do. I need you now... More than ever..."

"Okay then, I'll get things set up in the O.R. and have Elise come in to get you ready for surgery. Hang in there, Krys. Baby will be out soon and this will be all over," Dr Parker said soothingly.

"Hopefully this... won't end with me... in the morgue..." Krys gritted out.

"Not on my watch, my dear friend. Not on my watch," Lina replied.

Dr Parker left the room and Krys' nurse, Elise, came in smiling, "Hi Boss, let's get you ready for your C-section. I'll start your IV now, okay?"

"Yeah, let's get this... show on the road..." Krys breathed through the contractions.

Rick was still pasty white, silently sitting on a chair, letting Krys continue to crush his hand as she struggled through the pain. He had already called Natalie and told her what was happening, so he was expecting her to show up soon. Tony was staying at home with *all* of the kids – Natalie's four, Krys' three and Tony's four.

Within minutes, Krys was wheeled into the surgical suite and Rick was swept into the scrub room to prep with Dr Parker.

He really didn't know how he was going to cope if something bad happened to his Princess...

CHAPTER 154

March 8, 2015

Krys

Krys' baby was delivered safely into the world at twenty minutes past midnight and laid upon her chest for a quick moment of Mother-Baby bonding to show Krys that her baby was alive and well.

"Oh! It's so tiny!" Krys said, crying tears of relief and joy as Baby took a deep breath and gave a healthy cry, making her cry even harder.

"Sure is, Krys. Rick, would you like to cut the cord?" Dr Parker offered, turning to face him.

Krys smiled at him and nodded her head in agreement.

Rick was honored at being given the chance to perform something so wondrous and jumped head-first into it, since he was on tour and missed when his own daughter, Anya, was born. "You bet I do!"

He was given the scissors and cut the umbilical cord, laughing with pure joy. Baby was then placed in the warming unit, assessed, cleaned and wrapped up while Krys was attended to by Dr Parker.

Elise walked over to Rick and offered the baby to him to hold. He happily accepted the tiny bundle and cradled it close to his chest, looking into its face and smiling serenely.

"Kryssie, what's the name?" Rick asked, cuddling the baby close.

"I don't know! Lina, you didn't tell me what the gender is," Krys said as she suppressed a laugh.

"Oh! I'm so sorry! In all the excitement, I forgot! It's a girl!" Lina revealed.

Krys closed her eyes and let the tears fall. "Her name is Abigail."

Lina smiled warmly. "What a lovely name for her, Krys."

"Yes, it is," Krys croaked, her voice overflowing with emotion.

Rick was oblivious, cuddling Abigail to him and cooing at her quietly.

Krys looked at him...

And wished that he was Darryl...

CHAPTER 155

March 8, 2015
Krys & Natalie

Natalie arrived while Krys was in surgery, so she waited with some of the staff in the waiting room. She knew most of them and thankfully, it was a slow night in Labor & Delivery. There was only one other mother there who had delivered her baby earlier in the evening.

Dr Parker came into the waiting room at one in the morning to find Natalie and told her the good news. "Hi Natalie, good to see you. We had to do an emergency C-section because Baby was in distress, but she's fine and so is Krys. Rick is in there with them," she informed her.

"*She*? It's a girl?" Natalie smiled excitedly.

"Yes. Robust and healthy for being a couple of weeks early and having the cord wrapped around her neck three times. Krys has been telling me about what's been happening between her and Darryl and Rick. I'm really sorry to hear how crazy her situation is. I'm surprised she didn't go into labor earlier than this! Just shows how strong our girl is, huh?" Dr Parker said, pride lacing her words.

"She sure is! Can I go in and see them?" Nat asked excitedly.

"Absolutely! Krys has been asking for you," Dr Parker smiled happily.

Natalie entered the room and saw Krys in her hospital bed, breastfeeding the baby. Rick was sitting beside her with his arm around Krys, her head resting on his chest. They looked the picture of a happy family and for all intents and purposes, they were.

"Oh Kryssie! A baby girl!" Nat squealed as she rushed to the bedside and crawled in on the other side, sandwiching Krys in the middle and stroking the baby's tiny, bald head.

"Yup, daughter number three," Krys smiled tiredly.

"And her name is?" Nat asked.

Krys evaded the question and instead turned towards Rick. "Would you text the kids and ask them to come after breakfast to meet their baby sister? I'd also like a few minutes alone with Natalie, okay?"

"Of course. I'll be just outside," he replied, kissed her cheek, then left the room to give Krys and Nat some alone time and to do as she asked of him.

"I named our daughter Abigail, the name Darryl and I decided on if we ever had another daughter," Krys said sadly.

"Do you want me to tell him for you? He's still in a holding cell at the police station," Nat said.

"Yes. Natalie, he knew *she* was pregnant and he kept that from me! Did he think I would never find out, even though he isn't the father? That kind of deceit I just cannot tolerate. I'm going to divorce him..." Krys trailed off, the tears flowing freely down her face.

"Oh Krys, are you absolutely sure that's what you want to do?" Natalie asked sadly.

"Darryl's name will be on the birth certificate, but that's all the acknowledgement he's getting from me. He'll be able to see Abigail and our other children, but he'll have to arrange it through the lawyers. Rick and I will raise this baby together. I *never* want to see Darryl again," Krys added.

Krys finished nursing Abigail, gave her to Natalie and promptly fell asleep out of sheer exhaustion.

Rick knocked softly and poked his head around the door. "Is it safe for me to come back in?"

"Yes. Krys just passed out so I'm going to go home," Nat smiled, nodding at Krys.

"Thanks for being here, Natalie. We really appreciate it," Rick said, giving her a quick hug.

Natalie hugged him back and left the little family to settle into their first night together, wondering how she was going to break this devastating news to her brother.

CHAPTER 156

March 8, 2015
Natalie & Darryl

Natalie arrived at the police station at nine in the morning to visit Darryl, but she wasn't looking forward to telling him the news that he missed the birth of his daughter. He was brought in to the visitor room and they sat across the table from each other.

"What's the latest news about this shit show?" Natalie asked.

"They're letting me go in a bit. The forensics team found the knife used to stab her and lifted fingerprints from it that they positively identified are NOT mine. Plus, the DNA test came back and I am absolutely, one hundred percent, NOT the father, like I told them. And that makes me sick to my stomach," Darryl bit out.

"Why? I thought you'd be relieved!" Nat asked.

"Chew on this thought, Nat. How many other guys do you think she was fucking besides me?" Darryl made a disgusted face and stuck out his tongue.

"Oh, wow... I never considered that. You better get yourself tested for every STD there is and for HIV! Seriously, Darryl, don't delay! Krys won't let you get near your kids if you've gotten something from Cynthia!" Nat insisted.

"You're right. How is she? I'm sure hearing that news was no picnic for her," Darryl asked.

"I, uh... I have something to tell you..." Nat started.

Darryl sat straight up, concern on his face. "What? Is Krys okay? Is it the baby?"

"Darryl... the baby was born early this morning," Natalie said quietly.

Darryl's mouth dropped open and he looked like he was going to scream. "Which part of this nightmare put her over the edge?" Darryl asked angrily.

"All of it, but especially the part where you knew Cynthia was pregnant and didn't tell her," Nat answered.

"Shit. I didn't tell her because I knew I wasn't the father. I just needed proof. Are they both okay?" he wondered, looking away from her to focus on the wall.

"Yes, Darryl, your wife and your daughter are both healthy and well. She was born by emergency C-section," Natalie relayed.

Darryl's head snapped back to face his sister. "Daughter? Emergency C-section? What happened?"

"Baby went into distress. The cord was wrapped around her neck three times," Nat told him.

"Fuck! But they're both okay?" he repeated.

"Yes, they're both fine. Krys named her Abigail," Nat confirmed.

"Abigail? That's the name we picked if we ever had another little girl," Darryl said as he looked out the window and smiled.

"There's more, Darryl. She has put your name on the birth certificate, but she wants nothing more to do with you. She said... she wants a divorce... and that her and Rick are going to raise Abigail together," Natalie told him.

"Are you fucking kidding me? No way am I giving her a divorce! NO WAY! Krys is *my* wife and this baby is *mine*! Not *his*!!!" Darryl screamed, snapping out of his momentary idyllic bliss.

Is this really it?
Has she really given up?
Have I fucked things up permanently?

CHAPTER 157

March 8, 2015

Darryl

Late on Sunday afternoon, Darryl was released from jail and cleared of all charges. His dad came to pick him up and took him home.

"Did you and Mom go see Krys and our baby in the hospital this morning?" Darryl asked.

"Yes, we did. Baby is a cutie. Nice little round, bald head. Strong and solid. Good set of lungs, too," Owen said with grandfatherly affection.

"Did Krys mention me?" Darryl asked, hopeful.

"No, son. She didn't. She was in a good mood and we didn't want to ruin that for her. She's been through a lot and she needs rest, not more stress," Owen suggested.

"Dad, how did things go so far off the rails? Have I messed things up so badly that there's no going back?" Darryl asked his father.

"I really don't know, son. You hurt Krys pretty badly, on many levels. But right now, let's go home to your mother and have a nice Sunday dinner with her. She's worried about you.

We know you've been cleared of all charges, but there's still someone out there who murdered that poor girl you were with. You need to cooperate with the police and help them with their investigation any way you can," Owen told Darryl.

"Yeah, I guess so," Darryl replied.

The quicker this murder gets solved, the quicker I can start trying to make things right with Krys...

CHAPTER 158

March 2015

Cynthia

Detective Ian Martin and the Winnipeg Police Service did their due diligence with their investigation, swiftly solving the crime of who murdered Cynthia Rockford and who fathered her baby.

They were NOT the same person.

The father was identified through DNA testing. He was the scumbag lawyer at the law firm where Cynthia worked, the same scumbag lawyer she gave the blow job to in payment for him drawing up the false divorce papers.

Who the murderer was, was a whole other sordid story.

After canvassing the neighborhood, places she hung out and talking to the few people she knew who didn't hate her, Detective Martin confirmed that Cynthia was, in fact, entertaining a revolving door of men when Darryl wasn't home. But there was one man who was seen most often coming around, the same one who was seen running out the back door the night she was murdered, leaving a trail of blood behind him.

He was short, balding, weaselly and bug-eyed...

Mickey Nielson was positively identified not only by his bloody fingerprints on the murder weapon, but by three different people in a police line-up, one of them being Chuck Davenport, Mickey's bartender and co-owner of ILLUSIONS. When he was questioned, Chuck told the police everything he knew of Mickey and Cynthia's relationship.

Chuck was not only an honest man, he was smart, too. When he and Mickey had signed the papers for Chuck to become co-owner of ILLUSIONS, there was a clause indicating that if something should happen to one of them, be it illness, injury or incarceration, the other would assume full legal ownership, free and clear, and not require buying the other out. It also looked as though Mickey and Cynthia were planning Chuck's eventual demise when police found all sorts of chemicals and other paraphernalia to make poison at Mickey's place during their search. Mickey had also taken out an enormous life insurance policy on Chuck and was clearly planning on cashing it in at some point as Chuck's death would be a permanent solution to Mickey's money problems.

When Mickey was arrested, he confessed, breaking down and confirming what Chuck had told the police about his long-standing jealousy of a love not returned because of Cynthia's obsession over Darryl, ruining any chances Mickey ever had at getting her to commit to him.

Cynthia had called Mickey after she and Darryl had fought. Mickey rushed out of ILLUSIONS and when he got to her apartment, she told him that she was pregnant and Darryl had left her because of what she did with the false divorce papers. Mickey completely lost it and strangled her in an angry, jealous rage, then stabbed her in the belly, believing that the baby was

Darryl's. She never got the chance to tell him that baby was, in fact, *not* Darryl's, but fathered by someone else.

Chuck had seen Mickey slip out of the bar and decided to follow him, watching from his car. Mickey had been inside Cynthia's apartment no more than twenty minutes when he came rushing out the back door, threw himself in his car and sped away. That's when Chuck got out and noticed the blood trail leading to where Mickey had parked.

Mickey was charged with several major offences and had the book thrown at him. He was going to jail for the next twenty-five years with no parole. And he was going to do so without his business, without his money, without his friends... and without Cynthia.

CHAPTER 159

March 2015

Krys & Rick

"I can't believe Abby is eight days old already! And look what she can do, Krys! She's already holding my finger and looking at me like she knows who I am!" Rick giggled, cuddling Abby close and closing his eyes to absorb all her sweet baby goodness.

Krys smiled happily. She was rocking slowly back and forth in her rocking chair, her slippered feet crossed at the ankles on the ottoman. She watched as Rick wandered around the room with Abby in his arms, every now and then stopping to stand in place to coo at her.

Rick was quite the doting father to Abby and an even more doting partner to Krys. He insisted that she use her breast pump and fill a couple of bottles every night before she went to bed so he could get up with Abby at night and feed her, allowing Krys to sleep. He also made Krys breakfast in bed, allowing her to eat in peace while Rick tended to Abby, changing her diapers and marvelling at her daily changes.

Rick looked at her and smiled, saying softly, "Thank you, Princess."

"For what?" Krys replied.

"For letting me back in your life and giving me this incredible gift of fatherhood," he admitted quietly.

Krys knew he was referring to the baby they'd lost so many years ago. "Rick," she whispered, her eyes tearing up.

He came close, bent down and kissed her softly on her cheek. Then he smiled at her, love and devotion shining out of his eyes. "This is our second chance, Princess. I've come to terms with the fact that when you were pregnant with *our* baby, it wasn't the right time and fate intervened. I know I'm not Abby's biological father, but I feel like her father in every other way that matters. And I thank you for this, Krys. It means so much to me," Rick's voice cracked.

Krys' phone rang, breaking the sweet, tender moment between them. She looked at the display screen and frowned deeply, then answered sharply, "What do *you* want? I told you to talk to me through our lawyers if you –" she started but stopped abruptly as she was interrupted.

"Krys, Mickey was arrested for Cynthia's murder and went to jail yesterday. They just found him dead in his cell, awaiting trial. He hung himself," Darryl blurted.

"What? I can't say I'm surprised. Fitting end for a coward," Krys spat.

"I agree. Now Chuck is the sole owner of ILLUSIONS, free and clear. I'm glad for him. He's put up with a lot over the years from that weaselly asshole," Darryl said.

"He sure has. Thanks for telling me. I have to go now," Krys said, ready to hang up.

"KRYS! Just a minute, *please*," Darryl begged.

Krys sighed, closed her eyes and exhaled loudly. "Okay. One minute."

"Can... Can I come by... and meet Abigail?" he whispered.

"Have you called your lawyer and discussed visitation with him yet? If you haven't, then you had better get on that so he can work out something with mine. If you want to see our other three kids, contact Julie and she can drive herself, Lucas and Kayla to your parents' place. I'm recovering from major surgery and childbirth and I need peace and quiet to recuperate, not drama," Krys answered, hanging up before Darryl could utter another word.

"Kryssie, are you okay?" Rick asked, standing close to her and still cuddling a now-sleeping Abby.

"Yeah, I'm okay, only because I have you. Thank you, Rick for being here for me and Abby. I really don't know what I would have done if you hadn't been here with us, through all of this," she said as she reached up to kiss him.

"It's simple, Princess. I love you. I told you once, a long time ago, that I would never give up on us, that I would always love you, and that I would always be here for you. I've kept my word and I'm not about to break it, no matter what," he replied, crouching down beside her rocking chair and holding her hand.

Krys smiled and leaned forward, then stopped, her face contorted in pain. "Oh damn, this incision hurts!" she groaned as she sat back, holding her lower belly with both hands.

Rick stood up, placed Abby in her cradle and came back to Krys. He helped her to stand up and pulled her into his arms, holding her tenderly. "You'll heal, Krys. After all, it's only been a week since your C-section and you've been through a lot!

Give yourself time and cut yourself some slack," Rick said as he kissed her cheek.

"You're so good to me, Rick. I'm so lucky to have you in my life," she said, loving the feel of his arms around her.

"So am I, Princess," Rick said quietly.

They looked at each other and just as their lips were about to meet, Krys' phone rang again. She closed her eyes in frustration and answered it with a sharp, "Hello?"

"Kryssie, it's Nat. I just got a call from Darryl," she began.

"Is he getting you to do his dirty work for him now?" Krys ground out.

"Krys, he IS Abby's father. Please show some mercy and let him come to meet his daughter. Tony and I will be there and I'll be a buffer between you both, okay? And he IS my brother. I feel like the monkey in the middle," Nat grumbled.

Krys was still in Rick's arms, stiff and agitated. "Fine. As long as you stay in the room with us," Krys relented.

"Thank you, Kryssie. We'll be there soon," Nat said, hanging up.

Krys hung up, tossed her phone onto the rocking chair seat and wrapped her arms around Rick's neck, burrowing her nose into his throat.

"Lemme guess, you caved and now I'm going to be booted out so he can come to see Abby, right?" Rick deduced.

Her face still in Rick's throat, Krys replied a muffled, "Yes."

Rick smiled tightly and said, "I get it, Krys. He's Abby's father. He should be allowed to see her."

"Thank you for being so understanding, Rick. This is such a shitty situation, all the way around," Krys sighed, emotionally exhausted.

CHAPTER 160

March 2015
Krys & Darryl

A short time later, Darryl drove up just as Natalie and Tony arrived at the house. They walked to the front door together, Darryl hugging his sister close. "Thanks for doing this, Nat. I really appreciate you putting yourself out and having my back. This is such a shitty situation, all the way around."

"You're my brother and Abby is your daughter, Darryl. It's the right thing to do. Now just keep your temper in check and don't say anything to upset Krys. She's been through a lot and doesn't need the drama, okay?" Natalie lectured.

"Duly noted, little sister," Darryl grinned.

They rang the bell and waited until Rick opened the door. "Krys is upstairs in the nursery with Abby. Tony, let's go to the studio for a while. I have some great ideas for a few new songs," Rick said as he looked directly at Darryl, daring him to pick a fight.

Darryl didn't.

Rick and Tony took off, leaving Darryl and Natalie alone in the front foyer.

They walked up the curved staircase into the nursery where they saw Krys rocking slowly in her rocking chair, nursing Abby. She was humming and Darryl recognized the tune. It was "Princess".

He stood transfixed as he watched her. Then his eyes moved to the newborn cradled to her breast. "Oh, she's so tiny," Darryl said in awe, moving slowly over the plush carpet towards her.

This is the most beautiful sight, my wife nursing our daughter...

"She's nearly finished," Krys said softly, gazing lovingly at her daughter as Abby's tiny little rosebud lips popped off Krys' breast and she fell limply to sleep in her arms.

Darryl caught a glimpse of Krys' bared breast and a surge of lust rocketed through him. He averted his eyes, trying not to act on his desire to pull her into his arms and kiss her breathless.

I still love her...

I have to find some way to make things right between us...

Krys realized her breast was exposed from feeding Abby, so she rearranged her robe to cover herself, but a lusty feeling crept over her, making her blush.

I still love him...

Is there any way we can make things right between us again?

Darryl looked back at Krys and smiled, gingerly holding out his arms. "Can I hold her?"

"Here's Daddy, Sweetling," Krys said as she placed Abby in his arms.

Darryl held his daughter up to his face, feeling an avalanche of shame wash over him as he stared at his baby. Tears fell down his cheeks as he whispered, "Krys, she's absolutely beautiful."

"She looks just like you, Darryl," Krys replied as she eased herself up out of her rocking chair to stand beside him and admire their baby's cuteness.

Natalie moved to the corner of the room to give them some privacy.

Suddenly, Darryl handed Abby back to Krys, turned sharply and began to walk out of the nursery.

Krys grabbed for his sleeve and asked him, "Darryl, where are you going?"

He turned back to Krys, his face wet with tears. "Krys, I fucked everything up for us and I'm so, so sorry. I fucked everything up and it's not fixable. None of it is fixable. I fucked everything up and lost everything in my life that meant something to me. *Especially you,*" Darryl said, his voice gruff and full of emotion. He jerked his sleeve out of Krys' grasp and ran down the curving staircase, heading towards the front door to escape.

Krys gave Abby to Natalie and went after Darryl, calling out and catching up to him as he held the door open, one booted foot in the middle of taking a step over the threshold. "Darryl! Stop! *Please!!*" she begged, holding her belly and wincing in pain, pulling in a sharp breath as she grabbed onto his sleeve again to balance herself.

Darryl stopped when he heard the pain in her voice and felt her hand on his arm. He pulled his foot out of the doorway and lowered his head, still facing away from her. "Krys, I need to leave. I can't stay here and see you like this, happy with a man who would never hurt you the way I have. It's killing me. I'll talk to my lawyer about visitation and I won't contact you directly anymore. And when you start divorce proceedings,

I won't fight you on it. You can have whatever you want and whatever you need for our children," Darryl said, completely defeated.

Krys began crying. "Darryl, please, don't leave me like this, *please...*"

Darryl stood still as Krys' anxious voice reverberated through his head, *"'please, don't leave ME like this, please...'"*

He dropped his hand from the door frame, turned to look at her and pulled Krys into his arms as he said out loud, "What the fuck am I doing? Kryssie..." he cried as he wrapped himself around her and pulled her close to him, his face buried in her neck while sobs ripped free from his throat.

"Don't go..." Krys whispered as she wept, holding onto him tightly. "Please, don't go... Our kids need you... I need you..." she pleaded.

"I don't know how to fix this... I just don't..." Darryl admitted defeat into her hair, cupping the back of her head and holding her around her back as they wept together.

Krys pulled away to look at Darryl's still-handsome face, placing her hands on either side and sweeping her thumbs under his eyes to brush away the tears. She noticed that since his birthday, when he looked haggard and bloated, he was no longer looking rough as he had then. Now his clothes were wrinkle-free, his eyes were no longer bloodshot and the bags under his eyes were gone. He was cleanly shaved and his skin was back to looking clear and healthy. "We'll figure something out, Darryl. Both of us, together, we'll figure something out that will work for all of us. We have four children together now and we have to show them that we can figure this out and make it work," Krys said, her voice tremulous.

After everything, EVERYTHING, I still love him...

"Alright, Kryssie. But right now, I'm going to go. Natalie is here with you and we'll talk later, okay?" Darryl said, his voice hoarse.

"Okay," Krys agreed.

They were still wrapped in each other's arms, so Darryl decided to throw caution to the wind and kissed Krys softly on her lips.

She kissed him back.

And it was beautiful.

He looked at her gorgeous face and smiled lovingly at her, then let go and left without another word.

If it's the last thing I do, I'm going to figure out a way to fix this mess and get her back...

CHAPTER 161

April 2015 to June 2015
Rick

Ever since the day that Darryl came to see Abby, Krys had been pulling away from Rick. He could sense a difference in her that wasn't sitting well with him. When he tried to broach the subject with her, she always had a ready-made refusal to hand him why it wasn't a good time to talk about it, not to mention the fact that since Krys got cleared at her six-week check up to resume all previous activity, the most she'd allowed Rick to do was kiss her cheek.

That was it.

Nothing more.

What. The. Fuck?

On Mother's Day, he said nothing when he saw a large bouquet of carnations in shades of white, pink and yellow, with lush greenery in a beautiful crystal vase, wrapped with a white satin ribbon and placed in the middle of the dining room table.

Rick knew Darryl had sent them to her.

He was trying really hard to not let it get to him, but Rick was feeling like Darryl was slowly edging him out and Krys was doing nothing to discourage him.

He wasn't sure how much more he could cope with.

Now it was June and the last time he and Krys had sex was just after New Year's, more than six months ago! She had been uninterested in sex during the last couple of months of her pregnancy. Once Abby was born they'd been so tired from having a newborn and three teenagers in the house, and with Krys recuperating from her C-section, they'd totally abandoned their once-energetic, daily sex life.

They were like two ships passing in the night.

He needed to resolve this ASAP.

CHAPTER 162

June 2015

Rick

For Father's Day, Rick was going to spend the day with his daughter, Anya. She was fourteen and quickly growing up into a lovely young woman.

He left Krys in the kitchen with a kiss on her temple and a quick side hug before taking off in his black BMW SUV to pick up his daughter.

He wasn't sure if Krys cared that he was leaving.

Fuck...

CHAPTER 163

June 2015
Darryl

Darryl arrived in the driveway ten minutes after Rick left. He got out of his SUV and walked through the front door because Krys had told him he could.

After all, it was still his house.

Since their reconnection and mutual meltdown when Abby was eight days old, they had forged a truce, discussing their situation amicably without the intrusion of lawyers. He did notice some strain in Krys as she was trying to balance having both him and Rick in her life. Darryl was hoping that she would make a decision that would impact all of them in a positive way, namely boot Rick's ass to the curb and ask Darryl to come back to her. He wanted her back with a vengeance and he was willing to do anything to make that happen.

One fact Darryl had on his side was that he had been celibate since before Halloween. He had only had sex with Cynthia a couple of times when he went back to her in October. Afterwards, he was so disgusted, he couldn't get it up for her anymore. But Darryl had absolutely no problem getting a raging hard-on whenever he thought of Krys.

He had been scared shitless after the coroner's revelation about Cynthia being pregnant with another man's baby and Chuck's equally shitty revelation about Cynthia's legs being wide open for a surplus of different men to screw, so he went to a clinic and got tested for every STD known to man, and for HIV. He got all his results back and thank the merciful fates, he was clean.

Darryl knew that Krys had slept with Rick when she was pregnant with Abby and that burned him, but under the circumstances could he blame her with how HE'D acted? However, he didn't know if they had resumed that part of their relationship since Abby was born or since Krys' six-week postpartum check up. Darryl remembered after their other three kids were born, they hadn't waited very long to get horizontal, but they were much younger then, and their situation was much different now.

He'd been gauging Krys' behavior and it seemed that she was pulling away from Rick and gravitating more towards Darryl.

This gave him a glimmer of hope.

Now it was Father's Day and Rick was spending the day with his own daughter, so Darryl was going to spend the day with his wife and four children.

He had his test results folded up in his wallet and was going to show them to Krys today. If that didn't tell her what was on his mind, then he was at a loss...

CHAPTER 164

June 2015

Krys

Darryl walked through the patio doors into the backyard before lunch and looked so good, Krys nearly jumped him. He was wearing a faded vintage AC/DC concert t-shirt and dark gray cargo shorts with sport sandals. His hair was still damp and messy from the shower, just how she liked it. It was still dark blond, but Krys noticed that there were some distinguished-looking white strands starting to thread their way through. He also smelled so good, she couldn't help herself and took a deep breath when he came near her sitting in her lounge chair.

Darryl leaned down and kissed her on her cheek, a kiss that lasted just that little bit too long. His touch on her bare skin electrified her and she wondered if he felt the same way. Judging by the bulge in his shorts, she was pretty sure he did.

Krys hadn't felt this strong a sexual desire in a long time...
Not since the day Darryl came over and met their baby...
Everything kept coming back to that day...

CHAPTER 165

June 2015

Krys & Darryl

Julie, Lucas and Kayla were in their bathing suits since the weather outside was perfect for running through the sprinkler. Abby slept in her bassinet in the shade beside Krys, who was reclined back in her lounge chair wearing a navy tank top and khaki yoga shorts with her feet bare.

When he kissed her, Darryl felt an electric current jolt through him at their touch and wondered if Krys felt the same way as he obviously did. He pulled up another lounge chair and parked it beside Krys, with Abby tucked safely between them. "Thank you for today, Kryssie," he began.

Krys chuckled. "You're welcome, but we haven't done anything for you, yet."

Darryl scorched her with a lusty look, glanced down at his shorts and smirked, "Yes, you have."

Krys blushed, then leaned down to pick Abby up from her bassinet. She hugged her close, kissed her forehead and passed her to Darryl, cooing, "Time to go see Daddy for your first Father's Day together, Sweetling."

Darryl winked at Krys as he gently took Abby from her, amused that she was blushing. He snuggled Abby close to him, absorbing all her baby sweetness.

There's still something there between us...
I can feel it...

Watching Darryl holding their baby so lovingly made Krys melt into a puddle.

Something is still there between us...
I can feel it...

The family of six spent the day outside together, barbecued for supper and genuinely enjoyed each other's company.

After supper, the kids stayed outside while Darryl pulled Krys inside. "I have something I want you to see, Krys," he said, a serious look on his face as they stood together at the kitchen island.

"Okay," she said, feeling uncomfortable at what that *something* could possibly be, as Darryl reached into his wallet. He took out a folded piece of paper, opened it up and handed it to her. "These are test results for STD's... and HIV... All clear. Is this... yours?" Krys asked, confused.

"Yes. I made the biggest mistake of my entire life when I left you and went back to Cynthia. I only slept with her a couple of times –" he began.

"Darryl, stop right there. I don't want to hear this," she interrupted, holding up her hand.

"I need to tell you this, Krys. Please, will you listen?" he requested.

She sighed, put her hand down and gave him her full attention. "Okay, I will."

"I never slept with her past Halloween. Actually, it was before Halloween, and I've not been with anyone else, either. The thought of getting anywhere near her scared my dick into hiding. When I thought of you then, when I think of you now, only you, I get a raging hard-on," he grinned, taking her hand and placing it gingerly on his current raging hard-on over top of his cargo shorts.

She didn't remove her hand.

In fact, she may have stroked his raging hard-on a little...

"And?" she asked, her voice raspy.

"When I found out that Cynthia had been sleeping around, I got tested. I didn't want to come to you or our family with anything that I could pass on, in any way. I'm one hundred percent clean," he gritted as Krys started lightly rubbing her hand over his now rock-hard hard-on.

Darryl was leaning back with his ass against the quartz marble counter top, gripping it so hard he hoped he wasn't going to break off a piece. It felt so damn good to have Krys' hands on him again after so damn long without them...

"You haven't had sex since October?" she asked quietly, rubbing a little more forcefully while inching a little closer to him.

Darryl groaned and closed his eyes, then opened them and ground out, "That's right."

Krys licked her lips and gifted Darryl with the sexiest smirk he'd ever seen. "I can't say I've been celibate as long as you, but the night before your birthday was the last time I was with Rick..." she trailed off, letting her confession sink in.

"Kryssie, I'm... You better stop that before the kids walk in and find us in a compromising position," Darryl growled as she moved even closer and kept rubbing his hard-on.

"Oh? And what do you consider a compromising position?" Krys asked innocently, lightly squeezing him the way she knew he liked, her body nearly touching his own.

"Kryssie... Oh fuck, I've missed you," he moaned as he wrapped his arms around her. One hand came up and cupped her head while the other snaked down the back of her yoga shorts. He grabbed her ass, crushing her to him as he tipped her head back and kissed her, his tongue invading her mouth.

Krys let go of Darryl's cargoes and lifted one arm to grip his shoulder while the other slid through his hair. She pulled him close and kissed him back with savage lust.

They were tangled this way for several minutes until they heard the patio doors open and saw Julie coming inside, carrying Abby. Krys and Darryl stayed fused together with their arms wrapped around each other, but ended their searing kiss and turned their heads towards their oldest and youngest daughters, standing cheek to cheek.

Julie stopped cold, holding Abby upright on one shoulder. Her mouth dropped open and her eyes widened comically. "Uh, Abby needs her diaper changed," she said slowly.

"So go and do it. Your mother and I are in the middle of a very important conversation and you're interrupting," Darryl smiled and winked at Julie, knowing full-well how much their kids wanted their parents back together.

Julie took off upstairs to the nursery and returned in record time, Abby freshly diapered and smelling delightful.

The entire time Julie was upstairs with Abby, Darryl kept Krys enveloped in his arms and they just looked into each other eyes, smiling lovingly.

Once Julie took Abby back outside, they began kissing again. Darryl took this as an invitation and started to move them towards the curved staircase.

Krys stiffened and halted them. "Darryl, as much as I want to do this with you right now, and so help me, *I do*, I've slept with another man in our bed. If you and I are going to do this, I want it to be a clean slate for both of us. Let me have some time to figure things out with Rick, then I'm all yours," Krys proposed.

"Okay, but please hurry it up. I don't know how long I can hold out for," he growled, grabbing her ass in his hands again and grinding his pelvis into hers.

She gave him another sexy smile and kissed him lightly on his lips before extracting herself out of his embrace and heading back outside.

He waited a few minutes, talking down his hard-on before he went to bid his kids goodnight.

When he drove back to his parents' home that night, he did so with a spring in his step and a song in his heart.

I'm nearly there!

CHAPTER 166

June 2015

Julie

Whoa! Mom and Dad were really going at it with each other! Maybe this means I'll get my chance with Rick, after all!

CHAPTER 167

June 2015

Rick

Rick got home later than he planned because he wanted to make sure he avoided seeing Darryl at all costs. The bastard was just looking too damn smug these days.

He'd had a great day with his daughter, but he missed Krys.

When he walked in the front door just after nine that evening, Julie saw him and went right over to him, pulling him aside. "Rick, I think you have some stiff competition. My Dad was all over my Mom today and she didn't seem to mind. In fact, it seemed to me that she liked it and even encouraged it. I haven't seen her this happy in a long time," Julie declared.

Rick's mouth thinned into a straight line and his eyes glittered with anger and jealousy. "Is that right?" he growled.

"Do you really want to be with a woman who can't make up her mind between the two men in her life? A women who is married to one and has four kids with him, but has nothing holding her to the other? Maybe it's time for you to find another woman to be with who will give you all of herself, not just a tiny part, and other parts you'll never have," Julie taunted.

Rick wasn't a stupid man. He knew that Julie was telling him her version of the truth as she believed it, indicating that SHE wanted to be that woman. He didn't need to have a Masters Degree in Psychology to figure that out.

Julie was right about one thing. Perhaps it *was* time to gracefully bow out of this unwinnable fight for Krys and find another woman to give his heart to.

CHAPTER 168

June 2015
Rick & Julie

Three days after Father's Day, Rick was sitting out on the deck in a lounge chair drinking beer and enjoying the peace and quiet. School was finished for the year, so Krys was visiting her parents with Kayla and Abby while Lucas was at the school grounds playing basketball with some buddies. Julie was out with Carly and he had the house all to himself to ponder his life.

Do I still want to be in Diamond Angel?
What else will I do if I'm not playing guitar in a rock'n'roll band?
Will I ever find another woman to love?
If I do, will she be able knock Krys out of my head and my heart, once and for all?

While Rick was in the middle of his pondering, Julie came home. She breezed onto the deck through the patio doors, looking fresh and pretty in a pale yellow sundress with tiny sunflowers all over it, and white leather wedge sandals on her feet.

Rick looked distractedly at her as she walked towards him, smiling.

Fuck, she's the LAST person I want to see right now...

Julie flopped onto the other lounge chair, stretched her legs in front of her and crossed them at the ankles. She glanced at Rick's beer, grabbed it and took a sip.

Rick stared at her, then asked, "How come you're home already? Weren't you out with Carly?"

"I was, but then we met up with some of her University friends and I lost interest, so here I am," Julie explained, taking another sip of beer from Rick's bottle.

"Julie, what are you doing?" Rick questioned.

"Having a drink with you. Is there a problem?" she replied, trying to sound seductive.

"Yes, there is. Where's your boyfriend? I haven't seen him around lately," Rick asked, taking the bottle of beer back from her.

"Oh, Liam. We broke up," Julie told him, flipping her hand in an I-don't-care gesture.

"Why?" Rick inquired.

"I just wasn't feeling it with him anymore," Julie told him.

"You don't seem very upset about that," Rick replied.

"I'm not. We've been drifting apart for a while. It was amicable," Julie said, smiling at him through her eyelashes.

"Is there someone else you're interested in?" he asked, taking a swig of beer.

"Yes, Rick... *you*," Julie answered immediately, smiling as Rick stared at her bluntness in disbelief.

NOW I've got his attention...

"Julie, I'm still with your Mother," Rick said, composing himself. "You're only eighteen and I'm a hell of a lot older than you. I told you months ago that you and I are NEVER going to happen, so you need to get this ridiculous idea out of your head, right now," he concluded, exasperated.

"Really? Going by what I saw the other day, my Mom is very much back with my Dad. I know you tried to make it work with her, Rick, but she belongs to him. She always has and she always will. They are each other's true loves and have been from the very start. I've never seen any other couple with a relationship like theirs, except Gramma Lily and Grampa Jack. So that leaves you and me, free and clear," Julie declared.

Julie was right. It was obvious that Krys and Darryl DID belong together. Sadly, after more than twenty years of loving her, Rick finally had to admit defeat. He knew how lucky he was to have gotten the piece of her that he had, and doubly lucky, because he got to be with her not just once, but twice in his life.

"You and me *free and clear* to do what, exactly?" Rick asked.

"Give me a chance to be the woman you deserve in your life," she said, full of confidence. "You already know all there is to know about me and I know all I need to know about you. Besides, I have no great love of my life like my Mom did at my age, so I come to you with an open heart." Julie got up from her seat, moved over to Rick's side, perched on the edge of his lounge chair and placed her hand on his chest.

Rick recoiled at her touch, feeling incredibly uncomfortable at her brash behavior. He pushed her hand away from him, incredulous at what Julie was proposing for the two of them. "Are you frigging serious? I'm more than twice your age!"

"Mom raised me to go after what I want. And you, Rick, are what I want. What do you say?" Julie proclaimed as she leaned in closer to him.

"I think it's time there were some major changes made around here, starting with me," Rick said, pushing her away from him.

"What are you talking about?" Julie asked, dejected.

Rick stood up and looked down at her as he spoke. "I've told you Julie, many times already. You and me? NEVER going to happen. EVER. So get that through your head once and for all, because I will not tell you again. It's time for you to grow up and stop this ridiculous, childish fantasy of having me as your boyfriend. You are *not* what I want in a woman. Go and find yourself someone your own age and maturity level and leave me the hell alone, already. I'm fed up with you stalking me with your sexual suggestiveness and emotionally destructive attitude, prowling around me, trying to catch my eye, thinking that if you flip your hair or smile at me a certain way, I'll drop your mother and take up with you. You couldn't be more wrong and so pitifully mistaken. Not to mention badmouthing your Mother to me. Now if you'll excuse me, I have some long overdue business to attend to."

With that, Rick went inside the house to the bedroom he shared with Krys, sat on the edge of the bed and began planning out the rest of his life.

CHAPTER 169

June 2015

Krys & Rick

Krys came home in time to make supper while Lucas and Kayla lounged in the family room watching Bugs Bunny cartoons on TV.

Rick was no longer out on the deck drinking beer, where he had been when they left earlier.

Krys went up to the nursery with Abby and found him sitting in her rocking chair, an odd look on his face. "Hi. What are you doing in here?" she asked as she swiftly changed Abby's nuclear waste diaper and deftly tossed it in the diaper pail, then sanitized her hands and picked Abby back up.

"Waiting for you," Rick said, his voice flat.

"What's wrong? You look... miserable," Krys said as she searched for the right word to describe his facial expression.

"Krys, I think it's time we accept that we just aren't working. I know you're still in love with your husband. You always have been and I've finally realized that I can't compete with him. It was just a matter of time before things worked out the way they have between you two. I've seen the signs for a while," Rick began.

Krys stood there, dumbfounded, but the expression on her face confirmed that he was correct. "I'm sorry, Rick," she whispered.

He stood up from the rocking chair, took Abby from Krys' arms and placed her gently in her crib. He smiled sweetly at her and covered her up, then turned to Krys, taking her hands in his. He smiled sadly at her and said, "I moved all my things out this afternoon, back to my old place. When I leave this house today, I won't be back. Here's my key," he said quietly as he took her hand, turned it palm up and dropped the key into it.

She reached up with her other hand and caressed his face in a sad, accepting gesture and nodded slowly, tears sliding down her cheeks. "I'm so sorry, Rick. I love you and part of me always will. Twice, you saved my soul from emotional ruin and I'm grateful for that. I wish for you to find a woman who can give you her entire heart and soul, as I was never able to."

Rick gathered Krys in his arms and held her close while she cried. She wrapped her arms around his back and pressed her face into his neck. He lowered his head, buried his face in her hair and cried with her.

When they were cried out, they stood back from each other and just stared sadly into each other's eyes. Then Rick leaned in and kissed Krys' lips softly and sweetly, once.

He let go of her and walked over to the crib where Abby was sleeping peacefully, unaware of the huge drama unfolding beside her. He bent over the crib and kissed her downy soft head, his breath hitched in his throat as he said quietly to her, "Bye for now, Sweet Angel, you be a good girl for your Mommy. Love you lots, Little One."

Then Rick stood up, walked out of the nursery and out of Krys' life.

She heard him talking quietly to Lucas and Kayla downstairs as she sank into her rocking chair and just sat there, immobile, tears falling down her cheeks.

A few minutes later, she heard the front door close and a fresh wave of tears fell from her eyes. Lucas and Kayla came into the nursery and comforted their mother as best as they could, since they were crying, too. Rick had come to mean a great deal to both of them over the past several months and they needed to mourn the loss of him from their lives. Krys pulled her children into her arms and they cried together at their mutual loss.

Julie was nowhere to be found.

CHAPTER 170

June 2015
Rick

When Rick walked in the door of his old bachelor pad, he sat on the couch, cracked open a bottle of whiskey and started drinking.

Now what?

CHAPTER 171

June 2015
Krys & Natalie

A couple of hours after Rick left, Krys finished crying and called Natalie. "Nat, wanna come over? I've got something to tell you."

"You mean about you and Rick splitting up and him moving out?" Nat replied.

"What the hell! He told Tony already?" Krys grumbled.

"You know those boys, they're worse gossips than a bunch of barnyard hens," Nat chuckled.

"You got that right," Krys agreed.

"Are you okay? You don't sound like I thought you might," Nat asked.

"I'm sad, but really, I'm more relieved. Darryl and I..." she started.

"You and Darryl, WHAT???" Nat screeched in excitement.

"Don't get ahead of yourself, Nat. Darryl and I are getting along well and we're going to see where things take us. But it's weird, though. This is the first time in our lives that neither one of us have another relationship hanging over us in the background. For so many years, I had Rick pining for me and Darryl had Cynthia panting after him. Now, Rick is the one who took the initiative and broke things off with me before I could, and Cynthia is dead. I want things to work out with Darryl and I'm pretty sure he does, too," Krys confessed.

"Well, of course he does, Krys! You two are soulmates. You belong together. It was written in the stars!" Natalie gushed.

"There's just a few things I need to do, first, before we take this last step," Krys said mysteriously.

CHAPTER 172

July 2015
Krys & Darryl

On July 10, Krys and Darryl celebrated their twenty-first wedding anniversary.

When Darryl arrived at the house, his heart soared as he noticed that Krys was wearing her sapphire earrings, necklace and ring set. She was also wearing her engagement and wedding rings that she had taken off in October, the day he left.

Krys noticed that Darryl was wearing the engraved Rolex watch that she gave him for his birthday so many years before. He never had taken his wedding ring off.

Natalie came to babysit Abby for the evening so Krys and Darryl could go out, just the two of them.

"Thanks so much for coming to stay with your sweet baby niece, Auntie Natalie. It means a lot," Krys said, hugging her excitedly.

Nat replied, "I'm more than happy to! I'm also happy as all hell that things are getting back to normal between you two! Now go and have a great time together. Things here will be fine," she finished as she hugged Darryl and pushed them out the door.

Krys and Darryl drove out to Nick's Inn in Headingley. After they finished devouring bacon cheeseburgers and battered onion rings, they drove to Assiniboine Park to walk off the heavy food.

Darryl parked his Navigator, took Krys by the hand and they began walking on the well-kept trail around the park, chatting about everything and nothing at all. Every now and then, Darryl would stop, pull Krys close and kiss her lips, then continue walking, grinning in satisfaction at the lusty look on her face.

After an hour of walking, talking, kissing and holding hands, they headed back to the SUV. Instead of getting into the front seat, Krys silently climbed into the back seat, pulling Darryl with her, smiling seductively at him.

Darryl had barely closed the door behind him before Krys swiftly unzipped his cargo shorts, releasing his rock-hard erection. She lifted up her sundress, pulled aside her thong and straddled his lap. Then she grabbed his cock and slowly slid her slippery wetness onto him, taking him in all the way and sighing in utter satisfaction as she linked her fingers behind his neck. He grabbed onto her ass and began thrusting into her as he kissed her throat and nuzzled her neck.

Since neither of them had had sex in many months, it didn't take long for them to orgasm together. Darryl held Krys down on him by her hips as he groaned through his release. Krys grasped Darryl around his neck and shoulders as she moaned through hers.

When they were both spent, Krys sagged against Darryl's chest and giggled into his neck, "Well, I guess that seals the deal between us, don't you think?"

Darryl grinned in triumph, but decided to play dumb. "What deal is that, Kryssie?"

Krys smiled and whispered, "That you and I are officially, finally, and permanently, back together."

Darryl kissed her throat as he replied, "About damn time!"

"Then you'll be needing this," Krys said as she sat back, dipped her fingers into her bra and pulled out his house key. She took Darryl's hand and turned it palm up, placing the key into it.

Darryl closed his hand into a fist and pulled her close, kissing her sweetly. He looked at her and grinned. "Did you plan for all this to happen?"

Krys returned the grin. "Of course I did! We *finally* got to have sex in the car!"

Darryl's grin faded a bit as he asked, "Why aren't you freaking out that we didn't use a condom? Do you want another baby?"

"No. Besides, I can't. I got my tubes tied when Abby was born," Krys answered.

"Neither can I. I had a vasectomy after Cynthia told me she was pregnant, even though I *knew* it wasn't mine," Darryl revealed.

"Well then, no more babies. Are you sad about that?" Krys asked.

"Nope. Abby is the perfect finale to our family. Now we can have sex without worrying about another '*surprise*' happening again!" Darryl laughed.

"Let's go home. I want to break in our new bed," Krys smirked.

"New bed?" Darryl asked.

"Yup. The day after Rick moved out, I bought a new bed... for us," Krys admitted.

Darryl smiled devilishly and kissed her neck, then licked his way to her mouth, kissing her lovingly. "I never get tired of kissing you," he said, sighing happily.

"I never get tired of you kissing me," she responded.

Darryl and Krys climbed out of the back of the SUV and into the front seats, giggling like randy teenagers, then drove home holding hands like they did when they were younger. Darryl made quite the show of taking his key out of his pocket, inserting it into the lock with a flourish, turning it and pushing opening the front door. He ushered Krys in front of him, a look of smug satisfaction on his face as he grabbed her ass.

Krys giggled with glee and called out, "Nat! We're home!"

Natalie came down the stairs with her finger to her lips and whispered, "Abby went to sleep about twenty minutes ago, right after her bath. She should be out for a few hours," she said, winking saucily.

Darryl hugged her. "Smart woman, my sister."

Natalie grinned. "I'm gonna go. Julie, Lucas and Kayla are going to stay at my place until tomorrow, so you have the house to yourselves for the night, except for Abby."

Krys hugged Natalie close, saying softly, "Thank you, Nat. We really need to spend tonight alone. You're the best!"

"My pleasure," Nat replied, hugging Krys back.

Krys climbed up the curved staircase to the nursery to check on Abby while Darryl stayed behind to say goodnight to Natalie. "Thanks for everything, Nat. Love you, little sister," Darryl said as he hugged her again.

"Love you, too, big brother. Like I said, it was my pleasure. I'm so happy you two are back together," Natalie smiled happily as she hugged him back.

"Me too, Nat," Darryl said as he sighed contentedly, locking up the house for the night. He went upstairs and found Krys in the nursery standing at the crib, watching Abby sleep. He stood behind her and kissed her neck as he wound his arms around her waist. He laced his fingers with hers and gently rested his chin on her shoulder. "We did good, you and I," he said softly.

"We sure did. Welcome home, Darryl," Krys said, her voice tremulous with emotion as she turned in his arms to face him.

They stood together in the dark, holding each other, delighting in the feel of each other. Then they both moved to kiss each other at the same time, a soft, sweet kiss in the presence of their baby.

When the kisses started heating up, Darryl led Krys out of the nursery and into their bedroom, keeping contact the entire time.

Darryl whipped off his short sleeved button-down and Krys pulled the straps of her sundress down her arms, wiggling it down her hips, letting it puddle around her ankles. Darryl yanked his cargoes down his thighs to the floor and kicked them aside while Krys pulled off her bra and flung it aside.

She hooked her thumbs into her thong, but Darryl stopped her. "Please, allow me the privilege."

Krys bit her lip in anticipation and did as he requested.

He knelt down in front of her and leaned forward to kiss her belly. He closed his eyes and placed his hands around her hips as he nuzzled her abdomen, tears tracing down his face.

Krys placed her hands on his face, felt the tears and asked, "Darryl, why are you crying?"

"Because... I nearly lost all of this... Nearly lost you... And I'm so grateful to have you back. I love you so very much, Kryssie," he confessed.

She tilted his head to look up at her as she smiled down at him with tears in her eyes. "I love you, too, Darryl. You have me now and we have each other for the rest of our lives."

Darryl smiled up at Krys, then slipped her thong off her hips and helped her step out of it. He looked back at her belly and saw the scar from her C-section. "I'm so sorry I wasn't there with you when Abby was born. And I'm even more sorry you've got this scar to mar your skin because of me," he said, tracing the scar with his finger, shame lacing his words.

"Don't be sorry. Abby was born through my belly, but she's healthy and well. And so what if I have a scar? It doesn't bother me, so please don't let it bother you, okay?" Krys told him.

"You forgive me, then?" Darryl asked in a small voice.

"Of course I forgive you! We're back together and happily in love with each other. Now, can we continue where we left off in the nursery? We need to make sure all areas of this bed are to our liking," Krys said as she winked lewdly.

Darryl sighed in relief and kissed her scar, then licked a trail down to her wetness and dipped his tongue into paradise. Krys' legs wobbled and Darryl smirked in satisfaction.

We did it!

We found our way back to each other!

He stood and picked her up, then threw her onto the bed and watched her bounce across the king-sized mattress. He crawled on top of her and she welcomed him into her arms, kissing him as they laughed together.

Darryl leaned his weight onto his forearms, his hips cradled between Krys' thighs, her knees bent on either side of him. He kissed her mouth sensuously, then kissed and licked his way down to her breasts.

It had been some time since she had nursed Abby, so Krys held her hands on Darryl's head, keeping him close as he suckled her, easing some of the pressure on her breasts. "Do you want me to go get Abby so you can feed her? I can tell you're uncomfortable," Darryl offered.

"No, not yet. Let's continue. She can wait, I can't..." Krys rasped.

Darryl smiled sexily and moved farther down Krys' body, kissing her C-section scar again, making no further mention of it. There was no need since Krys absolved him of that sin.

He threw her legs over his shoulders and dove into her wet heat with his lips, tongue and fingers, devouring her as if he hadn't had a meal in a year.

Krys felt lightning strike as her orgasm ripped its way out of her body, making her go limp as Darryl kissed and licked his way back up her body. He kissed her deeply and slid all the way into her in one powerful thrust. It was like plugging himself into a light socket as Krys re-energized. Her eyes flew open, her arms and legs returned to solid strength, coiling around him and caging him within her embrace. Darryl started moving slowly and Krys met him thrust for thrust, moaning in pleasure.

Darryl rolled them over so Krys was on top straddling him. His hands grasped her hips as her hands gripped his shoulders and she rode him hard, building up to another orgasm.

Before she could come apart at the seams, Darryl sat up and wrapped his arms around her, one hand in her hair and one hand around her waist to keep her moving with him. She wound her arms around his shoulders and hung on, grinding down onto him as they kissed each other hungrily.

Krys could feel the burn starting in her lower belly. Darryl also felt the burn starting in his balls, moving steadily up his spine. A few thrusts later, they groaned in mutual deep pleasure as their orgasms swept through them like a hurricane. They held each other tightly, his cock still twitching inside her while her core still spasmed around him, savoring the feelings flowing between them.

"I think the bed works for me," Darryl said, unable to contain his laughter.

Krys giggled and kissed his jaw as she looked into his eyes. "Me too."

They both turned to the baby monitor as they heard a soft squawk.

"Do you want me to go get her now?" Darryl repeated his previous offer.

Krys looked at the clock on her side of the bed and replied, "Yes, please."

She lifted herself off Darryl and he went to get their baby. He returned a moment later cradling Abby close to him, then placed her lovingly in Krys' arms so she could feed her. He crawled into bed beside his wife and nestled her close into his side. Darryl held Abby's little head to Krys' breast, ecstatic to be involved in this intimate moment with their baby as she nursed.

Krys' heart burst with love for her husband. She kissed him sweetly while Abby drank greedily. They sat together marvelling at her until Krys switched Abby to the other breast, where she continuing to nurse greedily.

When she was finished, Darryl took her from Krys' arms, her little rosebud mouth slack, her body limp and belly full, and settled her back to sleep in the nursery.

He returned to find Krys laying on her side, watching him with hooded eyes. "You're not done with me yet, are you?" she husked. His semi-hard cock hardened all the way and Krys grinned when she spotted it.

"Not by a long shot," he growled, moving towards her like a wild animal, eyes locked with hers.

She rose to her knees and met Darryl in the middle of the bed. He pulled her close and kissed her passionately, then grabbed her legs and swung them around his hips. He walked forward on his knees, pressed Krys back against the headboard and drove inside her, thrusting in and out, again and again, kissing her mouth and burying his head in her neck.

Krys smiled with joy at being with Darryl again, how good he felt inside her and how happy she was that they were finally back together. He began thrusting harder and not long after, Krys came again, wringing another orgasm out of Darryl.

They collapsed against each other in total exhaustion, smiling happily at each other in between kisses. Once they both caught their breath, Darryl shifted back from the headboard with Krys still in his arms. He slipped out of her and lay them both down, he on his back with her propped up on his chest. They looked at each other, grinning from ear to ear.

"Now THAT'S a welcome home," Darryl laughed, smiling at Krys.

"It sure is," she agreed, smiling back.

They fell asleep shortly after and slept deeply the rest of the night wrapped in each other's arms.

Bliss...

Pure bliss...

CHAPTER 173

July 2015
Darryl & Kayla

Natalie dropped off Lucas and Kayla at home the next morning. They heard Journey's "Open Arms" playing on the stereo and wandered into the kitchen where they found Krys and Darryl together, laughing and teasing each other lovingly, as always.

Krys was wearing her deep pink satin robe, standing in front of the griddle, flipping pancakes.

Darryl was wearing his deep blue terrycloth bathrobe, sitting at the table reading the morning paper.

Kayla stood there with her eyes bugged out, staring at her Dad.

He looked up, smiled warmly at his daughter and said, "Hi KayKay. Want to share my pancakes?"

She flew at him and threw herself in his arms, hugging him fiercely. "YES, Daddy, YES!!!" she screamed, tears of elation falling down her cheeks. "Are you... really home? Are you and Mommy... finally back together... for good?" she said between crying fits.

"Yes KayKay, we are," Darryl said, hugging his excited daughter back as he looked at Krys and closed his eyes in pure happiness.

CHAPTER 174

July 2015

Krys & Lucas

When Lucas saw his parents together in the kitchen, he felt a warm, tingly feeling shoot through him. The way they were looking at each other and talking to each other, it was like the past ten months never happened.

Kayla had thrown herself at their father and screeched so loud, she nearly shattered the windows.

Lucas played it cool and sauntered over to his mother. "So, are you and Dad back together?" he asked casually, feigning indifference.

"Yes, Luke. Do you feel the same as your sister?" she asked, grinning.

"Yeah. It's a good thing," he replied, as he tossed his cool demeanor aside and hugged his mother tightly to him.

The music changed and "Love Will Keep Us Together" by Captain & Tenille began playing.

"It sure is," she said as she hugged her son and kissed his cheek, smiling happily while looking at Darryl, pure joy filling her heart.

CHAPTER 175

August 2015

Diamond Angel

Tony, Rick, Bryan, Alex and Diego were sitting in Bryan's back yard drinking beer and shooting the shit, teasing each other and behaving like frat boys.

Rick cleared his throat. He was unsure how his news was going to be received. "Uh, guys? I'm glad we're doing a greatest hits album and I've really enjoyed remixing our songs, but as of September first, I'm going on hiatus from the band."

The air crackled with disbelief.

Tony spoke up first. "You're not leaving the band, are you? Because if you are, this is a fucked up way to do it!"

"No, Tony. I'm not leaving Diamond Angel. I just need to take some time away from music. We've all done solo projects over the years and we have our remixed greatest hits coming out soon. I'm very proud of all we've done, but at the same time, I'm tired of it all. I've had a hell of a year and I want to do something different and not music related for a while," he explained.

Diego spoke next. "I agree, *mi hermano*. I wouldn't mind taking some time off to do nothing for a while with my woman and my son. Maybe we'll make another baby?"

Bryan chimed in. "I'm going to be working on some classical music with the Winnipeg Symphony Orchestra. They've asked me to write a few music scores for them and I'm really interested in pursuing that for something different."

Alex added, "I've been offered some session work with a couple of new bands that Global Music has just signed. I'll be like a mentor to these newbies. Might be fun! Especially since one of the groups is all female! Hubba hubba!"

Tony breathed in heavily through his nose and exhaled out through his mouth. "Well then, I guess once we wrap up next week, we'll go our separate ways for a while. How long do you guys want this hiatus to last?" Tony ceded.

"I've taken a one year term position at the University of Manitoba in the Psychology Department. I'll be teaching Child Stress and Trauma and I start after the September Labor Day weekend. I'm finally getting my chance, after all these years, to put my Master's Degree to good use," Rick smiled happily.

"Wow, man, that's really fantastic. I'm happy for you," Tony said as he clapped Rick on the back in congratulations.

Later that evening, the boys of Diamond Angel parted ways...

CHAPTER 176

September 2015
Rick

Rick's first day of teaching went well. Many of his students came up to him throughout the day and told him how excited they were to be learning from him, partly because he was a famous musician and partly because he was down-to-earth, knowledgeable and approachable.

He met some of the other professors in the Psychology Lounge during his lunch break. One in particular he hit it off with right away was Lauren Yates. She had her Masters Degree and had been teaching at the University of Manitoba for the past twelve years. In fact, she was teaching right next door to him. Lauren was 5'5" with golden brown hair cut in a shaggy bob and bright green eyes, a total opposite of what Rick usually went for in a woman...

They got to talking and found that they had a lot in common outside of their current professions.

Lauren was divorced, had a teenage son and had once been in the entertainment industry as a back-up dancer. She also sang and played the guitar. She was two years younger than

Rick, which made topics of conversation plentiful and easy to choose from.

As they got to know each other over the course of the month, Rick noted that she got his sense of humor, she got his moods, she just *got him*...

They spent their coffee breaks together, lunch breaks together and even spent time together after work in the evenings.

One weekend, they met for lunch and brought their kids with them – his daughter, Anya, and her son, Kevin. Anya was now almost fifteen and Kevin was fourteen. Funnily enough, their kids got along as a step-brother and step-sister would...

Maybe the universe is trying to tell me something...

CHAPTER 177

September 2015
Julie

After Rick so cruelly blew her off in June, Julie felt unattractive, lacking her usual confidence, and moped around all summer.

Nothing any of her friends could say or do cheered her up.

Even her parents getting back together didn't pull her out of her funk.

Then on her first day of classes, in her second year in the Faculty of Architecture, Jeff Osborne sat down beside her. He gave her a heart-stopping smile and drawled, "Hey, Jules."

Jeff Osborne!!

OHMIGOD!!!

Jeff Osborne knows my name and just said HI to me!!!

He was the lead singer of Blood Justice, *THE* premiere University of Manitoba classic rock'n'roll band. They had quite the cult following because they were *amazing* and everyone *loved* them.

Over the next several days, Jeff sat beside Julie in all of their classes. After she got over the shock of Jeff knowing who she was, she relaxed around him and they got to talking, finding that they had lots in common. They had lunch together every day and talked about their assignments and projects coming due, and decided to work together with a few other students. Soon they became the powerhouse combination to be beat.

Jeff was clearly more than scholastically interested in Julie, and after the second week of school, he asked her out and Julie heartily accepted.

They began spending all of their time together and quickly became inseparable.

It was just the relationship Julie was looking for.

CHAPTER 178

October 2015
Rick & Lauren

After a few weeks of tiptoeing around their mutual attraction for each other since the day they met, Rick and Lauren decided to start seeing each other exclusively. As professors, they weren't exempt from engaging in personal relationships with other faculty members.

Lauren insisted that they go out on dates like teenagers for a few weeks before they slept together. Waiting in sweet anticipation rewarded them with several stratospheric orgasms and declarations of love on both sides.

Rick finally found a woman he could love and give his heart to, who would love him and give him her heart in return.

He remembered thinking, *She may be out there, but where is she and when will I finally find her?*

Finally...

I found her...

CHAPTER 179

March 8, 2016
Everyone

Krys and Darryl mingled with their guests. They were throwing Abby a First Birthday Party and invited Krys' family, Darryl's family and all of Diamond Angel with their families.

Even Rick was invited, as was Lauren and her son, Kevin. Rick's daughter, Anya, was there with her mother, Holly, and her new husband, Randy.

Rick came over to Krys and hugged her lightly to his side while Darryl stood on Krys' other side, his face impassive. For once, Darryl felt no spark of jealousy or deep-seated hatred towards Rick. They even shook hands in an even-matched gesture of *TRUCE* that was not lost on Krys.

When Diamond Angel went on hiatus and Rick started teaching at the University, everyone noticed a huge change in him, especially once he met Lauren. She was *the one* who finally snapped Rick out of his life-long addiction to Krys.

"Krys, I have some wonderful news to tell you," he said excitedly.

"Oh? What's that?" she asked, intrigued.

"Look what we did!" Rick beamed as he held up his and Lauren's left hands. On Lauren's ring finger was a large, sparkling diamond solitaire engagement ring in white gold, with a wedding band of pave diamonds also set in white gold, and on his ring finger was a simple black titanium wedding band.

"I... What? When did *this* happen?" Krys cried, genuine excitement flowing from her.

"Rick proposed to me on February twenty-seventh, then we went to the Justice Of The Peace the next day on the twenty-eighth and *got married*!" Lauren said excitedly, beaming with happiness.

Krys threw her arms around Rick's neck and hugged him tightly, whispering in his ear, "I'm so happy for you, Rick. I always hoped you would find someone who would give you her whole heart, and I see that Lauren has. I'm so glad you found each other."

"I've finally put what you and I had together in the past, where it belongs. Now I understand how you feel about Darryl, because I feel the same way about Lauren." Rick said, love and joy emanating from him.

Krys' eyes were shining with tears as she and Rick hugged one last time.

It was then, that after more than twenty years, Krys and Rick were *finally* able to let each other go.

Darryl pulled Krys into his arms and they stood together, happy and secure in their marriage. He looked at her beautiful face and asked, "Are you good, Kryssie?"

"Yes, Darryl. Everything is all good now, just as it should be," she answered as she kissed his jaw and squeezed his waist gently, giving him a taste of what to expect when all their guests left and their four kids were packed off to their grandparent's for the rest of the night...

Natalie and Tony came over with their arms around each other and joined in congratulating the newlyweds.

There was absolutely no tension in the room between any of the couples.

All was well in their world as "In And Out Of Love" by Bon Jovi played on the stereo...

EPILOGUE

May 2016

Krys and Natalie were sitting outside on a beautiful Sunday afternoon, drinking margaritas on Krys' deck, while their husbands and children were at Assiniboine Park.

Nat took a sip of her drink, turned to Krys with a smirk on her face and asked, "Krys, if you wrote a book about your love life and named it after a song, what would you call it?"

Krys looked thoughtful for a moment, then looked Natalie directly in the eyes and replied with a clever grin and a sparkle in her eye, "Oh, that's easy, Nat... ***IN AND OUT OF LOVE!***"

THE END

CPSIA information can be obtained
at www.ICGtesting.com
Printed in the USA
BVHW030357100221
599415BV00001B/1